Prophet Of Eden

Book Three

The Boy had become the Prophet... the mystical Healer and white-winged Angel standing with him as One

The battle for the heart and soul of mankind was about to begin

Amal Guevin

Prophet Of Eden

Prophet Of Eden is the electrifying conclusion of the Into The Mystic Trilogy, the story of the boy destined to become the Prophet, the beautiful and mystically gifted woman he loved, and their white-winged Angel, as they stand together as One to defend the people of the new and powerless post-Flare earth against the rising forces of an old, ancient, and evil enemy.

The children of Miracle Island have begun to discover the unusual gifts and amazing powers given to them at birth... Adam's close and miraculous relationship with his God, Nylah's power to heal and prophesy, and Angel's ability to talk to the creatures of the sea. Protected by their osprey guardian angel, Moses, as they grow from childhood into young adults, they find both love and heartache on the challenging path to their destiny.

Only one quarter of earth's population survived the irreparable loss of all electrical power after the Flare, but it gave man and the earth he almost destroyed a chance to recover and blossom in the way the Creator first intended. But many still chose to follow the violent and destructive ways of the past, and of the Darkness... the archenemy of God who sought to destroy the young Prophet sent to guide mankind back to the Light.

Skylark's prophecy begins when Adam, Nylah, and Moses are sent on their first mission, and their enraged nemesis fights with all the powers of hell to prevent them from bringing love, hope, and faith to the peoples of the new Garden of Eden on earth.

The epic adventure saga of Daniel, Alea, Matt, and the Tribe of Miracle Island now travels the globe from the lush and tranquil islands of Eleuthera and Spanish Wells, Bahamas to the dark and mysterious Amazon rainforest, and finally into the vast but troubled wheatfields of the Ukraine, where the Prophet, the Healer, and the Angel will meet their first and most difficult test.

Books By Amal Guevin

The Into The Mystic Trilogy

Into The Mystic 2019

Inherit The Earth 2020

Prophet Of Eden 2022

Prophet Of Eden

A Speculative Fiction, Action & Adventure, Sci-Fi, Romantic, and Spiritual Novel

This is a work of fiction. Names, characters, events, incidents, and business establishments portrayed in this book are used fictitiously or are products of the author's imagination. Any resemblance to actual persons, living or dead, is entirely coincidental. References have been made to existing countries and locations, but some alterations and enhancements were created regarding geography, history, and physical properties for the purpose of this story.

Cover Art by BetiBup33 Studio Design

ISBN: 9798839746695

Cast Of Characters from Into The Mystic and Inherit The Earth

Daniel Devereaux - son of James and Dolores Devereaux, owner of Devereaux Fishing in Boston, ex-husband of Karen Sullivan, married to Dr. Alea Gabrielle.

Dr. Alea Gabrielle Devereaux - Pronounced Uh-Lee-ah. Orthopedic Surgeon, married to Daniel Devereaux, mother of Adam.

Adam Devereaux - son of Daniel and Alea, the Prophet of Eden.

Nylah Kennedy - daughter of Matt and Skylark, born as her mother died and gifted with special powers from the Great Spirit.

Moses - the white osprey, Angel Protector of Adam, and the Miracle Island Tribe.

Matt Kennedy - one of Daniel's two best friends, once secretly in love with Alea Devereaux but who finally found his soulmate and love with Skylark.

Skylark Miacoda Kennedy - the spiritually gifted Mi'kmaq Indian woman from Nova Scotia, Canada, who captured Matt's heart and gave her life to save Adam.

Chief Lonecloud Stewart - grandfather of Skylark, Mi'kmaq Chief and leader.

Chief Eagle Claw Stewart - father of Skylark and grandfather of Nylah.

Karen Sullivan - Ex-wife of Daniel, institutionalized with severe bipolar disorder but who escaped to become the leader of the cannibalistic Lunatic Fringe.

Ronny Robello - Daniel's other childhood friend, married to Pearl, with son, Robbie, and daughter, Gypsy (don't call her Rhonda!).

Benjamin Knowles - Owner of Knowles Marina & Boat Repair in Spanish Wells, Eleuthera, friend of James, Daniel, Ronny, and Matt, father of William and Gilbert Knowles. Murdered by the Barracuda gang from Nassau.

Dr. John Garner - General Practitioner from Boston, married to Josey, a schoolteacher, and father of Noah, Sammy, and daughter, Angel.

Dr. Armand Gabrielle - Cardiovascular Surgeon, married to Nadia Soliman, Surgical Nurse, father of Alea Gabrielle and Roger Gabrielle, Neurosurgeon, married to Loreen Sweeting of Spanish Wells.

Table Of Contents

**Playlist Mood Song*

Prologue The Prophet's Call

Adam leaped into his mother's arms, a damp and sandy mess, laughing uncontrollably with Bear playfully nipping at his toes as Moses fluttered down to the back of Alea's chair and folded his wings, his black eyes staring intently at Matt. Brandy dropped into the cool shade at Matt's feet, her tongue lolling out in a satisfied smile.

Nylah giggled and climbed up her father's leg, her long black hair loose and wet, her fawn-colored skin tinted pink from the sun, and flung her arms around Matt's neck.

"Papa, Papa, I talked to Mama again today! She told me to tell you she's sending you a present!" she exclaimed, her high sweet childish voice ringing with excitement.

Matt and Alea's eyes met instantly. He gently pulled his daughter's arms from around his neck and looked deep into her glowing gray eyes. For a moment, he saw Skylark smiling back at him. His heart twisted in pain, but he kissed her tenderly.

"And what did Mama say, sweetheart?"

Nylah smiled confidently.

"The lady with the golden hair will be here soon, Papa!"

She wiped away the single tear running slowly down her father's cheek.

"And you'll never be lonely again!" *Inherit The Earth

****

Alea lifted Nylah from Matt's lap and set her feet down on the soft sand, his stunned expression worrying her.

"Nylah, sweetie, why don't you and Adam take the dogs and run back to camp? Your dad and I will be there shortly."

Adam grabbed Nylah's hand and pulled her towards the beach, Bear and Brandy scrambling to follow.

"Come on, Nylah! Betcha I make it to the firepit first, even before Moses!"

Nylah grinned and turned to wave goodbye to her father, her eyes now a sparkling green. Shaking off Adam's hand, she broke into a full run, the dogs and boy racing to catch up.

Alea looked at Matt, sitting motionless in his chair. After the discussion they had just had about Nylah's unique ability to predict the future, she wasn't sure what to say to her friend, who was obviously in emotional turmoil. She took his hand... and waited.

Matt could barely breathe. No. No one could ever replace his beautiful Skylark, who had sacrificed herself to save Adam. If he lived the rest of his life on earth alone, he didn't care. His heart and soul belonged only to her... forever. This one time, Nylah's prediction had to be wrong. Besides, the location of Miracle Island was the Tribe's secret. Not even their family and closest friends that lived on Eleuthera and Spanish Wells knew where to find it.

He felt Alea gently squeeze his hand, drawing him out of his mournful silence. Her lovely hazel eyes glistened with tears as she leaned towards him, and he could feel her love and compassion. Forcing a smile, he squeezed her hand in return.

"I'll be okay, Alea... As much as I love my daughter and respect her spiritual gifts, I'm having a hard time believing this one. She's only four, for heaven's sake. She probably senses how much I miss her mother and was trying to help."

"Well, I can honestly say, Matt, that everyone in the Tribe is worried about you. Try to keep in mind what we discussed earlier about connecting with someone new when we go to Spanish Wells in the spring."

She released his hand and sat back in her chair. "You need to relax your guard and at least give the ladies a chance to get to know you better. I care about you so much and would love to see you happy again. Skylark would want that too."

He sighed, forced to admit she was right... as usual. This spectacular woman he had once thought he was in love with had become as good a friend to him as her husband, Daniel, whom he had known since childhood.

Trained as an orthopedic surgeon, she had saved his unborn daughter by surgically removing her from her dead mother's womb, resuscitating the tiny limp form with her own breath, and had nursed Nylah along with her infant son, Adam. Her doses of common sense and loving heart had helped to soothe and comfort him after Skylark's violent death, and he trusted her opinions and advice.

"Alright, Alea... I promise to give what you said some serious thought. But we won't be leaving for Spanish Wells until the first of May, so for a few more months, the ladies will just have to wait," he chuckled wryly.

She shook her head with a smile as they both stood up and started walking back to camp, Matt carrying the basket with the grouper he had speared earlier. He glanced at the sky over the tree line. "Looks like a storm might be coming our way from the west. We may have to batten down the camp before bed tonight."

Neither one had noticed that Moses had not followed the children. The white osprey was silently perched on a branch above them, listening intently to their conversation until they finally rose and disappeared down the beach.

His black eyes suddenly turned to the turquoise waters of the bay, and he grew still, listening to a voice he alone could hear. A moment later, he whistled his joyful response.

Spreading his wings, he rose into the air and headed west over the tops of the trees.

****

Adam took a last spoonful of grilled fish with lemon sauce, unable to eat another bite. The soft, flickering glow of the campfire danced on his face, highlighting his locks of dark brown hair, caramel brown eyes, and tanned skin.

"Momma, I'm done. Can Nylah and Angel go swimming with me?"

"It's getting late, Adam. I think you and the girls should go and wash up now before heading off to bed," Alea told him as she collected his wooden plate to add to the pile needing to be sand scraped and rinsed.

"What about Noah and Gypsy? Don't they have to go to bed too?" he pouted. "And Sammy and Robbie?"

Fifteen-year-old Noah and fourteen-year-old Gypsy had finished eating and were sitting on a driftwood log, talking quietly, Noah focused on Gypsy's every word. Sammy, his ten-year-old brother, was leaning against the other end of the log and absentmindedly eating a banana as he read his anatomy book by firelight, ignoring everyone around him. Gypsy's twin brother, Robbie, was chiseling out a mortice and tenon joint from two short lengths of buttonwood for his latest building project.

"They're older than you, son, and get to stay up longer," Daniel reminded him. "Do what your mom told you and we'll come in to say goodnight in a little while. There could be a storm later, and we have to prepare."

Gypsy gave him a wide slapstick grin. "Listen to your dad, Adam. Time for the *children* to go to bed!" Noah poked her in the leg but couldn't keep himself from laughing anyway.

The four-year-old little boy scanned the faces around the campfire hopefully, seeking any assistance for his cause from the rest of the Tribe.

His grandparents, James and Dolores Devereaux, waved goodnight in support of Alea's decree, as did John and Josey Garner and Ronny and Pearl Robello.

Ryan McCarthy and his wife, Sarah, who had followed Matt on the difficult odyssey to Boston, then chose to travel on with him to Miracle Island, smiled at him apologetically, their one-year-old son, Dylan, trying to climb off Sarah's lap to run to Adam, always ready to play.

Matt gave him the *What can you do?* look and shrugged his shoulders, but as far as bedtime for the three youngest children was concerned, Alea and Josey ruled the roost.

John and Josey hugged their little tow-headed daughter, Angel, who had been born on Miracle Island five years before in a long and perilous birth that almost cost both she and her mother their lives. Even at her young age, she'd more than earned her title of *The Little Mermaid of Miracle Island,* spending most of her day playing, swimming, and diving in Osprey Bay, and surprising all of them by demonstrating a curiously close connection to the myriad of creatures that lived in the ocean.

Matt kissed Nylah's cheek tenderly and the two girls, arm in arm, scampered off to the women's bath shack on the north side of camp, Adam to the men's shack on the south. After brushing his teeth and taking a shower with the hose from the overhead water container, he headed back to his family's treehouse, a line of torches illuminating the well-worn pathway. Nylah and Angel were already secluded in Nylah's room, whispering and giggling until Josey or John arrived to take Angel home.

Resigned to the inevitable, he climbed into bed, nestling into the homemade mattress stuffed with leaves, moss, and dried seaweed, and covered himself with his favorite blanket. The February night was comfortably cool and moonless, the slight rustle of casuarina tree boughs in the evening breeze and the steady, rhythmic pulse of the bay waters brushing the sandy shore the only sounds.

He closed his eyes and relaxed. Although he'd never admit it, even to Nylah, this was the time of day he relished the most, quiet, tranquil, and reverent, when he imagined he could feel the movement of the earth turning beneath him... breathe the fragrance of exotic flowers from distant lands he had never seen.

As he drifted with the night, a soft glowing light began to surround him, wrapping him in a protective cocoon of calm and peaceful serenity... and he waited for what he knew would be coming next.

Turning his head slightly to one side, the gentle, familiar Voice whispered in his ear, speaking words the child did not always understand. But he could feel the tender love in the Voice, and even more so, the power emanating from it, the same power that flowed out from deep within him whenever he inadvertently caused something unusual to happen.

His earliest memories were of his parents reading to him from the Holy Bible, amazing stories about the people and prophets of old, and about Almighty God and His Son, the Lord Jesus. From the innermost core of his young spirit, he sensed the truth of the Word, and believed.

In the boy's heart, he knew the whispering Voice could be no other, and his soul was filled with joy as he prayed. These moments of intimate communion with his God were a secret he shared with no one... nor did he ever share the frightening experience that followed it, as it had every night for the past three months.

A gust of cold biting wind suddenly blew the blanket off his chest, the glowing light and sense of peace vanishing. The stars dimmed in the heavens, the sounds of wind and wave faded away, and the air grew heavy with a dank, foul odor.

Adam braced himself.

The Darkness had returned...

Whenever the black, chilling, faceless fog drifted into his room and hovered above him, he hid under the covers and prayed even harder, quivering with fear until the evil entity eventually withdrew, gloating with pleasure at the terror of the child. For some strange reason, it never touched him, but he couldn't help wondering why God didn't keep such a scary thing away from him.

But on this night, he was filled with a strength and courage he had never felt before and heard the command from the voice of the Lord Himself as clear as day.

Feeling no fear for the first time, his eyes slowly opened, lit with a brilliant golden fire!

The Darkness screeched as if burned, breaking away from the boy with an angry snarl and disappearing in a toxic cloud into the night sky.

Adam now understood what he was meant to do.

The battle had finally begun.

Chapter 1 The Catira

"How in the name of God did I get myself into this?"

Pierce Covington struggled to stand up, but the sudden plunge of the deck in the tempestuous cross chop of the angry sea hurled him back down, the rain pelting his cedar brown hair and already drenched clothing with cold hard beads, his hazel-green eyes flashing with anger at his own helplessness.

With no way to control the boat at all, he was sure it was only a matter of time before *Piranha* sank into the depths of the Gulfstream, taking his very valuable cargo with it.

At least, that's where he thought they were...

The only thing keeping them from capsizing in the swells were the improvised outriggers attached to both sides of their flat-bottomed, fifty-foot riverboat, one of the two boats that had motored Pierce, the Horizon Studios production crew, and his two difficult, pain-in-the-ass Hollywood stars up the Amazon River almost five years ago.

The makeshift sail had been ripped away by the violent storm that appeared out of nowhere, just as the tip of the Florida Keys came into view. *Piranha* had now been adrift for three days, propelled towards the eastern Atlantic Ocean, and their doom, by the power of the storm.

The sky grew even darker with dusk approaching, and he finally ordered everyone on deck to return below. No one complained. Most were ill from seasickness, taking turns vomiting over the rail while one of the others kept them from being flung overboard by the unrelenting waves. He had stoically remained above, hoping beyond hope to spot land.

Of the original contingent of fifty people, only six were still alive... But due to Pierce's skills as a survivalist and guide, and with a great deal of effort on his part, his two megastars were also alive, guaranteeing him a monstrous paycheck once he returned them to Horizon Studios in LA.

The check would be more than enough money to allow him to comfortably retire at the relatively young age of forty-two and reunite with his sweet and beautiful twenty-three-year-old wife, Meg, and newly born daughter, Nora. Well, Nora would now be five, and Meg would be twenty-eight.

His jaw clenched at the thought of missing so much of his precious little daughter's life, and his heart ached when he pictured his Meg as he had last seen her, her long waves of honey-colored hair and amber eyes moist with tears as he waved goodbye.

****

A representative from Horizon Studios had contacted his Los Angeles-based company, Wild Outback Adventures, with a request for Pierce to personally guide their production staff for eight weeks of onsite filming in Brazil for the most highly anticipated movie of the year, The Refuge.

Initially reluctant, with Meg still in recovery from Nora's birth, he eagerly accepted the assignment when he was told who he would be guiding... and the amount of money the studio was offering him to do it.

Chase London and Morgan Monroe.

The two biggest names in Hollywood... their second film together only one year after their first, Private Message, shattered every box office record in the history of motion pictures.

If he knew then what he knew today, he never would have taken the job, not for all the bitcoin on the planet.

Chase London was a tall, drop dead gorgeous, raven-haired, six-packed prick who couldn't keep his roaming hands off an attractive woman if she was within ten feet of his mesmerizing emerald-green eyes.

He'd swept the innocent eighteen-year-old Morgan off her feet on the set of Private Message, becoming the darlings of the frenzied paparazzi until the night she caught him in her own bed, sandwiched between a pair of extras. But even Pierce had to admit the man could act, taking Hollywood by storm when he first appeared onscreen in a bit part at age twenty.

Morgan Monroe was a golden-haired ethereal beauty with sky-blue eyes, long sweeping dark eyelashes, and the dreamy face, glowing porcelain skin, full red lips, and curvaceous figure reminiscent of her namesake, Marilyn.

But she had the mouth of a dockworker and an attitude to match... a complete opposite of the role she played in her debut movie, The Novice, that won her an Academy Award for Best Actress when she was only fifteen years old. Since that major success, she'd gone on to make hit after hit, her name even rumored to be attached to a script creating a studio bidding war.

He'd made all the arrangements well in advance for their moviemaking adventure and chartered a flight from LA to Manaus International Airport, a city in central Brazil on the Amazon River.

After depositing his contentious stars, the famous director, Robert Silverman, his eight-year-old son, Michael, and their security in a five-star hotel, he escorted the rest of the film crew to their less extravagant accommodations nearby.

The next morning, Pierce visited the dockside offices of the Amazon Riverboat Company, where he had reserved a pair of fifty-foot, flat-bottomed cruisers that could easily house the entire cast and crew and all their equipment. *Piranha* and *Caiman* also provided luxury suites with Jacuzzi tubs for his demanding and petulant stars.

He made sure the boats were stocked with enough food, water, alcohol, and supplies for the eight week or possibly longer voyage up the far reaches of the Amazon River and into the remote, primal, and mysterious rainforest, as per Bob Silverman's specific request.

As they cruised, Silverman scanned the banks, ordering a halt when he determined a location was perfect for filming. Pierce preferred the boats anchored near the shoreline, but if it was too shallow to do so, the equipment and personnel were loaded into inflatable dinghies and motored to shore. Filming might take one or two days in that spot until Bob was satisfied, and the boats would move on to scout the next location.

They'd been in the field for three weeks, the intense humid July heat and swarms of giant insects on the bank of the river making the shoot extremely difficult and uncomfortable.

Chase walked off the set before noon, grabbing the hand of his well-endowed blonde stylist and refusing to leave his air-conditioned cabin. Silverman continued to roll with as many scenes that Morgan, always the consummate professional, could perform without Chase until he finally called it, much to everyone's relief. After an early dinner, both of the boats gradually grew silent as, one by one, cabin doors closed for the night.

Pierce woke up from a deep sleep, not quite sure what had awakened him. But his windowless cabin was in complete darkness, even the LED numbers on his digital clock blacked out. Feeling around for his clothes and shoes, he dressed quickly and opened the door to the hallway. Darkness greeted him there as well, the rest of the film crew not yet awake.

Palming the walls of the corridor, he made his way up the stairs to the cockpit. Bright sunlight illuminated the room, but the instrument panel was blank. The captain's head suddenly appeared from beneath the panel, a wrench in one hand and muttering curses in Portuguese as drops of sweat trickled down his furrowed brow. Resting for a moment on his elbow, he noticed Pierce's worried face above him.

"What's going on, Captain Diego?" Pierce asked.

Roberto Diego set the wrench aside and wiped his tired face with an oily rag. "I hope you're not in a hurry, amigo, because we're not going anywhere. Every electrical system on this boat is dead."

****

Desperately gripping the rail of the foundering boat, Pierce hung on, a powerful gust of wind almost catapulting him over the side. After surviving four years in the rainforest of the Amazon, he refused to let his life end like this, drowned in the stormy Atlantic, never to see Meg and Nora again. As another crashing wave broke hard on the bow, he couldn't help but remember when the nightmare first began.

****

It had become painfully clear after several days with no power that the engines, navigation, and communication systems of both *Piranha* and *Caiman* were not coming back. Cellphones and laptops had stopped receiving any signal the further they traveled upriver, but no one could explain what had happened to all the electrical systems on the boats.

With thirty-three film crew, two major stars, the director and his son, three men and two women security guards, the captain and his six staff, and one worried survivalist guide, a total of fifty people were now stuck on the crocodile, snake, and carnivorous fish infested Amazon River, and in a dark, dangerous, and unforgiving jungle that appeared untouched by modern man. With no way out.

Perfect for a movie plot... deadly for them.

Pierce immediately took control. With all contact lost, the studio would certainly send out a search and rescue team, but until they arrived, order had to be maintained.

Enlisting the support of the security guards, he announced a strict rationing of water. The dozens of five-gallon water bottles were stored below deck with each boat's freshwater tank and put under lock and key.

A large stone-lined firepit was assembled onshore, with the chefs of *Piranha* and *Caiman* put in charge of maintaining the fire and cooking any food that required refrigeration first. Two guards were posted during prep and mealtimes for protection from wild animals, semi-automatic pistols loaded and ready on their belts.

Separate clearings not too far into the forest canopy were designated as the men's and women's commode. No one was to visit the commodes during the day without escort from one of the guards, and Pierce arranged for a private place to squat over the gunnel of the boats at night.

His orders were met with sullen resistance by most of the film crew, not used to deprivation of any kind, with Chase leading the rebellion. But their resistance vanished when one of the cameramen, disgruntled by the small amount of fruit, toasted bread, and cheese served for breakfast, and tired of the constant heat and humidity, impulsively decided to go for a swim by himself.

A shrill scream cut through the sultry air as the stunned onlookers on shore watched the massive jaws of a twenty-foot Amazon crocodile, the caiman, clamp down on Bart's waist and drag him underwater, a trail of blood rising to the surface as the water gradually grew still.

Pierce never heard another complaint.

After Bart's death by crocodile, no one dared go near the river, and bathing became an urgent issue. A few of the braver men made quick dashes to the shoreline with buckets, but the amount of water they retrieved was barely enough for a spit bath, a hard pill to swallow for the spoiled LA crowd used to spa tubs, pedicures, manicures, massages, and hair salons.

Crocodiles weren't his only concern. No rescue party ever arrived, and over the course of the next month, five people died from fever and infection. One female guard, who must have thought her pistol was enough to protect her when she foolishly chose to visit the forest commode by herself, was heard screaming in terror as she was dragged away by what he later determined was a jaguar, based on tracks in the mud.

Chase whined incessantly. Unable to tolerate his hot stuffy cabin during the steamy daytime hours, his assistant used bed sheets to create an outdoor shade canopy, where he held royal court from his comfortable lounge chair.

Pierce couldn't stand the man but allowed the ridiculous practice to continue because of the way the twenty-two-year-old arrogant star seemed to calm the anxious crew, gifting them with the rare privilege of direct access into his protected bubble of fame, and entertaining them with juicy backstage gossip and stories of his wild bachelor life in Hollywood.

It also ensured him a variety of bed partners whenever he was so inclined, which was often, and embarrassingly loud.

Although she could also be an unpredictable handful, Pierce respected nineteen-year-old Morgan much more than her ex-boyfriend and leading man. She tended to keep to herself, spending most of her time with Bob Silverman and his son, Michael, who had an obvious crush on the beautiful star.

But she had no qualms about pitching in to help with even the most menial tasks, earning herself well-deserved kudos for her enthusiasm and willingness to work, the crew also enjoying her bawdy sense of humor and spicy jokes.

She wore loose pants and long-sleeved shirts to protect her fair skin from the scorching South American sun, her golden hair tucked beneath an old, battered hat she found in her cabin. Often mistaken for one of the men until she spoke, her unmistakable, rich, throaty voice echoed through the canopy of the lush green rainforest like a warm summer breeze.

With each passing day, Pierce found himself liking her more and more.

Their stock of dry and canned goods was rapidly depleting. Captain Diego kept his men busy fishing from the decks of *Piranha* and *Caiman*, supplementing their meager meals with peacock bass, redtail catfish, pancake sting ray, the delicious tambaqui, arapaima, and the surprisingly tasty piranha fish, but Pierce knew they would have to start hunting very soon.

This would mean stalking big game in the depths of the rainforest, with dangerous and uncertain outcomes. Their ammunition was limited, and although Pierce had years of experience making handmade weapons, he was the only one able to use them. It would take time to train the others, but he had no other choice... they were teetering on the edge of starvation.

He searched the forest to find the proper wood, then spent a week carving out three bows with twisted hemp bowstrings and twelve fire-sharpened feathered arrows. He'd make more if the first hunt was successful and planned to teach the entire crew how to snare small game as well.

A crowd gathered to watch his first demonstration. After tying a satchel to a tree at the edge of the forest forty feet away, he jogged back and drew a line in the dirt. With bow in hand, he stood behind the line, faced the tree, took aim, and fired.

Bullseye! As the cheering died down, he held out the bow to the admiring group, waiting to see who would volunteer.

To his surprise, the only one to step forward was Morgan. Meeting his questioning eyes with a Mona Lisa-like smile, she took the bow. Tipping up the brim of her hat, she nocked an arrow, raised the bow, pulled back firmly, and released.

A hard, resounding thud was heard, and the feathers of the arrow quivered in the center of the bag! The crowd roared its approval as Morgan turned with a grin and dipped low in an exaggerated theatrical bow.

Suddenly, the crew fell silent. As she rose, Morgan could see the fear on their faces and quickly spun around.

Standing against the edge of the rainforest canopy was a line of twenty silent, brown-skinned native warriors, their black eyes shining with hostility, their bodies covered with intricate tattoos.

Wearing nothing but maroon loin cloths and headbands that secured their chin-length, straight black hair tight to their skulls, each one held a cane tube to their lips with a deadly looking, red-tipped dart in the other end. As still as statues, they could have been mistaken for wax figures in a natural history museum display.

Suddenly, a native in the center jumped forward with a shout, startling Morgan! She quickly stepped backwards, tripping on an exposed tree root before Pierce could catch her. As she fell, his arm inadvertently knocked off her old, battered hat, her long wavy hair cascading down her back, shining like a golden halo in the midday sun.

The man abruptly held up a clenched fist and barked out a command to the warriors, who lowered their weapons, their eyes growing wide at the sight of Morgan's golden hair as he continued to speak. All at once, every warrior dropped to the ground, prostrating themselves before her.

No one moved... no one breathed.

Pierce nudged the captain, who was standing next to him.

"What did he say, Diego?" he whispered.

The captain could not contain his wonder and relief at their astounding stroke of luck, once he had deciphered a few words of the man's obscure tribal dialect.

"He is Chief of the Mayoruna... and he said their Goddess has finally returned."

****

As they shared the meager amount of food they had with the warriors, Pierce and Diego tried to convey their urgent need to return to Manaus, but Chief Bedi only shook his head and repeatedly dabbed his finger towards the sun.

"Ushe! Ushe!" he exclaimed.

Confused by what he meant, but knowing they'd never make it alive on foot, Pierce ordered both riverboats secured to the shore and proposed they all take a vote on the offer they had received from the chief.

Continue to wait for a rescue that might never come and risk death by starvation... or accept his generous offer and follow the Mayoruna warriors into the forest.

The vote was unanimous to join the tribe. If they wanted to live, there was really no other option.

They traveled with the Mayoruna for four years, moving with the clan of one hundred men, women, and children from one remote and isolated area deep in the jungle to the next, then returning to the banks of the Amazon River to fish, camping for no more than a full cycle of the moon in any location.

They never saw another human being.

It was a strenuous and difficult existence. The tribe knew nothing about cars, radios, electricity, or cellphones, living the same way the ancient ones had done for thousands of years. One might call them primitive, Pierce thought, but without their intimate knowledge of the rainforest and the river, the animals, birds, fish, insects, and reptiles in their environment, and their hunter/gatherer skills, none of the crew would have survived.

It took months to learn the ways of the people and to hunt with blowgun, bow and arrow, spear, and snare, but the contributions of the fledgling hunters to the communal food bank ensured their continued acceptance by the tribe.

Nothing was discarded or taken for granted. The women and children gleaned from the earth as they moved through the living forest, plucking, digging, gathering, and hunting small game. By the time they stopped to make camp for the night, even a meal of skewered green iguana, fire-roasted caterpillars, giant guinea pig, beetles, praying mantis, and katydids was considered a feast to the hungry crew.

Pierce was intrigued by their religious practices, but it was the Festival of the Moon, from which women were banned, that fascinated him the most. If they did not interfere and remained silent, he and his men, including Michael, were permitted to observe the sacred ceremony.

Morgan, however, played a vitally important role in this spiritual celebration, a role the Mayoruna people believed guaranteed the health and happiness of their tribe, and a place of eternal rest at the feet of the Goddess.

On the night of the full moon, the men of the tribe lifted her to their shoulders and carried her deep into the forest to a prepared clearing. Dressed in a red ceremonial gown and wearing an intricately carved headdress made of bronze and crusted with flecks of pure gold, her hair fell in loose curls to her waist, reflecting the light of the moon.

Lowering her gently to a high pile of skins and furs topped with the pelt of the sacred black panther, the warriors knelt before her, but as the drums and flute began to play, a grunt from the chief brought them to their feet.

Chanting songs of praise to the living Goddess, they danced joyously under the moonlight until the drums finally stopped and the sound of the flute faded away into the trees, the forest now eerily silent.

The shaman materialized at her side, muttering the last incantation of the sacred ritual. Lifting her wrist, he pierced it quickly with the tip of a sharp blade that had been scraped across the slimy skin of a rare jungle treefrog. The wrist of each warrior was then also pierced by his acolytes.

With a soft sigh, Morgan instantly fell into a trance, her body collapsing on the bed of furs, the warriors dropping to the ground where they stood.

When she awoke hours later, a sheltering cage of entwined branches covered her, the shaman and his acolytes waiting anxiously until she groggily sat up. With a shout of great joy, the shaman announced the Goddess had returned from the heavens, the Mayoruna again granted favor and protection!

Although Pierce questioned her many times about what she had experienced while she slept, she refused to discuss it, a faraway look in her eyes.

The awakened men, on the other hand, displayed physical abilities far beyond his human comprehension, performing incredible feats of strength and agility, and running mile after mile through the dense, hot, and humid rainforest without even breaking a sweat. Their senses of hearing, vision, and smell became super-sharpened, their aim with bow, spear, and dart even more deadly.

Pierce could see how these enhanced abilities enabled the men to protect the tribe against any danger and hoped that he might someday be deemed worthy to participate in their mystical ceremony.

But it was the Mayoruna's uncanny ability to communicate without speech that astonished the seasoned guide. In all his years and intimate contact with many and varied indigenous tribes, he'd never seen anything like it!

Small clusters of Mayoruna would come together briefly in a silent circle, and then, with no words spoken, begin a task in perfect sequence and unity. Individuals would meet, touch foreheads for a moment or two, smile, nod, and go their way, in total understanding.

But what shocked him completely was that the reigning Queen of Hollywood, the matchless Morgan Monroe, was able to communicate with them in the same way from the very beginning!

The day they first saw the Mayoruna, the warriors rose from their prostrate position on the ground, and Diego paled when he heard their chief issue an order to his men to have the rest of the crew slaughtered as a sacrifice to honor the reincarnated Goddess!

How she knew what the chief said was a mystery at the time, but a horrified Morgan immediately strode towards him to protest and plead for mercy! But before she could utter a word, the chief's eyes grew wide in surprise.

Bowing low to her in an obvious display of repentance, he made a great show of warmly hugging each member of the entourage, one by one, and from that moment on, they were all accepted by the tribe, which continued to worship Morgan year after year as their Golden Goddess in the flesh.

But the years had taken their toll as well. Of the forty-nine Catira, the word their indigenous hosts called their white-skinned blood brothers, only fifteen had survived.

Those with underlying conditions that required regular medication had died first. Animal attacks, infections from flesh-eating bacteria, malaria, venomous snake and insect bites took the rest. One of Chase's bedmates died in a long and agonizing premature childbirth, her tears and cries of pain still haunting the crew as they buried both her and the tiny baby girl.

That was the night Pierce made his decision, Meg's loving smile forefront in his mind, his loneliness unbearable.

It was time to go home... or die trying.

Chapter 2 Into The Mist

The entire tribe stood along the line of trees where their warriors first saw the Goddess and raised their hands in a sad final farewell. Then, silently melting away into the lush canopy of green, they disappeared.

When the Goddess told them that the spirit of the sun had demanded she return home, they understood, and when she raised her arms to bless them with fertility for their women and success in the hunt, the celebration went on for days.

Pierce and his remaining party of fourteen watched them go with heavy hearts. The Mayoruna were their friends, as well as having been their only hope in the beginning, and would never be forgotten. The daunting task ahead of him suddenly felt insurmountable, but he fought back his fear and squared his shoulders... It was his job to get these few who had ultimately survived safely back home.

“Okay, man, what do we do now? You said you’d get me back to Beverly Hills. I need a real drink! I’m sick of that crappy ceremonial shit.”

Chase London was still a prick.

Pierce smiled with amusement, clasping a friendly hand on Chase’s shoulder. But his fist followed next, hammering the famous jaw hard, the cocky actor hitting the ground.

“I’ve been waiting four years to do that,” he said with a satisfied grin. “Now, let’s get to work.”

****

After setting up a shoreline base camp and stone firepit, repairs began on one of the boats, and the women gave it a thorough cleaning. In the afternoon, two hunters set out to search for a tasty tapir or an armadillo. The Mayoruna had taught them well.

Pierce outlined his plan that night to the dirt-streaked but hopeful faces highlighted by the flames of the campfire.

They would sail *Piranha* downriver to Manaus. Diego and his two surviving sailors were tasked with creating a mast and the long push-poles they would need to keep the hull from becoming lodged in submerged trees, branches, and mud. With only the basic hand tools and machetes they'd left in storage on the boats at their disposal, it would be a difficult task.

The Mayoruna had shown Morgan and the women of the crew how to weave and dye the material they used for their minimal clothing needs, and Pierce asked if they could make a sail. Any captured breath of wind, their push-poles, and the current flowing towards the Atlantic would enable them to propel and guide the boat with some measure of control.

Preparations began the next morning. Diego and his men located the proper size tree for the improvised mast, cut it down, and hauled it back to camp to strip the bark and trim to shape.

With the now thirteen-year-old, dark-haired, blue-eyed, and well-trained Michael standing guard with bow and arrow, Morgan and the last two surviving women, Cassandra and Nada, began gathering coconut fronds, reeds, grasses, and other natural fibers gleaned from the forest and riverbank to begin the time-consuming process of weaving a sail.

It took weeks to complete all their projects. With the mast solidly installed, the homemade sail ready to hoist, and with plenty of dried food and bottles of fresh water in storage, they push-poled off the shoreline, feeling the current of the river catch the hull and start to carry them downstream. A loud cheer echoed off the trees of the Amazon rainforest as their journey began.

Little did they know what was yet to come.

****

The last reading on the boat's GPS that Pierce remembered before the power went down was that they were at least four hundred miles from Manaus, a trip that could very well take them two months to complete.

Silverman had insisted on using the real Amazon jungle in his film, not green screen, and he'd gotten exactly what he wanted. Multiple cameras with both digital and 35 mm film footage were stored in his cabin, priceless after what they'd been through for the past four years.

The studio would make an incredible fortune, not only from the completed movie, but from the breaking news of their two major stars return to civilization, their life with the Mayoruna sure to become a highly sought-after script in its own right.

Pierce could envision his agent negotiating a book memoir megadeal, the proceeds to supplement his paycheck from the studio, the number of zeros trailing the first digit or two left for his attorney to haggle. But what he really cared about was seeing Meg and Nora again.

As *Piranha* floated slowly downstream, the current and push-poles substituted for the mostly absent wind in the sail, all hands constantly on watch for obstacles in the river. In the afternoon, they would anchor the boat near shore to hunt and to cook a meal, on alert for any danger from the water, sky, or forest.

Signs of human habitation gradually began to appear after fifty days. They were approaching the outskirts of Manaus, the boat drifting past riverfront warehouses, docks, shacks, and overgrown side streets. But curiously enough, they saw no lights anywhere at night, the skies remaining dark, with the illumination of the moon and stars the only exception.

When the tall buildings of the city finally came into view, all fifteen weary travelers were more than ready to tie up at the Amazon Riverboat Company, hail a taxi, and check in to the nearest five-star hotel with steaming hot showers, soft beds, and a restaurant with a well-stocked bar.

But what they saw was not the bustling, exotic riverfront they had departed from.

Manaus was now a city of the dead.

****

As they walked the powerless streets, Pierce and his scouts realized the city was deserted. Buildings were in an advanced state of decay, the trees, vines, and vegetation of the ancient rainforest already reclaiming its birthright to the rich, fertile land that had been commandeered over the centuries by greed-driven men.

What had happened?

It was Michael who spotted the young boy, darting from a wrecked car to an alleyway in a poor attempt to tail them as they picked their way back to the dock. Motioning a silent alert to Pierce, he waved for him to keep going and ducked behind a concrete pillar just as the lone figure crept past him.

Snatching the sleeve of his threadbare and tattered shirt, Michael grabbed the boy, who began to cry, pleading for his life in rapid Portuguese. The other men backtracked to the scene, where Diego knelt down and calmly spoke to him in his own language.

The frightened tears stopped. Michael released him and the boy wiped his wet nose with a dirty hand, nodding or shaking his head in response to Diego's questions. Looking wide-eyed at all the armed hunters surrounding him, he launched into a lengthy and detailed explanation that had

Diego's bushy eyebrows lifting sharply in surprise, his tan, weather-beaten face growing pale.

"What's wrong, Diego?" Pierce asked in alarm.

The man rose, visibly shaken.

"The boy's name is Juan. He said the sun exploded when he was just a small child... and people began to die."

"What's the kid talking about, Pierce?" Chase growled scornfully. "The sun never exploded! It's right up there in the sky where it's always been. He must be crazy!"

Diego ignored him and spoke directly to Pierce.

"Do you remember the day when the power went down on the boats? That's about the same time Juan claims there was a bright flash from the sun very early one morning that temporarily blinded all who saw it, and everything stopped working... his father's car wouldn't run, the television and lights went out, the ice melted in their freezer. And he said the electricity never returned. Dios mio, what could cause such an extreme effect of that sort?

Pierce's expression grew solemn, his thoughts immediately turning to his family in Los Angeles.

"There's only one thing that has the power to do what he described, Diego. An electromagnetic pulse... or EMP for short. And there's only two possible places it could have come from. An atomic bomb... or a solar flare."

"This boy wouldn't even be alive if it had been an atomic blast," Michael replied. "The explosion would have leveled the city, and in the aftermath, radiation would kill anyone who re-entered. We've seen very few skeletons lying in the debris, so I'm thinking it was a solar flare. Without power, people probably left the city when they ran out of food, and we all know first-hand how deadly the rainforest and river can be. Ask him about his family, Diego."

Diego helped Juan to his feet and spoke to him again.

"His mother died last year from a pit viper bite. His father, uncle, sisters, cousins, and a close neighbor's family have an encampment not far from the edge of the city. Juan is often sent in to scavenge for parts and tools. He says they rarely see anyone else, which is why he followed us."

Pierce made the decision in an instant. "Thank him and let him go, Diego. Let's get back to the boat and tell the others what we've learned. I think I have a plan."

****

"So, are we in agreement?" Pierce poked the fire with a stick as he waited for an answer.

Bob Silverman glanced around at the silent faces for any signs of dissent. Seeing none, he spoke for the whole group.

"I think we'd all rather take our chances in the states than stay in the Brazilian bush for the rest of our lives. My wife, Giselle, Michael's two brothers, and little sister might still be alive in Los Angeles. And what if President Graham was able to fix the U.S. power outage quickly? Brazil is a third world country. Perhaps what we're seeing is their government's inability to reboot their power grid after such a catastrophic event."

Chase swatted at a giant cockroach on his leg. "And I could be having a Starbucks cinnamon latte right now instead of roughing it in bumble fuck Manaus," he grumbled.

Controlling his irritation, Pierce tossed the stick into the fire. "Okay, let's review this one more time. The river widens considerably from here to the Amazon Delta, where it drains into the Atlantic. The current, the sail, and our push-poles will keep us moving in that direction, as long as the boat doesn't get stuck. But our biggest problem will be when we hit the Atlantic.

"*Piranha* is a flat-bottom river boat, extremely unstable in rough seas. Diego has suggested we build an outrigger on each side of the hull. The ancient Hawaiians used outriggers to counterbalance their ocean-going canoes very successfully. With this technique, we can sail up the South American coast into the Caribbean and on to the tip of Florida, where I'm hoping things will have returned to normal. But if not, we'll continue sailing into the Gulf of Mexico, where we'll aim for the Texas coast.

"From there... we'll walk to California."

****

The evening they entered the delta of the Amazon River and first saw the open waters of the Atlantic Ocean should have been cause for a major celebration, but a weary coconut water toast was all they could muster before Pierce ordered them to drop anchor for the night near a tidal sandbar.

Their journey from Manaus had not been without great loss. Bob Silverman had collapsed, clutching his chest as he push-poled through shallow, reed-tangled water. Pierce and Michael carried the body to shore, where the boy dug his father's grave himself, refusing help from anyone.

Morgan cut and tied the branches for a wooden cross and pressed it into the earth, tears streaming down her cheeks. Gathering Michael in her arms, they wept as Pierce gave a stirring eulogy for the famous director... and his very good friend.

One of Diego's men, Martino Estevez, who could work wonders with an ax, fell ill from malaria and died in his bunk, feverish and sweating, whispering his wife's name.

Several days later, as they drifted through a narrow section of the river, a hail of arrows suddenly peppered the boat from the shore, killing four men standing on deck. Nada and

Cassandra, Morgan's hair and makeup artists, dove for cover too late, arrows protruding through their necks.

Diego and Chase poled as hard as they could, with Pierce, Michael, Morgan, Diego's mechanic, Ishmael Sanchez, and cameraman, Frank Carter, firing back with their own bows and arrows, the camouflaged raiders unsuccessful in their murderous attempt to hijack the boat.

Later that day, they lowered the bodies into the river, the splash of the first crocodile reminding them once more of the many unexpected dangers that could claim their lives at any moment.

Early the next morning, they pulled anchor. *Piranha's* two mahogany outriggers stabilized the hull as the sail filled with wind, and she began gliding through the delta towards the sea. Their hands firmly linked together, the seven survivors bowed their heads in a grateful prayer of thanks, hope rising in their hearts.

They were on their way home.

****

The violent Caribbean storm continued to rage as Pierce scanned the black sky above him. Damn it, they'd been so close... the Florida Keys visible in his binoculars ten minutes before the storm blew up out of nowhere. If they didn't find land, *Piranha* would be swept into the open Atlantic, death by starvation, dehydration, or drowning a certainty.

It had taken over eight months from the time they left the Mayoruna to reach the northeast coast of Venezuela. Pierce had forced them to go slow and steady, hopping from land mass to land mass, taking a week or two at each location to hunt for game, dive the bright blue waters for lobster and fish, refill the water bottles, and perform any repairs on the sail and boat.

A month earlier, Frank had been killed right off the most beautiful Venezuelan beach Pierce had ever seen, dragged into the depths by a hungry shark while diving. Besides himself, only five remained alive... Morgan, Diego, Ishmael, Chase, and Michael. Gladly leaving the continent of South America far behind them, *Piranha* had sailed northwest on the open sea, passing between the islands of Cuba and Haiti in their quest to reach Florida.

Another cold wave lashed him hard. He turned to fight his way below, resigned to accept whatever end had been slated as his destiny by the Almighty God, when a flash of brilliant white against the dark and stormy sky stopped him in his tracks.

To his utter amazement, a white osprey was hovering above him, unaffected by the torrential rain, hurricane force winds, and slashing seas! The bird whistled twice as it gazed directly at him, its black eyes searing deep into his very soul.

The hatch to the cabins below flung open as Morgan, her hat secured low and tight on her forehead, pushed her way out. Spotting him at the rail, she frantically waved for him to come inside. At that exact moment, a bolt of lightning struck the mast with a sharp crack! The boat shuddered from the impact, and as the pole splintered in two, the top section of wood tilted towards her.

Without a second thought, Pierce ran forward and pushed her away with such tremendous force that her feet lifted into the air! She flew backwards, her head slamming against the wall of the cockpit, knocking her unconscious as the mast crashed down, crushing his chest into the deck.

He gasped, unable to draw a breath. With a final sigh, he released and gave in to the inevitable, watching the osprey still hovering above him, realizing he'd never see Meg and Nora again.

The osprey's wings began to flutter as the bird retreated into the sky with a final whistle. But in its place, a swirling white mist began to form, and the face of an unknown woman slowly took shape.

The beautiful face shone with an unearthly light, the locks of her midnight hair brushed by a gentle, wildflower-scented summer breeze, her sparkling light gray eyes and ruby lips smiling at him with compassion and tender love. Even as he lay dying, he was entranced, his heart filled with a peace he had never known before.

The beautiful vision tilted her head to one side and lifted her chin, drawing his attention behind her as she faded away.

His dimming eyes filled with tears of joy as the face of his beloved wife Meg emerged from the mist, her long, honey-colored hair draped over a tiny squirming bundle held in her arms... and he knew he had finally made it home!

Nora gurgled happily as Meg reached out her hand, and he took it. She smiled... and pulled him into the mist.

Chapter 3 Nylah's Dream

"Adam, you're so quiet this morning. And why aren't you eating your breakfast, sweetheart? Did the storm frighten you last night?" Alea queried. They were sitting together at the campfire as the sun rose above the cliff line, waiting for the others to straggle in for the morning meal.

"You were already asleep by the time the rain began to fall and we came in to say goodnight, so we chose not to wake you. I must say, and your father agrees with me, that it was very unusual to get such a powerful storm during the dry season in February."

He looked up at his mother's worried face, replacing his own thoughtful expression with a smile.

"I'm just not hungry right now, Momma. I think I'll go up to the overlook for a while."

Alea studied him a moment longer, but saw nothing that concerned her, although she knew that breakfast was his favorite meal. He often went off alone by himself, walking up to the top of the sixty-foot-high cliff where John's wooden cross memorial to his friend from St. Thomas still kept watch over the vast Atlantic Ocean. He could spend hours on the cliff, seated on his favorite fallen tree trunk, but what he did while he was up there, he never discussed.

It wasn't that she was worried about him in the least. All the children, from Nylah to Noah, were as confident and sure-footed as mountain goats on the rough terrain and heights of Miracle Island, and she had no fear for their safety from other people, with only the Tribe in residence.

No, this was a mother's intuition. Something had changed in the sweet, young, carefree Adam she knew from just the day before, but she couldn't put a finger on what. A burst of love filled her heart as she smiled and brushed his soft dark hair with a gentle hand, nodding her approval.

She and Daniel had wanted to have many more children, but since Adam's birth, she was unable to conceive again. As the years went by, their love, passion, and desire for each other had only grown stronger, but no matter how often or enthusiastically they tried, they were still denied the joy of giving Adam a brother or a sister.

Swallowing their disappointment, they counted themselves fortunate and blessed to have this one son, this very special son, to love and cherish until the day the destiny that Skylark had predicted, and died for, would call him from their side.

The boy jumped up and hugged his mother's waist hard before dashing into the bush.

As soon as he disappeared, she fell to her knees in the sand, her face buried in her hands, and wept.

She had no idea why.

***

In the four years since Matt had been rescued from the heartache of Boston and brought to Miracle Island, many improvements and creative innovations had been made, the population having grown from only Daniel and Alea, when they were first marooned, to a total of nineteen people.

After discovering that Alea and Adam had already left for breakfast, Daniel walked out to the porch of the treehouse, contentedly surveying what had now become a small village on the shores of Casuarina Cove.

Five additional treehouses had been built to house James and Dolores, John's family, Ronny's family, Ryan, Sarah, and their son, Dylan, and Matt and Nylah. Walking down to the connecting pathway, he headed over to Matt's.

The Flare had obliterated all electrical power on the planet with one catastrophic solar event that no one could have predicted, the old way of life never to return without the manpower and massive infrastructure to bring it all back. Billions of human beings had died in the aftermath, unable to survive without the artificial support of electricity and the convenient daily services and sybaritic personal luxuries it offered... the empty, lifeless cities now nothing more than crumbling concrete wastelands.

The existence of mankind itself had depended on quickly finding new ways to adapt to a powerless environment. Those who survived the death and chaos did so by grouping together in small rural clusters and returning to the time-honored, ancient ways of the earth, hunting, gathering, and farming... utilizing the plentiful bounty that nature freely provided, if nature's limits were not exceeded.

Success was achieved through hard work, cooperation, and planning, with each clan, tribe, or community learning how to obtain and preserve the meat, poultry, vegetation, fish, and water necessary to survive.

Without power... the way man had lived for a million years until the dawn of electricity only two hundred years before.

The six men of the Tribe had discussed many different ideas of how to transport fresh water from the Black Hole reservoir all the way across the narrow island to an 8-foot-wide, 6-foot-deep limestone hole close to the village. They finally settled on the windpump, an older method used for centuries in undeveloped countries to draw water up from deep wells, and that required no electricity.

They spent six months gathering old metal pipe, metal rods, and sections of PVC pipe from Eleuthera and Spanish Wells to create the ingenious wind-catching machine that drove the water piston into the reservoir with a simple bell crank... no gears or pulleys required.

Two tall mahogany trees were felled and cleared for the fan blade pole on one side of the reservoir and the shaft support pole on the other, then set into the ground and braced with mounds of rock and straps. To capture the wind, they used the leafy ends of coconut branches, tightly interwoven with reeds and grasses to create wide, light fan blades.

After much trial and error, they eventually ended up with a functional windpump that pistoned water out of the Black Hole and directed it into hollowed out troughs made from thin tree trunks. The troughs were connected to one another until the homemade pipe system spanned the entire mile and a half to the limestone hole at the camp.

In order to provide water for Alea's proposed garden on the plain, a second offshoot trough system was in place and ready to go once the soil had been prepared.

On the day the windpump was to be tested, the women and children of the Tribe stood around the rim of the new well, watching the end of the pipe anxiously, with Noah ready to run to the Black Hole to let the men know whether or not their project was a success.

A loud cheer sounded when the first drops trickled out! Even with some evaporation from the open troughs, and the expected gradual absorption into the porous limestone of the well, an unending supply of clean fresh water was flowing straight to their door! The troughs would be screened later with thin woven material to keep leaves from filling them in and clogging the flow.

Alea, Josey, Pearl, Dolores, and Sarah hugged each other in excitement, the children happily joining in. That night, the celebration around the campfire was one to remember, the men finally able to relax from the hard work and stress of such an important project.

Water dripped constantly into the well, with a stronger flow when the wind was high. But now, anyone could draw up a bucket, even the kids! There was no need for the men to strap the five-gallon water bottles to their backs, fill them at the Black Hole, then carry the heavy, forty-pound load the entire distance back to camp.

Walking up the front steps to the porch, Daniel announced himself. "Matt, you awake?"

The door opened and Matt came out, finger-combing his long red hair behind his neck and securing it with a strip of leather. "Morning, Danny. What's up?"

"I want to check the pump this morning for storm damage, and I could use your help."

"No problem. Meet you at the campfire in five minutes."

Walking back inside, he saw Nylah standing pensively at the window, watching Daniel retreat down the pathway. Her eye color this morning was the same deep ocean blue as his own, her expression thoughtful.

"Are you okay, sweetheart?" he asked.

A smile flitted over her lovely face. "Yes, Papa. I had a dream last night about a strange boat that made me sad, but Momma told me it was meant to be and that all would be well. I get a little impatient, though, when I have to wait."

Matt's chest tightened when she mentioned Skylark. "Do you want to tell me your dream? Maybe I can help."

"No, you have to go now... and I need to talk to Adam."

"Nylah, if there's anything bothering you, I'll move heaven and earth to fix whatever it is."

"I know you would, Papa. I'll see you later, after you bring them all home," she declared as she blew him a kiss and raced out the door.

Matt shook his head. "What the heck did she mean by that?" he muttered. "Bring who home? There are times I just don't understand that girl."

As Nylah ran towards the beach, she giggled.

"Oh, but you will, Papa... you will!"

****

Their backpacks weighted with tools, Matt and Daniel headed west on the well-trodden trail between the camp and the Black Hole. Neither one spoke, simply enjoying the warmth of the sun rising behind them in the east. The cool, crisp morning air smelled fresh after the violent storm, the wet leaves, sticks, and debris brought down by the winds and rain releasing a pungent earthy perfume with each crunching step.

The windpump came into view as they emerged from the tree line, the three fan blades looking slightly battered, but catching the wind and rotating in the breeze properly. The bell crank was turning as it should, with plenty of water pumping out of the main pipe.

"Well, no need to worry, thank God," Daniel said with relief. "The pump is working, and the pipes to the camp and the garden look intact, but at least we came prepared."

Matt gave each pole a shake and stepped back with a satisfied nod. "I was sure that such a powerful storm would have ripped off the fan blades, at the very least. Hey, why don't we check the garden while we're here? Save the girls a trip later on."

Walking over to the opposite side of the Black Hole, they stopped at the edge of an expansive acre of neatly tilled soil. Row after row of potatoes, cassava root, lettuce, tomatoes, peas, pumpkin, onion, garlic, and a variety of aromatic herbs greeted them, unaffected by the storm, and in fact looking well-watered and perky. They harvested some ripe tomatoes, lettuce, and potatoes to bring back for dinner, stuffing their booty in their backpacks.

The garden was Alea's brainchild, only a dream until she and Daniel discovered the Black Hole, and the windpump was built. But once the pump was operational, and with an abundant supply of water and a delivery method finally at her disposal, she and Josey brought seeds, cuttings, starts, and roots from Spanish Wells, and the whole Tribe helped prepare the rich black soil for planting.

The growing season was the reverse from their northern hometown of Boston. In the Bahamas, crops were planted in October and harvested by May. With nighttime temperatures rarely plunging below fifty-five degrees in the winter, it was an ideal climate to nurture the plants that supplemented their daily diet of fish, crab, conch, lobster, and any edible native fruits and vegetables.

Alea had devised a way to use potatoes and cassava root to make a delicious grill-top flatbread and desserts sweetened with quick jams made from banana, mango, lemon, and sea grape. She loved to cook, and when the girls were a little bit older, she planned to teach Angel and Nylah how to make many of her original recipes that used only the vegetation and spices that grew on the island.

Before the solar flare, John had been a busy general practitioner and Alea a skilled orthopedic surgeon. With pre-Flare pharmaceuticals no longer obtainable, they used many of the herbs, roots, bark, fruits, and leaves gathered in the bush for medicinal purposes.

John's youngest son, Sam, had shown a keen interest in medicine early on. He accompanied both of them on their daily forages for the many available natural substitutes for medication and worked right alongside them on the pre-testing and healing applications for the Tribe's injuries and illnesses. An eager listener and active participant at their fireside chats and discussions, he impressed them with his intelligent, probing questions and immediate grasp of each topic.

Daniel was pleased as he surveyed the garden. The plants had survived the storm, their food supply practically ensured through the spring. Since the Flare, even a minor disruption to an important food source could spell disaster.

He was turning to go when Matt suddenly gripped his arm. "Daniel! Look at the cliff!"

What he saw caused his jaw to drop.

Impaled on the rocks, the splintered prow of a ship was pointing straight up into the air.

****

Perched on his fallen log, Adam closed his eyes, the crash of the waves against the rocks below vibrating in the cliff beneath him. Since his calling the night before, his senses seemed to have come alive! The boy could feel the depths of the ocean stirring, rolling, sweeping against the crust of the earth, could hear the whoosh of air passing over the wings of a seagull in flight. As he absorbed these new feelings and sensations, the warm rays of the morning sun caressed his skin, the soft, refreshing ocean breeze enveloping him in its comforting arms.

Lifting his face to the sky, he let the love in his heart flow unfettered towards the God of heaven and earth! Time stood still as he worshipped, lost in the music of the universe, until Moses fluttered down beside him, whistling a greeting before fluffing his wings and folding them neatly at his side.

With a last whisper of praise, he opened his eyes with a sigh, the powerful sense of the eternal mystic slowly fading.

His eyebrow lifted quizzically as he peered at the contented bird. "And where have you been, Moses? At least this time you only disappeared for a day."

He started at the sound of skittering rock close behind him, a pebble flying past his head and falling over the edge of the cliff. Twisting around on his log seat, he saw Nylah silhouetted against a passing cloud of white, her black hair lifting in the breeze, her lips curved in a gratified smile.

"We came to tell you... they're finally here!"

****

Matt stood at the top of the rocky rise, the hull of the ship facing him, the bow high overhead. The waves and swell had dropped considerably since the passing of the storm, but the partially submerged and broken stern of the boat continued to be pounded by the occasional set.

"It looks like it's pretty well stuck, Daniel. I think the two of us could climb onboard without the whole thing falling off the rocks."

Daniel lowered his backpack to the ground and opened it. "I'll bring a crowbar and a hammer with me. Go on ahead and start climbing, Matt. I'll be right behind you."

The fiberglass hull of the boat was pitted with deep divots and tears. Matt planted his boot in the nearest hole, and using one hand and foot at a time, climbed up the starboard side, grabbed the railing, and hauled himself over the edge.

Impaled on a jagged spike of rock, the flat-bottomed boat was lodged at a forty-degree angle against the cliff. Balancing on the edge of broken deck boards, he was surprised to see what appeared to be makeshift outriggers dangling from both sides of the hull, cracked and splintered.

A flat-bottomed boat on the ocean? Outriggers? Where did this strange vessel hail from?

The homemade mast was broken in two, the fallen section pointing towards the bow and rolled against the main cabin hatch. Matt suddenly tensed when he spotted a body trapped underneath.

Daniel climbed up over the railing behind him, the tools tucked into his belt. "I wonder what the story is here?" he asked as he glanced around the shattered deck. "This boat is a river cruiser."

Matt pointed at the body. "From where I'm standing, I can't tell if it's a man or a woman, but God rest their soul. And the mast is blocking the hatch. There could be people trapped in there, Daniel. We need to get it open!"

They climbed down to where the body lay. It was a man, his chest crushed to almost half its size, but what affected them the most was the expression on his frozen face, one of tremendous peace and joy. Matt and Daniel looked at each other, their eyes glistening. Whoever this man was, he had died happy.

Using their combined strength, they lifted the end of the mast off the body, the muscles of their arms bulging with the effort, and heaved it towards the starboard rail, where it rolled to a stop, the hull shuddering ominously under their feet. Matt gently closed the man's eyelids and covered the stiff body with the tattered sail before they dropped to one knee for a moment of silent prayer.

With the hatch to the interior now accessible, they went over to investigate. Daniel gripped the twisted handle and pushed down, but it refused to budge. He was pulling the crowbar and hammer off his belt when Matt heard a groan coming from beneath a pile of rope and seaweed.

Someone was alive!

He carefully picked his way through shards of glass broken out from the crushed window of the bridge. After sifting through the water-soaked mess, he found a still form lying underneath, wearing a battered old hat and rain gear.

"Daniel, this man is alive! I'm taking him up to the rise and I'll come back to help you!"

Gently lifting the limp body and positioning it over his shoulder, he retraced his steps through the glass and climbed down the side of the boat. The man he carried seemed as light as a feather, and Matt was concerned that the occupants on the wreck may have already been starving to death even before the storm struck.

Laying the man on a flat section of rock, he pressed his finger into the main artery at the neck. The pulse of blood was barely there... To give the hapless victim a chance to breathe easier, he tried to unzip the raincoat. But when it refused to slide open after several attempts, he gripped the front firmly, and with one powerful pull, tore it apart.

Two eyes suddenly flew open, mouth gasping for air!

Matt reared back sharply as his now wide-awake patient bolted upright and scrambled away from him on all fours like a startled crab, the battered old hat falling to the ground.

A mass of long, wet, tangled golden hair fell around her shoulders as her sky-blue eyes stared at him in shock.

“Who the hell are you?!”

Chapter 4 The Rescue

Speechless, Matt could only stare.

Was this scrappy wildcat really who he thought she was? He had seen that incomparable face a dozen times on the silver screen, his hand poised over his forgotten popcorn as she drew him into whatever magical persona she portrayed.

Many was the night he'd returned to his boat, *Solitude*, after dinner and a movie with a casual date or with Daniel and Ronny, lusting for the unforgettable vision that kept him tossing and turning in his lonely bed until dawn.

The power of an actress to affect him that way had stunned him, but he'd chalked it up to his usually unappeased sex drive and simply applied himself more vigorously to his work at Devereaux Fishing. Eventually, the memory of her sky-blue eyes, golden hair, and womanly curves faded... until he saw her in her next film. Then it all began again.

But the day he met Alea, the unattainable vision was quickly replaced by his new passion. And when he finally found the love of his life, his soulmate, his beautiful Skylark, he forgot about her completely.

Until today.

"Where's Pierce?!" she screamed, wet hair flying as she searched frantically in every direction. "What have you done with him? Where am I? Where are my friends? Where's Michael?" Before he could answer, she lasered him with a threatening glare as she pulled out a knife from beneath her raincoat, her magnetic eyes blazing.

"If you've harmed them in any way, Tarzan, I'll fucking kill you myself!"

Climbing to her feet unsteadily, her hand shot to the back of her head and came away red with blood. She looked at Matt, surprise suddenly registering on her beautiful face as she fell to her knees, the knife slipping from her grasp. The last thing she remembered before losing consciousness was two powerful arms scooping her off her the ground and clutching her tight against a hard chest.

With his lips close to hers, Matt muttered the first thought that came to his mind.

"What a bitch."

****

Her body now limp, he laid her down. Removing his t-shirt, he covered her as best he could before climbing back up the hull to help Daniel, who was working the frozen lock furiously with the crowbar.

"Matt, someone's pounding on the other side!"

He jammed the tip of the crowbar into the crevice between the door and frame again, and this time both he and Matt took hold of the bar. Gritting their teeth, they pulled with all their might until they heard a satisfying pop, and the door swung open.

Framed in the gangway were four wet and shivering men.

****

Matt carried the unconscious Morgan as Daniel followed, guiding the weak and stumbling men the short distance across the plain towards the Black Hole. Using his backpack as a pillow, Matt laid her in the grass near the base of the windmill and re-tucked his t-shirt around her body.

"My God, that's the famous actress, Morgan Monroe! Do you recognize her, Matt?" Daniel whispered.

Matt only nodded, gently wiping the oozing blood from her wound with a clean cloth from his bag.

Daniel shook his head in disbelief as he drew up a bucket of water for the thirsty men. He gave each of them a small coconut shell from the pile they kept handy while gardening, which they quickly dipped in, drinking cup after cup of the life-giving liquid.

"Thank you, sir," Diego gasped between gulps. "My men and I were trapped inside the boat when the storm threw *Piranha* onto the rocks during the night. She broke in two and the upper half of the hull crunched down, leaving us no opening to escape. Seawater from the breaking waves kept pouring in through every crack. We would have died from exposure and starvation if you hadn't found us."

He looked at the well-tended garden and the windpump system over the Black Hole. "May I ask where we are?"

"My name is Daniel Devereaux, and my friend over there is Matt Kennedy. You shipwrecked on our island in the eastern Bahamas," Daniel told him. "Where were you coming from, and where were you headed?"

"Don't tell him anything, Diego!" one of the men barked out. "We don't know this guy or what he's got planned. The red-haired dude is already manhandling Morgan!"

"Dios mio, Chase, will you just shut up for once?" the older, gray-haired Brazilian captain exclaimed. "These men have graciously saved our lives. If they wanted us dead, they could have left us in the bowels of *Piranha*. Show some respect, you fool, and perhaps a little appreciation."

Daniel noticed that the middle-aged Hispanic man and the teenage boy sitting near Diego said nothing but were on alert and listening intently.

Matt stood up and carefully studied the suspicious, dark-haired man with flashing green eyes. Holy Moly. The mouthy jerk was none other than Chase London! What were two major Hollywood stars doing on a jury-rigged river boat in Caribbean waters five years after the Flare?

"There was another man with us, Daniel. Did you rescue him as well?" Diego asked.

"I'm sorry," he replied sadly. "He was already dead... his chest crushed by your broken mast."

The three men looked at each other in horror, the teenage boy crying out in despair.

Diego crossed himself. "Pierce Covington was a good man... and my friend," he choked out, his voice husky with emotion. "He was our leader, and did his best for many years to keep us all alive."

A heartbreaking sob rang out from the grass, where they saw Morgan struggling to sit up. "Pierce!" she wailed, her agonized face lifting to the sky.

"He died trying to save me."

****

Matt threw the last shovel full of dirt on the shallow grave and stepped back, wiping his brow with the back of his hand. The teenage boy, whose name he learned was Michael, kept his arm tight around Morgan's waist as they kneeled beside the mound of soil. With tears streaming down their own faces, Diego, Chase, and Ishmael each laid a comforting hand on Morgan and Michael's shoulders, the bond between the five survivors clearly evident.

Daniel recited the Lord's Prayer, the only other sound that of the west wind whistling across the plain. When the prayer was finished, he asked if anyone wanted to speak.

His stubbled cheeks streaked with dirt and tears, Diego nodded and took Daniel's place.

"Mis amigos, what first began as an exciting movie-making adventure five long years ago ultimately led each one of us on a strange, dangerous, and mystical journey we could never have imagined, and Pierce Covington guided us every step of the way. He was strong when we were weak, wise when we were foolish, and never gave up hope, no matter the odds.

"He had the courage of the mighty jaguar and the loving heart of a father for us... his adopted children. But the yearning of his soul was to be with his wife and daughter, and although he was not given the joy of seeing them once more in this life, I pray that God will bring them together again someday, safe and happy in the clouds of heaven."

Morgan's shoulders shook, her grief inconsolable as she fell against Michael's chest.

Matt watched her, unable to look away. So, underneath the sharp and edgy exterior, there was a heart in there after all, he thought, and allowed himself to feel a bit sorry for her. She must have really cared for the dead man, and he, of all people, should have understood how pain could affect a suffering human soul. He imagined the gentle lecture he would have received from his tender and loving Skylark for such a lapse of kindness.

Daniel noticed the fiery red ball of the setting sun touching the horizon. "I'm sorry, folks, but it's getting late, and we need to get going."

The travelers slowly rose to their feet, Morgan still wrapped in Michael's arms. Catching sight of Matt's unreadable stare, she disengaged herself from the boy with a look of thanks and found her own shaky footing. With a parting glance at Pierce's grave, she lifted her chin proudly and turned to follow Daniel as he led the way through the trees.

Tired beyond measure, she forced her legs to keep moving. The path was unevenly sloped to the east, and she stumbled more than once. Angry at her own weakness, and knowing that the silent, red-haired Matt was watching, she refused to accept Diego's offered arm and kept trudging forward.

But as they walked, she found herself questioning her curiously negative reaction to the man. She was told he was the one who first saw *Piranha* impaled on the rocks and found Pierce's body under the mast. He and Daniel broke open the hatch, saving the lives of her companions. And apparently, he'd found her crumpled under a pile of rubble and carried her to safety himself, washing and tending the bloody split on her head.

What was it about him that irritated her so much?

He was certainly beyond attractive, but looks meant nothing to her, Chase London being Exhibit A, his heart-stabbing and embarrassing betrayal the reason she stopped dating, much to the dismay of the tabloids. She had resisted his many attempts to win her back while they were with the Mayoruna, choosing to live alone in her own small tent. Beauty and brawn were a dime a dozen in Hollywood, and if Chief Bedi had taught her anything, it was that the spirit, heart, and courage of a man was what made him beautiful in the eyes of the gods.

She'd learned some difficult lessons when she was a young and budding star, naïve and impressionable. *Rely only on yourself, always maintain control, trust no one.*

But her years with the wise and gentle Mayoruna had shown her a different way of relating to people that had challenged her hardened stance of protective self-reliance, and she knew that any Mayoruna warrior would have been proud of the selfless actions the man she found so disturbing had demonstrated. Her companions had expressed their appreciation to him repeatedly... She couldn't even make herself say the words.

She shrugged her shoulders. Now wasn't the time or place to decipher such puzzling thoughts. Pierce had given his life to save her, and she knew, deep in her soul, that she didn't deserve such a sacrifice. A wave of anguish overwhelmed her, and her knees suddenly buckled.

A strong arm encircled her waist, pulling her to her feet.

"Thank you, Mic…." She did a doubletake at the dark blue eyes just inches from her own.

"You're welcome, Miss Monroe," Matt said quietly, his deep voice rumbling in her ear before he released her and fell back to the end of the line.

How had he reached her so fast?

"I don't need your help," she murmured to herself. "I don't need any man's help," and kept walking.

****

The weary travelers emerged from the bush at the top of the bluff, the calm, turquoise-blue waters of Osprey Bay shimmering like a jewel just beyond the trees. A sleek cruiser with the name, *Into The Mystic*, was anchored out in the bay alongside two sailing catamarans. Stopping in their tracks, they marveled at the incredible scene before them.

A village of treehouses was nestled in a forest of pine-green casuarina, mahogany, and yellow elder trees. Orange and red tropical flowers lined both sides of a smooth connecting pathway that ran between the houses and meandered down to the beach. The smell of roasting potatoes, grilled fish, and hot bread wafted enticingly in the air from a large firepit near the sparkling white sand of a small, picturesque cove. Voices filtered up to the bluff, growing more excited as the residents noticed the return of Daniel and Matt.

"Welcome to Miracle Island!" Daniel announced, with a proud sweep of his arm presenting the panoramic view of Osprey Bay and the treehouse village below them. "We call ourselves the Tribe, and you are all our guests. I know you must be hungry, and I think you'll find that my wife, Alea, makes a very tasty fish stew and a terrific cassava flatbread on the grill!"

The five newcomers looked at each other, any suspicions they may have harbored now gone. As he started down the hill, they followed him eagerly, the promise of hot food in their shrunken stomachs too good to be true.

The rustle of branches ahead caught their attention. Two young children darted out of the trees and raced up the slope to meet them, the little boy and girl stopping directly in front of Morgan. What lovely children! she thought. The girl is a rare beauty, even at such a young age. And those sparkling light gray eyes...

A vague and foggy memory began to vibrate deep in the hidden recesses of her mind. I've seen those eyes before... but where?

The child reached out and took her hand, smiling happily.

"Hello, Morgan. I've been waiting for you."

Chapter 5 What A Day

Morgan felt embarrassed at being so obviously recognized. The days of screaming fans and flashing cameras were far behind her, and over the years she'd forgotten both the thrill and stresses of being an award-winning actress and a sought-after public figure.

It suddenly hit her what the girl said... *she'd been waiting for her*. But how did she know she was even here? Morgan sniffed the air. Was the child wearing perfume? The scent of wildflowers drifted lazily in the breeze.

"My name is Nylah, and this is Adam," the girl said as the dark-haired boy gave her a searching look and held out his hand. "Uncle Daniel is his dad."

Morgan shook Adam's hand, then smiled at her young fan. "What a lovely name! How old are you, Nylah, and which one of my movies did you like the most?"

"I'm four. I've never seen a movie, but Papa told me about them. Were you in a movie?"

Morgan was puzzled. Daniel had confirmed their initial suspicions that an enormous solar flare had obliterated all electrical power worldwide five years before. This girl was only four, and she'd never seen a movie... How could she have recognized her?

Nylah beamed as Matt joined them. "And this is my papa!"

Matt lifted his giggling daughter into his arms and gave her a big kiss, not giving a hoot that the truculent Morgan Monroe was watching.

"Hey, sweet pea. Did you miss me?"

"I always miss you, Papa. And you brought them all home, just like I told you!"

Matt froze, suddenly remembering her confusing parting words. Nylah smiled at him, her gray eyes sparkling with light. “I hope you like Morgan, Papa. She’s the present that Momma sent for you!”

Matt’s face turned to stone.

Nylah broke away from his embrace and hugged Morgan’s waist. “You’ll be staying with us,” she declared decisively. “There’s an extra bed in the loft, and you can tell Adam, me, and Angel all about movies! Come on, Morgan, I’ll introduce you to our Tribe!” Grabbing Morgan and Adam’s hand, she pulled them down the hill towards the firepit, where the rest of the survivors had gone with Daniel.

Morgan peeked at Matt over her shoulder, standing like a statue at the top of the bluff. What was Nylah talking about? And what did any of it have to do with her? She was a present... for Matt... from the child’s mother? Whoa! Morgan had seen and heard a lot of strange things in Hollywood, but this one almost topped the list.

She belonged to no man... and planned to keep it that way.

****

“Don’t be shy, Ishmael. Please take as many as you want.” Alea handed him the platter of coconut fritters fresh off the grill.

“Gracias!” The grateful man accepted her offer, loading his plate with half a dozen more fritters before passing it on to Michael. The entire Tribe had gathered around the firepit to meet the newcomers, except for Matt, who disappeared as soon as Nylah escorted Morgan to the beach.

Michael managed to offload a fritter or two before Chase snatched the platter away. He took a bite of the steaming treat and chewed slowly, savoring the sweet taste. As he swallowed, he glanced up to see Angel across the fire, gazing at him with an expression of innocent adoration.

The corners of his mouth lifted slightly in an amused smile, recognizing that he was most likely the object of an infatuated crush, something he had grown used to with the young Mayoruna girls. But she was simply adorable, and even shared the same birthday with him, November 17th, a fact the child excitedly discovered during all the getting-to-know-you conversation before dinner.

At thirteen, he was already a highly skilled and stealthy Mayoruna hunter and trained warrior. A growth spurt at age eleven had shot him up to an impressive five feet ten inches tall, and still growing. With a pair of striking ocean blue eyes, a muscular physique, and a mane of untamable dark hair, the marriageable virgins of the tribe had begged their fathers to request the bond.

As the leader of the Catira, Pierce made a show of seriously considering each proposal. With great sadness, however, he was forced to explain that Michael had dedicated himself to the Goddess until he was twenty, and if he were to violate his oath, disaster would fall upon the entire tribe.

Chief Bedi and the shaman approved his wise decision, and when the next Festival of the Moon approached, Pierce and Michael were invited to participate.

The boy had dropped to the earth moments after the tip of the blade pierced the blue vein in his arm, the mysterious substance from the skin of the tree frog coursing through his body like lightning, sending his mind on a fantastic journey through a dreamlike universe that unfolded before him like the petals of a rose, his visions both splendid and fearful. He sensed the presence of a powerful guiding spirit, whoever or whatever it was never revealing itself.

But before he returned to consciousness near dawn, his final, unforgettable vision was that of a glowing crystal in the shape of a woman rising slowly from the depths of a sea of iridescent turquoise-blue, awash with the soft blue glow of bioluminescence.

At that very moment, the light of the full moon emerged from behind an ominous dark cloud and struck the gem. The core of the crystal ignited, and a single ray of brilliant white light shot straight into his heart! The crystal shattered into a million shimmering pieces that floated up into the night sky, and in its place stood a magnificent woman of flesh, her face concealed by a veil of light. She reached out her arms... and Michael knew he was finally home.

****

"Earth to Michael, Earth to Michael... Hey, kid, I asked you ten times to pass me that bread. Wake up."

Chase leaned across Michael's lap and grabbed a piece of fresh-baked cassava flatbread straight off the grill, tossing it back and forth until it cooled enough to eat.

Michael's expression darkened but he said nothing. Chase had started taunting him not long after his father died. His friendship with Morgan had not gone unnoticed by the jealous ex-boyfriend, even though Michael was only eight when the trip to Brazil first began. But as he grew older and his dark good looks started drawing attention, Chase went full throttle on his malicious campaign to destroy their close relationship and re-ingratiate himself with the actress. It hadn't helped matters that young Michael had earned the respect of Chief Bedi and his warrior-hunters for succeeding at skills that Chase outright refused to attempt or failed at miserably.

The legendary day Pierce punched Chase in his famous jaw still made Michael smile. But Pierce was gone, and it was up to him to assume control, not only of Chase, but of his own life. He was no longer a boy. He was now a man.

He was about to speak when Angel leaped off her seat and planted herself in front of Chase, her hands on her hips.

"You're mean! We don't talk to people like that on my island!" she declared. "You should tell him you're very sorry, Mister Chase."

Chase didn't know what to say, challenged by a five-year-old girl in the presence of a group of complete strangers who controlled his access to food, water, and shelter. So, with a winning smile spreading across his flawless face, he did what he always did.

"Aw, honey, I was just joking with Michael. He and I have been through a lot together, and we're actually really good buddies, okay?" He tried to ruffle her hair, but she backed away from his touch, riveting him with a look that told him she didn't believe him for an instant.

Her flashing azure blue eyes met Michael's, and he was immediately drawn into their astounding depths. He stood and offered the child his hand, a look of wonder replacing her righteous anger towards Chase. The Tribe was silent as he escorted her to her chair, and as she settled into her seat, he bowed gallantly, dropped to one knee, and lifted her tiny hand in his own.

"My Lady Angel, I pledge myself, Sir Michael, to be your defending royal knight. My bow, my spear, and my dart are yours to command from this day forward, on my honor as a warrior of the Mayoruna," and touched his forehead to her hand as the Tribe clapped and cheered.

Her heart racing with joy, she decided to gift her knight with the most wonderful thing she could imagine.

"Sir Michael, would you like to go swimming with me?"

****

Pushing his way savagely through the bush, Matt somehow found himself at Alea's Secret Spot down the beach on the shore of the bay, far enough away from camp that he was spared from seeing or hearing whatever was taking place.

Falling to his knees, he howled with pain, blinded by his tears, his cries echoing across the water.

"Skylark! My darling, my heart... where are you? I need you so! Please let me see you!" Nylah seemed to see her all the time, telling him she shared long conversations with her momma, but he only saw her in his dreams.

"This woman cannot be the one. She's not you, my love, no one could ever be you! Your beauty, your faith, your sweet spirit... you were made for me, and I was made for you. We belong together. Why, God, why did you take her away from me? I believed in You... *I trusted You*!" he shouted and fell to the ground, pounding his fists into the sand.

As he sobbed, the Darkness suddenly materialized out of the ether, alerted by his hopeless cries. The noxious cloud cackled with glee, a tentacle of evil snaking down towards the tortured man lying in the sand, invited in by his outburst of doubt, ready to inject him with the venomous essence that would spawn a new host, eager to obey the commands of the Dark Master. But a second before its razor-sharp tip could touch his skin, it burst into flame!

Adam emerged from behind the trees, his eyes fiery orbs of golden light. "Where God has made His home, you have no power! Begone, foul beast... This man is sealed by the blood of the Son and can never be yours!"

The entity withdrew with a hiss, the tentacle snapping back up into the cloud.

"Ah, the boy has become His Prophet... But you are no match for me, mortal worm! The world will once again be mine, and I will watch them destroy themselves the same way they did before. I may have lost this man's soul, but there are many more left to harvest. You have no power to stop what is to come!"

"The Lord is my light and my salvation; whom shall I fear?" Adam's words of faith caused the Darkness to recoil with a shrill screech, and it slunk away, the scent of the air changing from heavy and foul to pure and sweet.

The intense golden fire of Adam's eyes softened, changing back into his usual shade of dark brown. He knelt at Matt's side and touched his shoulder.

"Uncle Matt, what can I do for you?" the boy asked gently.

Surprised, Matt rolled over and sat up, his face lined with pain, unaware of the invisible spiritual battle that had just occurred. "I still miss my wife, Adam..." he confessed, "and something Nylah said made it even worse."

"You mean, what she told you about Morgan?"

"Yeah."

A soft breeze brushed his ear, and Adam heard the loving Voice whispering the words that Matt so desperately needed to hear.

"Uncle Matt, my mother told me that Skylark took the knife that was meant for me. The Lord God permitted the Darkness to cause such a terrible thing to happen, and for you to suffer the agony of her loss. But the Evil One has no clue *why* He allowed her sacrifice. God's plan is always for our good, even if He doesn't share it with us. Our job is to *believe, trust, praise, and obey*, and one day, we'll see how perfect His plan was from the very beginning."

Matt listened, now the child and Adam his teacher. Skylark would have told him the same thing, he realized, and he felt his strength returning. "Thank you, my boy. Your mom was right. There are times you seem years older than you are, and a heck of a lot wiser than I ever was."

"Give her a chance, Uncle Matt. If you're listening to your heart, and she's really not the one... you'll know."

****

They walked back to camp together, and after a heartfelt hug, they parted ways and headed for home. The Tribe had retired for the night. Michael was bunking at the Garner's, much to Angel's delight, Chase was at Ryan's, and Ishmael and Diego were staying with James and Dolores.

As Matt walked up the steps to his front porch, he could hear peals of girlish laughter and giggling in Nylah's room. "I'm home, sweetheart," he called out. "Can I come in to say goodnight?" The laughter suddenly stopped. He heard the rustling of a blanket, then the room went silent.

"Okay, you can come in now, Papa."

He pushed open the door and saw her blanket mounded unusually high. Picking up an edge, he flung it off.

"Surprise!" she squealed, and Matt did a double take.

Nylah and Morgan were sitting cross-legged in the center of the bed, wearing headbands with white feathers tucked beneath, their faces painted with red clay stripes.

"Momma was from the Mi'kmaq tribe, and Morgan lived in a land called Brazil with the Mayoruna tribe! This is how the Mayoruna girls decorate themselves during festivals!" Nylah exclaimed, beaming with happiness. Her partner in crime, on the other hand, appeared completely mortified, looking anywhere but at Matt. Her shiny golden hair was clean and dry, falling in soft waves to her hips.

"Morgan's sleeping here with us, Papa, up in the loft, but we were waiting for you to come home. I made you a plate of food if you're hungry."

"Okay," he said gruffly and turned to leave without another word. The woman certainly was a jaw-dropping beauty, he had to admit, as images from her many movie roles flooded his mind.

Locating his plate of food, he took it out on the porch to eat. The light of the incandescent full moon flooded the sky, the bright and twinkling stars of the Milky Way hidden from sight. The night was windless... the silence a soothing balm for his weary soul. He took a bite of grouper and forced his thoughts to focus anywhere but back in that room.

Bedtime was generally geared to the setting sun on Miracle Island, or later on moonlit nights. It was too dangerous to use any kind of fire inside the highly flammable treehouses. If the occasional candle was needed, it was set into a glass container for safety and carefully guarded.

In the five years since the Flare, the lead plates in the deep cycle marine batteries had sulfated, rendering them unable to accept a charge, and with that failure, the ability to collect solar power also failed. And with gasoline for the outboards no longer available, the Tribe now had to rely on wind and fire as their only sources of energy.

Blinded by greed and convenience, the race of man had been systematically killing their planet with overpopulation and pollution that had caused the extinction of thousands of species over a short period of two hundred years. Then the Flare shut down the modern electronic age... and mankind was hurtled back to square one. Apparently, nature had the last laugh after all.

Finishing his meal, he blew out a deep breath, unable to think of any reason to keep him from going inside. What a day... He was bone-tired and ready for bed, and whether he wanted to or not, he'd have to deal with Morgan the best he could while she was living in his house. But if that's what made Nylah happy, that's exactly what he'd do.

Setting his plate on the counter, he noticed the laughing had stopped, and risked a peek into Nylah's room.

His daughter and Morgan were curled up together on the bed, sound asleep. He had to smile at the sight of the red paint staining their pillowcases and the scattering of white feathers on top of the blanket. They were each so lovely, in their own very different way...

As he watched them, his brow suddenly furrowed, and his heart stopped beating. "Momma," Nylah murmured in her sleep, and her head turned towards Matt as her eyes slowly opened.

There, in the moonlight, the beautiful face of Skylark smiled at him tenderly... and then she was gone.

Chapter 6 Mystic Memories

The pace of life on Miracle Island quickened with the arrival of the five shipwrecked travelers, each with their own unique personality, talents, and quirks.

Moses had immediately vanished as soon as Nylah led them into camp, but it certainly wasn't the first time the angel bird had flown off, reappearing days, or sometimes even weeks later, swooping down from the sky to perch on Adam's small but welcoming shoulder. No doubt home to recover from missions ordered by heaven, Alea said.

Diego and Ishmael hit it off immediately with James, their mutual love of boating and woodworking resulting in an exciting new project... the building of a sailboat from scratch!

Into The Mystic was permanently moored in Osprey Bay, her powerful engines rendered inoperable by the Flare. The lifespan of the Tribe's two forty-five-foot fiberglass sailing catamarans, *Barefootin'* and *Dances With Wind*, were at risk from the constant debilitating effects of salt and humidity, the materials needed to maintain and repair their hulls no longer obtainable. They would eventually need new sailboats for fishing and travel between the islands, and this meant drawing on every bit of knowledge they had of the craft of boatbuilding.

Matt and Ryan had observed the remarkable skill of the Mi'kmaq boatbuilders in Nova Scotia firsthand and were able to offer invaluable information on many of their ancient techniques. They combed the island searching for the proper trees for the ribs and planking and devised a method to create the sticky pitch that was essential to seal the seams of the hull. The sounds of hammering and sawing at the cove became commonplace, the stacks of timber shrinking as the new boat's form began to take shape.

With the project in full swing, Daniel, John, and Ronny assumed all fishing and diving duties, with Sammy, Robbie, Noah, and Gypsy tending the gardens, caring for the animals, and joining Alea and Josey on their foraging walks. Sarah already had a full-time job with her one-year-old son, Dylan, while Pearl and Dolores instructed Adam, Nylah, and Angel in their daily lessons, made lunches, and prepped for dinner.

Every morning, Michael, Chase, and Morgan were asked to select which work detail they preferred to join that day. Two young, strong, healthy men were an important addition to the Tribe, and Daniel wanted to ascertain what their talents might be. Morgan, however, was more of a question mark, her contributions yet to be determined.

Michael was eager to learn whatever might be required of him. Daniel was impressed with how quickly the intelligent young teen adapted to any new situation he was presented with, and he frequently offered suggestions that showed surprising insight and creativity.

He talked and joked with ease as he acquainted himself with every individual in the Tribe, who already viewed him as one of their own. Little Angel latched on to him as soon as he sat down, and it did not go unnoticed how patient and kind he was with the smitten child.

Chase, on the other hand, was a completely different story. It didn't take long for any crew to sigh in quiet resignation if he chose them. He'd be no help at all, and more than likely, a hindrance to their chores, always finding an excuse to wiggle out of an assigned task and repeatedly trying to engage them, at the worst possible moments, in distracting conversations about his celebrity life in Hollywood.

Daniel was disappointed, wracking his brain for a way to turn the superstar into a productive citizen of Miracle Island. But the night that Alea mentioned feeling ill at ease with his flirtatious behavior on a forage for fruit, he'd had enough!

The next day, Chase was permanently assigned to the dive boat, under the direct supervision of Ronny.

Ronny snorted with amusement when Daniel explained the reason for the actor's assignment. The man must have a death wish, messing with Daniel's wife! When *Barefootin'* anchored that afternoon, a much quieter Chase London disembarked, barely able to walk, and went straight to bed.

Morgan was relieved. Unless she chose to go out with the dive boat, she wouldn't see Chase again until the communal meal at sunset, spared for most of the day from the pressure of his constant pleas to reunite. During their years in the jungle, the handsome playboy had no trouble at all finding a willing partner to bed, but Chief Bedi never permitted a man to touch the Golden Goddess in a sexual way, under pain of death... and Morgan hadn't complained.

During their journey from Brazil, he started pushing again, but was held in check by Pierce. Now, with Pierce dead, he'd doubled his efforts to bed her. No matter how often she turned him down, he refused to take her seriously, the lust in his eyes rolling her stomach. Shoving him firmly away, she quickly hailed whoever was near, leaving Chase to deal with his all too frequent physical dilemma however he chose.

Although she bunked in Matt's loft, they went out of their way to avoid unnecessary contact. Matt kept himself busy all day with the new boat build while she rotated working with the other crews, their paths only crossing briefly. He never talked about Nylah's mother or even mentioned her name, and although curious, she felt it wasn't her place to bring the subject up, especially not with Nylah... In fact, no one in the Tribe ever discussed or dropped any kind of hint about Matt's past, and she decided not to pursue it.

The most uncomfortable moment for them both was each night after she finished telling Nylah a bedtime story and wished her sweet dreams. She'd close the door behind her, only to find Matt sitting rigidly at the table, waiting his turn to see his daughter, his face cold.

As she climbed the staircase to her loft, she would force herself to say goodnight, his response nothing more than a grunt in return. Jerk. Well, he *was* allowing her to live in his house. But all the same, it bothered her.

But what bothered her even more were the vivid dreams that began haunting her sleep ever since they shipwrecked on Miracle Island, dreams that both disturbed and thrilled her, resurrecting memories that had been locked away in the deepest recesses of her mind. With the exception of Chief Bedi, she had never spoken a word to anyone of the strange, and often incomprehensible, phenomena she'd experienced while in trance during the Festival of the Moon celebrations.

As soon as her forearm was pierced by the tip of the knife coated with the sticky tree frog substance, her spirit lifted out of her body and hovered above it. As she studied the inert flesh lying on the furs, she wondered why she had been limited with such a burdensome encumbrance when the twinkling stars and breathtaking universe beyond beckoned so enticingly.

A wildflower-scented white mist would begin to surround her, and she could sense what had now become a familiar presence approaching. The mist would then part to reveal her spirit companion, a young and beautiful woman with midnight black hair, fawn-colored skin, and sparkling gray eyes, who offered her hand with a loving smile.

Come away with me once more, my Chosen One.

With perfect trust, Morgan would take that hand, and together they traveled to the distant lands of planet Earth.

She was guided to many different places to watch people she knew were not spirits like herself and her companion, their faces always out of focus. She could feel their emotions and hear their thoughts as they went about their daily lives, the mysterious woman drifting down occasionally to speak to one of them, with Morgan by her side. A white bird with wise, black-masked eyes would fly alongside them as their escort, his feathers haloed with radiant light.

They visited one man often, his face shrouded in a dark haze, and she could feel the grief and sadness emanating from his tortured soul. For some reason, this man's sorrow touched her own lonely spirit, and she was caught off guard by the surprising feelings of love and caring for the unknown sufferer blossoming in her heart. She longed to hold him, to comfort him, to offer him whatever solace she could to ease his pain.

Whenever she asked the woman his name, the answer was always a cryptic smile and a slow shake of her head.

He will find you someday...

A loving hand then encircled her own and together they soared through a tunnel of dazzling light until she floated back down to her bed of furs, her companion releasing her with a soft farewell as she reluctantly slipped back into her sleeping flesh.

When she awoke with the dawn, the dream gradually began to fade until all that remained were pale shadows of her journey in the night. After they left the Mayoruna, the dreams disappeared... until she arrived on Miracle Island.

The travelers had been living with the Tribe for a month when she stepped off the porch one morning to join Alea for a trek into the bush for fruit. A flock of white-faced duck drew her attention as they flew across the bay and landed near the beach to hunt for insects and seeds. She stopped in her tracks, then turned and bolted towards the dirt path that led to the Black Hole.

Alea was pouring herself a cup of hot tea while she waited, surprised to see Morgan suddenly dash away into the bush. Matt was nearby, already at work on the boat, and she waved her arms to draw his attention. He dropped his hammer and raced over to where she stood.

"What's wrong, Alea?"

"It's Morgan. She was on her way here to meet me, but I saw her run off on the path to the west. She didn't look right, Matt. Can you go after her and make sure she's okay?"

He rolled his eyes, and Alea sighed in exasperation.

"Hey, it's obvious to everyone there's some issue between the two of you. The tension's so thick you could cut it with a knife, but for the life of me, I can't imagine why. Nylah adores her, and so do the rest of us," she chided gently as she laid a hand on his arm. "Maybe this would be a chance to clear the air, if you feel like it. But she's one of our Tribe now, and I'm concerned about her. Please, Matt? Do it for my sake, at the very least?"

With that request, he relented. "The path west, you say? If she was working with you today, why in the world would she be going over there? I'll grab my pack and track her down."

She gave him a grateful hug. "Thank you, Matt. The kids are swimming in the cove before breakfast, so I can't go with you, but let me know when you and Morgan get home."

Retrieving his travel gear from his bedroom, he started up the hill, jogging at a steady pace. Not even breaking a sweat, he reached the Black Hole in less than ten minutes.

Nothing looked disturbed. The windmill was turning in the brisk morning breeze, water pouring into both troughs. He peered into the sunless abyss of the reservoir opening, just in case she had stumbled in. The vexing woman was nowhere to be seen. Where had she gone?

A loud bang brought his head up, the sound coming from the direction of the ocean. Had she gone back to the wreck of *Piranha*? He sprinted through the garden and over the plain to the base of the cliff and began to climb. The bow of the boat still pointed to the sky, but the weatherworn hull was barely hanging on, shuddering from the pounding waves of a northwest swell.

Reaching the top, he could see the tip of the bow start to slip a few inches, then stop, then slip again, rocks dislodging from around the hull and splashing down into the churning water. She was inside! Why? And would the vibrations from her movements be enough to cause the remnants of the boat to tilt backwards off the cliff and sink to the bottom? She would surely drown, trapped thirty feet below the surface in the wreckage.

Tossing his gear to the ground, he gripped the rotting wood of the hull and hoisted himself up the side, finding toeholds for his feet. *Piranha* creaked and groaned as he reached the rusty metal railing. Streaks of mud from her moccasins led to the broken hatch door, the gaping maw of the entry wet and forbidding.

"Morgan, it's Matt!" he shouted as he picked his way to the opening. "Where are you?"

"I'm in my cabin, but I can't get out! Something in the hallway collapsed and the door is blocked!" There was no disguising the panic in her faint voice.

"Hold on, Morgan, I'm coming! Keep talking so I can find you!"

His command suddenly triggered the memory of her spirit companion's prediction. *He will find you someday.* But the memory instantly vanished as she was thrown off balance by a jarring downwards shift of the hull.

"Please help me, Matt! This boat is falling apart!" Despite her growing panic, she kept talking as he requested.

"I came back here for what I thought was a good reason, but maybe it was kind of stupid after all. You guys don't need anything I can do. The Tribe is surviving just fine without me. I guess I was feeling a bit useless and thought I'd found a way to contribute something valuable. My foolish ego got the best of me... and now I've put you, Nylah's father, at risk because of my actions. I'm so sorry, Matt. If I don't make it out of here, I hope you can forgive me someday for all the trouble I've put you through."

Tears filled her eyes as she reflected on how badly she had treated him since her arrival... but why? It was still a mystery she hadn't yet solved.

"I want you to know how much I care for your daughter," she continued. "Nylah is very special. I wish my childhood had been as happy and carefree as hers. I fell into a stardom I'm not sure I really deserved, but my parents kept pushing me. Sometimes I loved it so much... the lights, the cameras, the attention, the challenge to transform myself into a character completely different than who I am and make people believe it. And they did. Unfortunately, I think I let it go to my head.

"I haven't told anyone what happened during my years with the Mayoruna tribe in the Amazon. Because my hair was the color of gold, I was worshipped as their Goddess, and that worship saved the lives of my crew. It was a role I was forced to play for years until we came here, and now... I'm lost. I don't know who I am anymore, or what I have to offer.

"It's pretty obvious that you hate me, Matt, but I'm afraid... I'm afraid I have no future, no purpose, no reason to go on living. I'm stuck inside this ship because I thought I'd found a way to make myself feel worthy again. But all I've done is put you, the selfless man who rescued us and allowed me to live in his own home, in harm's way."

The door to her cabin suddenly swung open.

"You can shut up now. Take my hand and follow me."

She quickly clutched his hand, and before she could take a second breath, he pulled her through the door and slung her over his shoulder. Scrambling up the piles of debris crowding the vertical corridor, he burst into the light.

Piranha's bow was slowly tilting away from the rock wall, the bones of her hull shaking under Matt's feet. With Morgan wrapped around him, he leaped over the rail as she screamed in terror, landing hard on the top of the cliff, his powerful legs absorbing their weight. Their hearts pounding wildly, they watched as *Piranha* fell backwards into the ocean and sank below the surface.

Matt turned his head to look at her, his mouth just missing her famous lips. "What the hell is poking me in the neck?"

She beamed from ear to ear as she readjusted the items strapped to her back, strands of her lustrous hair loose and blowing in the breeze.

"It's the reason I went to the boat in the first place. I had to get my bow and arrows!"

****

"They're back!" Nylah pointed to the top of the rise as Matt appeared, with Morgan right behind him. She brushed off her sandy wet hands and stood up.

"Don't you want to finish our sandcastle?" Angel asked with a pout. "They probably just came home for lunch. Mom told me we're having grilled conch and french fries." Her expression suddenly brightened. "And Michael is eating with us today!"

"We can finish it tomorrow," Nylah declared, her eye color shifting from pale green to a light gold.

"Are you sure, Nylah?" Adam was concerned for his best friend. He already knew why she was so happy, and her predictions were never wrong. But the Darkness was always watching... listening... seeking to destroy human hopes and dreams out of its hatred for the Creator.

"Yes, Adam, I'm sure," she insisted, her face glowing with excitement. "My prayer was answered. Today's the day God is giving me a new mother!"

****

With a brief nod to Morgan, Matt left her alone to rest, and veered off to Daniel's treehouse. He called out a hail before walking up the steps to the porch as Alea held open the door. Dropping his heavy backpack to the floor with a thud, he collapsed into a swinging hammock chair suspended from the ceiling rafters, his body aching with fatigue.

"Well, you're both back in one piece, I see." Alea gave him a humorous smirk as she handed him a glass of lemonade.

"If you hadn't convinced me to go after her, she'd be dead."

Alea swung back and forth in her own chair, listening to his story of Morgan's precarious rescue.

"You know, the travelers really don't talk much about their years in the jungle. Maybe we need to encourage them to tell us more about their experiences and what they learned from the Mayoruna. Their knowledge of that culture could be very helpful here, and if Morgan is having personal issues she's struggling with, the men may be as well. I would never have guessed she was feeling useless to us. I'll talk to Morgan, and Daniel can speak to each of the men privately."

Matt lifted his lemonade, but his hand froze before the rim touched his lips. "She could have been killed today, but she was willing to risk her life for that bow. I wonder how good she actually is with a weapon like that?"

"How long has it been, Matt, since you've used a bow? I remember that any mention of the Mi'kmaq was a difficult reminder of Skylark when you and Nylah first got here, but I'm told you were a master with bow and arrow as a hunter of Reindeer Camp."

His eyes clouded, but despite himself, his lips curled up in a small smile. “Oh, now and then Ryan and I take the bows we made here on the island to a clearing out in the bush for a bit of practice time. But since there’s no big game to hunt, there really hasn’t been any use for them.”

His forehead suddenly wrinkled. “What the heck was she planning to shoot anyway?”

An amused voice suddenly spoke from the doorway. “From what I just heard, I think the Tribe’s long overdue for some fun of a different kind.” Daniel walked in and kissed his wife before grinning at Matt.

“It sounds like we have three contestants for an archery tournament!”

Chapter 7 The Contest

Matt stepped up to the line drawn in the sand and took his stance. He eyed the grass-stuffed, thick red pouch of material tied to an enormous piece of driftwood fifty-yards away in the sand along the bay. Piece of cake... for him. And maybe for Ryan, standing to his left.

The question mark was Morgan Monroe, on his right.

She had agreed to participate when Daniel approached her with the idea, her cryptic expression leaving him clueless as to its meaning. As soon as he left, she disappeared into her bedroom with her bow, the quiver of arrows, a container of coconut oil, and a cloth, re-emerging only minutes before the contest was to begin.

The entire Tribe watched from behind the line, seated on chairs carried over for the exciting competition that Daniel had announced would begin after lunch. Team Matt, Team Ryan, and Team Morgan cheered their chosen champion as they arrived at the beach, with Daniel remaining neutral as the contest judge.

Ryan held a simple white ash bow, carved with the ancient Mi'kmaq symbols for the Great Spirit and for Heron Camp, the fishermen of the tribe. He had honed his skills on the 700-mile odyssey from Nova Scotia to Boston, where a bow and a quiver of arrows had meant food, and very often, the difference between life and death.

Robbie, Noah, Sammy, James, and Dolores cheered as he waited to take his turn, with Sarah holding a squirming Dylan on her lap, guiding his tiny hand in an encouraging wave to his father.

Team Matt included Ronny, Pearl, John, Josey, Gypsy, and Adam, waving casuarina branches and whistling loudly, with Bear and Brandy howling their support as well.

When Morgan appeared, her bow and quiver hidden by a cloth, Diego, Ishmael, Michael, and Chase leaped to their feet, clapping and hooting enthusiastically. But when Alea, Angel, and Matt's daughter, Nylah, came over to join them, they paused, looking at each other in surprise.

Diego and Ishmael slid over on their log to make room for the unexpected new additions to Team Morgan as Michael lifted Angel to his lap, the happy little girl wrapping her arms around his neck, her blue eyes shining.

Daniel faced the noisy crowd, the competitors standing behind him, their bows ready.

"Sit back and relax, my friends, because this afternoon I have some very special entertainment for your enjoyment! Our very own Mi'kmaq and Miracle Island archers, Ryan McCarthy and Matt Kennedy, and Morgan Monroe, who is representing the Mayoruna of the Amazon, have agreed to dazzle us with a demonstration of their skill with bow and arrow!" he proclaimed.

"Now we've all heard that Matt was a member of Reindeer Camp, the big game hunters of the tribe. He was called Red Bird, and was renowned for his deadly accuracy, more so than many of their own warriors. And Ryan, of course, *claims* to have some skill as well, even though he was a fisherman with Heron Camp."

Team Ryan booed, pelting him with handfuls of prickly casuarina pinecones as they jeered raucously, Morgan and Matt's teams breaking into laughter.

Daniel waved his arms for silence. "Morgan retrieved a very interesting bow today, risking her life to do so, yet has never mentioned having any experience as an archer. Can she really shoot...? Can a woman of unknown ability defeat our two expert Mi'kmaq bowmen?"

Ishmael and Diego leaped to their feet, pointing at Daniel, and shaking their fists playfully.

"You doubt our Morgan? You will see, Daniel, all of you will see! These men do not stand a chance against her!" Michael, Angel, Chase, and Alea stood and clapped for their champion, but Nylah remained seated, her chin resting in her hands, her eyes sparkling.

Daniel chuckled at their display of loyalty, pleased that the crowd was getting caught up in the spirit of the game.

"The distance for round one is set at fifty yards, and the competitors will alternate shots twice. The two archers to score closest to the black bullseye will advance to the next round with one shot at sixty yards, and finally, one shot at seventy yards.

"The prize, you may ask?" he said enticingly. "Something that none of us have had for a very long time. The winner of our archery contest will receive two weeks off from work! Their treehouse will be kept clean, their laundry done, and they will be served their choice of entrée for every meal, as well as an entire jug of my wife's famous mango wine, to enjoy by themselves or share, if they choose. Consider it a Miracle Island tropical vacation!"

A groan of envy sounded from every chair. Living on the island was idyllic, even with the lack of electrical power, but it was also hard work; fishing, diving, gardening, harvesting, cooking, repair and maintenance of the treehouses, latrines, and boats, and the care and feeding of the farm animals. Two weeks with no responsibilities was a marvelous treat that all of them could appreciate.

Daniel turned to the three silent figures standing at the line in the sand.

"Let the games begin!"

****

Matt raised his bow, the shaft of the arrow straight and true, and took careful aim. The roughened buttonwood of the grip felt like the warm handshake of an old friend as his fingers curled around it. When Karen stole their truck on the road to Boston, he'd lost his treasured Mi'kmaq bow, a gift from Chief Lonecloud, Skylark's grandfather.

Starfire had been a magnificent creation, carved out of black oak, the beautiful face of Skylark and her shapely body flowing around the upper and lower limbs, the only image of her he possessed.

When he first arrived on Miracle Island, he was still in mourning, but gradually began to miss the feel of a bow in his hands. It took him a year before he could bring himself to carve an adequate replacement. It would never be *Starfire,* just as no woman could ever be Skylark, but it gave him back the confidence he'd lost after Karen's vengeful rampage that cost Skylark her life. But with no big game to hunt, he and Ryan occasionally hiked inland to a clearing in the bush to practice, for the simple joy of the sport.

The center of the bullseye slowly came into focus over the tip of his arrow as he prepared to release. It was a natural and familiar action he had taken a thousand times before, and always with accurate results.

So why, he asked himself, was he trembling? To those watching, imperceptible, but shocking to him.

He remained locked in firing position, willing his body to stop its frustrating betrayal. He sensed Morgan's surprise, as if she somehow knew he was in trouble... and he didn't like it. But his distaste was exactly what he needed to break him out of his inertia.

A millisecond later, his feathered arrow slammed into the target with an audible thump. A cheer burst out from Team Matt, but his heart sank.

The tip was buried deep in the target, yes, but it was impaled on the border between the three-inch-wide black bullseye and the red cloth of the pouch.

He struggled to keep his expression neutral as Ryan took his place, clapping his old friend and archery instructor on the back. “Nice shot, man! Let’s see if the student can beat the teacher!”

With a wave to his team, Ryan steadied himself and aimed. The bowstring vibrated as his arrow struck home in the red, an inch outside the edge of the bullseye.

“Next round will be better,” he reassured his disappointed fans, and relinquished his spot to Morgan. “I’m just getting warmed up!”

She nodded her thanks as she moved into position at the line, shrugging the bow off her shoulder and removing the cloth. The Tribe gasped in awe when her weapon came into view.

The dark mahogany wood of the one-piece, six-foot long bow curved in gracefully to the narrower handgrip, then out again, like the elongated figure eight of a woman. The grip itself was tightly wrapped with fine woven cordage, designed to prevent the archer’s hand from slipping.

The mahogany above and below the grip was ornately carved with the sacred spiritual symbols of the Mayoruna, the deeper indentations between the labyrinth of intricate symbols dyed a rich, dark maroon. The raised surfaces of the symbols had been hammered with a layer of 14-carat gold, gleaming like angel fire in the hot Bahamian sun, with a tassel of thick gold thread attached to the bottom.

The bow was spectacular, and the woman holding it a vision of undeniable beauty, her coiled hair as brilliant as the golden object she held. There was no doubt in anyone’s mind that this bow had been made specially for Morgan, but other than the crew from *Piranha*, only Matt knew the reason why.

Their surprise was complete when she slowly withdrew a four-foot long, featherless arrow from her gold-encrusted crocodile skin quiver and positioned it over the top of her hand holding the grip. The sleek arrowhead was made of black obsidian, with a glinting, razor-sharp tip.

Taking her stance, she studied the target leisurely, and took aim. Then, with a hint of a smirk curving her lips, she slowly turned her head to look directly into Matt's eyes... and released.

With one deafening shout, Team Morgan leaped to their feet! The arrow was dead center in the bullseye!

Her eyes never leaving Matt's, she lowered the weapon and stepped back from the line as her team crowded around her; Diego and Ishmael in tears, Chase grinning proudly, Alea, Angel, and Michael hugging her happily.

Matt felt a small hand slip into his own. He broke away from Morgan's challenging gaze to find his daughter by his side.

"You did good, Papa," she whispered quietly. "You'll find the way. Listen to your heart."

Her tender love instantly calmed his anger and frustration, but there was another, less defined emotion affecting him that he couldn't explain. Setting his own confusing issues aside, he dropped his bow in the sand and scooped her into his arms.

"I don't always understand what you tell me, my darling, but I know you love me... and you know I never give up, no matter what. That loss stung, but I'm a grown man who may be in need of some humbling, however much it may hurt. Perhaps this is God's way of teaching me that lesson. I was proud of my archery skills, and that's where He's poking me in the ribs right now. She's good. But the next round could be different."

"Archers on deck for your second shot," Daniel announced. He had already walked over to the target, documented the position of the arrows, and pulled them out.

After lowering Nylah to the ground, Matt ruffled her hair before returning to the line. Daniel gave him the go ahead, and with no hesitation at all, he raised his bow, drew back, and released.

His arrow drove into the same hole Morgan had made in the center of the bullseye!

His team exploded with cheers and whistles, Brandy and Bear jumping and barking along with them! Morgan nodded her congratulations but appeared somewhat shaken.

When order was finally restored, Ryan took his shot. His arrow landed outside the black bullseye circle by two inches.

"I guess I should just eliminate myself, Daniel."

"No, Ryan, Morgan still has a turn. Let's see how it goes," and he waved her to the line.

Her shot imbedded itself one inch away from center. She was obviously in second place.

"Okay!" Ryan exclaimed cheerfully. "I'm done. May the best man... or, uh, woman, win."

Daniel paced off ten more yards from the target, and as the Tribe picked up their chairs to move, Matt and Morgan stared at each other, the tension palpable between them.

"Morgan, you're up first," Daniel called out.

Tearing herself away from Matt's unflinching gaze, she turned and ran to the new line.

Matt's insides were left churning with a rush of disturbing emotions. As she darted down the beach, he watched the grains of sand spraying high into the air behind her with each pounding step, and for a brief moment, he longed to call her back. Shaking his head in disbelief at his own weakness, he shouldered his bow and followed.

This time, she was the one trembling, overwhelmed by his provocative scent of sea salt, sweet pine, and man sweat as they passed at the line, her knees growing weak with a long forgotten aching need, and she almost stumbled right there in front of him.

Some Goddess, she chided herself, letting a man, no matter how good-looking he was, affect her like that.

A hush fell over the crowd as she took aim, fighting for control. As her arrow soared towards the target, she closed her eyes, refusing to look at what she assumed would be an embarrassing disaster.

A roar erupted from Team Morgan, and the entire Tribe went wild!

Her arrow was again dead center!

Matt strolled up beside her, the heat from his body searing her exposed skin, his eyes doing the same as they locked onto hers.

"Good shot. But now... it's my turn."

She couldn't move until Daniel took hold of her arm and gently tugged her away. A corner of Matt's mouth lifted as he raised his arrow... and let it fly.

The Tribe was speechless, the only sound the soft whisper of waves on the shore of the bay.

Matt's arrow had split Morgan's in two!

****

"The target is now at seventy yards! Before the Flare, that was almost an Olympic gold medal archery distance," Daniel explained to the breathless crowd. "Whoever is closest to the center of the bullseye, with a single shot, will be the archery champion of Miracle Island, and the winner of the prize!"

He smiled at Matt. "Okay, my friend, good luck."

Nylah gave him an encouraging thumbs up, and Matt took a deep breath to relax. His daughter's love always gave him such strength, as had the love of his cherished Skylark.

Morgan's open challenge of his abilities had thrown him off balance, and her strange and baffling effect on him was disconcerting. It bothered him tremendously that no other woman in his past had ever made him feel this way, and although he didn't know why, felt compelled to keep her at arm's length, despite her unbelievable beauty and fire that both drew and antagonized him at the same time.

And it was important for him to keep this whole situation in perspective. The archery contest was nothing more than some much needed entertainment for the Tribe, and perhaps a test for his inflated ego. He would take his final shot and let the God of all wisdom decide the outcome.

Taking careful aim, he zeroed in on his mark and released, letting the chips fall where they may. But the reaction from the crowd told him all he needed to know.

His arrow was vibrating dead center of the bullseye!

Morgan's face fell. He'd done it...

Now she didn't care about a two-week vacation or her choice of entrée. It was up to her to bring honor to Chief Bedi and the Mayoruna people she loved.

She had to split his arrow.

Casting a sideways glance at the Tribe sitting in complete silence, Morgan pulled an arrow from her quiver. She noticed Adam watching her intently from his seat in the front row, but her attention was suddenly drawn to the sky above him.

Barreling down from the clouds was a large white hawk... and the predator bird was heading straight for Adam, who didn't see it coming!

Without a second thought, she quickly nocked her arrow and aimed, desperate to kill the dangerous creature before Adam could be harmed.

But before she could release, she was tackled to the ground by a solid wall of muscle, her arrow arcing harmlessly into the air! The weight of a man's heavy body crushed her into the sand, and she struggled to breathe as she found herself face to face with Matt, his eyes blazing into hers.

"What the hell were you doing?" he shouted. "That bird is Moses, Adam's guardian and protector, and believe it or not, he's an Angel!"

"He's a what?! How was I supposed to know he was a pet bird, you fool! I thought he was going to hurt Adam! Get off me!" she screamed. When he didn't move, she became even angrier, pushing against his unyielding iron chest.

"What are you going to do now, Matt? Kill me?"

"No," he replied, in a surprisingly calm voice, "I'm not."

And he kissed her.

Chapter 8 Tapestry of Life

His lips drank her in, his thirst suddenly unquenchable! She moaned beneath him, and he wasn't sure if it was in protest or pleasure. But he didn't care. He needed her. He hated her. He wanted her. At this moment, there was nothing he desired more than Morgan Monroe... tasting her, breathing in her sweet scent, her luscious body beneath him, warm, soft, and... struggling?

Gradually coming to his senses, he opened his eyes. Her own brilliant sky blues were wide open and staring at him wildly, her perfect mouth trying to speak. But with his lips crashing into hers, passionately possessing her with a life of their own, no words were possible.

Oh, God, what had he done?!

He raised his head. Tears began spilling down her cheeks as she released a heartbreaking sob. He turned to look at the Tribe, stunned and silent witnesses to his heinous crime.

He rolled off her and leaped to his feet, holding out a hand to help her up, but Daniel blocked his way.

"Matt, why don't you head on home. Morgan will stay with Alea and I tonight."

The rest of the Tribe were discreetly filtering away, Moses perched on Adam's shoulder as they disappeared over the berm. The bird whistled and cast a last backward glance at a stricken Matt. Orders from above had been followed, and he was content with his day's work.

Alea broke out of her shock and helped a shaky Morgan to her feet as Chase raced to assist her, glaring at Matt as he swept her up to carry her to Daniel's treehouse, the rest of *Piranha's* worried crew on his heels. Matt tried to follow, but Daniel and Ryan moved to stop him.

"Let it go, Matt," Daniel cautioned him. "There'll be time enough to talk to her later, but you need to apologize to that woman. Weeks of treating her like you couldn't stand her, and now this? And in front of the kids?"

"I'm so sorry, Daniel. I don't know what came over me. There's no excuse I'll even try to offer. Morgan didn't deserve that."

Daniel's stern expression softened. "Matt, I know how hard it's been for you since Skylark was murdered. Ryan and I were there. We saw it happen. If it had been Alea, I'd be standing in your shoes right now."

He wrapped his arms around his friend and held on tight.

"You need to let Skylark go, Matt. You have strong feelings for Morgan. Maybe no one else can see it, but I can. And you keep pushing her away, finding every excuse in the book to deny what's growing in your heart."

"Well, it's pretty clear to me after seeing that kiss!" Ryan piped in.

He could only listen, but his guilt started to lift.

Daniel stepped back and looked him straight in the eye.

"What would Sky have wanted for you, man? I can tell you she'd want you to be happy and find that special woman to love and be your partner and friend. To give Nylah a mother, and perhaps have more children. To live out the miracle of your life that our Lord blessed you with. Make Skylark's death count for something, Matt. She told us she died for Adam, who she predicted would be used by God in a way we are not yet able to see. And I believe her, knowing my son. But I also believe that each of us on Miracle Island will have some role to play as well, and that definitely includes you."

Matt wept unashamedly as Daniel spoke. It was as if Skylark was speaking to his heart from the world beyond, trying to tell him once more what he'd refused to hear for four years.

His daughter had predicted the golden-haired woman... Skylark had answered his plea and appeared to him while

Nylah and Morgan slept... His own loving dreams of her in spirit form...

He'd see her again in heaven, that he knew. But while he was on earth, it was time to spread his wings.

****

The sun was sinking low as Alea softly closed the guest room door. Morgan had finally fallen asleep after a long, intimate, and heart-wrenching conversation that had Alea's mind reeling. When Daniel at last came home, she ran to him, burying her face in his chest.

"Are you okay, sweetheart?" he asked, kissing her fragrant hair. "It's been quite a day, hasn't it?"

"Oh, Daniel, what a tapestry life is! We are interwoven with others in ways we could never predict, in whatever manner and for whatever reason our God deems best. It's humbling, frightening, and wonderful, all at the same time. And we can't even begin to comprehend the complexity of it all."

"You obviously spoke with Morgan. How is she doing?"

Alea sighed. "She's confused, of course. He's treated her horribly since she got here, then throws her to the ground and kisses her passionately in public, the kids totally bug-eyed! Matt has very ambivalent feelings for Morgan, and I will tell you, she feels exactly the same way. A pair of star-crossed lovers, if ever there was!"

"Well, they'll both have plenty of time to figure it out. He left for Hurricane Hole to be alone for a while, and I'm not sure when he's planning on coming home."

"At least he kept her from killing poor Moses," Alea said with relief.

Daniel stroked his chin thoughtfully. "Hmm. She meant well, but could our Angel Bird be up to something here? I find it rather suspicious that he picked today to show up after being gone for a whole month, *and*, I might add, right in the middle of a heated contest of wills between Matt and Morgan, who've been at odds ever since she arrived."

She laughed as she pulled him towards the supper table. "Well, after seeing the burst of sparks flying back and forth between them during the contest, and knowing Moses like we do, I wouldn't doubt it in the least!"

****

The fire burned hot and steady as chunks of fresh lobster seared on long skewers, their juices spitting into the flames and causing them to flare. Matt leaned forward on his log seat, elbows on his knees and stubbled chin resting on his clasped hands, staring into the flickering light as he waited for his meal to cook.

The wind howled through crevices in the rock walls, filling the cavernous expanse of Hurricane Hole with a symphony of sound. The night air was chilly, and he was grateful for the blanket around his shoulders. Not that he deserved any comforts after his graphic performance on the beach...

He told Daniel where he was going and ran the entire three miles to the cave, tossed his gear on a platform bed, ripped off his clothes, and dove off the cliff into the water with his spear. Two lobsters later, he climbed up the side of the cliff, his frayed emotions under better control.

What was she thinking, he wondered? Did she hate him now? He'd been determined to keep her at arm's length, for Skylark's sake, but lost it when he tackled her to the sand, the feel of her body beneath him shattering his resolve. Had he misread the crazy attraction between them during the archery competition? He cringed when he thought about how he had forced himself on her. It was only a kiss... but what a kiss!

Rather than hash through it all again while he was so tired, he decided to try and get a good night's sleep. Tomorrow, he'd be able to think more clearly. He ate the lobster right off the skewers, dragged himself up the stairs, and collapsed on the bed.

****

My warrior, I am here.

Her sweet, gentle voice echoed in his dream, and his lips curved into a happy smile as he drew the blanket up higher over his shoulders. "Skylark..." he murmured, drifting ever deeper into the spirit world.

He awoke, his body floating in an endless sky of brilliant blue, the multitude of stars surrounding him shimmering like diamonds. The awesome magnificence, the glory, the majesty, of the powerful and almighty Lord God's infinite universe humbled his soul to its very core, and he wept in remorse and shame for his many human weaknesses and failings.

But before he could fall into irretrievable despair and regret, a swirling white mist slowly arose from the ether, and she appeared, her ruby lips parted in a dazzling smile, her gray eyes sparkling with light. She walked towards him with her arms spread wide, her long midnight hair flowing behind her in a warm, wildflower-scented breeze.

"I am with you, my love," she whispered. "I will always be with you." Her arms encircled him, and he pulled her close with a cry of joy, their lips meeting in a tender embrace.

"We will be together forever, my darling," she promised. "In His house, we will be one soul, one spirit, as we praise and worship His Holy Name for all eternity."

"Come back to me, Skylark! I need you. Our daughter needs you. You are my only love, my life, my heart," he pleaded. The mist slowly began to dissipate as he spoke, and he clung to her, fearful of losing her once more.

Her hand cupped his cheek, and her eyes grew sad. "I must leave you now, my Matt. My task is complete, and I will not be permitted to visit you again in this outer world until we are reunited one day in the paradise of His kingdom! But I have sent you a gift, a gift that will bring you back to the life the Great Spirit meant for you to live."

"Morgan... Morgan is your gift." He knew who she meant, but he was still conflicted.

"You love her, but you resist out of devotion to me. There is room in your heart for many loves; for me, for Nylah, for your friends, and for the golden-haired one. Release me now, my love. She was chosen for you by He who is all-knowing and wise. You are free to love her, as our daughter does, as I do."

She kissed him one last time, and slowly retreated into the mist, their arms reaching for one another.

"You will not see me again, my warrior, but I will always be with you," she breathed, her voice echoing through the stars as she faded away. "Listen to your heart..."

For the first time since her death, he was finally at peace.

****

Adam held Nylah's hand tightly as she silently wept. They had both seen the vision.

"Is there anything I can do for you, Nylah?"

"No, Adam. She told me this would happen when we said goodbye. I'm glad Papa will be happy, and that the Darkness has been defeated once more. It just hurts to know that after tonight, I'll never see my momma again."

****

Morgan breathed a sigh of relief as the door to the guest room closed. The emotional talk with Alea had drained her, but it felt so good to tell her tale at last, and she appreciated Alea's willing and non-judgmental ear.

It wasn't comfortable for her to reveal her tumultuous life in Hollywood before the Flare, and her brief but passionate affair with Chase London. The many deaths that occurred in the Amazon and as they sailed away were also painful to discuss... especially Pierce's sacrifice to save her.

It was the final revelation that worried her the most as she described the worship she had received from the Mayoruna while playing the role of their beloved Golden Goddess. The harmless deception had spared the crew from slaughter, she explained, and the tribe then accepted them into their camp, where they lived for years as one of the people.

Alea's eyebrow's rose when she relayed how the Festival of the Moon celebrations had taken her disembodied spirit on mystical journeys to visit people in many different places all around the earth, and at times, into the very cosmos itself.

She realized that her stories of pagan worship and celestial travels were being told to a woman who was clearly devoted to her faith in the Lord Jesus Christ, and who had personally experienced what sounded to Morgan like actual miracles from a powerful and loving God. But when she described her spirit companion and guide, Alea clutched her heart, unable to breathe, her face pale.

"A woman with long black hair and gray eyes, you said, Morgan? And a white bird accompanied you?"

Yes, Morgan had replied, and went on to tell her of the man they visited most often, a man in great emotional pain, whom a dark haze had prevented her from seeing... the man who had somehow captured her heart... and the man she despaired of ever meeting.

Alea said nothing but enveloped her in comforting arms. “Sleep, my dear friend,” she told her. “With your permission, we’ll tell Daniel your story tomorrow, but right now, you need to get some rest.”

After Alea left, Morgan fell backwards onto the bed and stretched wearily, then covered herself with the blanket. Running a slow finger across her lips, the memory of Matt’s kiss returned... a kiss she’d never be able to forget. Why had she resisted? She rolled onto her side with a groan.

The weight of his hard muscled body had excited her, the heat and passion of his mouth intoxicating, yet she suddenly panicked, shoving him away in fury and fear. He had only acted innocently and impulsively on the strong but veiled attraction between them, something she’d refused to admit to herself, let alone to him.

And now, she’d ruined any hope of even a passably friendly relationship with him after the scene she’d made in front of the entire Tribe, making it look as if she was the unwilling victim of his unwanted attentions. She didn’t deserve such a man, and despite the distressing fact she would no longer be living in the same house as Nylah, would request a move in the morning.

The man in her dreams? Is that who she was waiting for? He was no more than that, just a silly dream... a ghost... a mirage... He wasn’t real, no matter how much she wished it to be true. She needed to wake up and stop wasting her life hoping to meet a fantasy man who didn’t exist.

Her eyelids grew heavy as she willed sleep to spare her from her own disquieting thoughts. Tomorrow was another day, and she was determined it would be a new day for her.

****

My Chosen One, I am here.

Morgan slowly awoke to find herself floating in a brilliant sky of electric blue that stretched into the vastness of infinity, surrounded by a halo of stars that shimmered with glorious light... and she knew she'd been here before.

She felt her companion before she saw her, emerging from a cloud of swirling white mist, her midnight hair streaming behind her, her sparkling gray eyes glowing with unearthly love. The woman reached out her hand, and she took it, an overpowering joy filling her soul.

"Who are you?" Morgan whispered, finally daring to ask the question she had never done before.

"I am Skylark, my child. I have been sent to reveal your destiny, a destiny that was ordained for you from the dawn of time."

With a radiant smile, Skylark swept her through a tunnel of light, their journey slowing when they reached the arched entrance of an enormous cave. She could hear the sound of waves crashing into the rock cliffs just beyond and saw a fire burning in a hearth near a pool of water.

They drifted inside to hover over the wooden platform of a bed. Lying on it, his face hidden by a dark haze, was the figure of the man she loved!

Morgan caught her breath, looking at her companion in shock. But before she could speak, Skylark passed her hand over the haze, and it slowly dissolved.

The man lying on the bed was Matt!

Peace lit Skylark's beautiful face as she gazed at him.

"I must leave you now, Morgan, and I give you the beloved of my heart. Do you remember what I once told you? *He will find you someday.* He did find you, but neither of you were yet ready to fulfill your destiny. He is ready now. You are ready now. Go to him, my sweet girl, and love him with all your heart, with my blessing, and with the blessing of the Father."

Morgan looked down at Matt, his sleeping face relaxed, with a serenity she had never seen on him before. It had been him all along! How could she not have recognized him?

"Will he know me, Skylark? I have shamed him in front of the Tribe, and he may hate me."

Skylark's eyes were ablaze with a mystic fire, her image already fading. "Do not fear, Morgan, he waits for you. And be assured, my dearest one, you and I will someday meet again... in another world."

****

Morgan bolted upright, her chest heaving. "Oh my God, my dreams were real!"

She scrambled out of bed and tore open the bedroom door. The house was dark and quiet, its occupants having retired hours earlier. Bear lifted his head from his pad on the floor but seeing no challenge to his duties as a guard dog, went back to sleep.

She had to find him! Her heart was racing wildly as she pushed open the front door and ran out on the porch. The full moon cast its glow over the still waters of the bay, the occasional splash of a fishtail the only sound.

"He's not here, Morgan."

She skidded to a halt before reaching the stairs and turned towards the source of the voice. There, sitting on a stool in a corner, was Adam.

"Oh, I'm sorry, I didn't see you there, Adam," she said in surprise. "Who are you talking about?"

"You're looking for Uncle Matt, aren't you?"

She studied the boy curiously. She'd never noticed before that his eyes had golden highlights. "Well, you're right, I am looking for Matt... But how did you know that?"

She couldn't shake the odd feeling that she was talking to a much older and wiser person than the average four-year-old boy.

He smiled but didn't reply.

"I really need to talk to him, Adam."

"I can take you to him."

"It's got to be after midnight. You should be asleep."

"She told you he was waiting for you, Chosen One. You must go to him. He is your destiny."

The hairs on the back of her neck stood up, and at that moment, she understood. "You've seen her too... you've seen Skylark. Who is she?"

"She was Matt's wife, killed by an evil and vengeful woman who wanted me dead. Skylark stepped between us and was stabbed in the neck by the knife that was meant for me. My mother cut Nylah from her womb after she died."

Morgan was stunned! The man in her dreams, Matt, had suffered terrible, agonizing pain... and now she knew why. But standing before her, an even greater mystery was yet to be solved.

"Adam, *who are you*?"

****

They walked down the winding path leading to Hurricane Hole, the light of the full moon guiding their way. When the tall, arched entry to the massive cave came into view, Adam drew to a halt. "He's inside."

He took her hand, his eyes gleaming gold in the moonlight. "I can take you no further, Morgan, but remember what you promised. Don't tell anyone who I am... even Matt. God chose you for a reason. Matt is your destiny, but the Tribe will also need your strength, your courage, and your love in the future."

She started to drop to her knees, but he stopped her. *"You must worship the Lord your God and serve only Him."*

"Thank you, Adam, for showing me the way... in more ways than one."

He hugged her, suddenly a four-year old child once again. "Bye, Morgan. Say hi to Uncle Matt for me!" he said with a mischievous grin and ran back to camp.

****

The night sky glowed with ambient light as Morgan stood at the entrance to the cave. The coals of the fire were red hot, the aromatic perfume of sweet smokey driftwood filling the air, reminding her of the long and treacherous voyage on *Piranha*. She gazed up at the moon, a smile playing on her lips.

"I'm home, Skylark," she whispered softly. "I finally made it home."

And she walked inside.

Chapter 9 Phoenix Rising

The glow from the slowly dying fire cast dancing shadows on the high ceiling above, the rest of the enormous cavern in complete darkness. She squinted to see beyond the circular border of rock that contained the sizzling coals, skirting the edge of a wide pool of water as she walked.

The pool was the lowermost of three that appeared to be continuously fed from a spring that emerged from the left side of the cave wall. As the first pool waterfalled into the second, and the second into the third, it filled to the top, the crystal-clear water then cascading into a natural stone trough that eventually disappeared underground.

She noticed a pile of driftwood near the firepit. Selecting several good-sized pieces, she added them to the coals until the fire burned bright. Dusting off her hands, she stood and surveyed the spacious interior of the cave.

What a wonderful place! she thought. All the comforts one could desire for a hurricane hideaway, including what looked like a bathroom in the rear. She noticed a wooden shelving unit against the right wall and went over to examine it.

Covered baskets lined the shelves, several filled with both dried and fresh fruit. One held salt-cured fish, another with flats of cassava bread, with thin sheets of white sea salt laid out in neat rows on an upper shelf. Curious. Matt couldn't have carried all of this food with him when he left, and how could anyone have possibly predicted she or Matt would be coming here?

The face of Adam came to mind, and she smiled.

Although she was interested in exploring further, there was only one question to be answered.

Where was Matt?

She scanned the perimeter of the cavern beyond the circle of light. There, towards the rear, was a flight of stone steps, barely visible in the darkness.

A dozen pre-made torches were leaning against the wall that matched the ones the Tribe used at night. Picking one up, she sniffed the ball of dried sea oat grass secured to the end, the odor of fish oil wrinkling her nose. Pushing it into the fire, the grass ignited, and with flaming torch in hand, she climbed the stairs.

She found him asleep on one of the dozen large platform beds on that level, covered with a blanket, his dark red hair disheveled on the pillow, his handsome face relaxed and at peace, exactly as she had seen him in her dream.

She watched his hard muscled chest rise and fall with each breath, aching to touch him... to apologize with all her heart... to tell him how unfairly she had judged him... to tell him how she really felt... but ultimately chose not to wake him. After the emotionally stormy day they had both been through, she understood he needed some time to rest, but couldn't keep herself from inhaling the scent of sea salt, sweet pine, and sweat that had so surprisingly excited her during the contest.

Reluctantly backing away from the bed, she retraced her steps and quietly tiptoed down the stairs. Suddenly feeling hungry, she grabbed a mango from the basket of fruit and bit into it as she returned to the warmth of the fire.

The sound of the cascading water from the pools drew her attention. I'm so exhausted, she realized, but a bath would be heavenly! There was even a pile of towels stacked at the side of the pool, and what looked like bars of homemade soap, as well as a basket of dried natural sea sponges.

Thanking Adam once again, she quickly polished off the mango, kicked off her moccasins, stripped off her shorts and top, and uncoiled her hair. Lowering herself down to the smooth rock edge, she slid into the lowest pool.

The water was cool, clear, and refreshing, the lulling sounds of the tinkling waterfall from the second pool relaxing. With a grateful sigh, she sank below the surface and remained there, enjoying the weightlessness and the feel of the water caressing her skin.

Floating back up, she inhaled a deep breath, already feeling invigorated. Picking up a sponge and a bar of soap, she noted the fragrance of coconut and an unidentifiable flower, with an undertone of sweet herbs.

Alea and Josey's doing, no doubt, she mused, and began lathering her body thoroughly before beginning the time-consuming process of washing her long, wavy hair.

She knew that her unshaven legs, hairy underarms, and curly, unkempt bikini line would have garnered her finger-pointing shame in the media before the Flare, as would her unmanicured natural fingertips and toenails. But since her years in the Amazon jungle and at sea, these trivial matters were no longer of any importance.

The women of the Tribe kept themselves clean and groomed without the use of modern tools. Razors were impossible to come by anyway, and wax was a relic of the past. Their hair and nails were trimmed with a knife or scissors, their teeth brushed and whitened with sea salt and flossed with the stringy fibers of coconut leaves, their bodies moisturized with coconut oil and the aloe vera plants that grew everywhere on the island. And their men didn't seem to mind a little extra hair... anywhere.

She moved under the waterfall to rinse, her clean golden tresses feeling like soft, luxurious strands of silk running through her fingers. But her soothing private time was cut short by the clatter of a pebble rolling towards the pool and stopping right at the edge.

Looking up, she saw Matt staring down at her from the top of the stairs, his blanket wrapped around his waist.

Quickly swimming to the pile of towels, she snatched the first one she found. Holding it draped in front of her body, she stood up in the waist deep water.

"Morgan. What are you doing here?" he asked as he made his way slowly down the stairs.

She clutched the towel, more nervous than she'd ever been before. "I... I came to see you," she stuttered.

"*You* came to see *me*?" he asked, moving closer with each step, his eyes never leaving her.

With her hair dripping wet, but her head held high, she met his steady gaze straight on.

"Yes, I did, Matt. I came to apologize for how I acted in front of the Tribe today."

He stopped a few feet away, his skin glowing with a reddish hue in the firelight. "Why?"

This wasn't exactly going the way she'd been expecting. Skylark said he was waiting for her, but it sure didn't seem like it. She began to get a little angry.

"Look, I was being a jerk during the contest, and I... well, I overreacted to what you did."

He took a step forward. "And what did I do, Morgan?" he asked softly, his dark blue eyes lit with a fire of their own.

"You know what you did."

"I want you to say it." He took another step forward.

"Okay... you kissed me."

"Yes, Morgan, I did," his eyes lasering into hers, "and I thoroughly enjoyed kissing you. So why did you really come to see me?"

Her body began to tremble under the heat of his gaze. "Oh, why are you making this so hard?!" she exclaimed. "Okay, yes, I came to apologize because my reaction made you look like some kind of pervert in front of the Tribe... and I feel bad!"

He moved closer, so close she could smell him.

"And why do you feel bad, Morgan?" He lowered himself into the pool, the heat radiating from his body warming her chilled skin. She stared at him until he stopped directly in front of her, what was left of her composure finally cracking.

"Because I wanted your kiss! Because I wanted *you*!" she blurted out wildly. "Because I'm crazy in love with you, you big, red-headed fool! There. I've said it. I'm leaving."

Before she could run, he yanked the blanket from his waist and slung it around her, pulling her hard against his chest. She gasped as his powerful arms encircled her, and for the first time since she met him, he smiled.

"Well, if that's the case, shouldn't we give it one more try?"

And he kissed her.

****

His lips were tender, and as soon as they touched her own aching mouth she melted against him, weak with need, his tongue seeking her leisurely as he held her tight against his naked body.

She wrapped her arms around his neck, and they were lost in the intoxicating magic of their first exploration of each other; tasting, feeling, their breath mingling. She broke their embrace and stepped back, her flashing eyes repeating what her lips had already told him as her towel fell into the water. He pulled her against him again, and this time, the heat from his loins burned into the softness of her flesh, their hands frantically seeking one another as their passion grew.

"Matt," she whispered between kisses, "I need you... I need you inside me."

He swept her into his arms and stepped out of the pool, water dripping behind them as he carried her up the stairs and laid her on the bed.

"As much as I want you, my love, I don't want this to end too soon."

He slid a blanket off an adjacent platform and knelt by her side, drying her arms and legs as she lay unresisting.

"You called me *your love...*"

Hearing the shaky, vulnerable tone in her voice, he paused his ministrations. "I so want to do this right," he said gently, and took her hand.

"Morgan, I fell in love with you the moment you yelled at me after I carried you off *Piranha.* The attraction was strong, but I refused to admit it to myself... until today.

"You told me your story this morning, but I've never told you mine. I met and married Nylah's mother in Nova Scotia after my ship was beached there after the Flare. She was the love of my life... my heart... my very soul. But she was also the Spirit Singer and Healer of the Mi'kmaq tribe, with mystical gifts and amazing powers that most people would find hard to believe.

"She was pregnant when we journeyed to Boston to search for my parents and sisters. I was too late to save them from the wrath of Daniel's insane and vengeful ex-wife, and on the very day he arrived on *Barefootin'* to take us to Miracle Island, my wife was murdered, sacrificing her life to save baby Adam. Alea cut my unborn daughter out of my wife's womb minutes after she died, and I've been in mourning ever since, unable to fully move on from my grief.

"Over the years, she has often appeared to me in my dreams to comfort me, but tonight I had a dream where she released me to find a new life with the woman I'd fallen in love with... her gift... and that woman was you. I love you, Morgan... and I thank God that you love me too."

"Oh, Matt," she whispered, her heart racing in shock, "I have something to tell you. But first, what was your wife's name?"

"Her name was Skylark."

****

They lay together under the same blanket, her cheek resting on his shoulder, the sky outside the cave brightening almost imperceptibly with the coming dawn.

Matt had paled when she told him of her visit from Skylark, and of the mystical journeys in the past with her companion, where she was shown the suffering man who had captured her heart, who she now knew was Matt.

"She spoke to you tonight, Morgan, at the exact same time she came to me," he said, his voice shaking with awe.

Her story confirmed his own message from his beloved, and Matt's heart rejoiced. He would never stop loving Skylark, but she had freed him from the bondage of his guilt, remorse, and pain to live a whole life once more.

She rose to her elbow. "Well, if this is how God works, I guess I'm a believer. I wasn't very good at being a pagan Goddess anyway," she chuckled.

"Do that again."

"Do what?"

"I love when you smile."

She batted her eyelashes, her perfect sparkling white teeth displayed in a wide slapstick grin. "You mean, like this?"

"I love your mouth too."

"Prove it."

He rolled on top of her, his damp hair brushing her cheeks. "You mean, like this?" he murmured as he kissed her, her soft moan only inciting him to delve even deeper.

The feel of his smooth, warm skin and the firm muscles running along the length of his spine was tantalizing. She gently caressed the solid twin globes of his rear, his thick, engorged member pressed tight against her belly. She felt so small beneath him, his massive body as chiseled and well-defined as that of a trophy-winning bodybuilder.

His lips suddenly deserted hers as his kisses traveled along the curve of her slender neck, and then further down to her large, firm breasts, enjoying the light salty taste of her creamy white skin. He sucked one of her rosy nipples into his mouth, swirling his tongue around the taut raised tip as she arched to meet him.

Matt was entranced! She was so lovely, even more so than when he had sat for hours in the dark movie theater in Boston, mesmerized, watching her longingly on the giant silver screen as she captivated his imagination… and his desire.

But it wasn't just her luminous beauty that drew him now. It was her inner fire, her tempestuous ferocity, her strength of character, and her protectiveness for those she loved that was irresistible to him.

She was so different from Skylark, but the compelling attraction he'd felt when he first saw her instantly connected to other elements of his being deep inside that had lain dormant and waiting until she materialized out of the blue that day on *Piranha*. A new Matt Kennedy was resurrected, rising like a phoenix from the ashes of his past, and now, with Morgan, he could finally spread his wings… and fly!

She moaned with delight as he indulged himself just a little longer, wrapping her legs around his waist and rolling her eager hips against him. He smiled, understanding what she so desperately needed, and slipped down between her thighs to kneel at the foot of the bed. With one quick motion, he slid her hips towards him, her knees draped over his shoulders, her golden curls only inches away from his hungry mouth. He dipped in for a long, slow swipe, and she writhed at his touch, crying out for more.

And he was happy to oblige.

She whimpered as he began to circle and tease her delicate folds, his tongue hot, rough, and wet. She was fragrant and delicious, and he was thoroughly enjoying the taste of her flower-scented juices when he found her tiny sensitive bud, already swollen and ready for his attentions.

He blew hot breath directly on the dot of quivering flesh and flicked it repeatedly with the tip of his tongue before finishing with a slow and luxurious circle. The results of his efforts were enough to make him grin even with his face buried between her thighs as she exploded into wave after wave of wildly throbbing pulsations that never seemed to end... and he made sure they didn't.

Again and again and again he brought her to the brink, then drove her over the edge until she finally begged him to stop. He carefully lifted her knees from his shoulders and crawled up on the bed to lay beside her.

"Had enough, my sweet? I can keep going if you like. It's definitely my pleasure." With a slow smile, he kissed her tenderly, her own aromatic juices on his lips.

She sighed, stretching out lazily like a cat in a midday sunbeam before sitting up and swinging a leg over his chest.

"That was amazing, my darling! But now... it's my turn."

She flipped around on his chest, slowly easing her hips backwards until her golden curls hovered directly above his face. Leaning forward, her famous red lips engulfed the glistening tip of his turgid organ before continuing their descent. When her nose brushed the hair of his groin, she ran her tongue along its length as she pulled back up to the top with gentle suction, before plunging down once again.

It was impossible to resist the inviting vision above him! Holding her hips firmly, his tongue dove deep into her moist passage, the double sensations from above and below making him growl with lust. They feasted until he tossed her off his body, his patience finally at an end.

"I'm going to take you now, Morgan," he panted as he rose above her, positioning his oh-so-ready member between her willing thighs.

"What took you so long?" she breathed, her hips surging up to meet him at the exact moment he plunged in.

"Oh, my God, Morgan, my sweet love!" he cried out as he sank inside her, her velvety softness bringing tears to his eyes, the exquisite feel of a woman only a distant memory for the last four lonely years. When he could go no deeper, he pulled back and began to thrust with a powerful and steady rhythm, electrified by the vision of incomparable beauty beneath him, her golden hair fanned out on the bed like a field of daffodils.

"I'm yours, Matt, only yours," and she met him, thrust for thrust, their bodies moving as one, slick with the sweat of their lovemaking and burning with an unquenchable desire. This exciting, wonderful, and sexy man felt so right... so good. Her brief affair with Chase London was nothing compared to this overwhelming passion, this melding of herself with another human being to the point where she couldn't discern where she ended, and he began.

"I love you, my Morgan," he murmured against her lips, her heart and body responding to his sincere and tender words with a savage orgasm that left her stunned by its intensity.

He drove in hard one last time with a cry, shuddering to a halt. She buried her face in the crook of his neck as she clung to him, feeling him pulse and throb until he was drained, then begin to move again more slowly until totally replete.

When he finally grew still, they remained locked together, gasping for breath.

"I could have beaten you, you know," she whispered in his ear.

"Maybe," he replied, "but there's one bullseye my arrow will never miss."

And he took her again.

****

They remained at Hurricane Hole for three weeks, a time of magic and passion and inexpressible joy, feeling complete and at peace, their every heart's desire fulfilled by nothing more than being together.

Every morning, after they had reluctantly disentangled themselves, a basket of fruit, vegetables, flatbread, and a jug of mango wine was waiting at the entrance to the cave, and Morgan had her suspicions as to who was responsible.

Matt dove for lobster and fish while she tended the fire and prepped the ingredients for their meals. Other than the necessary housekeeping duties that were required even in a cave, they spent their days and nights in a dream world of their own, eating, talking, laughing, and reminiscing.

When they finally fell silent, their lips sought each other again, their bodies intertwining wherever they might be; on their bed, under the waterfall, next to the roaring fire, in the rolling ocean... their cries of passion echoing off the walls of the cavern or resonating into the sky, heard by no one but the sun, the moon, and the stars above.

He missed Nylah so much but knew she would be well-cared for in his absence. In retrospect, his daughter had accurately predicted that Morgan was coming, and he would thank her when he finally brought her new mother home.

Her abilities staggered him, and he realized that God had called her to His service, even at such a young age. As a father, he feared for her... but as a believer, he rejoiced! Skylark had often told him that no matter what, God had a purpose in everything He allowed to happen in life, and he rested in that confidence.

As they departed on their last day, they hiked to the top of the winding pathway. Turning to look back at the cave, Matt reached for Morgan's hand, and their eyes met.

They had been healed of their heartache, pain, and regrets by the grace of the loving and powerful God of the universe, who had gifted them both with a second chance for love.

Their hearts safe in each other's care, Matt and Morgan could now travel together into the future, into the unknown... into the mystic.

Chapter 10 Angel's Gift

The Tribe slept in late that morning, gradually drifting down to the firepit, one or two at a time, until almost noon. Chores were forgotten, the unexpected drama between Matt and Morgan during the archery competition the day before the only topic of conversation.

Daniel arrived last and looked around curiously, blowing on the cup of hot coffee that Alea handed him. "Anyone know where Matt and Morgan are?"

The whispered discussions stopped.

"I haven't seen Matt," John replied. "Morgan either."

"Morgan might be resting in her own room this morning, but I can go get her, if you want," Pearl offered.

Moses was perched on the log next to Adam, and the boy offered the bird a piece of his hot biscuit. "They're not here, Dad. They're at Hurricane Hole. Morgan was pretty upset and looking for Uncle Matt last night. It was dark, and everyone was already asleep, so I took her there."

His announcement started a second flurry of animated conversation, Chase's expression souring.

"You took her all the way over to Hurricane Hole, and they haven't returned yet?"

"I wouldn't wait for them, Dad. They'll come home when they're ready."

Nylah plopped herself on the log next to Adam, wiggling with unrestrained excitement, causing Moses to fly off in a huff. "I got a new momma, Uncle Daniel! I love Morgan, and so does Papa!"

When Daniel's eyebrows could lift no further, Alea couldn't help but laugh. "Well, it's what I've wanted for Matt all along. Now, if they don't kill each other first, I think it's a match made in heaven!"

****

"All aboard if you're going on the dive!"

Ronny checked each of his arriving passengers to make sure they had their mask, snorkel, spear, towel, and water bottle. With the workday half gone, he and Daniel decided to take whoever wanted to go on a lobster dive out to a nearby offshore cloud break reef that never failed to produce. The kids enjoyed snorkeling there too, an adult by their side as they watched the divers bring up their catch.

Angel bounded down to the boat with her dive bag in one hand and clutching Michael's hand with her other.

"We're ready, Uncle Ronny!" she exclaimed, her lovely face beaming with joy. Being near Michael was all she dreamed of, and today she would show him her favorite place to dive, a place she could only go if the tender took her out. She loved Osprey Bay, but the deeper waters of the Atlantic drew her very soul.

Michael smiled at her enthusiasm. The little tow-headed girl pulled at his heartstrings in some inexplicable way that even he didn't understand. Her innocent infatuation was no secret to him or anyone else in the Tribe, but he handled it well and enjoyed her company, swimming, snorkeling, and diving together every day, her aquatic abilities at her young age astounding.

At thirteen, he was already an experienced hunter, warrior, and diver, but watching tiny Angel dart through the water like a fish and hover on the bottom for minutes at a time simply amazed him. The child didn't even need her fins to move through the turquoise depths at incredible speed, her white-blonde hair streaming behind her, and if she had suddenly sprouted a mermaid's tail, he would not have been in the least surprised.

But it was what happened as soon as she entered the water that gobsmacked his mind!

Her first splash and squeal of delight seemed to draw the creatures of the bay towards her, and as she descended below the surface, schools of fish swarmed around her in a protective silvery mass, with green sea turtles lifting their snouts for a quick breath of air before following her down below. She reminded him of a rock star with her adoring fans, and even his presence failed to deter them.

The first time he excitedly told the Tribe what he'd seen, they merely smiled and nodded their heads. Yep, that was Angel, they said. It had been like that all her life. She loved the fish and other creatures of the ocean so much that she refused to eat seafood anymore when she turned three.

But Ishmael, Chase, Morgan, and Diego understood his shock after they saw her too, Diego wondering out loud if the little girl was really a sea nymph, and what Chief Bedi and the shaman might have thought.

He climbed into the tender and lifted her to sit next to him on the bench seat. They were joined by Gypsy, Noah, Robbie, Sammy, Pearl, and Alea. Everyone grabbed a paddle, and they rowed through the pass and out into the Atlantic Ocean.

The reef was a quarter mile from the pass, the same reef Daniel and the boys liked to surf on a good swell. But today, the wind was non-existent, and the swell was low at just under a foot. Ronny positioned the boat a bit south of the spot and dropped anchor while the divers prepared to go in. The adults divvied up who they would supervise, with Daniel claiming Angel, Sammy, and Michael.

Already set to go, Angel waited for Michael to don all his gear. When he finally gave a thumbs up, they joined hands and fell backwards off the gunnel into the water with a splash, Sammy right behind. Together, they surfaced to see Daniel waving them over.

He pulled out his mouthpiece. "I see multiple lobbies right below us, guys. Michael, Sammy, are you shooting?"

They both held up their spears and nodded.

"Okay, let's all stay together. Angel, you're our spotter, little mermaid! Point when you see antennae. Anyone who gets tired, let me know and I'll swim with you back to the boat."

A wide smile split Angel's face, and she jackknifed and dove. Daniel shook his head when her feet flipped into the air before disappearing underwater. No fins again, as usual...

Michael hovered on the surface for a moment, enjoying a view of Hidden Cove he didn't get to see very often. *Piranha* had crashed into a cliff on the calmer Caribbean coast, but the Atlantic side was rougher and much more dangerous. Not only was he up to the challenge, but Angel had told him this was her favorite place to dive, and he couldn't wait to see what it was that so appealed to her. With spear in hand and snorkel secured, he tucked and dove.

He assessed the water depth at over thirty feet, the ridge of underwater rock running parallel to the cliffs and five feet below the waves. Ronny had chosen to start the dive on the more protected inside wall, where lobster hid in holes and crevices near the base.

Michael hadn't seen such colorful coral since *Piranha* passed through Mexican waters. He had plenty of dives under his belt and felt confident he could contribute to the evening meal. He saw Angel point to a dark hole in the reef and followed the direction of her arm. Spotting two sets of antennae, he kicked to start his downward drift.

The cooler was overflowing as the four teams brought up their catch, one at a time. Michael was proud of his eight bugs, all found by Angel, who never seemed to tire. He took a brief rest before jackknifing again, determined to shoot at least one more.

The flash of a light gray and blue tail caught his attention. No way, he thought in excitement! A Cubera snapper! And at least thirty pounds! The gray body with lighter gray vertical striping was unmistakable. What better way to display his skill and prowess with a spear to Daniel and Ronny! He'd caught this type of snapper before, but never one this big.

Without signaling to anyone, he cocked his sling and began a slow, steady descent towards the unwary fish, willing his body to become part of the very reef itself, and calling on every molecule of oxygen in his blood to sustain him as he drew closer and closer.

He released his grip, and the three prongs pierced the fish just above the gill plate, an instant kill! He shouted for joy, air bubbles from his mouth escaping his snorkel, and began to kick up, the fish rising with him on the end of his spear, a trail of blood in its wake.

He saw it coming when he was still twenty-five feet down... With its massive jaws apart, double row of sharp white teeth gleaming, and tail aggressively swishing from side to side, the fifteen-foot, sleek, brown-bodied shark with darker brown stripes began swimming faster and faster as it zeroed in on the intoxicating scent of blood. He'd seen tigers in the zoo as a child. This was a tiger of the sea.

He wasn't going to make it.

Almost out of breath and hoping that the shark would follow its normal prey, he let go of the handgrip, the spear and snapper falling into the murky depths. He had enough in him to make a run for the bottom and the safety of the rocks, but if he did, he knew he'd never see the sun again.

The ploy didn't work.

He closed his eyes, releasing his claim on life, his oxygen-starved mind singing the death chant of the Mayoruna warrior as he began to fade into unconsciousness, proud to die bravely and without fear... to die as a man.

His eyelids fluttered open slightly. Had he re-entered the Mayoruna world of dreams... or was he already dead?

The haze clouding his vision cleared just enough for him to see Angel streaking towards the shark, now only twenty feet away from his free-floating body, its eyes rolled back, ready to bite. She gently grasped its dorsal fin and pulled herself close to the creature's head, where she appeared to whisper into the pore that led to its inner ear.

The shark suddenly broke off its attack and veered to the left, Angel still riding with it until she finally let go and waved goodbye as the beast disappeared into the shadowy depths. She turned to him and smiled as gloriously as her namesake, then quickly swam towards him and gripped his rash guard. With her body smoothly oscillating like that of a dolphin, she towed his limp body to the surface.

After they pumped the seawater from his lungs, the only thing Michael could remember were her beautiful azure blue eyes welcoming him back to life.

****

"Thank God you're still here with us, Michael, and still in one piece to boot! Smart move... dumping the snapper to distract the shark," Diego declared with an approving nod. "I'm certainly glad it didn't turn out to be a repeat of what happened to Frank in Mexico."

The Tribe had gathered at John and Josey's house, where Michael lived with the Garner's. The great room was packed with people, candles casting their soft flickering light on the relieved faces waiting for the young man's response.

Michael felt somewhat guilty. When he first told the story of what happened, he chose not to volunteer every fantastical detail, still not convinced the whole scene hadn't merely been the result of a severe lack of oxygen. But if he were to make any sense of what he thought he saw, it was important to talk to Angel privately.

After the boat returned to shore and he'd had some time to recover, he found her, all alone, building a sandcastle on the beach at Casuarina Cove. Delighted that he had joined her, she handed him a wooden spoon and directed him where to shore up the walls.

"Angel," he started out, pressing a wet spoonful of sand into place. "Can you explain what really happened in the ocean today?"

"Did you like my reef, Michael? It's my favorite place to swim in the whole world! The water's so deep and blue, and I've made a lot of new friends there."

She scooped some loose shells and sand out of the moat, then whispered so only he could hear. "I never told any of the grownups about my friends in the ocean. I don't think they'd understand like Adam and Nylah do."

"The reef was beautiful, sweetheart, but I thought I was going to die. What did you do to that shark? You made it go away somehow."

She laughed as if he was the silliest person she'd ever met.

"Charlie's my best friend at the reef, and he thought you were going to hurt me with your spear. I just told him that I loved you, Michael, and that you belonged to me. That's when he understood and went home." Brushing off her hands, she gazed at him, all her heart in her eyes.

"I do love you, Michael," her expression suddenly growing serious as she gently touched his cheek.

"I'll love you 'til I die."

He pulled her into his arms and hugged her tight, only half listening to her last declaration, still trying to process the unbelievable explanation she had given him.

"I love you too, my little Angel. And whatever happened out there today, thank you for saving my life."

****

"I'm sure that snapper didn't go to waste, Diego." Michael watched Angel take a bite of her banana bread, and as she chewed, she gave him a conspiratorial wink.

"I don't know how my little five-year-old daughter got you to the boat!" Josey said in amazement. "Ronny said you were out cold when they hauled you onboard and started CPR."

"And I should have been keeping a closer watch on all of you." Daniel was upset about what could have been a terrible tragedy, and that while Michael was staring down a hungry tiger shark, he'd been helping Sammy wrangle a 10-pound lobster out of a hole fifty feet away.

"Daniel, you can't be everywhere at once," Alea wisely reminded him. "The whole point of teaching your students what you've learned is that someday they have to catch the football you passed them and run it in for a touchdown by themselves. It sounds like Michael did the right thing and had Angel to guide him back to the boat. Kudos to you both!"

While the Tribe congratulated Michael and Angel, Adam and Nylah gave each other a look. They had foreseen that Angel would handle the dangerous shark with her special gift, a gift only the three of them knew about, and hadn't even tried to warn the divers in advance.

If God had allowed Michael to be harmed by the Darkness, nothing on earth could have stopped it.

****

The next few weeks were uneventful but productive. The new sailboat was finally completed, despite Matt's absence, with the unveiling scheduled for later that day.

That morning, Nylah thanked Daniel and Alea for letting her stay with them while her father was gone but insisted on returning home. She had many preparations to make, she told them, and wanted everything to be perfect for his return.

How do you know he's coming today? Alea had asked, only to be met with a cryptic smile as Nylah darted out the door.

The Tribe headed down to the beach in the late morning for the anticipated unveiling of the new boat. Diego, Ishmael, and James stood waist deep in the bay, with James holding a rope attached to a parachute tarp hiding the vessel, which was anchored thirty feet away. When everyone in the Tribe had arrived, James hailed Gypsy.

"Gypsy, can you please come out here?"

She looked at Noah, then at Robbie, then at the rest of the Tribe. "Me?" she asked.

"Yes, you, girl! Get on out here. Don't you want to see your new boat?"

Her eyes grew wide, but her body refused to move. It took a gentle nudge from Noah to start her wading into the water, her waist-length sandy brown hair trailing behind her. When she reached James, he held out the rope.

"Whenever you're ready, my girl. She's all yours."

Gypsy flung herself into his arms. "Oh, Grampa James, thank you! Thank you so much!"

"You can thank Diego and Ishmael too," he said, his eyes glistening. "It didn't take a lot of discussion to know who deserved this boat."

After hugging both blushing men, she accepted the rope. "I guess I'll have to think of a name and paint it on."

All three men grinned at the same time. "I don't think you need to worry about that, Gypsy. I believe we already had just the right name in mind," James told her. "Go ahead, pull the rope."

She tugged, and the light parachute material fluttered off.

Floating gracefully on the pale turquoise-blue waters of Osprey Bay was Gypsy's long-held dream... the brand new thirty-two-foot sloop, *Gypsy Queen*.

****

Sammy was the first to see them when he noticed the bushes moving at the top of the western rise behind the village. Matt and Morgan came into view moments later, making their way down the well-worn path, hand in hand.

"They're back!" he shouted, his voice echoing through the treehouses. His medicine bag forgotten on the ground where he'd been digging, he raced to find Daniel.

Matt took a deep breath as he watched the members of the Tribe stop whatever they were doing and run towards them; astonishment on the faces of some, confirmation of their suspicions on the faces of others, anger on the face of Chase London. He felt Morgan trembling and squeezed her hand in reassurance. She was his woman now... it was as simple as that. But how would his daughter feel about Morgan joining their life in such a completely different way?

They were surrounded as they reached the border of the village with welcoming backslappings and cheerful cries of greeting. A brooding Chase stood at the edge of the excited group, staring daggers at Matt, his fists clenched.

Alea pushed her way through the crowd to hug him, unable to speak when she saw the peace on his face, his difficult and painful personal journey of five years finally at an end.

"Papa!"

The crowd parted as Nylah bolted towards her father and leapt into his arms. "I missed you, Papa!" she exclaimed as they hugged each other tight. "And now you're home!"

Wriggling out of his embrace, she gave Morgan a happy smile. "But this time, I think you brought *me* a present."

"I already love you so much, Nylah," Morgan whispered. She held out her arms and Nylah flew into them, her cheek pressed against Morgan's belly. Her eyes suddenly widened, and when they drew apart, she turned to look at her father.

"Have you decided on a name for my new baby brother, Papa?"

Without missing a beat, Matt answered her... his arm quickly supporting a shocked Morgan.

"Why yes, sweetheart, we have. His name is Max."

Chapter 11 Five Years Later

Adam loved his usual vantage point at the top of the cliff, the same favorite spot he'd been coming to for many years. With his lunch bag open but untouched, he relaxed on his well-worn log seat and gazed out over the dark blue ocean. From the dizzying height of sixty feet, he had a 180-degree view of the vast Atlantic, with nothing between him and the continent of Africa far, far away.

He would sit alone for hours at a time, leaning against the old weatherworn cross as he read the battered copy of his mother's Bible. The inspiring words and stories came to life in his mind and heart, as real as the earth beneath him and the heat of the midday Bahamian sun beating down on his dark, windswept hair.

Every so often, he lifted his face to the sky and spoke to his Creator of his love and adoration, giving grateful thanks for the amazing wonders of the earth, the sea, and the sky, and for the people in his life that he loved so dearly.

But his prayers went further than most. As he scanned the endless waters before him, he could feel the vibrations of the remaining men and women of earth from after the Flare who he could not see, people in distant lands who were in pain, suffering, weeping from loss, and crying out in fear, victims of heinous acts that the Darkness had inspired.

And there were others... others who were angry, full of rage and hate, jealous and power mad, driven by their depraved desires and furthering their corrupt ambitions by callous and remorseless abuse of the innocent. These were the souls the Darkness had easily possessed in their arrogant refusal to acknowledge their Creator, used as pawns in his unwinnable game to depose the Almighty God... and then laughingly disposed of when their task was complete.

The Darkness had no love, no loyalty. With him, there was no forgiveness or mercy, no redemption, no second chance for a new life or restoration from wrong. Men were merely fleshly tools to be invaded, influenced, and discarded, with the only eternal life offered to be lived in whatever nightmare they feared the most... a personal living hell.

His nightly communion with his Lord had continued over the past five years, the Darkness kept at bay by His servant, Moses. The boy's trust in his God grew deeper, his questions sometimes answered directly, but more often than not, left for him to pray about and seek his own answers from the Word. At the age of nine, he already understood he would have an important role to play as he grew older, but in his innocence, youth, and fervor, he longed to do battle with the Darkness now!

No, he was told, it was too soon. He still had much to learn and experience, and when the time of his apprenticeship was complete, he would then be sent out into the world to show them the way back to the Light, the way that would allow the earth to become, once again, the Garden of Eden that God had intended from the beginning.

Adam took a sip from his water bottle, wondering when the anticipated promise he was waiting for would come to pass. Not yet ready to read, he laid the Bible on his lap, his thoughts gradually shifting to the people of his Tribe, and the ones who had eventually left.

He knew his parents were heartbroken at not being able to have any more children. When he asked Nylah if there was something she could do to help them, she shook her head, but was unable to explain why her ability to heal was being withheld in this instance.

He smiled at the thought of little Max, the terror of Miracle Island! Now four years old, the boy looked exactly like Matt, but with Morgan's shiny golden hair. He was everyone's love and spoiled beyond belief. That was me once, Adam thought, and chuckled to himself. Max and Dylan were best buddies, and extremely hard to catch, especially at bedtime.

Morgan and Matt had revived hunting with bow and arrow after they returned from their Hurricane Hole honeymoon. Morgan was almost killed trying to retrieve her special bow from *Piranha,* but she had a very good reason to try. A flock of white-faced duck had flown into Osprey Bay and landed on the beach at Casuarina Cove. Recognizing their value as a source of food, and without telling anyone, she raced over to the disintegrating boat.

But what no one in Hollywood had ever discovered was that Morgan Monroe had practiced archery since she was a child, the therapeutic way she chose to relax from the pressures of her demanding work as an acclaimed actress. Her expertise had earned her even more homage from the Mayoruna, and on the day of the archery competition, the Tribe was unaware of the possible advantage she had over Matt and Ryan.

Ultimately, it all ended well, and now the three hunters brought in seasonal braces of ring-necked pheasant, quail dove, duck, and white crown pigeons to add to their mostly seafood diet, with the pigs and chickens the occasional tasty treat. Morgan was pregnant again, which hardly slowed her down, although Matt did his best to rein her in.

Adam laughed out loud. Well, good luck with that, Uncle Matt!

Daniel *invited* Chase London to leave Miracle Island after he attempted to ambush Matt the night before he married Morgan, thinking that if he could show his ex-girlfriend that he had dominated his hated rival for her affections, she would change her mind and race into his arms.

His delusional attempt to surprise a well-trained Mi'kmaq hunter and warrior backfired, resulting in two black eyes and a badly bruised ego when Matt smelled him coming and took him to the ground in less than three seconds.

A week later, *Gypsy Queen* deposited him at the dock in Spanish Wells with a lone bag of personal items and a wave goodbye from a grinning Gypsy and Noah. Last they heard, he was living with an admiring local woman and working in the community garden, weeding and tending the plants.

Sarah had given birth to twin girls two years before, Ella and Mila, their three active children quite a handful for her and Ryan. Dolores had been a godsend for their growing family until her unexpected death a year ago. No one, not even Nylah, was quite sure what had caused Daniel's sweet and loving mother to drift away in her sleep one night, a look of calm and peace on her face.

After her burial, there were too many memories for James on Miracle Island, and he asked Gypsy to take him back to Spanish Wells, where he would live at Bonefish Bay until he recovered.

Diego greeted him at the Knowles dock with open arms. The Brazilian captain had made the move to Spanish Wells one year after his arrival on Miracle Island, joining Will and Gil's boat repair business, and spearheading their latest venture of building wooden sailboats from scratch. Traders from all over the Bahamas were coming to Spanish Wells to barter for one of Diego's exceptional vessels, since fiberglass boats were no longer an option. They were also locating and propagating groves of Abaco pine, cedar, buttonwood, and mahogany trees, which were the essential woods needed for boatbuilding in the future.

Ishmael met his wife on his first trip to Spanish Wells, and eventually brought Essie to Miracle Island, where their son, Alonzo, and daughter, Esmeralda, were born.

Roger Gabrielle and his wife, Loreen, now had two girls and two boys. As his parents grew older, Roger had gradually assumed leadership of the Spanish Wells, Gun Point, and Bluff clinics. He also traveled with the Eleuthera United Care Teams for two weeks every four months, rotating with five other Bahamian doctors to provide medical care for every inhabited island.

After soaking up all the mathematics, biology, chemistry, and science that he could from his mother's island school classes, Sam Garner spent every January through May on Spanish Wells with Roger, Armand, and Nadia, adding their extensive medical knowledge to the volumes already passed down from Alea and John. The young teen hoped that if he could prove himself worthy, he might one day be considered a physician in the eyes of the community.

Robbie had enjoyed working with Daniel so much on the treehouses that he decided to become a builder. The process of designing and constructing hurricane survivable island homes was fascinating to him, even venturing into crafting comfortable homes in limestone caves as he had done at Hurricane Hole, cool in the summer and well-protected from storms. He supervised a group of young men and women carpenters who traveled with the Care Teams, trading their skills for food and a place to stay, their after-work parties becoming that island's hot spot for socializing and fun.

At eighteen and nineteen, Gypsy and Noah were content to remain on Miracle Island. With her boat, *Gypsy Queen,* at their disposal, the pair often set sail to nearby cays to help the surviving villagers as needed and meeting other young people their age. But Adam knew a wedding was inevitable... They were destined to be together, with a love that began from the moment they met as children.

Adam could understand that love quite well. That's how he felt about Nylah. As each year passed, she had grown more physically beautiful, with long, silky, midnight-black hair, tawny golden skin, sparkling light gray eyes, and a shapely figure. But it was her beautiful inner spirit that drew him the most. She radiated compassion and love with everyone she met, always seeing the best in a person, always kind and caring, warm, gracious, and accepting. Her special gifts of the Spirit were strong, but she never flaunted them. She was his best friend, his staunchest ally, and he trusted her as he did no other, even his father and mother.

When he first revealed his interactions with the Darkness, she wasn't surprised. She too had felt the presence of the entity, she said, had fought it each time she healed, each time she sang a spirit song of praise. But now, she understood. Together, he knew, they would be faithful warriors for God! And perhaps in the future, he hoped, something closer. It was the problem of Michael and Angel that puzzled him the most, and would need...

His thoughts were interrupted by Moses appearing in the open sky beyond the cliff and fluttering to the ground. The bird hopped up on the log and tucked his wings, leveling him with a baleful stare.

"What have I done now, Moses?" he groaned. "Or is it something I haven't done? I never know with you anymore."

The hawk's beak pointed out to sea, and he flapped his wings.

"Right... You want me to fly, is that it? I'm afraid I can't do that, boy. Angels can fly, humans can't. Stop trying to make me feel bad, okay?"

Moses insistently flapped his wings again as his feathers began to glow with an unearthly radiant light. Adam leaped to his feet, his eyes suddenly igniting into flames of gold as the Voice only he could hear began to speak.

"The time has come, My son. This is the day you begin your years of training. You have seen nothing of the new earth or of its people whom I love. You have not seen what the Enemy can do. You are My Prophet, and you must understand what you will face

one day. Go now, step out over the edge, and as you do, tell Me where you wish to go... and I will take you."

He pictured it in his mind... and in complete trust, stepped out over the edge of the cliff, the bird leaping after him.

And they vanished.

****

Michael lingered at his kitchen window, unwilling to go outside, dreading what he had to face. His duffle had been packed for hours. Noah was prepping *Gypsy Queen* for the sail while Gypsy hauled the last box of provisions onboard. Christmas and New Year's Day had come and gone, and his Care Team was expecting him to arrive in five days to begin their voyage to Emerald Bay in the Exumas, where the team of twenty-five would be building a community kitchen and repairing a crumbling boat dock.

Since he was fifteen, he'd been working with different Care Teams as a jack of all trades, returning to Miracle Island right before hurricane season in late May and remaining there until early January. When he was sixteen, Daniel offered to help him build his own treehouse, and he gladly accepted, although he loved living with the Garner family... and being close to his darling little Angel.

If leaving her was painful for him, it was particularly hard on the child, the final farewell before he boarded the most difficult moment of all as she bravely struggled to hold back the flood of tears that he was told would instantly stream down her cheeks after the boat disappeared.

She was ten years old, with a deep love for the ocean and all its creatures and for the people of her Tribe more than anyone he had ever met. Unfortunately, he also knew that Angel loved him in a way he'd never be able to return. He was eighteen years old, a young man who was stepping out into the world and forging a life for himself. And that life could never include a child, however much he cared for her.

He'd met someone last winter. Kayla Knowles was Ben's granddaughter, beautiful, exciting, and smart, and when he'd walked her home after their second date, she'd melted into his arms and gifted him with the best first kiss he could ever have imagined! His team would return to home base now and then over the winter months, and he planned to see her as often as he could. A lot of guys were interested in Kayla, and it worried him that he couldn't be there all the time. He'd even thought about moving to Spanish Wells but knew it would break his heart to leave his friends... really his only family now, on Miracle Island.

He started at the sound of a knock on his front door. With a sigh, he picked up his duffle and slung it across his back. Taking one last look around the room, he opened the door to see Josey standing on the porch.

"Are you ready, Michael?" she asked gently. It wasn't the first time she'd escorted him to the bay. He felt like one of her own beloved boys, and she would miss him terribly.

"I'm all set, Mom. Is she at the beach?"

Her smile wavered. "I don't think she's coming this time, Michael. I left her in her room. Maybe it's better this way."

His heart dropped, but perhaps she was right. "Please tell her I'll miss her and that I love her, okay? I'll be back before she knows it, and we'll swim and talk and picnic again, just like we always do."

"Yes, my boy, I'll tell her, but now you go and enjoy that lovely young lady you keep mentioning. Angel will be fine. She has plenty of other things to keep her mind occupied, and she'll probably forget all about you by tomorrow. The whale migration is due soon, and she's been itching to see them again."

They walked down to the beach together, arm in arm. After a hug and a kiss goodbye, he climbed into the tender as Daniel and Ryan manned the oars. He scanned the length of the shoreline hopefully, but Angel was nowhere in sight. Disappointed, he stashed his gear under a seat and turned away from the beach to see Noah waving from the deck of *Gypsy Queen*.

His excitement grew! Kayla would be waiting for him, and he smiled in anticipation.

****

Josey tapped at her daughter's door. "Angel, sweetie, can I come in?" She was met with a brief silence before the door cracked open, but the patter of scampering feet told her that Angel had run back to the safety of her bed. Sure enough, she had burrowed under her mound of blankets, the sound of her muffled sobs unmistakable.

Sitting on the edge of the platform bed, Josey gently drew back the covers. Angel was curled up in a ball, her eyes swollen with tears, her nose running with moisture that she quickly tried to wipe away as soon as she saw her mother.

Josey reached for her and pulled her into her arms, cuddling her as she once did as a baby, and rocking her back and forth in an effort to soothe the heartbroken child.

"Angel, I know you care deeply for Michael, and that it hurts when he has to leave. He understands why you didn't come to say goodbye and told me to tell you that he loves you and will miss you too."

"Momma, if Michael loves me, why does he always leave me?" she whispered, fresh tears springing from her already reddened eyes.

Josey kissed the trembling cheek and held her close, her own heart breaking over her child's pain, pain she could do nothing to fix.

"Angel, Michael is a grown man. He's expected to go out into the world and live an adult life, to find work he loves to do, and eventually make a family. As much as he cares for you, he can't stay on Miracle Island and do those things."

"But I love him, Momma! Michael belongs to me!" she cried out in anguish. Pushing herself away, she leaped out of bed, her blue eyes blazing with an unaccustomed anger.

"I heard Robbie talking about a girl he likes in Spanish Wells! He never told me about her!"

Josey kept her voice calm. "It's because he didn't want to hurt your feelings, sweetheart. Angel, you're simply too young for Michael. He's eight years older than you, and to be honest, I think it's unhealthy for you to be suffering over him like this. You need to let him go. Someday, when you're older, you'll finally meet the boy who was meant for you all along, and you'll see that this infatuation, as real as it feels to you now, was only an impossible dream."

She could see the girl's anger deflate as she spoke, a weary sadness taking its place, her daughter suddenly appearing much older than her ten short years.

"I know you're right, Momma," she confessed. "I promise to try as hard as I can to do what you said." She climbed back into her mother's comforting arms, and Josey rocked her until she finally drifted off to sleep.

****

The wind buffeted the wooden cross, the swell pounding into the cliff, a crashing wave sending showers of white spray high into the air as Adam reappeared, stepping back onto solid ground, with Moses on his shoulder. The hawk whistled twice before lifting off and veering inland towards camp.

Adam turned and gazed out over the Atlantic, his eyes now a deep sky blue. Falling to his knees, he bowed low and praised the miraculous God of the Heavens and the Earth!

What he had seen had shaken him to his very core.

He now knew why God was making him wait. He could never defeat the Darkness until he had observed the peoples of the earth, watching, listening, and learning... feeling their love, weeping for their sorrows, and suffering with the pain in their hearts, to truly understand who the family of man really was.

Tomorrow, he would select another place to go, realizing that his education in the ways of the world, and of the true enemy, the Darkness, had only just begun.

Chapter 12 Just Desserts

"We'll only be gone about five days, my love," Matt assured Morgan, her growing belly pressed close against him. "Daniel promised Barris Hollingsworth we'd come if he ever needed us. Rum Cay is maybe half a day's sail to the southwest, but it'll take all our manpower to help his village build an above ground rain catch system."

She clung to him a little longer before relinquishing her claim. "I know... but I miss you so much, Matt, even when you leave for a day. We're so lucky to have the Black Hole on this island! It rains like crazy in the summer, but once our New Year's Eve celebration is over, it only rains now and then for a couple of months."

"That cistern will save Rum Cay in the future, and I won't have to sail back and forth every winter to refill their water barrels." He lifted her blouse and kissed the soft skin of her belly. "Then I can stay home with you, Nylah, Maxie, and our new baby until you beg me to leave again!"

Pulling her gently back into his arms, he captured her moist red lips with a lingering kiss that would have to satisfy his desires until he returned.

Ronny popped his head in the doorway, making them both jump. "Don't you two ever stop?! You realize you can only make one baby at a time, don't you?"

Matt picked up an avocado from a bowl on the table and pitched it, Ronny ducking quickly. "Can't a man say goodbye to his wife in the privacy of his own treehouse? Get thee hence to the beach! I'll be there in a minute."

"Okay, but Daniel, Ishmael, Ryan, and John are already at the boat. They sent me to kick you in the rear to hurry it up."

Morgan handed Matt his duffle bag. "You're all packed, sweetheart. Come on, I'll walk you guys down. Your little wild man is already there. Nylah and Adam are... oh, I never know where they are!"

John, Ishmael, and Ryan were standing in the shallows, their families waiting to see them off. When they saw Matt and Ronny walking over the berm, they jumped in to wait for them to board, with Daniel holding the tender in place. Alea and Pearl would ride out with them to *Dances With Wind*, then row the tender back to Casuarina Cove.

It wasn't unusual for the men to use one of the sailcats for a few days of offshore fishing, diving, and for Ronny, some exploring. Only the most trusted family and friends were given the coordinates of Miracle Island, and except for the Garner's chance arrival on *Barefootin'* after the Flare and *Piranha's* shipwreck five years ago, no one unexpected had ever shown up.

Michael, Robbie, and Sammy had left for Spanish Wells on *Gypsy Queen* the week before, captained by Gypsy and her first mate, Noah. All the wives and the nine children were staying home for this particular trip, but with the island's long history of seclusion, no one was concerned.

Maxie raced across the top of the berm and dove headlong into his father's arms. "Daddy, I wanna come too!" he wailed, his face scrunching in dismay. "I'm a big boy now!"

Matt smiled with amusement at his son's animated display and hugged him tight. "But I have a very important job for you to do, Maximilian Kennedy. I'm counting on you to take good care of your mom and sister while I'm gone. Have you been keeping your spear sharp in case you need to protect them?"

Earnest deep blue eyes stared back at him. "Yes, Daddy, I won't ever let anything bad happen to my family."

"Good. And make sure you feed the dogs. We've got a litter of puppies who'll be leaving for their new homes very soon.

Out of Bear and Brandy's six pups, have you picked out the one you want to keep?"

"I want the all-red one that looks like Brandy. His fur is the same color as yours, Daddy!"

Matt laughed, kissing his golden-haired son and beautiful wife one last time, and threw his duffle in the boat. He, Ronny, and Daniel pushed off the beach and jumped in, with many waves and calls of farewell following them out to the catamaran. The men climbed onboard *Dances With Wind* as Alea and Pearl steadied the tender.

"I love you, my darling," Daniel whispered to Alea, the tips of their fingers touching over the water.

"No more than I love you," she replied, her eyes glistening. It was always hard to see him go, but she was so proud of everything he did to help their neighbors in need.

Daniel watched as Pearl and Alea rowed back to shore. Only when the bow of their tender ran up on the wet sand did he turn away, beaming from ear to ear. "Hoist the sails, me maties! We're on our way to Rum Cay!"

****

Angel's head popped up from beneath the waves at the entrance to Hidden Cove, watching *Dances With Wind's* billowing sail disappear to the southwest. Since Michael left, she'd been pushing herself to swim farther and faster and dive deeper and deeper in an effort to distract herself from her heartache, sometimes swimming out as far as two miles from the cliffs.

A smooth, curved, light gray fin rolled in the water next to her, and she smiled brightly.

"Good morning, Miss Sally!" she said, before reminding herself that the dolphin didn't speak her human language and switched to Dolphinese in her mind.

"How is your family today?"

The dolphin rose out of the water and skidded backwards, the thrust of her powerful tailfin holding her aloft.

"Oh, that's good to hear, girl. My dad left today, and my brothers won't be home until summer."

Sally swam up close and gently nosed Angel's leg.

"Yes, Michael left too," she said sadly. Remembering her talk with her mother not long ago, she lifted her chin.

"But I'm really okay. I'm going to try something new, Sally! Sarah is a real artist, and is teaching me how to sketch and paint, and Morgan is showing me how the Mayoruna make natural paints and dyes from plants, berries, and clay. I see so much beauty in the ocean and on the reefs when I dive, and after I've had more practice, I plan to recreate some of the underwater scenes on cloth and wood! I can't be in the ocean all the time, even if it's the only place I want to be... if I can't be with Michael."

The dolphin chattered and Angel took hold of her fin, her melancholy temporarily forgotten. "Why yes, I'd love to see your new reef, girl! Let's go!" The two friends took a breath and sank beneath the waves.

****

Alea was up early the next morning. She always found it difficult to sleep without being able to curl around Daniel's warmth, and yawned as she lit the pile of tinder in the cold firepit to start a pot of coffee. Adam's bed had been empty, as usual. Where did he go in the dim, pre-dawn hours, long before the sun even rose above the cliffs?

Whenever she asked him about his lengthy and frequent absences, his answers were rather vague. He'd gone for a hike... he was exploring new places... he just needed some time alone. Moses always accompanied him on his forays, but she knew she'd get no answers from the bird.

Nine-year old's... she thought in exasperation, the age when children were attempting to stretch their wings and gradually break away from parental authority. She wasn't concerned for his safety. The dogs or Moses tailed him constantly and would alert her if there was any trouble. But she was already feeling the inevitable separation that would occur as he grew older. Josey and Pearl were still having difficulty dealing with Sammy's five month stay in Spanish Wells and with Michael and Robbie's travels with the Care Teams as it was.

She was about to toss another log on top of the fire for good measure when movement out on the bay suddenly caught her attention.

Rowing steadily towards Casuarina Cove were two wooden skiffs, each with six men at the oars, and a tall, dark-haired passenger wearing a wide-brimmed hat standing at the bow of the lead boat! Dropping the log, she raced into the village, slipping into Essie's treehouse first.

"Essie," she whispered, "As quietly as you can, leave right now and take Esmeralda and Alonzo to Hurricane Hole! Two boatloads of what look like pirates will land here in minutes. Take the dogs and all the puppies with you too! I'll warn the others."

Without waiting for a response, she ran to Josey's with the same directive, then to Sarah, Pearl, and Morgan.

"I'm not leaving, Alea," Morgan stated firmly. "I'll send Max with Pearl, but Nylah left earlier with Adam."

"Morgan, just go. I don't want them to know the rest of you are here. Yes, they'll see the treehouses, but I'll tell them that everyone left for an early morning fishing trip. Maybe they're only searching for food and water. I can offer them that."

"Well, thirteen pirates don't row all the way across the ocean in skiffs. There must be a bigger boat anchored outside that couldn't make it through the pass, and there may be more men waiting out there." Morgan slung her quiver of arrows over her shoulder and picked up her bow. "I'll stay hidden in the trees while you talk to them. That way, I can keep an eye on what's going on. Don't worry, Alea... I got your back."

As the last woman and child vanished into the bush, the two boats slid up onto the beach. The men jumped out, the one wearing the hat leading the way forward to where Alea was standing at the firepit.

She studied them as they approached. The men were a mix of ethnicities... black, brown, white, and she could catch bits and pieces of English, Spanish, and what sounded to her like French Creole. Except for their dapper leader, their clothes were worn and mismatched, some wearing a different shoe on each foot, and carrying antique swords, machetes, and knives. Definitely pirates, she thought, and began to worry.

The leader stopped in front of her, his men lining up behind him, staring at her silently.

"Hello, pretty lady!" He glanced around the village, pleased with what he saw. "Very nice... very secluded... We happened to spot your cove and decided to investigate." His eyes slowly devoured her from head to foot.

"Are you all alone, my dear?"

Alea leveled him with a stony stare. "My friends are fishing and will be here soon. If it's food and water you need, I'll be happy to provide enough for all of you... to take back to your ship as you leave."

The man laughed, his men smirking as they gazed at her with unconcealed lust. "Oh, my foolish beauty... food and water are not the only things we need."

She turned to run, but two men quickly darted forward to seize her. The leader casually strolled over and toyed briefly with the neckline of her shirt. Then, with one swift pull, he tore it down the middle, exposing her heaving breasts.

He smiled as he caressed a nipple, Alea struggling to free herself from their grasp. “Regretfully, we cannot partake of the delightful feast before us. A closer inspection of your village and boats for whatever treasures we can find will have to satisfy us for the time being.”

He motioned to the men holding her. “Keep her here… but do not molest her. This one is for the captain.”

****

Angel skimmed along the bottom of the bay, searching for unbroken seashells. She loved the first rays of the sun as it rose in the morning, the light gradually changing the water from the darkest black of night to a clear turquoise blue.

Spotting a perfect empty conch shell, she pulled it from the sand and shot to the surface. Blinking the water from her eyes, she was surprised to see unfamiliar rowboats anchored at the beach. She gasped at the sight of two men restraining a bare-chested Alea as others gleefully hauled out armfuls of clothing, utensils, tools, and dive gear from the treehouses. Several men were carrying their valuable five-gallon water bottles to the rowboats and stowing them aboard.

Where was the rest of the Tribe? She searched the grounds of the village but saw no one. And where was Adam? He could have stopped them. But perhaps there was something she could do!

Dropping the conch shell, she dove and began undulating out the pass. Coming up for a quick breath of air, she saw a sixty-foot sailboat anchored slightly offshore, with more men scattered on deck. Ducking underwater to avoid being seen, she continued her way out to sea.

****

An angry Morgan watched as Alea's shirt was ripped in half by the pirate leader. Quickly nocking her arrow, she took aim and was about to release when she realized that Alea was not in any immediate danger and lowered her weapon. But as the men filtered into the village to plunder, she had an idea.

Melting into the bush, she crept around the perimeter until she reached Josey's house. Hearing scuffling and muttering inside, she chanced a peek through one of the windows. A scruffy-looking pirate was examining each item greedily and chuckling with pleasure as he loaded his booty into a sack. Once he had stripped anything of value from the rooms, he lifted the heavy bag and opened the front door.

The tip of an arrow was aimed straight at his head... and Morgan smiled.

****

Alea glared as the leader sauntered over to where she was being held, his bag of stolen goods bulging.

"This has been quite fun and very productive! Perhaps we'll stay for a while and surprise your friends when they return. Are there young and beautiful women with them? My men are most anxious for some female companionship."

"Trust me, it would be far better if you left now. You have no idea who you're up against."

"Please, call me Raoul. And your name, my sweet? I'll be taking you to Captain Fernando's bed, but I insist on making a proper introduction first, before his... unconventional, shall we say, intimacies commence."

A shout sounded from Matt's treehouse as one of the pirates ran out on the porch. "Skinner, Tatum, and Buzzy are dead! Shot with an arrow! We're being hunted!"

Raoul glanced at Alea, whose lips were curved in a ghost of a smile. With a roar of anger, he backhanded her across the face, sending her flying to the ground.

"Return to the boats! Bring whatever you can carry! The woman comes with us." Dragging her to her feet, he slung her into a skiff, her mouth pouring blood. The pirates piled their loaded bags into the boats, quickly pushed off, and scrambled aboard. The oars plunged into the water as they sped away from shore, Raoul's boat leading the way.

An arrow whizzed past his ear like a buzzing bee, leaving a bloody nick. He turned to see Morgan standing on the berm, drawing her bow again. She released, but they had moved out of range and her arrow fell short. With an angry snarl, she determinedly re-set and shot again, but to no avail.

He tipped the brim of his hat, his black eyes twinkling with anticipation. "We shall return soon with reinforcements, my golden-haired queen! And you're for me!"

"Raoul, what the hell is this?!" a rower cried out in utter astonishment, staring over the bow.

The crew turned to see a pod of six humpback whales rolling and diving through the pass and into the bay, heading straight towards them. But what shocked them all was what they saw riding on the back of the lead whale!

A beautiful girl child was gripping the whale's large dorsal fin, her waist-length white-blonde hair streaming behind her like a Valkyrie riding the winds of a storm, one arm pointing at their boats! As the fifty-five-foot humpback dove, she rode with it, laughing with glee as it rose to the surface.

"Jesu Christos, it is a demon of the sea!" a swarthy-faced pirate shouted.

"Keep rowing!" Raoul ordered. "The whales will pass us by, no doubt searching for krill." He rubbed his eyes. The girl had to be a hallucination, he thought, but how could they all be seeing the same thing? He yanked Alea to her feet.

"Tell me what you see out there, woman!"

Alea was just as amazed as the superstitious pirates. That was sweet little Angel riding that enormous whale! Her mind was reeling, but there was no way she'd give her captor an ounce of satisfaction.

She shrugged off his hand. "I see your doom."

The pod suddenly disappeared underwater. Silence fell over the boats as the pirates peered fearfully into the depths.

Suddenly, the lead whale exploded into the air, Angel diving off its back only seconds before the fifty-ton animal crashed down on the rear skiff! When the splintered pieces floated up, six crushed bodies bobbed up with it.

The remaining oarsmen froze in place, not knowing what to do. A horrified Raoul stood at the stern, scanning the bay behind him while Alea gripped the gunnel to maintain her balance, the boat pitching and rolling from the tremendous splash. A small hand suddenly shot out of the water, grabbed her tattered shirt, and pulled her over the side.

Before Raoul could react, the water exploded again, and the sky above him grew dark. He smiled ruefully and tipped his hat to the woman and girl watching from a short distance away as the massive behemoth took him and his screaming men down forever to the bottom of the bay.

****

With Angel's help, Alea stumbled to shore and collapsed on the sand, breathing hard, as Angel knelt beside her.

"Thank you for what you did, Angel," she gasped. "But I don't understand what just happened."

Angel bit her bottom lip, pondering how to answer. Adam and Nylah had told her this day would eventually come.

"Auntie Alea, you know about Adam's gifts, don't you?"

Alea nodded. "Yes, Angel. Daniel, Matt, and I have known for many years, but I didn't know that you did."

"And about Nylah too?"

"Yes, the whole Tribe is aware of her healing abilities and gift of prophecy."

"Well, I have a gift that only Adam, Nylah, and Michael know about. I can talk to the creatures of the sea, and I can swim just like they do! They're my friends, Auntie Alea, and today, I asked the whales to save you from those bad men."

Alea wrapped her arms around the girl, pulling her in tight. Had the immeasurable amounts of magnetic energy from the Flare somehow affected all the babies carried in the womb or conceived that year? And what could God's purpose possibly be for their unusual powers?

"Angel! Alea! Are you alright?" Morgan's feet pounded the sand as she raced towards them, her bow on her shoulder.

"I saw what happened!" She looked at Alea curiously, then at Angel with a raised eyebrow. "Are the scumbags all dead?"

"They're no longer a threat, Morgan, thanks to you and Angel. After we bury the bodies, we can tell everyone it's safe to come home."

Angel got up, relieved that her secret was finally revealed. "Not just yet, Auntie Alea. There's still something I need to finish." She waved goodbye and dove into the water.

Alea rose to her feet, brushing tiny pink shells and mossy debris from her legs. "Morgan, can we keep the truth about Angel between the two of us for now? We're going to need more time to prepare the rest of the Tribe for this one!"

****

Captain Fernando paced the deck, his bored crew leaning against the railings while they waited for Raoul to return.

"They've been gone for hours! Find them!" he ordered.

All at once, six giant humpback whales broke the surface and circled once around the boat before blowing their air and disappearing underwater. Seconds later, all six behemoths leaped high into the sky and simultaneously crashed down on top of the sixty-foot sailboat, the men shouting in terror as they were hurled into the water, the crushed and broken vessel capsizing and sinking rapidly!

The first fin broke the surface thirty feet away, and the pirates began to scream! Charlie and his family had been invited to dinner... and they had accepted the invitation.

****

Adam and Nylah stood hand in hand at the top of the rise, watching as the drama unfolding below came to an end.

"It was good that we were told to stay out of it, Nylah. Angel was so unhappy about Michael, but she needed to find herself, and the Tribe was saved, thanks to her. And after today, her life will change completely... They know about her now!"

Chapter 13 Pieces Of A Puzzle

Angel floated dreamily in the middle of the bay, a bank of white puffy clouds lazily drifting by in the sky above her, her long silky strands of white-blonde hair buoyed by the calm turquoise water. Michael was coming home today, after his usual stint with the Eleuthera United Care Teams.

She wouldn't be at the beach to greet him.

Her stomach clenched, and she flipped over. Her irritation grew as she glanced at the village, where the Tribe was in full blown preparation for Robbie, Sammy, and Michael's return. Huh. You'd think it wouldn't be such a big deal anymore after so many years, she muttered to herself, but it was still the same old silly brouhaha for their homecoming. Now, at sixteen, Michael's pending arrival couldn't even get her out of bed this morning.

Sammy was a different matter altogether. She adored her big brother, a handsome, twenty-one-year-old doctor who traveled with the Care Teams during the winter and spring months, leaving Roger Gabrielle free to serve the Spanish Wells and Eleuthera clinics until June. Armand and Nadia still practiced but had opened a school for teens from any island who displayed an aptitude for medicine.

Robbie Robello operated his own construction company that worked with the Care Teams, a free-wheeling, partying crowd that included both men and women who were skilled, detail-oriented carpenters and craftsmen with no marital attachments, coming and going depending on their personal circumstances. But it was Robbie's flamboyant, fun-loving, and daredevil personality that attracted the workers he recruited from all over the islands, their loyalty ensured by his solid core of commitment and caring for his crew, whom he also considered his friends.

After her incredible secret had been revealed to the Tribe, Daniel thanked her repeatedly for saving the families, and told her he'd never worry about the safety of Miracle Island again. The men watched in astonishment as she retrieved their dive gear and tools from the bottom of the bay, as well as valuable items from the sunken ship.

To the delight of the fishermen, she also began guiding them to offshore migrating schools of tuna, mahi mahi, and wahoo. Yes, she loved the creatures of the ocean, but she also understood the basic and unavoidable fact that both fish and human beings had to hunt and kill if they were to survive and reproduce.

She now had a flourishing business of her own too. Her colorful and realistic paintings of underwater scenery and ocean life done on wood and cloth were impressive, her late-blooming talent garnering her much praise from the Tribe. Her lifelike murals covered many walls and doors in all the treehouses, and her intricately detailed paintings on wood planks and natural fiber cloth canvas were trading well in Spanish Wells.

Local residents, as well as visiting sailors, traded for her popular wares at a small shop that Gil Knowles' oldest son, Bruno, had opened next to the marina office, with the artist's portion of the proceeds saved for her until one of the Miracle Island boats made the trip over once a month.

She turned away from the shoreline and plunged into the water, deciding to swim out to the Atlantic reef she now called her own. Angel's Reef had once been Sally's Reef, but when her dolphin friend had taken her brood and re-located south, she bequeathed her old home to Angel.

Reaching the reef, she slid herself up on a flat rock. At low tide, a smooth, weatherworn section stood a foot above the waves, and Angel loved to sit on top to comb the tangles out of her hair with her fingers and bask in the sun, all alone with nothing but a cool breeze caressing her skin and the deep blue ocean surrounding her.

The color of Michael's eyes...

The thought had popped into her mind unbidden, and she forced it back angrily. He didn't deserve to inhabit one square inch of her brain!

When he'd left her, *again*, at age ten, he'd run straight into the arms of that temptress, Kayla. For two summers it was nothing but Kayla this and Kayla that! Then he told Mom and Dad he was going to ask her to marry him. She'd overheard *that* devastating conversation from her barely open bedroom door, positive that the pain she felt was her real heart actually breaking in two.

He'd made an effort to spend time with her though, she had to give him that. And despite her heartache, they fell back into their old habits of talking, laughing, swimming, picnics, and watching the stars. It was then she realized she would always be in love with Michael, and that he really loved her too... just not in the way she had hoped and prayed that he would.

But when he returned the following year, Michael was a changed man. Kayla had married someone else during his absence. He spent most of his days alone, wandering the island, and often staying at Hurricane Hole for days. When he finally came back to camp, he was silent and moody and ignored her completely, choosing instead to engage in long private talks with Daniel, Matt, or her father.

She tried tugging on his sleeve once to get his attention, to offer him her sympathy and love, but he brushed her off like an irritating fly and resumed his intense conversation with his companion as if she wasn't even there. She was mortified and began avoiding him after that.

And that's how it had been for the last three years. As soon as he stepped foot on Miracle Island, she had as little to do with him as possible. They'd all noticed it... It was the talk of the Tribe, but nothing could change her mind. And when she heard he was dating other girls, she hardly spoke to him at all, the expression of hurt on his face secretly delighting her.

But this morning, in advance of his arrival, her mother sat her down and scolded her for her behavior.

"Angel, you know you upset Michael terribly every time he comes home. He doesn't understand what he could possibly have done to hurt you, and you always walk away before he gets close enough to actually speak to you. Yes, you politely say good morning and thank you in front of the others, but it's just not like you to treat anyone so coldly... and you've been doing it now for three years. He told me before he left that he was very worried about you. This problem has gone on much too long, Angel, and it's upsetting everyone in the Tribe. Won't you at least talk to him when he gets here... clear the air? I hate to see the two of you like this."

How could she even begin to explain to her mother that it was because she loved Michael so much that she couldn't do it? That if such a conversation were to begin, her heart would only be smashed to pieces by its inevitable ending? What was the point? But if it would make her mom feel any better...

Sighing in resignation, she slowly nodded. "Okay, Mom, I'll do it. When it feels right, I'll talk to him."

****

Adam reappeared and stepped back onto the edge of the cliff, his flaming eyes now a deep-sea green. Moses flew in from behind him, landing on the post of the cross.

"Thank you, my Lord, for showing me so much beauty!" he exclaimed. "But how does such a beautiful land become so full of war and hate?" He sat down on his log, the horizon in the distant Atlantic hazy with heavy clouds of rain.

"It's still what You've shown me all along, isn't it? The work of the Darkness and his minions. Why do You allow the Evil One so much power on earth? And why must I continue to wait and only observe? I'm fifteen! I'm ready! When will You let..."

"What are you doing up here, Adam?" A soft voice spoke right into his ear, causing him to jump. Nylah laughed and stepped over the log to sit beside him. "Sometimes you and Moses just seem to vanish. I search for you with the Spirit, but I can never find you."

He heard a whisper on the wind, the loving and familiar Voice explaining how to answer her. "You weren't meant to find me, Nylah, not until He wanted you to." He leaped up, unable to contain his excitement.

"I've been traveling... in a way you won't believe! For many years, God has been sending me to faraway lands every day to watch and listen and learn. The Darkness continues to forward his plans to destroy mankind, trying to lure them back into the old ways of turmoil, dissension, anger, and greed before the Flare. Once I'm ready, He will send me to them, to be His messenger, His Prophet of the Eden on earth that can be theirs, if they will only believe and follow the ways of peace! And just now, as we were talking, He told me that you and Moses will be going with me!"

Was he joking with her? Traveling to faraway lands? Every day? How? She knew that nothing was impossible with God, but really, Adam?

"Well, if you say so... but can you show me?"

Adam stood. He closed his eyes for a moment, and when he re-opened them, they gleamed with golden light. He smiled confidently, walked over to the edge of the cliff, took a step out into thin air... and disappeared!

Nylah shrieked in horror, collapsing to the ground and bursting into tears. "Why would you do that, Adam?!" she cried out. "How could you leave me like that?"

Moses did not follow Adam this time but flew to her side with a whistle and nosed her arm with his beak.

"You want me to look, Moses?"

The bird whistled again.

Crawling to the edge of the cliff, she peered down at the sharp rocks and pounding surf sixty feet below. He wasn't there! Backing away in confusion, she knelt at the base of the old wooden cross, wrapping her arms around the post and clutching it tightly. Where was he?

"Adam!" she sobbed, her heart breaking.

She felt a gentle touch on her shoulder. Looking up, she was amazed to see him standing right in front of her, holding a strange red flower!

"I brought this for you... so you'll believe. It's called a rose, and it grows in a beautiful green valley between two very tall mountains." Helping her to her feet, he offered her the flower. In awe, she accepted the perfect bloom, still wet with dew, and inhaled its intoxicating fragrance.

"Oh, Adam, how could I have doubted?"

He wiped away the tears running down her cheeks. "So, my Nylah, where would you like to go?"

Her smile was glorious as she tucked his magnificent gift into the deep pocket of her white blouse and took his hand.

"Take me to the land of my mother!"

****

Michael stood at the bow of *Gypsy Queen* as she slipped into the blue-green waters of Osprey Bay, breathing in the sweet scent of white beach flowers in full bloom. It was good to be home! He scanned the shoreline anxiously, looking for Angel, but she wasn't there. She was never there anymore.

He knew he'd blown it with her the summer he came back after Kayla left him, devastated that she had married Jonas Wilkes during the Christmas holidays while he was still on Miracle Island. He never saw it coming... and no one had dared tell him she'd been dating someone else while she was also seeing him, a young man who was an employee of her father's and who lived all year on Spanish Wells.

Even Will was kept in the dark until his daughter and her newlywed husband showed up at his door after a secret wedding at the church in Bluff, her pregnancy making their marriage more urgent. He and his shocked wife threw them a hastily planned reception, all the while wondering how to break the bitter news to the man she had betrayed when he finally returned.

Michael completed his Care Team assignments that winter in a dazed fog. Lying in his cold and lonely bed at night, he remembered how it had felt to hold her shapely body and caress her silky dark skin... how it had felt as he sank deep inside her for his first time, the steady rhythm of her hips as he plunged in again and again driving him mad, her cries of pleasure ringing in his ears. At that moment, he realized it wasn't her first time, but he didn't care.

They were together whenever they could manage, making love for hours in empty boat cabins. He couldn't get enough of her, but as each year went by, their lovemaking became the highlight of their relationship, with less and less to talk about when they weren't gasping in each other's arms.

Entwined in the aftermath, she frequently grew quiet and distant. When he questioned her mood, she only smiled and reassured him that she was fine, but he couldn't shake the nagging feeling that he was losing her.

He'd planned to ask her to marry him when he saw her again after New Year's, but he was too late. Her father had the unhappy responsibility of telling him his daughter had unexpectedly married another man two weeks before and relocated to Cat Island when he innocently knocked at the door, a bouquet of flowers in hand, asking for Kayla.

It hadn't gone well...

He realized that in his anger and misery he'd been rough, careless, and dismissive with Angel. He deeply regretted the insensitive way he'd treated her over the last few years, but at the time, his own emotional problems had overwhelmed him. He had alienated his closest and dearest friend, and now that he'd fully recovered from the impetuous youthful relationship that was probably doomed to failure anyway, he missed his sweet Angel tremendously.

But how to repair the damage he'd caused? And could she ever forgive him?

****

As *Gypsy Queen* entered Osprey Bay, the excited Tribe paraded down to the beach to welcome Robbie, Sammy, and Michael. Once anchored, the three young men manned the oars to return to shore, where they received hugs, kisses, and warm greetings from everyone.

Gypsy and Noah were greeted too, the twenty-four and twenty-five-year-old couple holding hands as they headed home to their own treehouse. They had married four years earlier on the bow of *Gypsy Queen*, a joyous wedding long expected by the Tribe. James and his new wife of one year, Elizabeth Pinder, and Diego, his wife, Alice Sweeting, and their two children, had sailed over for the event.

John and Josey eagerly embraced Sammy, who had grown tall and slender, his brown hair kept short, his hazel eyes snapping with intelligence and humor. Michael was next as Josey enveloped him in her arms before John could reach him, her heart full of love for her adopted son. But even as he hugged her, Michael searched the crowd, and his heart sank.

She hadn't come...

"I made sure to have a big pot of that bouillabaisse you love hot and ready!" Josey announced.

Glancing around hopefully one more time, he couldn't help feeling disappointed, but gave Josey a loving smile. "Thanks, Mom! I could almost smell it as we passed San Salvador."

He leaned over and put his lips to her ear. "Where is she?"

"She's been at Alea's Secret Spot all morning," Josey told him. "I think maybe, just maybe, she's ready to talk."

"Put that stew on simmer for me, Momma!" Dropping his duffle, he tore off his shirt, kicked off his shoes, and started jogging up the beach.

****

She saw him coming from a thousand feet away, her heart pounding despite herself. The waters of the bay offered an easy way to escape the inevitable confrontation... but she vowed she'd never run again. It was time to face her anger, and the man who had caused it.

As he jogged towards her, a light sheen of sweat glistened on his tan skin, the powerful muscles of his chest covered with a scattering of dark hair that narrowed and disappeared into the waistband of his trunks, his chiseled face clean shaven, his shoulder-length black hair secured behind his neck. When he finally slowed to a stop, his deep blue eyes lasered her with their intensity.

"You weren't there to meet us at the boat... again! Angel, when is this *thing* you're holding against me, whatever it is, going to end?"

His voice softened as he knelt in front of her and reached for her hands. "I miss you, sweetie, and I want us to be the way we were. You know how much I've always loved you."

Shoving his hands away in disgust, she sprang from her chair, and he fell into the hot, sun-drenched sand.

"You *love* me, Michael?! No... you have *insulted* me for three years! I was your friend! I cared about you! I showed you who I really was before anyone else knew! I could see you were hurting, and I tried to comfort you after that girl left you, but you tossed me aside like so much flotsam. And now, you want everything to be the way it once was? You want us to go on picnics together, swim in *my* ocean, hold hands and gaze at the stars at midnight, and talk about our lives, our dreams, our feelings, like nothing ever happened, just because *you* decided it was time? Ha! Those days are gone forever!"

She might as well have just shot him. My God, he'd hurt her so badly! And he never even saw it, his betrayal by Kayla blinding him for so long to the needs and emotions of anyone else.

But he did see the woman standing in front of him now.

She had always been an exquisitely beautiful child, but since he had last seen her, she had magically transformed into her heavenly namesake... an Angel of indescribable and luminous beauty! She wore a blue two-piece swimsuit, her silky, white-blonde hair falling in soft waves to her slender but curvaceous hips, her tanned legs long and shapely, her youthful breasts high and full, her dark-lashed azure blue eyes flashing like lightning.

The child was gone... a vision stood in her place!

He was humbled before her righteous anger, his foolish mistakes, insensitive actions, and cruel words spoken to the one person he cared for the most since arriving on Miracle Island stabbing him again and again. He didn't know what to say... what to do... how to fix this... his uncertainty and anguish clearly written in his eyes.

And in that instant, she forgave him!

Falling to her knees, her hands cupped his face as her lips crashed into his with a fire, a wild passion he'd never seen in her before! There was no time to think... no time to reason... He quickly caught her as they tumbled backwards into the sand, the purity and power of her love ripping apart the veil that had obscured the buried truth in his heart.

He rolled over until he lay on the lush bed of her curves, her body matching his perfectly like the pieces of a puzzle. Her long, firm legs wrapped around his waist, and he grew dizzy with desire, feasting like a starving man on her eager sweetness as she softly moaned beneath his lips, and all at once... his heart fell into place!

How could he not have seen it? How could he not have felt it? She had always belonged to him, and he to her! Now he understood why he had felt so natural, so happy, so free, so complete, whenever he was with her. She was the one meant for him... the true one... his beloved Angel!

From the first moment he saw her when he was thirteen, his young heart had been inexplicably drawn to the child, his spirit somehow, mysteriously, recognizing her importance in his life. He had logically interpreted his feelings at the time as nothing more than a warm and abiding affection for the loveable little five-year-old girl who had so openly adored him, but now, the electrifying realization of the truth could no longer be denied!

Their kiss deepened as their passion grew, her breath, her scent, enflaming him, her fingers running through his hair, his hands sliding down the curve of her neck to caress her breasts, when a sudden disturbing thought drove a razor-sharp spear straight into his soul...

Angel was only sixteen. He was twenty-four.

His heart and body aching, he pulled away.

She cried out with the loss of his touch, and they stared at each other, only inches apart, breathing hard.

Gently disentangling himself, he rolled off her and stood up as she lay in the sand, her beautiful eyes glistening with pain, waiting for the hammer to fall.

"I wasn't there for you when you needed me, Angel, and I'm so very sorry how I treated you. But I can't be here for you now... like this. I'm too old for you, my darling, and you're much too young for me. It's impossible. But there's one thing I can confess without a shadow of a doubt...

"I'm in love with you."

He turned and walked away.

Chapter 14 From A Faraway Land

When Eagle Claw first saw the giant obelisk of red rock, imbedded in the sand and pounded smooth by the tides of the southern Nova Scotia coast, he knew that the Great Spirit had led him to the only monument that could properly honor his father on the day of his death many years before.

The majestic rock had been sculpted by the elements over eons of time. During some long ago and distant age, a restless rumble from a crack in the lowermost parts of the earth had shaken the rock from its ancient berth in the cliff, causing it to fall into the surf below with a thundering crash that no man alive ever heard.

Using the same techniques that built the mighty Egyptian pyramids, the huge ten-thousand-pound stone had taken forty braves, heavy rope, and multiple logs to transport it from the sandy shallows to the top of the bluff, then set on the exact square of earth where the body of Chief Lonecloud had been discovered by his son early one morning, his arm reaching towards the sea, a look of joyous recognition on his old, weatherworn face. Eagle Claw's deepest regret was that the great Chief and spiritual leader of the Mi'kmaq had not lived to see his beloved granddaughter, Skylark, once more before he died.

Using his cane to navigate the uneven trail that led to the pine tree-covered bluff, he slowly made his way down until he came to a stop in front of the rock, the rays of the morning sun causing it to glow like fire. His braids were now brushed with silver, his skin as lined as his ancestors, but he stood straight and proud, his black eyes bright. As he watched the waves rolling in, the breeze off the ocean fresh and cool, he allowed his memories to flow unfettered through his mind, letting the Spirit guide them where He would.

Leaning against the stone to ease his aching hips, he saw a white-winged osprey sweep up from below the cliff. When it saw him, the bird flew straight towards him and landed at his feet. The unusual black-eyed, masked hawk showed no fear, surprising Eagle Claw by calmly folding its wings and turning back to the cliff with a whistle.

A strange white mist began to rise from the green grass before him, thick enough to obscure his view of the ocean, and suddenly, a young man and woman walked out of the mist, their eyes a radiant gold, their fingers intertwined. The girl's long midnight hair lifted in the breeze, and she smiled at him, her eyes gradually changing to a sparkling gray.

He clutched his heart, unable to breath, but before the Chief of the Mi'kmaq tribe fell unconscious to the earth in front of his father's monument, he reached out his arm and whispered her name...

"Skylark!"

****

Nylah raced to the fallen man's side and touched his damp forehead. Adam knelt down next to her with a slight smile but said nothing.

"Adam, this man is my grandfather!" she exclaimed. "He thought I was my mother! He'd been told by the man named Bjorn that she was murdered by that evil woman in Boston, and I look so much like her that seeing me was simply too much of a shock."

She looked at him disapprovingly. "You've already visited this place, haven't you? And why can he see us?"

"The Lord will allow us to be visible for now, but they never saw me before, Nylah. I only came to observe. I heard all the stories about the Mi'kmaq from Matt and Ryan and wanted to see for myself. They're good people who follow the wise teachings of the Great Spirit and are not very far off from the true way to heaven through Christ.

"Those who accepted the Way of the Light through your mother many years ago have drawn some of the people to God, but many still cling to the old and ancient beliefs. The Darkness knows of them and fears their influence. He has already poisoned the Others who live on the lands nearby, hoping to instigate the destruction of the Mi'kmaq people, and if he succeeds, there may be war very soon."

Eagle Claw stirred, his eyes opening. His lost daughter was leaning over him, but he knew it could not be so. He touched a lock of her hair in awe. "Who are you, my child?"

"I am Nylah, my grandfather, the daughter of Skylark and Matt Kennedy. I have come to you from a faraway land to meet the people whose blood I share."

Eagle Claw studied the handsome young man who knelt beside her, sensing the love between them, and another, more mysterious bond. He allowed himself to be helped to a sitting position and leaned against the rock.

"You came from the mist! How is this possible?"

"I'll let Adam share that story with you, Grandfather."

"You are the image of your mother! When I was told how she died, I could not speak for many months. Bjorn and Marcel would come to sit with me, telling me all they knew of her journey, of her love for Matt, of her murder, and of the infant who was drawn from her womb, but I refused to end my mourning, so much did I love her. I could not... It felt as if she still lived, if only in my heart."

"But she *is* alive, Grandfather! She came to me as a spirit when I was a child, but as real to me as you and Adam are right now, and we talked and laughed together every day! She was called back to heaven when I was four years old, after she arranged for Papa to meet the woman chosen for him, to finally fill his lonely heart."

He gazed into her eyes, feeling the truth in her words. "I want to see her again someday, Nylah. Can you make this happen, you who have the power to ride the wind?"

"No, Grandfather, I can't. But *you* can! If you freely choose to believe in the Lord Jesus Christ, and that His terrible death on the cross paid for every one of your mistakes and sins in the eyes of the most pure and holy God, and humbly ask His forgiveness, you will be born again into His kingdom forever! As mother was... as Adam and I are. And I promise, you will see her again!"

He gripped her hands tightly, his eyes glistening with tears, his granddaughter reminding him of the message of hope and faith that Skylark had often tried to share. His heart now open and ready, Eagle Claw spoke the words that gave him the gift of eternal life.

****

The Darkness, with a gaggle of his cackling demonic beings surrounding him, glared from the shadows of the forest as a ray of pure white Light shone down from the heavens upon the old man. Only his hated nemesis, the Prophet, was able to see the radiant beam, and looked directly into the forest with a triumphant smile.

Snatching a demon who had the misfortune of standing too close, the Evil One tore off its head with a shriek and threw it at Adam, where it rolled and bounced until landing at his feet and disintegrating into thin air. Adam merely chuckled and turned back to Eagle Claw and Nylah, who were unaware of what was taking place.

Another soul saved from eternal torment, he rejoiced! And in the Lord's wise and all-knowing plan, a man who would be influential with the Mi'kmaq people, joining Bjorn, Marcel, and the other believers of the tribe in not only speaking of their faith and trust in God, but in demonstrating how to walk in the ways of the Holy Spirit.

They helped Eagle Claw to his feet. He took an unsteady step forward with his cane, Nylah and Adam staying close by his side, as he led them up the path to Thunder Lodge. But before they even reached the porch, people passing by stopped dead in their tracks, gasping in shock at the sight of Nylah, unable to believe what they were seeing.

"Skylark has returned from the dead! The Healer's power has brought her back from the realm of the Spirit!"

The front door flung open. An older, white-haired woman ran to the rail, staring in amazement, the back of her hand pressed against her mouth. "My daughter! Is it really you, or are you a ghost, lost and wandering the earth?"

A smiling Eagle Claw turned to face the rapidly growing crowd. "The merciful Great Spirit has blessed me! This is Nylah, the daughter of Skylark and Red Bird!" he cried out and raised his arms victoriously.

"My granddaughter has come home!"

****

Adam leaned on the armrest of the old, overstuffed couch, enjoying the scene unfolding before him. The morning after their arrival, Eagle Claw had dispatched runners to summon one camp each day to meet his granddaughter, starting with Warrior Camp.

After lunch, Nylah was seated like a royal queen as each member of Warrior Camp filed in to meet her. Those who were old enough to remember the beautiful Skylark had retold the story of her powerful spirit gifts, her great love for her husband, Red Bird, her perilous journey from Nova Scotia to Boston, and her sacrificial death many times as they sat around the fire. Even the children were wide-eyed with wonder when they met Skylark's lovely daughter, the white osprey perched majestically on the back of her chair, his black-masked eyes carefully surveying each one as they shook her hand.

Adam knew that none of them were aware of Nylah's gifts, gifts of much greater power than Skylark herself. They would know soon enough... of that he had no doubt. There was a reason they'd been brought here.

Nylah was to be tested... here in the land of her people. The Lord had removed His hedge of divine protection from around her temporarily, an unblemished, sweet, and devoted soul that the Darkness had yearned to break for many years, and he prayed she would be faithful enough to pass through the fire that was to come.

The last of Warrior Camp had finally filed out and the door began to swing shut when it suddenly reversed direction and creaked open again. An enormous shadow fell into the room, followed by its equally large owner.

A giant of a man with blond hair and blue eyes walked in, dressed in buckskin breeches, moccasins, and a beaded shirt, his long hair tied behind his neck, a leather band encircling his forehead with the gray, white, and black feather of an eagle tucked beneath. Draped across his broad shoulders was the fur of a white cougar.

"My God, it's true! You could be her double!" he declared, his accent foreign and strange. The man approached Nylah, who lifted her chin bravely despite her trepidation at this frightening apparition. Dropping to one knee, he gently took her hand.

"My name is Bjorn, my dear, and I was with your mother on the day she died."

****

The coals glowed low in the hearth as they talked well into the night, Nylah listening raptly to the Norwegian's tale of the long, difficult, and tragic journey that her parents had taken to Boston.

He spoke of the mystical connection that had first drawn the couple together, of their passionate love, of their idyllic life with the Mi'kmaq tribe at Thunder Hills, and of their joy when they discovered a child was to be born. But when he described the many miraculous healings that Skylark had performed, Adam caught her eye. A slight shake of his head told her she was not to mention her own gifts just yet.

But Bjorn also told them of the suffering and heartache they had seen, and of the parents and sisters that Matt had lost to the treacherous Karen, the same debauched cannibal who had inadvertently taken the life of Skylark in her rage to kill baby Adam and Alea as vengeance against Daniel, her ex-husband.

"Skylark sacrificed herself to save you," he told Adam. "She prophesied that you were born to be a Prophet, sent by God to bring many to the Light... and to bring mankind back to a Garden of Eden on earth. She said a woman would walk with you, and that an Angel would protect you from harm."

He looked at Moses, who was busily grooming his feathers, and laughed. "You as the woman who walks with the Prophet I can understand, Nylah, but if that bird is your Angel, you should request a replacement!"

Moses glanced up at him dismissively before continuing his preening's.

Bjorn's expression grew somber. "We could use a Prophet right now. The Others, I mean, the community that resides on the public parklands to the north, have harassed us for many years, and it's been getting worse. Their borders give them only a few points of access to the St. Mary's River and none whatsoever to the ocean, so they especially covet the estuary and our miles of beachfront on the Atlantic.

"They have survived, yes, but they refuse to honor the land and waters that the Spirit gave us. They kill all the birds and animals to eat, taking their eggs as well as their young. They strip the forest bare of every leaf, bush, and herb, the trees cut and harvested with no thought to their replenishment, to fuel their fires and build their shacks. They run nets across the streams to do their fishing for them, leaving nothing alive to reproduce. It's no wonder they desire to take what we have fought so hard to preserve.

"In their greed and hatred for the Mi'kmaq people, they violate our agreement to respect one another's borders again and again, crossing over at night and stealing what they can when the camps are asleep. The ones that the guards catch are sent home unharmed, with fair warning. But they refuse to listen, growing bolder as time passes. I am White Cougar, now the chief of Warrior Camp, and I have counseled that if they persist, we may have to take stronger measures."

"Tell us of your family, Bjorn. My father said you left them in Boston to return to a girl named Leaping Fawn. Did you marry?" Adam asked. Nylah had moved to sit next to him on the couch, interested in what Bjorn would say.

A smile of love and pride spread across Bjorn's face. "She became my wife within the very month that Marcel and I anchored our sailboat in the river. We were blessed with two sons and a daughter, who, Nylah, is named after your dear mother. My eldest son, Thor, is about your age."

He stood up and stretched like a huge bear. "But it grows late, and you both must be tired."

Nylah rose from her seat and wrapped her arms around the big man's waist. "Thank you so much, Bjorn! I feel as if my mother had been sitting right next to me, you brought her to life so vividly."

Bjorn beamed with pleasure. "I will introduce you both to my family tomorrow," he promised. "And bring the Angel with you too!"

****

It took a week to meet the people of each camp, the nightly feasting and rejoicing continuing into the wee hours of the morning, the tribe celebrating the beautiful daughter of their beloved Healer and Spirit Singer, Skylark, and the happiness of her grandparents. It was on the final night that Eagle Claw raised his glass of blackberry wine and hushed the boisterous crowd from Reindeer Camp.

"I have been told... on good authority," he said with a wink at Adam, "that Nylah shares a special gift with her mother. I now ask my granddaughter to favor us with a song!"

The people stomped and cheered as Nylah bashfully rose from her seat and walked towards the large communal firepit, where a platform stage had been built for outdoor meetings and festivals. She stepped up and turned to the crowd, their faces illuminated against the dark background of the forest by the flickering fire.

Her heart went out to them, the people whose blood she shared, and she closed her eyes to seek Him, praying that in some small way, she could tell them of His greatness, His power, and His love.

When her eyes finally opened, they sparkled like stars, spotlighted by the soft glow of the fire, her jet-black hair falling to her hips, her slender frame wrapped in a fringed buckskin dress. The people fell silent, and she began to sing!

Holy, Holy, Holy, Lord God Almighty!
Early in the morning our song shall rise to Thee.
Holy, Holy, Holy, Merciful and Mighty,
God in three persons, blessed Trinity!

Holy, Holy, Holy, All the saints adore Thee!
Casting down their golden crowns around the glassy sea.
Cherubim and Seraphim falling down before Thee,
Which wert and art and evermore shall be.

Holy, Holy, Holy, Though the Darkness hide Thee,
Though the eye of sinful man Thy glory may not see.
Only Thou art holy; there is none beside Thee,
Perfect in power, in love and purity.

Holy, Holy, Holy! Lord God Almighty!
All Thy works shall praise Thy name in earth, and sky, and sea.
Holy, Holy, Holy! Merciful and Mighty!
God in three persons, blessed Trinity!

Her face alight with joy, her arms reached to the sky as her last pure, rich, and passionate note echoed into the forest and faded away. The brush of the wind in the treetops was the only sound. No one spoke... no one moved.

She was uncertain what to do. Had they disliked her song of praise? With her head down, she was about to slip quietly off the platform when she braved a look into the crowd.

Every eye was damp with tears... Couples clung to one another, mothers held their children close, even the braves who stood guard struggling to control their emotions, when suddenly, the crowd burst into thunderous applause!

Adam escorted her off the stage, where Eagle Claw met her and enfolded her in his arms. "My dear child, my life could not be more complete! You are a rare and special woman, Nylah, as your name proclaims!"

Crouched and hidden at the edge of the dark forest, a pair of dirt-blackened faces had watched the entire celebration, paying particular attention to Chief Eagle Claw's obvious love for the young teenage girl.

"She's his granddaughter, Cole! What do you think your father could do with that piece of information?"

His companion didn't answer immediately, still staring at the vision of delicate loveliness wrapped in the arms of the one crucial man he'd finally found the key to influence.

"I'm not even going to tell him, Marcus. He'd just use her as a pawn in his own twisted political games, and once he won, he'd probably kill her. I can't let that happen... I want her for myself!"

****

Nylah said goodnight to Adam and closed the door of her bedroom, the same room her mother had slept in many years before. She carefully took off the lovely buckskin dress Eagle Claw had given her and slipped back into her own blouse and shorts. Feeling restless, she walked outside to the balcony that overlooked the Atlantic. It was too dark to see the ocean, but she could hear the pounding of the surf below.

Funny, she thought, not long after she and Adam arrived, her mystical gifts completely disappeared... It felt as if an important piece of her inner being was missing, and it was strangely disconcerting to interact with others without the advantage of her foresight.

Too tired to think about it anymore, she turned to go inside when a man dressed in black stepped in front to block her way! But before her lips could even part to scream, a gloved hand from behind smothered her cry.

In the morning, her grandmother found the room empty, the balcony door wide open. Nylah was gone.

****

There was very little air to breathe in the bag her captors shoved her into, the gag stuffed in her mouth choking her. Slung across a muscled shoulder, her body ached from the constant shaking and bouncing as the man silently ran and jumped over what must have been rough, hilly terrain, and at one point, waded through a waist-deep stream. That was the worst part... when the water soaked the bottom of the cloth bag and her with it.

Why did they want her? Where were they taking her? And where were Adam and Moses? The minds of the two men were closed to her, and she felt lost and helpless without her ability to read them. God must have taken away her gifts for a reason, but what His reason could be completely eluded her.

Her muscles began to cramp in the confines of the bag. What had Papa always told her? *Trust in the Lord... no matter what*, and as she was taken deeper into the dark of night, she clung to that belief.

After what seemed like hours, she heard a door creak open, and the sounds of the forest grew mute. The man spoke quietly to his accomplice and footsteps padded away as her abductor closed the door, then lowered his burden to a cot, breathing heavily from his exertions. The bag wiggled as if being untied and slid off her head.

He couldn't have been much older than twenty, his hair color and features uncertain beneath a thick layer of black soot. His tall, well-conditioned body was dressed all in black, and he wore a belt with a holster on his hip that held a gun, similar to the pistols in her father's gun box.

He reached forward and she shied away, but he only pulled the gag from her mouth. Pushing the bag further down, he untied the rope at her wrists, but left her ankles secured.

Nylah licked her dry lips as she gingerly rubbed her sore and chafened wrists. "Who are you?" she demanded, "and why am I here?"

He picked up a full bottle of water and handed it to her without a word. Surprised, she accepted the offer and drank thirstily while the man opened a second bottle and poured it over his head, revealing a mane of sandy brown hair and intense green eyes. Under normal circumstances, she would have described him to Angel as being very attractive.

He dried himself off with a towel and sat down next to her. “My name is Cole McLaughlin. I already know your name, Nylah.” Tossing the towel on the floor, he lifted a lock of her silky dark hair. “You’re so beautiful.”

She flipped her hair away angrily, the lock slipping from his fingers. “My grandfather will come for me!”

“Yes, your grandfather *will* come for you,” he said with a confident smile, and took a sip of his water. “I’m counting on it... But you will refuse to return with him.”

“And why would I do that?”

“Because you belong to me now.”

Chapter 15 Baptism Of Fire

"Angus, he plans to take her to the old Elkhorn lodge later tonight and wasn't going to tell you until after he'd wooed and bedded the wench. Then, when she was swollen with his child, he said he could negotiate for access to Eagle Claw's land, with the girl supporting him with her grandfather. I helped him kidnap her, but I felt my first loyalty was to you."

"Aye, Marcus, you did the right thing, lad! My son always did have a roving eye, but this time, the object of his desire may be just what I need to force the old man's hand."

The grizzled leader grinned, the left side of his face scarred and twisted, one eye socket empty from the single swipe of a raging bear claw when he fought in the Pit years ago. He'd lost half of his eyesight, he liked to proudly boast, but the fur of the blasted bear lay beneath his feet.

"Cole's plan is actually very clever... but it will take much too long." He settled himself comfortably on his wolfskin-lined chair, waving Marcus over to take a seat beside him.

"Now that you've told me where she is, I'll take custody of her tonight, and send my proposal to the Mi'kmaq in the morning. Eagle Claw will come for her, perhaps even offer his own life in exchange for hers. I'll tell him the only two choices he has are the girl's life and marriage to my son, with the right of passage through his lands... or she dies and we go to war! If he agrees, I'll allow Cole to keep his squaw and breed her to his heart's content, and when he tires of her, he can dispose of her as he pleases. The animals in the Pit always need fresh meat."

"What about Warrior Camp? They'll be suspicious and will most likely speak against this agreement."

Angus leaned in, a macabre smile on his disfigured face. "They should indeed be suspicious, Marcus," he chuckled. "Because once we are permitted to move about freely in their lands, Bjorn's warriors will be forced to do nothing. But what Cole doesn't know is that after we've put them at ease for a month or two, I plan to mount an attack at night, when their warriors least expect it! Every Mi'kmaq man and child will be slain, but I'll let my men choose the women they want before the rest are thrown into the Pit to entertain us."

"Brilliant, Angus! But maybe leave the younger children alive as slave labor."

"I knew you had a head on your shoulders, boy! Bobby's midnight raiding party is leaving soon, and you should go along with them. I wouldn't want Cole to find out that his best friend is my spy. I'll handle this myself."

Marcus checked twice before cautiously slipping out the door, relieved to have been given permission to avoid the confrontation with Cole. One glimpse of the beautiful black-haired girl with the voice of an angel, and the extra-added bonus of a deliciously round bosom, had thrown Cole into a frenzy. They remained hidden in the woods until she was alone and kidnapped her from her own bedroom balcony, right from under the noses of the Mi'kmaq guards.

He'd give a tooth to know what was going on in Cole's cabin... Hopefully, his father wouldn't walk in on him in a compromising position. Oh yeah, he snorted, he'd give two teeth to be there for that one!

****

Nylah leaned in towards the fire burning in the hearth, dressed only in her white blouse, with a blanket wrapped around her waist. Her blue shorts hung on the arm of her chair and were almost dry. Her captor had barricaded the door, then untied her legs before allowing her a few minutes of privacy in the tiny, curtained off latrine.

She glanced behind her to see him pulling out a knife and fork in what looked like a primitive kitchen, secretly hoping he'd bring her something to eat. She was hungry, and not at all sure when she last ate, her stomach audibly growling. At least the fire was warm, and for that she was grateful.

"Here, eat this."

He was holding out a small plate with a slice of leathery meat and a scoop of wilted vegetables, but it was the sight of his pinched face that suddenly made her understand the generosity of his offer.

"Thank you, but that's much too much food for me. Would you like to share?"

His expression became guarded, but he sat down. "You take a bite first. We have a long way to travel tonight."

She tentatively sampled what looked like a carrot. The taste was bitter, but she forced herself to swallow. "Where are we going? Please, can't you just take me home?"

"Get used to me, Nylah," he said abruptly. "I'm all you got. Trust me, if my father found you, you'd be a lot worse off. You'd be his ultimate pawn in his ridiculous game of power, and he certainly wouldn't be offering you any food."

"How could I be important to him in any way?" she asked. Deciding to risk his anger, she placed her hand gently on his arm. "And why am I so important to you, Cole?"

He didn't answer. How could he tell her that the moment he saw her, he was lost? That her innocence and beauty had captured his heart, that her astounding voice that sang of love and praise and worship had electrified his very being? The fact that she was Eagle Claw's granddaughter... and a golden opportunity to bring about the changes that he and many of the other men secretly longed for... had somehow become less urgent to him now that he had her.

His father had led the first group of survivors to the public lands years before when the solar flare had driven them out of the dead cities. But even as a child, he was sickened by the way many of the men deliberately chose to live, slapping together rough log structures or rickety shanties, stripping the forest of anything edible, and killing every animal and bird they saw, with no thought to the unsustainability of their actions.

Angus instead preferred to send out armed raiding parties to plunder successful outlying groups that had worked hard to survive by planting, gathering, hunting, and fishing, thinking nothing of killing anyone who resisted. The widows and daughters of their victims were divided amongst the eager men, and with no birth control, the helpless women were kept in a state of perpetual pregnancy.

With nowhere else to go and lacking the necessary skills to survive alone in the post-flare world, they stayed for the food and lodging that was provided in exchange for their willing bodies, and for protection, praying they'd be given to the men who were the least abusive. But with the freshest and most nutritious plundered foods commandeered by Angus and his greedy cronies, many of the infants died after their time at the breast had ended.

But it was the depraved and bloody practices that his father had introduced that disgusted him the most. Their village had been established next to an old stone quarry, where rainwater collected in small pools around the top of the perimeter. The quarry itself was forty feet deep, but the rainwater drained away as fast as it flowed in.

Years ago, the men had grown bored with the daily grind of survival. To keep them amused and under his control, Angus ordered the capture of young predator animals to raise in cages, kept half-starved and regularly beaten until they were savage and vicious killers, ready to be used at his whim in the inescapable quarry he called the Pit.

A wooden elevator on a pulley was built to raise and lower the cages. Unfortunately, this lurid entertainment became so popular that armed volunteers were eager to enter the Pit and do battle with a raging bear, starving cougar, or snarling wolf, their prize either a week of unlimited food or a night with as many women as they chose.

If a man made six kills without losing a limb or an eye, he earned the title of *Beastmaster*, giving him both the right to bed any woman he wanted and unlimited food until the title was lost to another. The Pit bookies did a brisk business in trade whenever a reigning Beastmaster was challenged by a cocky competitor.

The Pit also became the courthouse of final judgement for any action or speech that displeased Angus McLaughlin. Men or women who were even vaguely suspected of resisting his rule or speaking against him were slowly lowered into the Pit on the elevator, pleading for mercy as their judge sat in his fur-draped chair with a jug of elderberry wine, laughing and joking with his sycophant friends.

The bloodthirsty men standing around the rim cheered when the elevator finally landed on the bottom, cheering even louder whenever a terrified woman tried to escape by digging her nails into crevices in the rock walls in a frantic attempt to climb out, only to have rows of jagged teeth and sharp claws pull her back down, screaming in agony as a pack of hungry wolves or a maddened grizzly bear ripped her body to shreds and devoured her remains.

Cole's own beloved mother had died that way, suspected by Angus of infidelity. He presided over her execution with no remorse, holding his young son by the scruff of the neck and making him watch as she was torn to pieces by a pair of cougars. He'd despised his father ever since.

Under cover of darkness, Cole was anxious to spirit Nylah away to the distant and deserted Elkhorn cabin. Until he had won her heart and loyalty, his father would never learn that he had kidnapped Eagle Claw's granddaughter. Then, with a loving hostage-wife, he could negotiate with the Chief of the Mi'kmaq and gain his permission to access their land and waters rich with fish and wild game.

And Nylah would encourage her grandfather to agree of her own accord, and because it would allow her, and the children she would bear, to visit her family whenever she chose. With such an important political victory to his credit, and with the powerful leverage it would give him, he could finally depose his father and put a stop, once and for all, to the abhorrent practices at the Pit.

The resourceful Mi'kmaq knew how to live off the land, as well as the secrets of how to keep the forest, rivers, ponds, and lakes healthy, and their many creatures thriving and plentiful year after year. The Mi'kmaq tribe and the people of Wolftown could be friends, allies... brothers. Nylah was not only the key to his plan, but in only a few short hours, had become the key to his heart.

Her sweet face was entrancing as she waited for his answer, but he couldn't reveal his true purpose until she was safe. Angus had no patience. He'd beat or torture her to force her grandfather to compromise quickly, and this Cole could not permit. And if she became useless to him, his father would throw her in the Pit without a second thought.

"You ask too many questions. Finish your food. Then we go," he said a bit harshly. The loss of her warmth when she pulled her hand away from his arm was devastating. She looked so forlorn that he almost broke his own vow not to touch her until she wanted him to.

"It gets cool here at night, even in the summer," he told her in a gentler tone. "You can wear my jacket."

They both jumped when someone banged on the door.

"I realize it's late, son, but can I come in?"

Cole stood up, the beat of his heart pounding in his ears. Why was his father here? He almost never came by... And why tonight? But to deny him entry was a dangerous move and risked his anger.

Quickly seizing Nylah by the arm, he thrust her behind the bathroom curtain, a finger to his lips to ask for silence, and she nodded. After closing the curtain, he strode to the door and swung it open.

"It's kinda late for company."

Angus smirked knowingly, angling for a peek over Cole's shoulder. "You alone, son? Did I interrupt you in bed with Raven again? Or was it the redhead tonight?"

"Dad, I'm bushed. Can we banter aimlessly tomorrow?"

"Of course, of course, so rude of me," he murmured as he pushed past him and ambled around the tight quarters. He stopped by the fireplace and bent down, retrieving a pair of blue shorts drying on the arm of a chair.

"So, you're not alone," he said with a sly wink. "Well, if she's good enough for my boy, I guess she should meet your old man! Richey, Joey, come in here," he called out, and his two bodyguards burst through the door.

"Find her."

****

Nylah was awakened by the splash of a bucket of icy cold water in her face, her bottom lip split and bleeding, one eye purple and swollen shut. Her wrists and ankles had been tied with rope, and she hung spread-eagled from the eaves of a smokehouse, her tangled hair matted with straw, dirt, and blood. As her eye slowly opened, she saw a man in front of her, his calloused fingers pinching her nipples.

"Finally comin' around, are ya'?"

The rough hands kept fondling her breasts, covered only by her white blouse, now smudged with the fingerprints of her sneering tormenter. She shivered, her blue shorts and thin blouse poor defense from the bitter wind that blew in through the open door.

Grabbing a handful of hair, the man yanked her chin off her chest, squeezing her cheeks tightly and jerking her face from side to side as he examined her carefully.

"The chief will be here soon to negotiate for your release. Can't have you lookin' too pretty... not enough incentive for your grandpa to agree to Angus' terms."

Her head collapsed limply when he let go, and he wiped the blood off his hands as he hocked up a ball of viscous phlegm and spit it out on the dirt floor.

With great effort, she struggled to look up, her one good eye meeting his contemptuous stare with compassion.

"I forgive you, sir... You don't understand what you're doing. I'll pray for your redemption from the Darkness to my Lord in heaven."

A loud crack sounded, and her head flew backwards, a fresh spray of blood spattering the wall. "You little bitch! Why, I ought to... Oh shit, now look what you made me do! Angus just wanted me to smack you around some, take the shine off the penny, so to speak."

A lecherous grin suddenly spread across his face.

"Hmm, bet I'd be the first to get a taste of your sweet little honeypot, girl. Might as well enjoy myself if I'm gonna get in trouble anyway, and that's the one place the old man would never complain about a little bit of blood," he snickered as he unzipped his pants.

"Louie, they're coming! Cut her down and bring her out!"

With a foul exclamation, he wrestled his zipper back up. Pulling out a knife, he sliced through the ropes at her ankles, then at her wrists. Nylah's body fell, bouncing off the hard ground. Slinging her over his shoulder, he carried her into the center courtyard of town where Angus and a throng of men with guns and clubs were waiting and tossed her onto a pile of hay.

Her vision was hazy, but off to one side she saw Cole being held by four men, struggling and shouting like a madman. Directly in front of her, a silent procession was making its way into the town square. When they finally came to a halt, a lone man with a cane hobbled forward until he and Angus stood face to face.

"Where is my granddaughter?"

Angus gave a short, harsh laugh and stepped to one side, sweeping his arm like a circus ringmaster presenting the star of his show.

Eagle Claw saw her then, lying on the hay, blood dripping from her torn and swollen cheek and lacerated lip, gazing at him one-sidedly with love. His black eyes snapped back to Angus, his expression inscrutable.

"What is it you want from me, that you have done this thing to an innocent?"

"My messenger delivered my terms. What is your answer?"

"The Grand Council will convene today. You shall have your answer in the morning." His cane suddenly lifted and struck the ground! "But I warn you, man of the Others, if she is harmed any further, the God of Heaven Himself will judge you. And it is far better that you throw yourself into the darkest depths of the ocean than to face His wrath for the evil you have done."

****

Thunder Lodge was silent, the delegation already on their way to Wolftown when Adam walked into the empty great room. Dark clouds had rolled in from the ocean and the light was dim, the air chill. Reindeer Camp had just left to gird for war, all the camps now on high alert.

Bjorn and twenty of his finest warriors had accompanied Eagle Claw on his heart-wrenching journey, and once they returned, the Grand Council would convene in this room to deliberate the life-changing demands made by the leader of Wolftown.

He looked up into the rafters of the high cathedral ceiling. Moses clung to a beam, his wings folded, staring glumly off into space.

Without Nylah, nothing was the same.

But it couldn't be helped. He and Moses could only watch and wait. This was Nylah's cross to bear... her baptism of fire. If she was to serve at his side, she had to be sifted, measured, and weighed. The purest of gold must first be melted in the fiery furnace and refined, and the Lord was preparing to test her heart for His glorious purpose, which had not yet been revealed.

A difficult decision was about to be made, a decision that would significantly affect the lives of the Mi'kmaq people for many years to come. No matter what, the choice would be theirs, but Adam was prepared to give the Council a gift they would never expect...

Knowledge.

****

"They ask to pass through our lands to fish in the estuary and in the ocean," Red Beard declared. "If it will avoid war, what is the harm? As long as they stay on the path around the perimeter, we'll never even see them. Nylah will marry the boy, and our lives will go on as usual."

Bjorn jumped up, his fist slamming the table.

"I don't trust them! Why kidnap her in the first place, then beat her like a dog to force a loving grandfather's heart? Why have they not come to us before, like honest men, seeking our help? No, they enter our land without permission and steal in the dead of night. I saw their village... They live in hovels, with the smell of death in the air. I saw no crops, no happy groups of workers weaving or working the skins and meat of fresh kills. I saw no children at play. If we agree to his terms, I predict disaster for our people!"

The members of the Council and their wives murmured amongst themselves, the debate continuing until dusk. Eagle Claw's wife brought in trays of hot food, and when they had finished eating, the shaman rose to speak.

"Perhaps we have been too harsh with the people of the Others. Does not the Great Spirit offer the precious gift of life to men of all races and colors? Are we not all one in His eyes? Our history has made us resent the white man, but do not all men love, weep, suffer, and then return as dust to the earth? It is possible that we are being asked to bring them into the light of the Spirit, to teach them a new way to live, in peace and harmony with their neighbors, as it was intended from the beginning."

His wise words brought many nods of agreement as Eagle Claw stood, looking tired and drawn.

"I and my wife were given a miracle when Nylah came to us from an island far away, a mystical wonder I do not yet understand. But she brought love and faith into my heart and home, so cold and dead after losing Skylark. She has been my greatest joy, the highlight of my old age until the day I finally meet the Lord. I cannot, I will not, lose her again. Therefore, despite my concerns, I must cast my vote for..."

"Wait!" Adam rose from his seat in the darkest corner of the room, where he had been quietly listening for hours.

"If you will permit me, Chief Eagle Claw and members of the Council, there is something very important you cannot know. I have been blessed with a special gift from God, and I ask your permission to guide you on a spirit journey before you vote. Perhaps what you hear and see will help as you choose your path."

The shaman, Wise One, lifted the hands of those beside him and nodded for the others to do the same. "Join us, my son. If the Great Spirit has truly given you this power, we cannot refuse."

Their eyes closed as they suddenly felt their souls being drawn into the eternal ether, and in what was only seconds in real time, they opened them again, unable to speak.

Eagle Claw slowly rose, every man and woman at the table rising with him, and in silent reverence, they bowed as one to Adam. Then he spoke, his voice trembling.

"The decision has been made."

****

She was thrown on the hard dirt floor of the smokehouse, her body splattering a congealed puddle of her own blood. The leering guard had reluctantly locked the door and left her to spend the long, cold night with no blanket, food, or water.

Rolling onto her side painfully, she rested her undamaged cheek on her arm with a sigh of relief, glad to finally be left alone. She tried to pray, but her anguished words felt as if they were bouncing off a stone wall. She had never felt so helpless or so lonely... so unneeded and unloved, and her thoughts traveled to her home on Miracle Island. She'd been spoiled and adored by her father and loved by the Tribe. Where were the people that loved her now? Had Adam and

Moses deserted her? Why was she still being held prisoner by these ruthless men? What had happened to her gifts?

For the first time in her life, she considered the possibility of her death. She had only heard the stories of what the Flare had done to humanity... the suffering, the desperate need, the acts of horror inflicted on the weak or undefended. She was now experiencing those sufferings herself, and her heart suddenly awakened with an explosion of understanding and compassion she had never felt before.

Tears of pity trickled from her lashes as she considered the afflictions of the broken people she had seen in Wolftown; the thin, starving children, the worn and hopeless faces of women too afraid to speak out on her behalf, even some of the men quickly averting their eyes, ashamed of their fear and powerless to help her.

"I forgive them all, my Lord. I am Yours, to do with as You will. Forgive me for my selfishness, for not seeing the plight of the people of Wolftown and thinking only of my own pain. Help them, Father, please! They need You. And if I am to die, then I know I will see You in heaven, in all Your glory. If I may but have a seat on the floor of the great hall of worship behind those of much greater love and faith than I could ever show, thank you!"

The dark and musty room began to glow with an unearthly light, and her cracked and bloodied lips smiled with joy.

Her prayer had been heard.

****

The Mi'kmaq contingent of armed warriors and the men and women of the Council walked solemnly into Wolftown, their nostrils bombarded by the foul odor of rotting flesh and the stink of animal feces exuding from the Pit.

Angus stood next to the post erected in the center of the square where Nylah was bound, standing tall, fearless, and proud as her grandfather approached the smirking leader. She saw Adam right behind Eagle Claw, and if he had any emotions about her bloody and battered appearance, she couldn't read them.

"I am anxious to hear your decision, Eagle Claw! Are you wise enough to avoid war, become our allies, and save the life of a young and beautiful girl? Or are you a fool who would see his own flesh and blood thrown to the wolves because you refuse to let my hungry people hunt and fish on your land?"

Eagle Claw planted his feet firmly and drew himself to his full height. "It would seem that neither of the choices you offered will change what you have already planned for us, Angus McLaughlin. The obliteration of my people has been your intention all along."

Angus froze. How could the Indians have discovered his plan? Had Marcus betrayed him?

The Chief of the Mi'kmaq gazed into the one undefiled eye of the only child of Skylark, the burden of what he was about to do causing his heart to crumble. She smiled sweetly in return, with a look of peace, acceptance, and incredible love.

"The Mi'kmaq refuse your deceptive offer! We choose to leave the fate of my granddaughter, and your ultimate fate, in the hands of the Almighty God of power!"

A gasp went up from the crowd! The Mi'kmaq had chosen war! How could they ever hope to defeat such skilled and well-trained warriors? Their leader had signed their death warrant to satisfy his own pride and greed.

"Untie her and throw her in the Pit!" Angus barked. "The wolves are hungry and waiting! Let the man who claims he loves his beloved granddaughter listen to her pitiful screams and witness her agonizing death as the animals tear her limb from limb! But if you agree to my terms within the next thirty seconds, Eagle Claw, I'll spare her life."

"Save the people, Grandfather!" she cried out. "Save *all* the people!"

As her ropes were being untied, her eyes sought Adam's. "Goodbye, my love..." she whispered. Then, surprising the men with her quickness, she wrenched her arms from their grasp and raced towards the Pit.

"No, Nylah, stop!" With a surge of strength, Cole escaped the grip of his guards, darting forward to intercept her. He'd almost reached her when a shot suddenly rang out and he stumbled to the ground, blood spurting from a bullet hole in his side.

Angus reholstered his weapon. "Let her die, traitor... and you with her!"

Without breaking her stride, her foot hit the rim and she pushed off, sailing high into the air before her body began its descent to the bottom. Time passed in slow motion as she fell, her dark hair streaming above her, and she smiled.

This was now her choice... her sacrifice.

With her death, her grandfather would no longer suffer with the temptation to reverse his decision out of his love for her.

Nylah closed her eyes, ready to meet her Lord and Savior.

Chapter 16 The Eternal Rose

With shouts of horror, both the Mi'kmaq contingent and the people of Wolftown rushed forward and slid to a halt at the edge of the Pit. All breath stopped... no one moved... the impossibility of what they were seeing shocking them to their very core!

Nylah was floating, her body suspended in mid-air... her slender form radiating a soft, luminous golden light, her arms extended like the wings of a bird preparing to ride the wind! Her joyous, unblemished face was lifted to the sky, her locks of midnight hair swirling in a ghostly breeze, her eyes golden orbs of liquid fire!

A pack of snarling timber wolves were frantically leaping straight up off the ground in a fruitless attempt to tear out chunks of her flesh, their foaming jaws snapping shut loudly as they fell back down in frustration.

The crowd gasped as she lowered her arms and slowly drifted to the ground, the wolves whining and backing away. The golden light faded as her eyes transitioned to a sparkling gray, and she smiled as she held out her hand.

One of the wolves began creeping towards her until her fingers brushed his nose. With a puppy-like yelp, he rubbed his muzzle against her hand and gently licked it, begging for her touch, the other scarred and battered animals coming forward to do the same.

From high above the Pit, a piercing whistle sounded as Moses swooped down to land beside her. Cries of fear and amazement rang out as the osprey spread his wings with a flourish and began to transform into his true likeness... a mighty and powerful Angel of the Living God!

The Angel towered above Nylah, clad in shimmering robes that draped to his feet, his eyes glittering crystals of flashing light, his magnificent feathered wings and silken strands of hair a glorious and dazzling white! He swept her into his arms and lifted into the air, and as he set her down at the edge of the quarry, the people fell back in awe.

She knelt at Cole's side, his blood soaking into the soil beneath him. He struggled to rise when he saw her, but she lifted his shoulders gently in her arms.

"Oh, you didn't do it after all," he gurgled hoarsely. "I'm so glad... and I'm so sorry, Nylah. I was a deluded dreamer. I never should have taken you from your home." He coughed, a dribble of blood running down his chin.

"Nylah, I love you. My last breath will be your name... my sweet, beautiful Nylah."

She placed her hand over the steadily pulsing wound. "The Lord of grace and mercy has seen your heart, Cole, a heart that loved and suffered for his people, and dared to try to help them. Your destiny has yet to be fulfilled."

The spellbound crowd risked moving in as close as they could with the majestic and fearsome Angel standing guard. Her hand began to tremble and shimmer with the soft glow of starlight, and she sighed as her healing power poured into his dying body. The weeping men and sobbing women cried out in disbelief when she drew her hand away.

The bloody wound was gone!

"No!" Angus drew his pistol and started towards them, firing wildly at the feet of anyone blocking his path. Bjorn quickly ran up behind him and struck his arm sharply, the gun falling from his hand and skidding across the ground. But before Bjorn could restrain him, he sprinted through the fearful crowd, his face black with rage.

"A traitor and his whore! I'll kill you both if it's the last thing I do!"

With a slight smile, Moses casually stepped aside to let him pass as Nylah clutched Cole tightly in her arms. But just as he reached them, determined to shove them over the edge, they vanished!

The piercing shriek of Angus McLaughlin as he flew over the rim of the Pit brought a quiet sigh of relief and a measure of justice to the families of the innocent men and women he had ordered torn to shreds. After the echo of the heavy thud at the bottom had faded away, the only other sound was that of the starving wolves finally getting what they had been so cruelly denied... a meal of fresh meat from their master's still living and screaming body.

****

Bjorn's commanding voice suddenly rang out, drawing the attention of Angus' shaken people.

"Men and women of Wolftown, your heinous leader has been judged by God, and has met the end that comes to all who hurt and destroy. His son, Cole McLaughlin, has been returned to you by the Spirit Healer of the Mi'kmaq. He is a man who seeks nothing but peace with his neighbors, and his heart of love, caring, and devotion for his people has been shown to us by the Prophet."

The Angel moved to stand with Bjorn, his feathered wings spread wide, his crystal eyes searching every heart.

"Choose you this day whom you will serve! Will it be on the side of the ruler of Darkness, who has brought you nothing but starvation, pain, and death? Or will it be for the Lord of Life, as witnessed by His Angel, and His servant, Nylah?"

The people fell to their knees. The miracles they had just witnessed had removed any doubt of the existence of God, and their hearts were now open.

"I choose God!" a man called out. "Teach us the way!"

"Forgive us and help us!" a woman pleaded. "My son needs food, or he will die. The animals in the Pit were given more to eat than Angus' own people!"

The light in the Angel's crystal eyes flickered as it bored into the man who had mercilessly beat Nylah. Prostrating himself at the feet of the Angel in shame, he wept bitterly. "I have done cruel and terrible things in my life, and I harmed the innocent young girl! How can God ever forgive me?"

Bjorn laid a comforting hand on the man's shoulder. "You have but to ask, my friend, if you truly repent in His name and sin no more."

The Angel opened his arms, and all the people rose to their feet. One by one, they tentatively approached him, touching his robe in wonder, some kneeling and pleading for their own forgiveness. Moses gifted each one with a radiant smile that took away their fear, and for many, it was the first time in their lives they had ever known such a feeling of pure, holy, and unconditional love.

"We will provide food for you and your children this very day," Eagle Claw announced. "Tomorrow, I will return to meet with your new leader, Cole, and the council he chooses from among you. Our people can live in peace and work together to share the bounty of the forests and ocean of Nova Scotia. We will teach you how to honor the earth and its inhabitants, that your own land may be healed and become the garden of plenty it was always meant to be." Lowering himself to one knee before the Angel, he bowed his head.

"How unsearchable are His judgements and inscrutable His ways. Blessed be the name of the Lord!"

****

Cole felt the place in his side where his father's bullet had entered. There was no blood, no pain, no wound.

He and Nylah were leaning against a tree trunk, a gurgling stream running past them, warm sunlight dappling through the rustling green leaves above. Nylah was humming a soft tune, a skylark perched on her finger and singing along with her.

"Where are we, Nylah?"

With a smile, she lifted her hand, releasing the bird back into the sky. "I brought you to the stream I like to swim in near my grandfather's house. You needed to rest for a while before you return to your people."

"How did we get here? The last thing I remember was you holding me. I thought I was dying."

She saw Adam standing in the trees across the stream, his voice whispering in her mind. "Adam is calling for me. Your people will tell you what happened, Cole."

"Nylah, please don't leave me! We could make a happy life here," he pleaded. "I love you!"

"There will be another for you, Cole. You are destined to fall deeply in love with a wonderful young woman very soon. Your heart was opened to me temporarily for His divine purpose, but I am not the one."

He felt her fingers brush his temple lightly. "Your feelings for me will fade, but I will never forget you, Cole. You will be a great leader." Her smile of farewell left him speechless.

"Your people are searching for you. It's time for you to go."

Before he could blink again, she disappeared.

****

Bjorn stood at the head of the table of the Grand Council, pleased to report the exciting progress made following the miraculous events of the week before.

"It has been decided. Cole will be moving their town to the banks of Keys Pond and plans to rename it *New Hope*. We have already begun to teach them better ways to construct their homes, how to properly glean fruits, greens, and nuts from the forest to conserve its bounty for the future, and the most productive ways to garden and farm. Our hunters and fishermen will share their knowledge as well, and others in the tribe will instruct them in the care and feeding of the pigs, goats, and chickens we have given them.

"The Pit animals were set free after Nylah healed their broken bones and festering open wounds. The quarry will be filled in, and Cole plans to make the site a memorial for all who died there by Angus' hand.

"Not everyone has been as accepting of the new ways that the majority of their people have wholeheartedly chosen. Cole's friend, Marcus, had been Angus' spy for many years. He and a group of his cohorts left town in quite a hurry after seeing the Angel, and probably for the best," he chuckled.

"Every human being is free to choose their own beliefs and must then accept the eternal results of that choice. But if their actions interfere with the peace and safety of the people of New Hope, they are more than welcome to move on and find a life that better suits them elsewhere.

"Many have asked to learn more of the Word of God. To fulfill their desire, our shaman's assistant, Tom, of Meadow Camp, and our good friend, Marcel, of Arrow Camp, will be traveling to New Hope twice a week to teach from the Bible. Nylah and the Angel have sparked the fires of belief and hope for a better future in a people who had lost their way."

Eagle Claw nodded in approval. "But there is one here who has not received his due." They all turned to Adam, seated at Eagle Claw's right hand.

"We have prayed and sought the counsel of God through His Word in all that we have done. But is there any other wisdom you can share with us, Prophet, that we, as mere men, may have been too blind to see? You are young, Adam, but God is in you, and with great power! Honor us with your thoughts. Command us, and we will obey."

The Council waited breathlessly as his chair slid back and he rose. What would he say to them, this Prophet of the Most High God? He looked like any one of their own beloved sons; tall, his hair dark and wavy, his body lean and muscled. But those eyes! There was the difference! Gleaming golden with power or green with intelligence, ocean blue with gentle love or hazel in prayer, each color reflecting another facet of this mysterious and complicated young man.

Every Mi'kmaq had heard the incredible story, told over and over by the witnesses who had been there. And if Nylah's miraculous healings of the sick were not enough for them, the presence of the magnificent Angel walking through the camps had everyone clamoring to read a Bible! Skylark's long-ago explanation that the Great Spirit and the Lord God were one and the same was now coming to life in the hearts of the people.

"I am only His instrument, my friends. My time to serve has not yet come. This was Nylah's journey, a true daughter of the Mi'kmaq. Her test was severe, and the power of the Darkness did all it could to crush her and conquer her spirit. But she rose above her human weaknesses and found the strength of her faith! God is pleased and has accepted her service, and I rejoice for her! She will follow me as I walk my path, both she and the Angel, Moses. We will serve Him as One.

"You have pleased the Lord as well! Your chosen path is blessed. Do not vary from it and nothing but goodness will follow. And if I can give you any simple, yet not so simple, words of wisdom, it is this.

"Believe, trust, praise, and obey... No matter what."

****

Nylah escorted Eagle Claw carefully down the path to the bluff overlooking the Atlantic Ocean where he first saw them, Adam, Bjorn, and the shaman following close behind. They came to a halt at Lonecloud's memorial rock, and Eagle Claw leaned against it to rest. For a time, they stood and watched the waves rolling in, the decaying hulls of *Four Winds* and the *Fury* in clear view just offshore, heavy gray clouds low in the evening sky.

Bjorn's voice broke the silence. "There will be rain soon."

"And so we must go." Adam's arms encircled Bjorn as the big man fought his tears.

"Thank you, Adam. Please tell Matt I am so happy for him! Never have I seen a love like he and Skylark once shared, but if the beautiful Morgan Monroe has captured his heart, he is indeed to be envied."

Adam said the rest of his goodbyes, saving Eagle Claw for last. "We will meet again someday, Great Chief, of that you can be certain."

"Take care of her, my son. I let my Skylark leave me to follow her heart, and she never returned. Promise me I will see Nylah once more before I die."

A flutter of wings drew their attention as Moses landed on Adam's shoulder and promptly swallowed the salamander he had caught.

"This angel bird of yours, is he the typical kind of angel that serves the Savior? Or is he, shall we say, unique?" Eagle Claw inquired.

Adam had to laugh. "Oh, I think he's pretty unique. And I do believe he enjoyed prancing around New Hope Village and all the Mi'kmaq camps, everyone bowing and kneeling at his feet in awe and practically worshipping him! I had to talk to him a couple of times, you know... bring him back down to earth."

Moses chirped in his ear. "Oh, and in answer to your request to see Nylah again, Moses said to tell you... yes."

"Grandfather?" Her soft, sweet voice humbly interrupted their laughter. She threw her arms around his neck, her eyes welling. "I don't want to leave you, but Adam says we must."

He patted her arm, gazing off towards the ocean. "There, there, Nylah, the Angel told me we will see one another again someday. I am comforted. Kiss me, my child, and go. Adam is waiting."

Adam clasped her hand, and as he did, a white mist began to rise from the grass, enveloping the two young teens.

"Goodbye, Grandfather! I love you!"

They walked to the edge of the cliff, hand in hand... and they were gone.

****

They appeared out of the sky together and stepped onto the cliff as Moses flew off Adam's shoulder, landing on a beam of the wooden cross.

"We've been gone for weeks, Adam! Papa might still be on Rum Cay, but Morgan and Alea must be frantic! We're gonna be in the biggest trouble! I bet they have search parties looking for us right now."

"Time has no meaning to God, Nylah. To them, we've only been gone since early this morning. We'll be home in time for dinner, and it better be lobster!" He enfolded her in his arms, and she clung to him.

"You understand why I couldn't help you, don't you?"

She pressed her cheek against his chest with a sigh. "I do, Adam. But I'm so glad you were there! And Moses too!"

He tipped up her chin, gently pressing his lips to hers. "I love you, Nylah. I've always loved you. And I've wanted to do that for a very long time."

She melted into him, radiant with happiness. "And I have always loved y..." Suddenly, she winced. "Ouch!"

Reaching into her pocket, she pulled out the red rose he had given her in what now seemed like ages ago.

"Oh, Adam, look!"

Her soot and blood-spattered blouse had been laundered and repaired in Thunder Hills, but the rose was somehow still in her pocket, as fresh as if it had been plucked from the bush only moments before, the ruby red petals heavy with dew, its delicate scent entrancing.

"How can this be?" she wondered.

He smiled and drew her back for another soft kiss. "Your rose will never die, my Nylah, just as His love... and mine... is eternally yours."

Chapter 17 Plots And Plans

"You can't stay on Miracle Island forever, Angel! You've refused to go to Spanish Wells with us since you were ten. There are people from all over the Bahamas who are anxious to meet the artist who creates the amazing pieces that Bruno sells for you in the gift shop."

John waited patiently for her reply, as did Daniel and Matt. They had asked to meet with her at the Black Hole, where privacy for their discussion would be guaranteed. It wasn't the first time they had tried to convince Angel into relinquishing her self-imposed isolation for their yearly end-of-spring trip. But ever since Michael had fled the island only one day after he returned in May the year before, her rigid stance had gotten even worse.

They all remembered how carefree and happy Michael had been when he took off down the beach, stripping off his shirt and tossing away his shoes as he jogged towards Alea's Secret Spot to see Angel again after being gone for so long.

They also remembered his dark and stormy expression as he came plodding back to camp, silent and alone, seeking out Daniel immediately with a special request for a ride back to Spanish Wells the very next day, and Gypsy agreed to take him. With a tight smile and blank, unreadable eyes, he told everyone not to worry, that he just needed some time to be alone, but it was no secret to anyone in the Tribe that his unexpected departure was due to the continuing problem with his once best and closest friend, Angel.

"I don't want to go, Dad. There's nothing for me in Spanish Wells. My home is here... My ocean is here... I create my art pieces on Miracle Island, and I'm glad that people enjoy and value them, but I really don't need much more. I'm content with holding down the fort whenever you guys leave for a while."

She allowed herself a small smile. "And you know you don't have to worry about me. My ocean friends are always around."

"Sweetheart, I'm your father. It's my job to worry about you. Constantly... I'd love to see you socializing with teens your own age and meeting some nice young men you might be able to build a life with. Don't you want to have a family of your own someday?"

She blew out an exasperated breath, combing back her long blonde hair with her fingers.

"And are these *nice young men* going to stick around when they discover that I'd rather spend my time underwater with sharks and whales and fish than on land? Or with people? That I can swim and dive like a dolphin and that I can talk to the creatures of the sea? I'd be labeled a crazy person, and everyone in Spanish Wells would avoid me as if I had some kind of contagious disease."

"She's got a point, John," Matt said. "Maybe we should stop pushing and let nature take its course. Angel is smart enough to know what's best for her."

"I have an idea." Daniel hadn't joined the conversation yet but thought he might have a compromise to suggest.

"Come with us just this once, Angel. At least meet some of the local folks who appreciate your work. Your presence would show respect for Bruno and all he's done to promote your art with traders from all over the Bahamas, and I suspect, from even farther away. If you do this, I promise we won't bother you again. You'll turn eighteen this November anyway, and your ultimate life choices will be your own to make."

"That's a great idea!" John and Matt burst out at the same time.

Angel considered the three wonderful men who loved her unconditionally. Not one of them had ever hurt her... would never hurt her. She'd do it... for their sake. But there was one question left to be answered before she agreed.

"Will Michael be there?"

Daniel, John, and Matt looked at each other, none of them wanting to be the one to tell her. Daniel swallowed hard and decided to take the leap. She had never asked before, but once on Spanish Wells, she'd find out sooner or later.

"No, Angel, he won't. Gypsy and Noah dropped him off last May at the dock, and no one's seen or heard from him since, not even the Care Teams."

She hesitated for only a second before she lifted her chin.

"Okay... I'll go."

****

Except for short fishing or exploratory trips on *Barefootin'*, *Dances With Wind*, or *Gypsy Queen*, Angel had never sailed more than two or three miles from Miracle Island.

She stood on the bow of *Barefootin'*, the brisk wind lifting her white-blonde hair into ribbon-like streams that danced in the air behind her. An unexpected feeling of excitement and the anticipation of adventure suddenly took hold of her as she scanned the horizon for any sight of land.

"We won't see Spanish Wells for a few days, but I'll make sure to point out the other islands as we pass by."

Matt leaned on the rail next to her, with eight-month-old baby Mariah safely berthed in her carrier on his chest. Behind him, eleven-year-old Max led his little brother, six-year-old Mason, to join them.

"Thanks, Uncle Matt! This is so cool! I'm really glad you sort of twisted my arm to get me to come. But I wish Nylah and Adam were here... Ishmael, Essie, and the kids too."

He laughed and gave her a quick hug. "You made the final decision, Angel. And I think you'll be glad you did, even if it's the one and only time you ever leave home." He leaned in conspiratorially, keeping his voice low.

"I suppose I shouldn't be letting the cat out of the bag, but I've been hearing rumors of parties, cakes, hairdos, and dresses from your mom, Morgan, and Alea. And I'm sure Bruno will plan something special for you as soon as you step off the boat."

She scrunched her nose at the mention of dresses and parties. "Bruno can't possibly know I'll be with you."

"True. Batteries were unaffected by the Flare, but with age they no longer held a charge, leaving our shortwave radios useless. Thank heaven Gypsy and Noah love to travel! Their regular monthly voyages to Spanish Wells keep us in the communication loop, but it's a slow process, not like in the old days with the lightning-fast internet."

"That must have been amazing, Uncle Matt! You could send a message all the way across the planet in seconds! It sounds like a miracle to me."

"In many ways, it was... But far too often mankind didn't use the unbelievable blessings we were given in beneficial ways. Greed and the lust for power corrupted men, and if the solar flare hadn't clobbered us first, we most likely would have destroyed ourselves anyway."

"That's what Mom taught us," she replied. "But if mankind didn't have electricity for hundreds of thousands of years, why was losing it seventeen years ago such a disaster?"

Matt nodded. "Good question, Angel. Electricity was first developed about two hundred years ago, but from that point on, we gradually became completely dependent on it, losing the knowledge and skills of how to survive, and the ability to live our daily lives without it.

"Some very helpful things were created because of it, but ever since the light bulb, the Darkness manipulated man's use of electrical power to send humanity on a destructive downward spiral of global war with sophisticated weaponry, as well as a pattern of fiscal greed and overpopulation that led to the pollution of the lands and oceans of earth. Before the Flare set mankind back 40,000 years, we were on the brink of sending the planet into another ice age.

"The final straw for God, I think, was when society became so jaded, decadent, and self-centered that even the mention of the name of His Son, Jesus, was an embarrassment to many people, who thought that following Him meant they couldn't do whatever they wanted or have the things of the world they selfishly desired. Their scornful rejection of the Almighty was exactly what the Darkness had hoped for, and I'm sure he couldn't have been more pleased.

"I truly believe, as do the Mi'kmaq, and as we all do on Miracle Island, that God permitted the Flare to heal the earth and the oceans and to bring us home again... home to Him, and home to the Garden of Eden he had prepared for us in the very beginning."

Lost in thought, she watched as the catamaran split the water, sending frothing lines of white wake to either side of the boat. She had always felt that her home, her Garden of Eden, was wherever Michael was. With that dream now in pieces, where *did* she belong?

"I often think about the terrible things you went through on your journey to Boston after the Flare. Have you finally found your home, Uncle Matt? Are you happy now?"

He looked at his daughter, sound asleep in her carrier, and smiled tenderly. "Happiness is not a place, Angel." He kissed Mariah's soft golden curls.

"Not even on Miracle Island. Happiness is being with the people you love, the ones you would do anything to protect, even if it meant sacrificing yourself. I was happy with my Skylark in a teepee, but I was given a second chance for love after she died. So, in answer to your question, yes, I'm very happy now, with Morgan, Nylah, Max, Mason, and Mariah in my life."

Mason tugged on her sleeve to get her attention. "I love you, Angel! You make *me* happy!"

Touched by his declaration, tears threatened to spill as she hoisted him to her hip and kissed his cheek. "And I love you too, my little big man. How about a nice swim in the ocean with me before dinner?"

His mouth split into a wide toothy grin, his mop of dark red hair ruffling in the breeze. "Okay! Let me know when to put on my swimsuit."

Max pulled him off her hip and onto his own. "I'm coming too! See you later, Angel."

Matt hugged her again, feeling her pain and aware of its cause, wishing there was some way to help her.

"Your happiness is out there, Angel. God is working. Trust Him. He loves you, and He'll never let you down."

As he herded his children to the main lounge, Angel gazed out over the blue Caribbean Sea, unable to control her tears any longer. Everyone else had found their happiness. Matt and Morgan, Adam and Nylah, Gypsy and Noah, Ryan and Sarah, Ronny and Pearl, Ishmael and Essie, Daniel and Alea. Her own parents. Even Grandpa James and Diego had found love again.

Why not her? She believed in and loved God. Who else could have made her the way she was? So why was she being denied the joy that all the other couples were given? Had she angered God... done something wrong? Or was she a bad person, undeserving of His favor?

All she knew for certain was that she had fallen completely and irrevocably in love with Michael the first time she saw him as a five-year-old little girl. Her happiness, her very being, depended on him, and except for the wonderful early years when they'd spent every waking moment together, the only thing he had ever done since then was reject her and let her down.

At this point in her life, she found it hard to believe that God would do any better.

****

By the end of her first week in Spanish Wells, Angel was exhausted. After being pampered, primped, and fussed over for hours by the Miracle Island ladies, and Nadia, Elizabeth, Loreen, and Alice, the never-ending parties began.

The potluck dinners... The church socials... The barbeque picnics... The invitations from old friends of the families... Drinking glass after glass of lemonade and sweet tea and munching slices of guava duff and pumpkin bread as she was introduced to the kind but curious folk of Spanish Wells, who were anxious to meet the exquisitely beautiful and talented young woman they'd heard so much about.

She wasn't used to so many people constantly surrounding her, as well-meaning and friendly as they were. The tranquil shores of the island were breathtaking, and the sea called to her with its siren's song, but she had yet to be able to break free to immerse herself in its soothing arms.

Her gills were drying up, she thought in dismay. She was determined to make some believable social excuse as soon as possible and jump into the cove at Bonefish Bay, the perfect and private place to begin her real exploration of Spanish Wells and introduce herself to the inhabitants of its waters. All the families and anyone who had ever lived on Miracle Island and their wives knew about her ocean abilities and wouldn't find her long disappearances unusual in any way.

But the highlight of her week had been on the second day, when all the ladies took her to meet Bruno Knowles at the Blue Starfish Gift Shop.

Bruno was the youngest grandson of Ben, and helped his father, Gil Knowles, run the harborside boat repair shop and organize the fishing fleet. An astute businessman with an artistic flare himself, he had opened a gift shop, attached to his repair shop office, to sell locally made artwork, wood and metal sculptures, pottery, jewelry, baskets, and hats to the many sailors and traders that arrived daily.

Once the trading boats received security clearance from Mr. Curry and his deputies, a variety of new and exciting goods flowed into the Spanish Wells economy, goods that had not been available for many years after the Flare.

Rum from Cuba, Barbados, and Jamaica. Aromatic coffee beans, bananas, herbs, and hemp for the weaving of rough cloth from Central and South America. Corn, beans, tequila, and yucca from Mexico. Oranges from Florida.

The lively, bustling waterfront was now reminiscent of old charcoal drawings from the early 1800's. The captains and crews of the traveling ships much preferred to deal with this safe, well-monitored harbor, confident they would not be robbed, cheated, or murdered by the citizens of the law-abiding community, unlike more questionable ports of call in Cuba, the Dominican Republic, Mexico, Costa Rica, and further south towards the equator.

Since the Flare, the only reliable source of power was wind, harnessed by windmill and sail. The pumping system devised on Miracle Island was becoming widely used throughout the Bahamas to draw water from deep wells and underground reservoirs, and Spanish Wells had become the main hub where parts for a windpump system could be obtained and partially assembled by trained craftsmen.

Boat repair services were available at the marina, as well as Diego's expertly handcrafted wooden sailboats in a range of lengths. Along the waterfront boardwalk, fresh baked breads, cakes, jams, pineapple, fruits, and vegetables were offered for trade at small colorful stands, and restaurants and bars catered to the never-ending influx of sailors from all over the Caribbean, Central and South America, and the U.S. east coast.

When Angel walked into the shop, she was impressed with the displays of lovely craft work in wood, stone, shell, and sea glass. Pieces of art hung on the walls, painted or etched on stretched fabric and wood. She liked Bruno immediately, his warm and low-key personality setting her anxieties at ease.

"I am honored to meet my most popular artist at last, dear Angel," he said as he engulfed her small hand in his two giant paws, his white teeth sparkling in a big smile. "Your work has found homes on at least seven islands and four countries that I'm sure of! My wife loves the piece you entitled *Whale Song* and insisted that I trade for it myself."

She couldn't help but blush at his compliments. "Thank you, Mr. Knowles. That one was very close to my heart. I'm glad she liked it."

"I don't know a Mr. Knowles, Angel. Please, call me Bruno! I have an appointment in my office right next door, but take your time and look around, all of you."

Josey examined a carved mahogany replica of a conch shell, polished to a brilliant sheen. "Angel, sweetie," she said under her breath, "This is really nice work, but your stuff is so much better!"

Alea had to agree. "No wonder Bruno said that everyone wanted to meet the artist."

"Would you be amenable to doing a mural while we're here, Angel?" Morgan asked. "I can already picture one on the big wall in the oceanfront living room at Bonefish Bay."

Angel didn't have to think twice. It was a legitimate way to avoid the constant socializing and the numerous parties she was expected to attend. Everyone was so nice, but she just wasn't used to it. Her art was relaxing and blessedly solo.

Now, if she could occasionally sneak away for a swim, being in Spanish Wells for a month might not be so bad.

"I'd love to do that, Morgan! Maybe Nadia can suggest a scene or theme she'd like to have. I can mix my own paints, or perhaps Bruno has some I can borrow."

Alea, Morgan, and Josey caught each other's eye. The first stage of their plots and plans for Angel was well underway.

****

The spectacular and vibrant mural Angel painted on the wall at Bonefish Bay was the talk of the island, and she was immediately inundated with orders. Mr. Curry was first in line, offering two prized goats for a scene depicting schools of colorful tropical fish swimming in and out of a coral reef that would cover the 12-foot walls and high arched ceiling of his daughter's bedroom.

She was proud of the positive reviews her art was receiving but began to worry. It was almost June, and the Tribe would be sailing home soon, their visiting and trading time at an end. It was only fair to tell Bruno she would have to decline the multiple requests he was fielding for one of her murals, and after the embarrassing surprise party that Morgan and Alea threw for her at Bonefish Bay, a getting-to-know-you evening attended by teens between the ages of sixteen and nineteen, she was more than ready to leave.

She decided to break the bad news personally. The next morning, she opened the front door of the Blue Starfish to find an exasperated Bruno in a heated conversation with a sulky-looking fourteen-year-old girl.

"You promised me, Kesha! I can't run three businesses by myself. Family is supposed to help. Middle school's out for the summer, and I need you here."

"I know I promised, but I can't just sit in this shop from morning 'til night for months, twiddling my thumbs! I want to be with Kelso and my friends!"

Angel tried to quietly back out the door, but Bruno saw her and waved her in. "It's okay, Angel, please stay. You've met my cousin, Kesha, yes?"

Kesha examined her manicured fingernails dismissively. "Yeah, we've met... the famous blonde artist my boyfriend can't stop talking about..." But she suddenly lit up.

"Why doesn't Miss Fancy Pants Angel run the shop for you this summer? I bet having the *famous artist* behind the desk would boost business. Maybe she could give lessons too."

Bruno seized her by the shoulders and kissed her on both cheeks. "Wonderful idea, my girl! You're off the hook."

He turned to Angel, standing stunned in the center of the shop, his excitement almost palpable.

"It would only be for the summer, Angel! Having you here would be great publicity for the shop, and for your art. You can use the back room to sculpt and paint while you wait for customers. It's got nice big windows that let in the breeze. And the idea of giving lessons is perfect! I'm aware of a few budding young artists with no one to teach them what I know you can, and over time, the Blue Starfish could well become the cultural mecca of the Bahamas!"

She stood like a statue, unable to move a muscle, but her thoughts were whirling! Her first realization was that she'd barely thought about Michael for weeks, the constant, dull ache in her heart gradually growing fainter and fainter, all the people and events that filled her days distracting her from her sorrow, events that she now fully suspected were being skillfully orchestrated by her mother, Morgan, Alea, and Nadia.

But would it be the same on Miracle Island, where every beach, every cove, every blade of grass held memories, both precious and painful?

Secondly, she'd be able to accept the numerous offers to paint the colorful undersea murals that were in such high demand, and the prospect of teaching her techniques to the young artists Bruno mentioned was appealing. She had to admit, his proposal sounded interesting.

Bruno wrung his hands as he awaited her reply. "So, what do you say, Angel?"

The radiant smile she gave him dropped his jaw.

"Bruno, you've got yourself a deal. I'll do it!"

Chapter 18 Happy Birthday

Angel wiped off her hands with a cloth, her eyes narrowing as she studied the canvas resting on the easel before her. Yes, the colors blended perfectly, the swishing tail of the striped tiger shark disappearing ominously into the inky blue-black depths of the sea. She smiled to herself, remembering her old friend at her favorite reef back home, Charlie.

Her six students had left right before lunch, promising to return as soon as their mothers released them from the table. The Blue Starfish was quiet for the first time that morning, giving her a chance to focus on her latest piece.

She hadn't expected to enjoy working at the gift shop as much as she did for the past month, the peaceful and artistic atmosphere soothing and allowing her creativity to blossom and flow. She kept eucalyptus-scented candles burning for ambience, which also masked the pungent odor of fish that constantly permeated from the docks outside.

Curious traders and sailors from distant islands and lands filtered through the aisles to trade for her wares, examining the intricately carved and polished wooden sculptures, the natural shell, conch, or prized sparkling sea glass jewelry, and the impressive art pieces displayed on every inch of wall space. Bruno had even allowed her to negotiate the trades herself, and her reputation had spread as being not only quite a vendor to behold, but also fair and pleasant to deal with.

Of necessity, she'd become a skilled diplomat at distracting the advances of the lonely sailors who'd been at sea for weeks at a time and were stunned by her rare beauty and innocent sweetness. The door to Bruno's office was always open, but she'd never needed to call for him. Spanish Wells was well-known for its stringent rules and severe consequences for violators, and not one sailor dared to push the boundaries of acceptable behavior and risk being banned from its safe and lucrative shores forever.

Instead, she was forming close friendships with many of her customers, who often sat in the shop holding a glass of offered sweet tea as they shared fascinating stories of their travels, their lives, and at times, their deepest troubles and heartaches. Angel began to see how isolated she'd allowed herself to become on Miracle Island, the education she was now receiving about her own fellow human beings and the outside world literally priceless.

Tossing aside the paint-spattered cloth, she walked out to the shop. When she closed up at three, she planned to finish the mural at Mr. and Mrs. Arthur Pinder's house. Where were those larger brushes she remembered seeing? She bent over to dig in a lower drawer when the entry bell suddenly tinkled, and the front door swung open.

"So, it is true! The Blue Starfish does offer some *extremely* attractive items."

She quickly straightened and spun around, her cheeks a hot pink. Speechless, all she could do was stare.

The most attractive man she had seen since arriving in Spanish Wells was standing in the center of the shop, his hands in the pockets of his hemp-woven cargo shorts as he gazed at her with a pleasantly surprised grin.

He was slightly older than she was, with short blond hair as well as wide azure blue eyes that matched her own, his jaw and cheekbones sculpted like a statue and covered in dark blond stubble. He towered above her, his lean, strong, and muscled limbs a golden tan.

"Does the vision speak?" he asked with a chuckle.

"Who are you?" she stuttered.

"Ah yes, a voice like a soft summer breeze!" He walked towards her until their toes almost touched, and she caught the familiar scent of the salty ocean.

"Let me introduce myself. My name is Jordan Russell. And you are...?"

She took a slight step backwards, his nearness and the heat emanating from his skin confusing her in some inexplicable way. "I'm Angel. Angel Garner."

"Of course, it could only be Angel." He held out his hand, his eyes twinkling. "Pleased to meet you, Angel Garner," and waited.

She stared at his courteously offered hand, but for some strange reason, couldn't move.

He smiled as he reached forward, took her hand, placed it in his own, and shook firmly. "There, was that so hard? I really don't bite."

Coming to her senses, she gave him an embarrassed smile. "I'm so sorry. I don't know what came over me. Welcome to the Blue Starfish. Is there anything I can help you find?"

"No... I believe I've already found what I was looking for."

****

The summer months flew by, and October brought in the moderate seasonal changes that had made the islands of the Bahamas so desirable to tourists from all over the world before the Flare. The high levels of humidity began to drop, the risk of major hurricanes lessened, and temperatures were becoming more bearable.

Weather permitting, Gypsy and Noah sailed over once a month with news from Miracle Island, and with strict orders from Josey, Alea, and Morgan to bring back a detailed report on Angel's new job and activities.

When they announced that she was dating twenty-year-old Jordan Russell, the ladies rejoiced, although they did give their husbands at least partial credit for convincing her to go in the first place. Her experiences on Spanish Wells were exactly what Angel had needed, and with a glass of mango wine in hand, they congratulated themselves on a job well done. Perhaps now she could move on from her tragic, star-crossed attachment to Michael, who'd been gone for a year and a half.

Her brother, Noah, however, did a little digging on Jordan Russell, and his confidential interviews with some of the locals revealed more than he could have hoped for.

Jordan was the eldest son of George Russell, the owner of the biggest lobster harvesting operation in Spanish Wells before the Flare. With his fleet out of commission, but with the demand for lobster still high, he had converted over to sailing catamarans that went out for one to two-day trips. The bugs could no longer be pre-frozen for shipment, but that proved no obstacle for the traders from distant ports. Livewells were fabricated right on deck, able to be drained and refilled regularly with fresh sea water by a long line of sailors with buckets, which kept their delicious cargo alive and healthy for the length of their voyage home.

The enterprising Russell had also opened a restaurant on the dock called the Conch Club, that offered boiled or grilled lobster and spicy conch salad to hungry boat crews, as well as hot corn bread, baked cassava root, fried plantains, peas and rice, fruit salad, and crackers with an herbed goat cheese dip. Payment for a meal was pre-bartered in trade goods, and the sailors never hesitated to pay whatever was asked. Rum and tequila were also available, but if a tipsy sailor got out of hand, the spigot was turned off and he was ousted from the premises with good-natured cat calls, his mates making sure he found his berth to sleep it off.

Jordan was at the top of his class at the Samuel Guy Pinder School but chose to join the Eleuthera United Care Teams after graduation rather than lobstering on his father's boats.

His passion was in teaching the island communities how to fish and harvest conservatively, in order to keep their supply of fish, conch, and lobster available on their shorelines for years into the future. Although a rather unpopular concept in the islands since the Flare had caused such desperate need, he discouraged the use of fish traps that stripped out and destroyed a reef in short order, taking years to repopulate. Once the people of a village understood the danger, however, they too refused to use the traps.

He had also worked after school with Diego's boat building business, learning how to create the twenty-eight-foot and longer sailboats that would enable the fisherman to reach schools of black and yellowfin tuna, king mackerel, mahi-mahi, wahoo, and marlin, fish who often ran well over 30-pounds and whose migratory routes were so far out to sea it made them impossible to catch without a boat.

And apparently, Jordan was quite popular with the girls. Rumor had it that he was serious about Angel, disappointing a number of hopeful young ladies. He took a break from his Care Team the day after he met her, choosing to spend the hours until Angel was free to join him refurbishing his two-story dome house that overlooked an isolated beach on the north side.

It took her a while to relax enough to trust him, although she chose not to share knowledge of her special gift with him. He seemed sincerely interested in her as a person, how she felt, what she enjoyed, what she believed... listening to her attentively, respectful of her point of view, yet bringing his own thoughts and opinions to the table as well.

Angel looked forward to their conversations and found herself liking him more and more. No, she thought, the first time he drew her close and kissed her, it wasn't the heart-stopping wild passion she felt for Michael, nor was it the fiery tsunami of desire that had swept her away the first time their lips crashed together. Perhaps this was something better... more stable and healthier for her mind and spirit, and she couldn't help wondering what it would be like to make love with him.

But her traitorous heart still rebelled whenever he kissed her... still waiting for the only man she'd ever loved, the man who had callously walked away when she had offered herself to him unreservedly, body and soul.

The more she thought about it, the angrier she became. Jordan deserved her love, not the coward whose only excuse was that he was older than she was, even though he'd finally admitted he loved her before turning his back on all they'd shared, her heart shattering into a million pieces when he vanished from her life forever.

The next time she was at Jordan's, things were going to be very different...

****

"Your eighteenth birthday is on November 17th, isn't it, Angel?" Jordan offered her a glass of fruit wine, then poured one for himself.

They were sitting out on his deck facing the Atlantic, the light cooling sea breeze salty and refreshing. The sun was setting behind them in the west, with long rays of sunlight dancing off the white-capped waves.

"Yes, it is. A month to go before I can officially drink." She winked as she took a sip, and Jordan laughed. "We make a mango wine on Miracle Island that I was permitted a taste of now and then, but I like this one much better."

He lifted her hand to his lips for a kiss. "You deserve only the best of everything, my darling. You know, before the Flare, people could travel on airplanes to any country in the world. If we could do that now, where would you choose to go?"

"I would never leave the Bahamas," she answered without any hesitation. "I can't imagine a more beautiful place to be! I have the Atlantic Ocean on one side and the Caribbean Sea on the other... the best of both worlds. What about you?"

He leaned back in his chair and swirled his wine in the glass. "I'd really like to see the Rocky Mountains. I've been told they're spectacular." He took her glass from her hand and set both their drinks on the table, then slid his chair close to hers and wrapped his arms around her.

"But I can't imagine seeing anything more spectacular than the woman I'm holding right now." He tilted up her chin and pressed his lips to hers as she opened for him willingly, his tongue leisurely exploring her mouth until he finally drew back, breathless.

"You're so beautiful, Angel. You have to know... I've fallen in love with you."

Her dreamy smile was enough for him. He lifted her in his arms and carried her inside, lowering her gently onto the couch in the living room. But when she pulled him down to the cushions to join her, he uttered a cry of joy!

He had wanted to wait for this until their wedding night, but the vision of her inviting eyes, silken blonde hair, and parted pink lips was too tempting.

She lay back as he pressed the length of his body against her, feeling the warm ample mounds of her breasts as she kissed him. He pulled away only to strip off his t-shirt and toss it to the floor, immediately capturing her lips again, her taste driving him wild!

Freeing her breasts from the confines of her blouse, he stroked and kneaded their firm roundness, pulling each taut nipple into his mouth, one at a time, as she murmured his name so softly he could barely hear her.

His ears pricked uncertainly. It was his name, wasn't it? Of course, who else could it be? But it was enough to make him stop and think about what he was doing.

He sat up and took a deep calming breath, running his fingers through his tousled hair. She was a virgin, that he knew, and with no birth control available anymore, the right thing to do would be to wait until she truly belonged to him before he made love to her. He was planning to propose on her birthday, which was only a month away, but he'd make damn sure the wedding would quickly follow.

"Angel, I love you, and I want you so much." He looked down at his tented lap. "And I think you can see how much. But it's too soon for us to take this step. Can we move a little slower for a while? There's so much I feel I don't know about you. There's a mystery to you that intrigues me, and I feel like a diver on a new and unfamiliar reef."

She sighed. Was it with relief, he suddenly wondered?

"I just wanted to make you happy, Jordan. You've been so understanding and sweet. But isn't sex what men usually want from their girlfriends?"

He had to laugh. "Well, yeah. But let's be different, okay?"

"Okay," she replied with a smile of genuine affection, and tossed him his shirt.

****

Except for Adam and Nylah, who sent their love and pleas for forgiveness, everyone from Miracle Island showed up for her birthday celebration, with Robbie and Sammy sailing in with their Care Teams from Abaco.

Planned and organized by Bruno, Nadia, and Loreen, the brand-new community center was the only indoor venue capable of seating the dozens of people expected to attend.

Even the traveling boat crews were invited, many of whom were friends with Angel.

Tables and chairs were arranged in front of the stage, with an array of hot and cold food lining the perimeter of the room. One table held a large double-layer vanilla sheet cake with the message *Happy First Day of the Rest of Your Life, Angel!* written in pink. Another table was gradually piling high with gifts for the birthday girl as the guests arrived.

A forest of tropical flowers and potted plants filled the stage, with a clear area left open in the center. A dozen local musicians were setting up their instruments in a corner, preparing to jam as soon as the festivities began.

In a dressing room down the hallway from the auditorium, Angel stared at the alien reflection in the mirror as Morgan brushed her long locks of hair into a silky veil that cascaded to her thighs. Seated around them, sipping tea and munching sugar cookies, were Alea, Josey, Pearl, Essie, and Sarah, who oohed and aahed when Morgan finished tucking a delicate pink hibiscus flower behind one ear.

"You are red carpet ready!" Morgan declared, her voice trembling with emotion. "Nadia found that dress in her attic in a box that had been unopened since before the Flare. It fits you perfectly! You do look like an Angel!"

"It's not too much?" she asked uncertainly. She'd never worn such a beautiful dress. Her usual attire on the island had been swimsuits, shorts, and tank tops.

"Of course not!" Morgan huffed. "This is a very important birthday. A girl is now recognized as a woman. She can make her own choices, decide her own path. Oh, and let me add, take her own consequences as well!"

The tea-drinking ladies booed, but Morgan shrugged.

"Got to keep it real. She needs to hear it."

Angel laughed. Morgan always knew how to lighten her mood. “Well, I really love it! But don’t you think it looks kind of bridal? I mean, it’s only my birthday.”

Alea canted an eye at the gown. “Hmm. Could work as double duty... No, it’s just a nice cocktail dress, even though it’s lacy and white. But I believe I might have something to complete the look.” Setting her teacup down, she pulled out a gold case from under her chair.

“Daniel and I have a present for you, sweetheart.”

As she opened the lid, everyone gasped! Lying on a bed of rich black velvet were a pair of diamond earrings, with a one-carat diamond at the ear and a two-carat teardrop hanging beneath. Next to the earrings was a slim, diamond-crusted bracelet.

“Daniel gave me these for our wedding, but we have no daughter to pass them on to. We want you to have them.”

Angel hugged her tightly, her eyes brimming with tears. “Oh, thank you, Alea! They’re absolutely stunning! I don’t deserve such treasures.”

“*You’re* stunning, Angel. I still can’t believe I was there for your birth, and now you’re eighteen.” Alea wiped her own eyes and sniffed. “Okay, let’s get this party started!”

****

“I’m so happy, Jordan!” she murmured as they swayed on the dance floor to a slow, romantic tune. “It’s been a long time since I’ve had so much fun.”

“You’re a beautiful, fantastic, amazing, wonderful woman,” he whispered. “You’re loved by everyone... and especially by me. Happy Birthday, my darling!” They paused in the middle of the dance floor as couples continued to sway around them, and he kissed her moist pink lips tenderly, the other dancers pretending not to notice. Breaking their kiss, he touched his forehead to hers. “Come with me?”

“Of course, Jordan. Where are we going?”

He only smiled and took her hand, leading her up the steps to the stage and into the open circle between the riot of flowers and plants. With that cue, the musicians drew their song to a close, and his friends who were aware of what he had planned began ushering everyone towards the front of the stage.

Turning her to face him, he dropped to one knee.

Angel’s fingertips flew to her lips in surprise, and from their position in the front row of the excited crowd, Josey, Alea, and Morgan hugged each other as they began to cry.

“Angel, you know I love you, and I want to spend the rest of my life loving you. I want to drink glasses of fruit wine on our porch as we watch day turn to night together and remind you again and again what a rare and exceptional woman you are. You would do me great honor, my darling, if you would agree to become my wife.”

Reaching into his pocket, he pulled out a small black box and opened it. Inside was a pearlescent opal ring, the stone shimmering and alive with sparkling fire and set in a silver band. Removing the ring from the box, and without waiting for her reply, he started to push it on her finger when he was suddenly distracted by a flutter of white wings directly above them. The ring fell to the floor and rolled away.

“Moses! What are you doing here?!” Angel cried out in shock. The osprey hovered above her, then whistled three times before flying out the double doors of the hall. The guests began to murmur as Jordan got up with an angry expression and began searching for the ring.

Angel was bewildered! What had just happened? Why had Moses disrupted such an important moment? Looking down, she saw that the ring had somehow rolled right in front of her feet. She picked it up, and as she did, something told her to look towards the doors where Moses had escaped.

Standing in the shadows was a man, dark and brooding, with a close-cropped black beard and blazing blue eyes that bored into hers with a burning fire she knew only too well.

"Michael!"

The fierce, all-consuming eyes that were calling to her very soul were the last thing she saw before she collapsed on the floor.

****

The crackling flames of the campfire lit the quiet night as Nylah lifted a spoonful of fish stew to her lips. Her spoon suddenly paused in mid-air, and she smiled at Adam.

"Moses did it. Mission accomplished."

He shook his head. "We need to pray, Nylah. The Darkness is still intent on destroying them. Michael and Angel's test is far from over."

Chapter 19 The Challenge

Moses flew out the double doors and lifted into the dark and moonless sky, the atmosphere above the community center heavy with the invisible presence of the Darkness. His white wings beat the air as he slowed to hover, and the bird's shape gradually changed into his true form of the Angel.

"What have you done, lowly servant of God? She was ready to choose him! Her unhappiness was guaranteed!"

The night sky shifted, re-forming into the foul and noxious black cloud of the Darkness. Hate-filled orbs of red locked onto Moses, who faced his ancient enemy unafraid.

"You think you can stop what I have set in motion, fish-eater? For a million years, I have controlled the destiny of mankind. I was on the verge of driving them to the brink of complete and utter destruction when it occurred to me that one simple planetary disaster could make it happen much more quickly."

Moses merely smiled.

"What do you mean that everything that happened was His plan from the beginning of time?" the entity sputtered as flames ignited within the black cloud. "And how dare you even suggest there were occasions that I had to be given *permission* by God to perform my perfidious acts on earth, then insult me with your outrageous claim that they were ultimately intended to fulfill *His* purposes!

"Who do you think sent the solar flare, you worm? I did! Who made certain that billions of men, women, and children died horribly in the aftermath? I did! Who arranged for the Spirit Singer and Healer to be murdered by the hand of my servant, Karen? That was all me! Who do you think causes death, pain, confusion, and terror all over the world? I do! Who enters a man and whispers in his ear that he may do my bidding? It is I! No one can defeat me! I should be the one ruling the unseen heavens! All should bow to me!"

Moses' crystal eyes shimmered.

"You ask if I've ever read the Bible? I know every word, from beginning to end! But what you don't understand is that *my* power, *my* glory, *will change* what has been written! It may take me another millennium, but I will do it! The destruction of mankind and his new earth will be complete!"

The Angel's wings fluttered slightly.

"Ah, the Prophet... he's been sent to help them, you say? If they rejected the one you call the Savior, the Son of God, who gave His life for them and offered them the opportunity to live forever in joy and happiness in heaven, why would they listen to a mere mortal human? I will never, in all eternity, comprehend why He loves these miserable creatures so much, even above His own angels, I might add, of whom I once had charge until I at last woke up! Bah, humanity will never change its selfish ways."

Moses smoothed a feather, and the Darkness cringed.

"It's possible, of course, but fortunately for me, loving self-sacrifice is not the first choice of most human beings. If it were, my task would be impossible. The young girl, Nylah, was an interesting anomaly. Too bad she's protected from ultimate damnation. She certainly would have been an angel feather in my cap, if you'll excuse the pun."

Moses smirked as a particularly foul-smelling odor emitted from the cloud.

"Yes, yes, the Mi'kmaq and the people of New Hope are now beyond my control, having made their decision for my enemy. But there are fields of wheat ripe for the harvest all around the planet, where my servants are already hard at work. They had their chance at redemption, so what else do the fools have to do anyway, damned for all eternity? Better to do my bidding on earth than endure the torment that lies below... for now."

Moses looked towards the heavens and nodded.

"Leaving, are you? Oh, we'll meet again, of that you can be certain. I know you believe that goodness was placed in men at the time of their creation, Angel, but the capacity for evil was also ingrained. My only goals are to stoke the flames of the many laudable sins that lurk deep in their hearts; envy, lust, pride, greed, wrath, selfishness, and corruption... and to keep them from discovering that their salvation is but one choice away."

Moses slowly began his metamorphosis back into the form of an osprey while the Darkness growled, frustrated that the bird was protected from his grasp by the power of God.

"I have plans for them all... the Prophet and his Mystic Rose, your precious Angel and Michael, and for anyone they touch. Take that message to the Prophet! I look forward to the day he finally finds the courage to confront me. And never forget, what appears to be the cruel and destructive acts of man are actually my glorious self in disguise, walking to and fro across the face of the earth, seeking those whom I may destroy!"

The noxious cloud withdrew into the night sky, and with an ear-shattering crack of thunder, it disappeared.

Chapter 20 Muchacho

Michael stood on the dock at Spanish Wells, his backpack hanging off his shoulder, watching as *Gypsy Queen* pulled anchor. Gypsy had hugged him goodbye and wished him well, but he could tell from her expression she thought he was making the wrong move. Noah had been more direct.

"What are you doing, man? You're in love with my sister. You've always loved her... Why are you running away from her now?"

"She's sixteen, Noah. I'm twenty-four. She's just a child. She hasn't really lived or experienced life. Hell, she's never even left Miracle Island."

"Then wait for her. Travel with her. Maybe her attachment will fade as she gets older."

"It's not fair to her," Michael said, shaking his head. "If I stay, she'll never let go. She needs to find someone her own age to build a life with. The Mayoruna always mated a girl with a boy born in the same year."

"But we're not the Mayoruna, Michael. I realizc you lived with them from the time you were eight years old until you were thirteen and engrained many of their ways, and you always were a little more mature than the rest of us kids, having been trained as a hunter and warrior in the Amazon jungle. But age differences aren't that important, as long as it's not too out of line and the couple's attraction is mutual. Mom told me that in some cultures, a sixteen-year-old girl was already having babies and running a household... and maybe married to a really old dude."

In utter dismay, Michael ran his fingers through his hair, realizing now that he'd overreacted. How could he have been so blind? He winced as he pictured her lying on the beach as he walked away, distraught and in tears. "So, what should I do here, Noah? I may have already blown it, and after what happened between us last week, I don't think she'll ever be able to forgive me."

"Well, I have a suggestion, but you won't like it."

"Just give it to me straight."

"You need to disappear... Do what you started to do and remove yourself completely from the equation. Let Angel discover what her life could be like without you. Sure, it'll hurt like hell, but we'll gradually nudge her out into society to find herself and meet some guys closer to her own age. Yeah, don't look at me like that, Michael... you wanted it yourself. Gypsy and I will only tell my mom and dad, Alea, Morgan, Daniel, and Matt the truth so they can all help my sister to move forward. Then, in a year or two, come back and see what happens."

He stared at Noah. My God, she was going to suffer, even more than from the heartache he'd put her through because of his infatuation with Kayla and after their break-up.

And *he* was going to suffer worse than the damned.

But Noah was right. It was the only way. If he went back to her now, he'd always wonder if he'd kept her from her destiny, kept her from meeting the man who could freely give her the love and security he had denied her for so long, out of his own clueless and selfish needs.

His gut twisted in agony. He'd do it, but what if he was too late? What if he lost her forever? But for Angel's sake, it was a risk he'd just have to take.

****

After *Gypsy Queen* had sailed, he sat down on a bench. What to do now? He could stay at Bonefish Bay or with any of his Care Team friends who might be in town, but for some reason, he couldn't decide where to go. He didn't move for hours, even after the sun started to set, his elbows on his knees, staring at the ground.

All he could think about was Angel.

He saw her as a child when they dove together in the sea, shooting up for a breath of air and laughing with sheer joy, her white-blonde hair spread out on the surface of the water like the fantail of a mermaid. He'd wrap a long shining lock around his wrist and pull her in close, her little arms tight around his neck as they rested for a moment or two before taking a deep breath and diving down again.

He saw her as a young girl when they snuck out of the treehouse at midnight and walked hand in hand to Alea's Secret Spot, where they would lay out on a blanket to marvel at the river of stars of the Milky Way and talk until dawn.

He saw her as a pre-teen, the love and compassion clearly evident in her eyes as she tugged on his sleeve, trying to regain his lost attention that had been stolen from her by the faithless Kayla... that he had allowed to be stolen.

And then, he saw her as she was only a few days before, almost a grown woman, but with a beauty, passion, and heat he could only imagine in his wildest dreams.

His tears stained the earth, his chest heaving with his sobs. He didn't care who saw him. He had hurt the only woman he would ever truly love.

He deserved the hell he had created for himself.

****

"Hey, amigo, you okay?" a heavily-accented voice asked as an insistent hand shook his shoulder.

Michael slowly opened his swollen eyes. It was night, and he was laying on the bench at the dock, his head splitting. He pushed himself up to a sitting position, the pounding in his brain getting worse.

"Yeah, I'm fine. You happen to have any water?" He looked up to see a dark, swarthy face grinning at him.

"Got better than that, my friend. You like rum?"

"Pepe, what are you doing with that drunk? Leave him alone and get back to the ship! We sail at dawn!"

"Si, si, Captain! But this man is not a drunk. I think he's afligido... troubled."

Michael saw a group of eight men approaching him from the restaurant down the way, led by... a woman?

She was as swarthy as the man who had checked on him, with brown eyes and short, black, man-cut hair. Dressed all in black, she wore a pair of pants that clung to her shapely thighs, leather boots, a long-sleeved blouse that revealed a generous cleavage, and a wide-brimmed hat with the blue-green feather of a peacock tucked into the brim. He saw a medallion of lustrous gold around her neck, engraved with the Mayan spiritual symbol, Chuwen, that he recognized as meaning infinity.

She looked him over from head to foot, a glint of interest flickering in her eyes. "I could use an extra hand."

"I could use a ship." Michael stood up, slinging his heavy backpack over his shoulder.

"You'll eat well, drink well, and I pay well, if the hold is filled with coffee plants, coffee beans, and corn for trade. Our route covers the gamut from the Caribbean to Mexico, and we've traveled as far south as Brazil. We're not pirates, in case you're wondering. I run an honest ship, but I expect my crew to work hard." She stuck out her hand and he shook it.

"My name is Michael Silverman."

"I am Captain Gonzalez of *Muchacho*. Welcome aboard!"

****

"Dios mio, Miguel, leave some for your campaneros! We are thirsty too!"

Michael raised his forehead from the table, his bleary eyes locating his shot glass. His fingers crawled along the rough planks until they reached it, dragging the sloshing contents towards his mouth and lifting it to his lips. Dribbles of rum ran down his chin until he slammed the empty glass down.

"Bartender," he slurred, "Another!"

At a separate table, Pepe and the rest of the crew shook their heads. Miguel only got like this now and then, but when he did, no one could talk to him. And if the sorrow took hold of him while they were in a port, it got even worse. His bottle of rum was the only one he'd whisper to, and oh what secrets that bottle must have heard!

After a year of trading along the coasts of Central America, Venezuela, and Brazil, *Muchacho* had dropped anchor in Havana, Cuba, now a city of only twenty thousand, much smaller than its pre-Flare population of over two million people.

But the sins of the historic past had changed very little in this popular port, where trade in the necessary staples of rum, coffee, corn, cassava, and hemp also included exotic women for hire, as well as dime bags of white powder and expertly rolled joints of high-grade marijuana.

Captain Rafia Gonzalez, unlike many of her counterparts, refused to deal in marijuana, or any kind of drug, much to the dismay of her newer crew members, but she refused to discuss her reasons. If someone foolishly reintroduced the topic, she snapped at the questioner harshly and assigned him to one of the more unpleasant jobs onboard. Her men had learned to leave that subject completely alone, unless they were gluttons for punishment.

She was twenty when the Flare struck, causing riots and chaos in her hometown of Mexico City. Her family made it to the coastal port of Altamira, where her father's seventy-foot ketch, *Muchacho,* was berthed, a boat that Rafia and her three younger brothers had cut their teeth on.

They immediately left port, avoiding people altogether, living off the sea and anchoring for only short periods of time to search for fresh water or harvest fruit and greens. One morning, Rafia and her brothers remained onboard while her parents rowed the tender ashore to harvest ripe papaya they'd spotted growing just beyond the beach. When there was still no sign of them by noon, she began to worry.

With strict instructions to her brothers not to follow, Rafia swam ashore. Locating the grove of papayas, she saw no one, but as she walked further into the jungle, she fell to her knees in horror.

Her mother and father had been hung by their ankles from a fruit-laden tree, their wrists slit open, their blood oozing into puddles beneath them, a handful of marijuana stuffed into their mouths. Written in their own blood on a piece of wood, a message had been nailed to the trunk.

No mercy to all who enter our fields

She became the captain of *Muchacho* that day, gradually assembling a skilled and competent crew, choosing hardened men with both sailing and fighting experience. One year later, she, Pepe, Emilio, and Mateo returned to the scene of the brutal murders, seeking vengeance, or the justice of God, as she liked to call it.

After scouting the fields and the encampment of the drug dealers, they came ashore in the dead of night and set fire to the jungle and the countless acres of product where their parents had lost their lives. The rest of the bewildered crew could not understand why the captain had destroyed such a valuable commodity, but one look at her face as she stood at the bow and silently watched the jungle burn put an end to any complaints.

The door of the bar burst open, and the captain strutted in, surveying the patrons carefully before joining her men at their table. Mateo pulled out a chair and she dropped into the seat. Without even looking, she raised her hand to accept the shot glass of rum the bartender placed in her palm before leaving the bottle on the table.

She swirled the rich golden liquid round and round before raising it to her lips. "Ahhh, that's good!" she exclaimed and set the glass down. Pepe refilled it instantly. She glanced at Michael, whose forehead had returned to the tabletop.

Her brow wrinkled in concern. "Again?" Fortunately, his drunken sprees only occurred when they hit a port where the rum flowed freely. She permitted no drinking on her ship while at sea. Of course, the bottle or two she kept hidden in her wardrobe was her own damn business.

"Has he enjoyed any *other* diversions while we've been here, Pepe?"

"No, Rafia. He never does... not even with the whores. It's not natural. I mean, most of us have a girl we like to visit in every port, but not the gringo. Madre de Dios, he must be a volcano ready to explode!"

The men burst out laughing and Rafia had to smile. More than once she'd admired the sweat-drenched muscles of his broad chest, his strong, sculptured arms and legs, and tight round buttocks as he worked in the hot sun. Not that she'd do anything about it. Crew was off limits.

"Hey, once, in the latrines, I saw what hides under those shorts, Captain! It's a fucking anaconda! A woman should fear for her life! It could swallow her whole!" Rodriquez made a terrified face and pretended to cower in his chair.

Michael moaned and tried to lift his head, bringing tears to the eyes of the already hysterical men, who pounded the table as they laughed even harder. After regaining control of herself, Rafia tossed back her shot and motioned to her navigator to take the seat beside her.

"Okay, it's now the end of May, Manuel. We have pick-ups and drop-offs to make in the Dominican Republic, San Juan, Grand Cayman, Jamaica, and Cozumel. Then, I think I'd like to put in for the worst of the hurricane season in Bocas Del Toro, Panama. In October, we'll shoot north to the Turks and Caicos in the southern Bahamas and finish this year's run in Spanish Wells by mid-November. Can you plot all that out and let me know the best course by tomorrow?"

"Aye aye, Captain. I'll have it ready by morning."

She picked up the bottle of rum and tucked it under her arm. "We're done here. Collect the gringo, gently please, and carry him back to the ship."

As her men scurried to obey, she tapped Pepe's arm. "Once they've put him in his bunk and left, you and Emilio bring him to my cabin. At least for tonight, he can sleep it off in a real bed."

****

Was this a dream?

He opened his eyes to find himself floating in an unending expanse of turquoise sea, a gentle swell raising and lowering his body as he gazed up at an electric blue sky filled with white clouds, the rays of the sun warming his skin.

It took no effort at all to stay above water and he was tempted to drift away into sleep, a soothing breeze brushing past his ears and lulling him into a peaceful calm.

"Michael..."

He turned his head to see her as she slowly rose from beneath the surface, her hair wet and glistening in the light of the sun, the azure blue of her beautiful eyes shining with love. His heart leapt with joy, but his tears instantly welled.

"I'm so sorry, Angel," he whispered. "Can you ever forgive me? I love you, my darling. I've always loved you."

She put a finger to her lips as she moved closer, and when she reached him, she took his face in her hands and pressed her mouth to his, forgiving him without a word.

He pulled her into his arms, her soft curves fitting against his hard body like a silken glove. Her long sleek legs wrapped around him, and his hands sought the perfect globes of her rear. Lifting her naked hips to meet his throbbing heat, he pushed the tip against her virgin opening.

"Angel!" he cried out as he plunged deep inside!

"Michael, I'm yours, only yours..." she whispered as he thrust wildly, again and again, her head tossed back, her eyes closed in ecstasy.

He couldn't stop, he couldn't get enough of her, pounding into her willing flesh until he finally exploded with a shout, clasping her tight against him as he drowned her with wave after wave of his essence.

Kissing her lips tenderly, he released her from his arms, and she floated away on the current, the distance between them growing farther and farther apart.

"I love you, Michael... I'll love you 'til I die..." Her sweet voice grew fainter until she gradually disappeared over the horizon. Devastated, he started to swim after her, but an invisible force suddenly pulled him underwater.

"Go back to sleep, my stallion. She's not here. But I envy the one you cry out for, your Angel."

Waiting until she heard him snoring lightly, Rafia sighed and relaxed back on her pillow, satiated and exhausted. He probably wouldn't remember any of this tomorrow, but for tonight, as drunk as he was, he belonged to her.

****

The pleasant summer months in Bocas del Toro drew to a close, and the crew of *Muchacho* prepped the ship to sail. The captain had planned two additional stops on their way to the Bahama islands after hearing word of a coastal town in Nicaragua with rice, red beans, and stalks of sugar cane for trade, and a village in Guatemala that made chocolate bars from cacao beans, a priceless treat!

The economy of the Caribbean and equatorial coastlines now resembled that of the old seafaring days, but with no official form of currency, trading had evolved around food, drink, and the basic, practical items that people needed to live. Gold, silver, diamonds, and other precious gems were now considered lovely but useless baubles.

Satisfied with her hold full of goods, Rafia ordered the boat to dock in both Jamaica and Cuba, where the men could spend a few nights with their women or reconnect with old friends. Several weeks later, *Muchacho* sailed through the strait between eastern Cuba and the western shore of Haiti and began island hopping as they traded their way to their final port of call, Spanish Wells, Eleuthera.

Michael grew quieter and brooding the farther north they sailed. He'd never been particularly conversant, but the crew had accepted him as he was after discovering he was a hard-working, trustworthy, and reliable shipmate that had their back in a barroom brawl or in a wave-battering storm.

When the night seas were calm, the men gathered in the main lounge to eat, talk, and share the tales of their lives, and when Michael told them of his years in the jungle with the Mayoruna, Rafia and her crew were fascinated. Not one of them had ever seen the isolated and legendary tribe of the Brazilian Amazon, much less lived with them for years. His stories of their people, customs, beliefs, and rituals were spellbinding, and when he described the fighting skills and deadly ancient weapons he was trained in, their respect for him grew a hundred-fold.

The story of his journey down the Amazon River with his director father on *Piranha*, then back to whatever civilization was left after the Flare had their mouths hanging open, and when they learned he had been the intimate companion of the two famous movie stars, Chase London and the beautiful Morgan Monroe, even Rodriquez was rendered speechless.

Of his life on Miracle Island, he picked and chose what to tell them, and never revealed its location in any way. But from the look on his face and the tone of his voice as he spoke, it was clear he had been happy there. Only Rafia knew there was much more to that story than Michael had revealed to his enraptured audience.

Now that she knew him better, she could see the shadow of sorrow in his eyes that never left him. She'd awoken early the next morning, but he was already gone from her bed. Whether he remembered or not, it had been a night that would live in her secret midnight memories forever, and decided it was best to leave matters as they were.

His dark hair still brushed his shoulders, his hard, lean, and powerful body without an ounce of fat, and he kept his recent growth of beard close-cropped and neat. But he had changed in the year and a half since leaving Spanish Wells. He had become a man who had finally found the core of his being, a man who had struggled through the fire of his pain and guilt and emerged victorious on the other side, free from his troubled past and ready to begin again... a man who knew exactly what he wanted more than anything else in the world.

They were two days out from Spanish Wells when she found him leaning over the bow rail, lost in thought, the pale light of the waning moon reflecting on the placid water as *Muchacho* rolled gently at anchor off a small uninhabited island. She could feel an edge, an uneasiness about him, and although reluctant to disturb him, she strolled up alongside.

"Am I interrupting anything, Michael?"

"Of course not, Captain. Please join me."

She leaned over the rail next to him, taking a deep breath of the cool salty air. "What a night! One might even imagine a beautiful mermaid combing her hair on the rocks in the moonlight and singing her siren's song, her tail rippling the water, with dolphins rolling in the sea all around her."

His eyebrow lifted. "You know, Captain, I may have seen just such a sight in my life."

"Oh? I wouldn't doubt it, after some of the stories you've told us."

He smiled, a faraway look in his eyes.

"She was so lovely... her hair a silky white-blonde, eyes as blue as the Caribbean on a sunny day. She didn't have a tail, but she swam like a dolphin. She talks to them too. And they talk to her. She saved my life once, from a tiger shark. She whispered in his ear, and the beast spared me because they were friends."

Rafia chuckled. "No such creature exists, Miguel, except in the bottom of a bottle of rum. Have you been drinking?"

"She loved me. And I loved her. But I was a fool, in so many ways. I don't even recognize that Michael anymore. He's dead and gone. And good riddance. No, I haven't had a drop since before Panama, Captain. When we get to Spanish Wells, I've got a mermaid to catch!"

She could see the joy, the hope, on his face, even in the moonlight. He's serious! she thought. Could this mermaid be the one he cried out for, his Angel?

"Well, good hunting, my friend. I wish you well."

She turned to go, but he captured her hand and brought it to his lips, gazing deep into her eyes. "Thank you, Rafia," he whispered with a soft smile. "For one wonderful night, you gave me the dream of my heart. I'll never forget that... and I'll never forget you."

****

It was dark when they finally cleared security and pulled into the Spanish Wells channel. They dropped anchor and locked the cargo hold before rowing to the dock.

"Where is everyone? Even the Conch Club is closed! How are we supposed to find something to drink?" Emilio wailed.

The sound of a band playing in the distance got their attention. "This way!" Pepe yelled. "Where there's rake n' scrape, there's always rum!"

Michael didn't want to follow. He needed to go to Bonefish Bay immediately and find out where Angel was. If she was on Miracle Island, he'd have to wait for Gypsy and Noah to show up this month or the next to take him there, and he wasn't sure if he could deal with any delay in seeing her again.

Realizing that their path to the musical event was on the way to Armand and Nadia's anyway, he joined the others. As the music grew louder, he saw it was coming from a brand-new building called the Spanish Wells Community Center. Scores of people were moving in and out of the wide double doors, with festive decorations covering the entryway.

"It's a party!" Pepe declared in excitement. "Anyone can go in. There'll be food and drink for us all!"

Rafia squinted in the dark. "There's a banner over the door that says *Happy Birthday, Angel.*"

Instantly recognizing the name, she spun around to find Michael, but he had already stopped dead in his tracks.

Oh God, it was November 17th... Angel's 18th birthday! His own 26th birthday. She was here!

Pushing and shoving his way through the crowd, he was frantically searching for a glimpse of her when he heard an announcement that chilled his heart.

"Jordan's about to propose to Angel!"

The crowd surged ahead of him, but he held himself back at the doorway to the auditorium, remaining in the shadows.

Then he saw her... a fantasy woman come to life!

Her short, white cocktail dress was sleeveless, with a lacy scoop neck bodice that highlighted the creamy mounds of her high, firm breasts, and with a sexy lace back that dipped dangerously low. High-heeled white shoes accented her long, slender legs, a diamond-crusted bracelet encircling her wrist and diamond earrings flashing at her ears.

Her white-blonde hair flowed like a waterfall to her thighs, a pink hibiscus flower that matched her lips tucked behind one ear. But what shattered Michael's heart into pieces was the look of happiness on her sweet face as she gazed at the man she was with.

She was on the dance floor, wrapped in the arms of a tall, handsome, blond young man, who leaned over and kissed her tenderly as the other dancers around them continued to sway, ignoring the lovers as they embraced. When their lips drew apart, he spoke to her briefly before leading her up to a stage filled with flowers.

Michael's hands clenched into fists of fury, shaking with jealousy and rage as this Jordan dropped to one knee and professed his love for Angel, then asked her to become his bride. Without even waiting for her answer, he started to push a ring on her finger.

Suddenly, appearing out of nowhere, Michael saw Moses hovering above the couple! Angel cried out in surprise and the ring fell from the young man's fingertips.

As Moses darted out the door, he slowed to catch Michael's eye and gave him a low whistle. He felt a powerful surge of renewed hope, and the pieces of his heart snapped back together. He would fight for her, no matter what!

Angel saw the ring at her feet and picked it up. But rather than turn to Jordan, she turned towards him, and their eyes locked across the crowded room.

He prayed to God as he poured his very soul into that look, his passion... his pain... his regrets and heartache, his lust and desire, his longing for her sweet and tender spirit, for her laughter and joy. She belonged to him, and no other man could ever, would ever have what was his!

Hear me, my dearest love, his burning eyes spoke. Listen to your heart. I am here. I'm coming for you, my Angel. You are mine. And I will never leave you again. We will be together forever. I love you... I love you... I love you...

He saw her lips form his name.

"Michael!"

Their eyes still locked, she collapsed to the floor.

Chapter 21 The Mission Begins

Something was different.

Nylah sat up in bed and listened. She could hear the usual chatter of seagulls and the rumble of the pounding waves outside the cliffs, the day promising to be lovely, the early morning sun rising over the eastern horizon in all its glory. She closed her eyes and searched the invisible mystic ether with her second sight but could find nothing to account for the anxious feelings that had kept her tossing and turning all night long.

Flipping off her blanket, she got up, quickly dressed, and set out to find Adam.

The firepit area was deserted. She and Adam were the only ones who had remained behind on Miracle Island while the others left for Spanish Wells to celebrate Angel's birthday. She flipped open the lid of a storage basket and found a bunch of almost too ripe bananas inside. Planning to make them a real breakfast later, she selected one for herself and tucked another in her pocket for Adam.

She couldn't sense him. It only happened now and then when he was traveling on a distant observation foray that he'd been called to do alone. On those rare occasions, even Moses was told to stay behind, the anxious osprey waiting faithfully at the cross until Adam at last reappeared on the cliff, no matter how long it took.

Well, that was certainly the most likely place to find him, she thought, and started up the hill.

As she came up over the rise, she saw him. He was facing the ocean, kneeling with his head bent low over his clasped hands, deep in prayer. Always hesitant to disturb him when she found him at worship, she waited until he rose and sat down on the log, wiping his reddened eyes.

"Adam, are you alright?" Her hand rested on his shoulder, and he covered it with his own.

"Sit with me."

She walked around the log and dropped to her knees at his feet. "You've been crying. How could I not know you were hurting?

He smiled ruefully and kissed her palm. "I have something to tell you, Nylah. Something wonderful, something terrible, something I am so grateful for, yet something that tore my soul apart."

She waited, unable to imagine what he was about to say.

"I met the Lord Jesus Christ last night... and I watched as He was crucified on the cross."

****

"After Moses returned from his assignment in Spanish Wells, you and I said good night and I went to bed. I was almost asleep when I suddenly felt an urgent need to come up here to the clifftop. Moses came with me... he felt it too... and we sat for quite a while, watching the stars and listening to the ocean. It was so beautiful, Nylah! The natural world of nature that God created never ceases to amaze me.

"It was then that I heard His call! But I had no destination in my mind. I was being asked to step out, in complete faith, not knowing where I was going or what I would be facing. Moses flew to my wrist, and we walked over the edge of the cliff together.

"Usually when we step out, as you know, we arrive at our chosen destination instantly. But that didn't happen to us this time. Instead, a hurricane of wind swept us through a tunnel of light! Light everywhere, Nylah, indescribable light that shimmered and danced with a kaleidoscope of colors I've never seen before!

"It didn't seem to faze Moses in the least. I guess he's used to various methods of heavenly transport as an Angel. But I was caught up in wonder and fascination at the might, the power, the majesty of God, a being so great that we as human beings simply cannot comprehend the magnitude of all that He is and all that He can do. I was being taken on a journey through time, space, and dimension, where the past, present, and future coexist in perfect harmony.

"Who could have conceived of such a thing? Who could have the power to control it? Who else but the Creator of the universe, the unseen God who asks us to believe *before* we can see!"

"Oh, how wonderful!" she exclaimed. "How long were you traveling?"

His golden eyes glittered, his excitement growing as he relived the amazing experience.

"I'm not really certain, but we finally slowed and drifted down like feathers to the earth, landing in the middle of a beautiful garden of cypress, eucalyptus, and pine trees. There were olive trees too, their fruit dark green and ripe, with clusters of colorful wildflowers scattered everywhere, their smell pungent and sweet.

"I was surprised when Moses transitioned into his form as an Angel. I didn't recognize where we were, but he pointed in a direction, and we started to walk. We hadn't gone very far when I saw a small group of men sitting on the ground, most of them fast asleep. *"Won't they spot us?"* I whispered, but Moses shook his head. No one could see us, he assured me, we were invisible to the human eye.

"I noticed another man at a distance from the others, all alone and kneeling at the base of a boulder, the moonlight illuminating the blue and white robes he was wearing. He was praying intensely, his dark hair brushing his shoulders and damp with perspiration, his voice laden with urgency and pain... and I suddenly knew where we were.

"We'd been transported over two thousand years back in time to the Garden of Gethsemane, Nylah, and the man was Jesus Himself, preparing for His vigil on the cross!

"I wanted to go to Him, to comfort Him, to pray with Him, but Moses stopped me. The Darkness was hovering above Him... laughing and taunting Him, its slimy tentacles of evil winding down towards Him. But He struggled to stand and faced the mocking entity, the tentacles bursting into flame before it vanished into the night sky."

Nylah was trembling as she listened. "It was really Jesus!"

He nodded mutely, unable to go on, and she laid her hand on his arm. "I know what the Bible says happens next. The temple soldiers arrive, led by Judas, who betrays Him with a traitorous kiss. His disciples rise to fight, and Peter cuts off the ear of one of the soldiers."

Adam regained control of his emotions and continued.

"Yes, Moses and I watched it all. Jesus scooped up some dirt from the earth and spit into it to make a smear of mud. While everyone else was fighting, He picked up the bloody ear with His mud-soiled hand and knelt at the side of the agonized soldier. His presence seemed to calm the man as He placed the ear gently against his head and held it there... and when His hand came away, the ear had been completely healed!"

"Oh, Adam, what a gift you were given by God! I've only dreamt of seeing Him in the flesh!"

"Everything happened so fast after that! Judas escaped their grasp and raced towards me. I was about to dodge into the bushes, but he ran straight through me like I wasn't even there! I could feel his confusion and regret, and I pitied him. I might have been able to spare him from what he intended to do if only I could have told him that even his misguided and cowardly act could be forgiven, if he only asked for it. But I could see the shadow of the Darkness following him as he ran from the garden, ready to collect another poor soul for his collection in hell."

"So, they took Him away at that point, didn't they? To be judged by the priests in the temple of His own people?"

Adam stared out across the ocean. "Not just yet... His disciples had all fled, but the soldiers decided to have a little fun of their own, punching and kicking Him and laughing as they did. One vicious blow laid Him out on His belly, only a few yards from where Moses and I were standing."

His eyes began to water at the memory. "I started to cry, Nylah. His face was battered and bruised, but He raised His head and looked deep into my eyes. He saw me, Nylah! The Savior saw me! And despite His pain, He smiled at me! Then, in my mind, I heard Him speak."

"From before the creation of the universe, you were chosen to be My final Prophet, he who will carry the last message of redemption to the people of the new earth.

"Go now, My son. Your mission has begun. The Darkness will resist you with all the powers of hell, but My Word, My Name, and My Blood are mightier than the enemy.

"I have given you the Healer and the Angel to stand with you as One. Bring My beloved people back to the light, back to the Garden of Eden, where they may enjoy their lives on earth in joy, peace, and prosperity before they join My Father one day in their eternal home."

"So, now it begins," she whispered. "I'm ready, Adam! I've been ready since Wolftown. He shows me more of what I can do every day, new powers He has given me that I may serve Him by your side! But what happened after He spoke to you?" Seeing the sudden flash of black sorrow in his eyes, she braced herself.

"You've read how the story continues after the events in the garden. Moses and I would materialize at different times and places. At His meeting with Pontius Pilate. When He was sent to meet with King Herod, then returned to Pilate. When He was beaten and tortured by the Roman soldiers. When the crown of thorns was pressed deep into His skull as they mocked Him. When He cried out to the Father in agony as the stained and rusty nails were hammered into His wrists and feet. The four recordings of His crucifixion in the Bible don't come anywhere close to describing what it was really like for Him... what cruel, vindictive, and hate-filled people put Him through. I was ashamed of the entire human race as I watched how they made Him suffer... and without a word of complaint falling from His lips.

"Do you remember Morgan telling us about a movie that was made before the Flare by a famous actor and director that portrayed the crucifixion? Remember how everyone wept that night as we listened to her describe it?"

Nylah was already quietly sobbing as he spoke, the only response she could make a slight nod.

"It was a thousand times worse."

Moses landed next to Adam and folded his wings as they held each other and cried. But when they finally dried their tears, he whistled for their attention.

"Yes, Moses, I was going to tell Nylah the most important part." Holding her close to his side, they watched the clouds on the horizon darken with rain.

"I saw Him die, Nylah... There was no doubt in my mind whatsoever that His Spirit had left His torn and bloody body behind. There was no breath, no movement, His skin a pale and ghostly white."

Adam's golden eyes suddenly re-ignited as Moses whistled joyously, his feathers radiant with light.

"Some people talk about the resurrection as if it were just an inspirational story meant to entertain them, without any real significance in their lives. But I can tell you firsthand, my love, His resurrection from the dead was very real! I saw it as it happened!

"Jesus Christ is alive, right now, this very minute, and has been and will forever be in control of the destiny of mankind, and of each one of us, His creations! And He has given you, me, and Moses the task of ensuring that every human being on this new earth gets their chance to hear the Truth, and to make the most important decision of their lives.

"Will they choose a joyful eternal home in heaven with their loving Savior... or will they risk an endless infinity of hopelessness and torment, clutched in the tentacles of the merciless Darkness?"

Chapter 22 Here We Go

Alea raced up the steps to the stage, Josey and Morgan right behind her, the rest of the Miracle Island Tribe pushing their way forward through the throng of concerned people.

"Angel... Angel, sweetheart, can you hear me?" she asked as she patted the girl's colorless cheek. When there was no response, she carefully examined her head for any sign of an injury as John slid over a planter to elevate his daughter's feet before checking her heartbeat.

Daniel stripped off his shirt, and Alea tucked it carefully under Angel's neck for support. "Please, everyone! I know you all want to help but stay back. She needs air!"

Jordan's worried face hung over Alea's shoulder. "Will she be okay? Why did she faint, Doctor Devereaux?"

"We haven't determined that yet, Jordan. It may be that the combined excitement of her birthday celebration and your surprise proposal was too much for her."

All at once, Angel's eyelids fluttered open and she moaned softly, appearing dazed. "Where is he?" she breathed.

"I'm here, Angel!" Jordan dove past Alea to clasp Angel's limp hand, covering it with kisses.

John stood up and walked over to join Daniel and Matt, who were standing nearby. "She'll be fine with some rest and something salty to eat. Her pulse is low, but steady."

"Is Angel actually engaged to Jordan now?" Matt asked uncertainly. "I never heard her say yes, and he's got the ring in his pocket."

"I'm calling that a no," Daniel said. "Until I hear her agree, he's only her boyfriend in my book." He didn't like the young man when he first met him but couldn't figure out why he'd reacted in such an unexpectedly strong way.

"We need to get her to Bonefish Bay and into bed. A bowl of hot soup, buttered toast, and a good night's sleep are my prescription," her father advised. "In the morning, we'll sit down with her and have a talk. And I agree with you, Daniel. I won't see her forced into anything she doesn't want, no matter how great a guy Jordan might be. Until I say so, he'll just have to wing it on his own."

****

"The Tribe's not coming back as planned, Adam. They're caring for Angel in advance of what's to come, and they won't be home for weeks after it happens."

He was quiet as he pondered Nylah's revelation. They were sitting on a log at the firepit, watching the sun rise over the Atlantic with a cup of hot lemonade.

"I really wanted to tell my mom and dad that the prophecy Skylark told them I'd been born for is about to begin. I don't think my mother ever wanted to admit to herself that I would be leaving her to do God's work someday. I'm her only child, and this will be hard on her. And I don't know how long we'll be gone on these missions. It might only be a few hours in their time... or it could be months.

"I never told anyone but you, Nylah, that I talk to Him every night, and I certainly never told the Tribe about my childhood experiences with the Darkness. But Moses and I have kept him at bay over the years. My mom, Dad, Noah, and Gypsy saw God's power work through me once to save them on their voyage to Boston when I was just a baby, but no one is aware how much my abilities have grown as I've gotten older, or that the three of us are able to step out and travel the earth to observe the struggles and sorrows of the survivors of the Flare in preparation for our mission."

"Well, everyone knows I'm a Healer and that I can predict future events, but that's all they know. Imagine if they knew the full extent of the gifts and powers we were given."

She smiled affectionately as Moses landed on the log next to her, carrying a freshly caught yellowtail snapper.

"And they've never seen Moses in any form other than an osprey! But they believe he's an Angel without ever having seen him transform into his true appearance. I think that's real faith, don't you, Adam?"

"If only more people had that kind of simple faith, my love. Moses performed several miracles on my parent's journey to Boston seventeen years ago to rescue Matt, his assignment to guard and protect them, and he was invisibly present on the day Angel was born, having received permission from God to retrieve both Josey and her baby from certain death.

"He has been seamlessly woven into the fabric of their lives from the very first day he guided my father to Osprey Bay, a perfect example of how God works. People that appear in our lives or surprising events that occur are often construed as chance or luck. It takes confident belief to see the hand of God in every little thing. Nothing is too small or too trivial for Him to care about!"

Nylah drained her cup and set it down. "So, do we wait for the Tribe... or do we go?"

As he helped her up, Moses whistled in excitement, the partially eaten fish forgotten.

"We do His will, Nylah, and His will is that we leave today for our first mission." He cocked an eyebrow and gave her a crooked smile.

"But it couldn't hurt to leave them a note."

****

"Can I get you more soup, Angel? Another piece of toast?"

Josey was reluctant to leave her daughter all alone in the studio guest house that Angel had claimed as her own when she first arrived in Spanish Wells.

The four-acre Bonefish Bay property was large enough to accommodate the two guest houses that James had designed and built in the years before the solar flare. A two-story with three bedrooms was positioned one hundred feet to the west of the main house and slept six to eight people.

But the studio cottage was well to the east and sat right on the beach facing the northern Atlantic, blocked from sight by a grove of mahogany, casuarina, and yellow elder trees.

Its isolation and proximity to the ocean was what made Angel fall in love with the cozy little cottage as soon as she saw it, the perfect and private location for her to explore the waters surrounding Spanish Wells, day or night.

She loved the floor to ceiling windows that allowed her to watch the waves from the comfort of the massive king bed, with a wall of mirrors serving as a headboard, a panoramic view of the ocean wherever she looked. The kitchen had no power, and although she had to cook, grill, and bake in the oceanside firepit, she mixed her own favorite bread dough and prepared her salads on the granite countertop.

The wide, covered front porch led to a partially enclosed outdoor shower that was fed from a raincatch water tank on the roof, water to bathe available with the simple pull of a cord. The composting commode had its own enclosed cubby next to the shower stall, with a door low enough to enable its visitor to enjoy the enchanting seascape before them.

On her own time, she had painted a mural on one of the cottage walls, depicting a dark-haired man and a mermaid with long, white-blonde hair streaming behind her, diving down hand in hand to a spectacular ocean reef alive with fish, dolphins, sea fans, and coral formations. If her mural had reminded anyone in the Tribe of her and Michael, no one had commented.

“Mom, I’ll be fine. The soup helped a lot. I feel much better now.” She pushed herself up higher in bed as Josey propped the pillows around her for more support. Morgan set a cup of hot tea on the table next to the bed, then sat down.

"If you need anything at all, Angel, just ring the bell on the porch. Matt and I can be here in seconds."

Alea walked in the door with a burlap bag in her arms and dropped it on the granite island.

"I brought fruit, salad, bread, and a big piece of birthday cake for you, Angel. Make sure you eat some, okay? I don't want to see you fainting like that ever again. Jordan is very worried about you, and he kept apologizing over and over when he realized you hadn't eaten a thing all night."

Angel nodded, but her expression was distant. "It wasn't his fault."

"Do you want to see him, sweetheart? I can have Matt or Daniel go get him," Morgan offered.

She panicked, her face blanching white again. "No, please, Morgan! It's so late. I just need to be alone and get some sleep. I'm sure I'll feel better in the morning."

The bewildered women glanced at one another but said nothing. Angel's reaction to the proposal to fetch Jordan was rather odd, but without further discussion, they kissed her goodnight and filed out the door.

She breathed a sigh of relief as she watched them leave. Ignoring the tea, she climbed out of bed and walked to the window, staring out sightlessly. Had it really been Michael... or had she only imagined seeing him?

But the slamming of her heart against her ribs told her the truth. Her hot breath fogged the glass, the dark ocean fading from sight. The old pain washed over her again like rushing water and she couldn't breathe, the room closing in around her!

Ripping off her white dress and diamond gifts, she tore open the door and raced to the ocean, splashing wildly into the shore break before diving in headfirst!

Darkness greeted her until the world below the surface slowly illuminated with the soft ambient light that made the ocean at night her own private playground. Had no one else seen him? And if he *was* there, they would have told her... wouldn't they?

Touching down on the sand and grass-covered bottom, her body was finally able to relax, suspended and weightless, her warm, salty tears blending invisibly into the cocoon of water surrounding her.

If it really was him, why had he returned on the very day she'd been weighing whether or not it was time to move on with her life with Jordan? And why did Moses show up like that, suddenly disrupting his proposal that he'd obviously pre-arranged to coincide with her 18th birthday? She knew the angel bird never did anything without a purpose... but what could it be?

A curious dolphin nosed her leg, breaking her out of her runaway thoughts. She shot back up, the dolphin rising with her to make sure the human with the unusual vibrations made it safely to the surface, and as the dolphin circled her, she offered her thanks for his kindness.

A human female that could speak their language? The pod needed to hear of this!

Waving goodbye, she undulated towards shore. Reaching the shallows, she rose from the waves and gathered her hair, squeezing the seawater from the long, saturated strands, her naked body chilling in the cool night air as she made her way to the outdoor shower.

She pulled the cord, enjoying the feel of the warmer water cascading over her skin, and turned herself in a slow circle, allowing the soothing flow to rinse away every last vestige of salt. Feeling refreshed and much calmer, she wrapped a towel around her breasts and tied a knot. That cup of hot tea did sound good.

With her tea reheated over the embers of the fire, she set the cup on the bedside table next to the candle and draped her wet towel on a chair to dry. Reclining back on the bed, she felt the tumultuous day starting to catch up with her.

I'll just lay here for a minute, she thought wearily, I'm so tired... and felt herself starting to drift.

She startled awake. The room was quiet and dark, the candle having burned itself out as she slept. Pushing up to her elbows, she looked around, her senses on high alert. Noticing movement near the door, she grew rigid when a dark shadow seemed to shift in the dim light of the stars.

Someone was in the room!

The shadow slowly moved in front of the window when a sudden strong gust of wind caused the firepit outside to burst back into flame, the figure of a man now clearly silhouetted between her and the flickering light behind him. The wind flared the firepit again, its light reflecting off the mirrored wall, and she gasped when she saw what it revealed.

The burning blue eyes of the man that had haunted her dreams were riveted on her with an intensity that caused her to shiver.

"Michael!"

****

"Are you ready, Nylah?"

The three of them stood at the edge of the cliff, Moses on Adam's shoulder. The cross behind them seemed to glow in the sun, the beacon they could always count on to tell them they were finally home whenever they reappeared from an observation journey.

"Yes, Adam. I left a letter for them on my father's desk he'll be sure to find."

He nodded in approval and looked up at Moses. "And you, Angel. Are you prepared as well?"

The bird whistled and gave a slight flap of his wings.

"Oh, I almost forgot!" Nylah reached into her pocket and pulled out the red rose, its petals as dewy and perfect as the day she received it. "I carry it with me always."

He smiled as she lifted the rose, her eyes closing in delight as she inhaled its rich fragrance.

"Well, here we go, my love."

"Where *are* we going, Adam?" she asked shyly, tucking the rose back into her pocket.

His eyes ignited with golden fire as he took her hand.

"Have you ever heard of a faraway land called Russia?"

Together, they stepped out over the edge of the cliff... and were gone.

****

She rose from the bed, naked, her eyes never leaving his, and walked towards him, stopping just before her nipples could brush his chest.

Suddenly, she drew back her arm and slapped him with all her might! His head twisted abruptly to one side, mottled fingerprints flaring on his cheek, but without a word, he turned back to face her. Furious, she slapped him a second time, but again, without making a sound, his eyes locked on to hers.

"You bastard!" she screamed. "You fucking bastard! How dare you come here!" She clenched her fist and aimed for his jaw, but this time, his hand came up and grabbed her wrist.

"I hate you!" The fingers of her other hand curled into sharp-tipped weapons as she shot them towards his eyes, but he grabbed that wrist too and swung her arms behind her.

"Why?" she wailed in agony, "Oh God, why?"

He pulled her hips against him as she struggled wildly in his grasp, arching as far away from him as she could.

"I thought you were gone from my life forever! Why did you have to come back today, of all days?" she cried.

His forehead dropped heavily to her shoulder, christening her breast with anguished tears of repentance, his chest heaving as he wept out his remorse, his shame, his sorrow, his guilt. Then, releasing her wrists, he clung to her waist like a drowning man in a raging storm.

He deserved her hatred. She deserved her revenge. Let her do whatever she wanted to him. She could hurt him no more than what he had done to himself.

But he'd never let her go again.

She felt him shudder, his body wracked with tortured sobs. Her fury dissipating like smoke in a strong breeze, her arms rose to encircle his neck, and she buried her nose in his hair.

This was her Michael... his scent, his touch, his heat, his tears. He was the only key to the locked door of her heart that Jordan had never once been able to open, and as he held her, the key turned in the lock... and her love burst forth, unbound and free!

She gently caressed his soft, dark, disheveled hair as his unbelieving, tear-stained face lifted, and she tenderly kissed the red and swollen marks her own hands had made, each touch of her lips an act of absolution.

"I love you, Angel," he whispered reverently. "You're all I need... all I'll ever want. It took me much too long to see it, to finally see you, but once I did, I vowed to never leave you again. I sailed the seas for almost two years, and all I could think about was how I had hurt you... and that I might be too late to hold you in my arms again.

"When I saw you with that other man, I almost went insane! I called out to you with every molecule of my being and prayed that you'd hear me... and that you could find it in your heart to forgive me.

"The merciful Lord God, in His infinite love, grace, and wisdom, brought me back to you on the very night another man was about to claim you as his own. I'll never be able to offer you everything he can, Angel, but I'm yours, if you'll have me, and I'm asking you now to become my wife."

"Oh, Michael," she breathed, "I've always been your wife."

And she kissed him.

Chapter 23 At What Cost

Thick deciduous forests of oak, elm, aspen, and ash had stood as the gatekeepers between the rolling hills of western Russia and the fertile plains of the Ukraine for thousands of years. Their evergreen cousins, the stately spruce and the versatile pine, had also made this land their home, the black soil nutrient rich and fed by the southern flowing waters of the Dnieper River and its tributaries.

For a land so lush and so beautiful, with the biting cold of winter mitigated by its location at the southwestern corner of Russia and bordering the Black Sea, and with as much wild game, fish, and greenery that men could possibly desire, the curse of war had unfortunately also taken root here.

For centuries, the breadbasket of the Ukraine had seen its share of alien conquerors, eager to plunder and control the millions of acres of wheat, corn, rye, and barley its rural inhabitants were famous for. Giant sunflowers, their pressed oil of great value for cooking and in cosmetics, were grown in vast fields, their yellow-crowned heads swaying gently in the breeze, a sight that dazzled the visitor's eye.

Once a part of the former Soviet Union, the Ukraine had sought and won their independence in 1991, and supported by the Europeans and the United States, had envisioned a new and more prosperous future out from under the cruel and repressive regime of the time in Moscow.

Tensions remained high, however, for many years, with violent incidents and thefts along the border between the two countries disallowed by the Russian government and media or blamed on the Ukrainians themselves.

But the four hundred townspeople of the small Ukrainian town of Pavel, situated on the western bank of the Dnieper River on the northern border, knew the truth.

They knew how many of their hard-working men had been senselessly slaughtered... how many of their young women had been caught unawares by patrols of laughing Russian soldiers and shamefully dishonored... how many trucks of grain had been ambushed and stolen...

Why? they asked, as they gathered in the town's municipal building to decide what to do about these crimes. We are of the same blood! We may not have agreed with their politics, but our history, our culture, is still the same.

They eventually concurred that their choice for freedom from repression had challenged the firmly established and autocratic premier and his body of ministers, who for their own incomprehensible reasons, chose to continue the old cold war ideology that saw the Republic of the Ukraine as a wayward child of the Soviet family conglomerate.

But how do we stop the bloodshed? How do we protect our women? How do we keep our farms from going bankrupt? Beyond sending formal requests for protection to their own government, who increased their drone surveillance of the border, there was nothing else they could do.

The final outrage came in 2017 when the Russian premier authorized the construction of Samovar Dam across the Dnieper River on the Soviet side of the border, with the Red Star of Russia emblazoned high on the center wall, a dam so large that an extra tax was levied on the Russian people to fund its creation. The gargantuan reservoir behind the dam flooded an area of 3000 square miles to a depth of 350 feet behind the dam, and Samovar Lake was then stocked with pike, carp, catfish, trout, sturgeon, and perch. Within two years from the start of construction, the flow of the mighty half-mile wide Dnieper into the Ukraine was reduced to no more than a fifty-foot stream.

The Ukrainian government protested the devastating loss of their main source of crop irrigation, but their cries fell on deaf Russian ears. Their urgent pleas to the international community brought no relief beyond a few token monetary sanctions from a hamstrung United Nations and an angry and sputtering U.S. president.

Premier Yellen, his ministers, and generals celebrated at the Kremlin, toasting their success with shots of premium vodka and an animated game of darts, with the inaugural photograph of the smiling American president in the center of the target. The eighty-inch television screen on the wall was tuned to the latest press conference at the White House to address the problematic Ukrainian issue.

"Their Commander-In-Chief isn't looking quite so cocky today, is he, Boris?" Premier Yellen asked his Minister of Defense as he set his empty glass down, the slinky blonde twins in the doorway pursing their lips and gesturing for him to follow.

"With the Ukraine on their knees, it will only be a matter of time before their people beg to be reinstated into the greatest and most powerful nation on earth... and we won't have fired a shot!"

And then, on July 29th of 2019, an unprecedented and earth-shaking event occurred that changed the world.

At dawn on that fateful morning, an ominous blood red rising sun exploded into a brilliant array of light and color that blinded every inhabitant of Pavel that saw it!

When their vision finally returned, the riotous sun had reverted to its usual glowing yellow, but the entire town had shut down... no cellphones, no television, no radio, no lights. Farm equipment and machinery had ground to a halt. Cars and trucks were stalled in the streets, with only a handful of older vehicles able to start. Although the people did not yet know it, their lives would never be the same again.

Both Russian and Ukrainian military units did their best to maintain order, but with food supplies becoming scarce, even loyal troops began to desert, one by one, to seek out their families before the deadly cold of winter set in.

The Flare was a catastrophic disaster that wiped out three quarters of earth's population in the first eight weeks of the die-off. With basic survival needs now the primary focus of the living, politics and war took a decided back seat.

But Boris Chenko had planned for every possible scenario during the course of his many years as the most important man in Moscow next to the reigning premier... and the most feared. He was an old-fashioned general from the bitter Cold War era. "A finger on a trigger is a sure thing," he liked to say to his cowering staff. "You can't enjoy watching your enemy die as a red blip on a radar screen."

He had studied the effects of an electromagnetic pulse from a nuclear explosion, and even the farfetched science-fiction possibility of an extremely powerful solar flare, both of which would render Russia's state-of-the-art satellite systems and computerized weaponry useless. But no EMP could affect the function of conventional weaponry, and its value could not be overestimated.

The completely solar-powered Samovar Dam had been his brainchild, and in addition to the army base adjacent to it, he had ordered the construction of a massive secret bunker in the lowest level of the dam, lined with steel plate to serve as a Faraday cage, and containing thousands of weapons, as well as limited tactical nuclear devices.

No fingerprint recognition bullshit for Chenko. He carried the only sets of keys to unlock the doors that led to the bunker, and to his own private luxury accommodations on three levels, where he, his mistress, Elena Popov, and his daughter, five-year-old Sasha, would lack for nothing for many years. His annoying wife, Madya, would be left to fend for herself, but he chose not to share that callous bit of information with Sasha.

With Samovar right on the Ukrainian border, he would have an ongoing supply of fish from the river and lake, timber and game from the surrounding forests, corn and grains from the rich growing fields of the Ukraine... and a source of labor for the planting and harvesting of those grains from the closest town of Pavel, to be kept under complete and strict control by his two hundred loyal troops at the base, all highly-trained single men.

He kept his personal security force, the legendary Elite 20, with him 24/7. Secretly recruited from ranks of the KGB with the permission of the chairman, his boyhood friend, Anton Vasilyeva, these twenty cold, hard, men of steel with no visible signs of emotion spied for Chenko, torturing and killing at his command.

The mere threat of their inhuman techniques used to draw information from their targets was often enough to get them whatever they asked for. To emphasize the message that complete cooperation was beneficial to one's health, an unimportant interviewee would occasionally be taken into custody and threatened with the instruments of torture. They were then released, with the *request* that they broadcast their reprieve from what could have been a horrifying death. This intimidating tactic was usually more than enough to ensure voluntary compliance from future victims.

The day after the solar flare traumatized Moscow, Boris Chenko, Elena, and Sasha were driven through the chaos and looting to Samovar Dam in a modified, solar flare-resistant Humvee, escorted by the Elite 20, who mowed down anyone who tried to stop them.

Upon their arrival, they descended to Level 4 on the solar-powered elevator. Chenko inserted the key and pushed open the double-wide steel doors. Flipping on the wall switch, lights softly lit the room as the surround sound stereo system played the soothing strains of Tchaikovsky.

“Welcome to your new home, my dears,” he announced to Elena and Sasha. “We’re going to stay in Samovar until this power issue is straightened out.”

“What about Premier Yellen, Papa?” Sasha asked. “Are he and Mama coming too?”

He smiled and patted his sweet girl’s arm. What he had ordered, on pain of death, was that his beloved daughter was never to learn that after receiving definitive confirmation of the power and extent of the solar disaster, he and his Elite 20 had marched into the panicked Mika Yellen’s office and shot him in the back of the head as he wept at his desk.

Fifty-five-year-old Boris Chenko was now the undisputed leader of Russia... or what was left of it.

****

Yuri surveyed the ripe golden stalks of wheat swaying in the breeze, the fields of grain stretching as far as the eye could see. The noon sun was straight above him, the heat making him sweat. But the thought of what the bleak winter months would bring to Pavel made him turn his face up to enjoy its warmth a little longer.

He had been a young child of seven when the Flare struck. The scythe of an angry and vengeful God, the priest called it as he stood at his pulpit every Sunday morning, trying to convince his hope-starved congregation that their terrible and grievous sins had brought the solar flare disaster, as well as their subsequent bondage, upon themselves.

But it was the face of Christ on the cross behind him that the people looked at, a face of such love, a face that gave them such a feeling of comfort, that the harsh words of the priest had little effect. However, even that consolation was taken away when General Chenko ordered the cessation of all religious practices, viewing them as a waste of time and energy. The church doors were boarded up and the clergy sent to labor in the fields with everyone else.

Then suddenly, three years ago, he inexplicably gave his permission to resume Sunday morning services. The brave souls who dared to go to worship entered the church on a walkway lined with armed troopers.

But what the people did not know, and that Yuri did, was that it was his daughter, Sasha, who had softened his heart.

Sasha... with her kind smile, luminous hazel eyes, and shiny brown hair, who came into town every Wednesday, protected by her armed escorts.

Sasha... who nursed the sick and comforted the dying.

Sasha... who brought her own treasured books to read to the children, who hungered to hear the exciting tales of adventure she brought to life.

His Sasha... the woman he had fallen desperately in love with, and who, by some miracle, loved him too!

They had bumped into each other as she carried a tray of bandages down the hall at the newly renovated hospital, a spark of instant attraction igniting between them. He was smitten by her humble sweetness, and made sure to visit hospitalized friends, and even the friends of friends, every Wednesday evening, their spark gradually blossoming into love.

But he mourned the fact that she was the daughter of the most feared and violent man in this corner of Russia, and to have her as his wife was an impossible dream.

Life was hard in Pavel. Kept alive by Boris Chenko to serve his needs and the needs of his troops, the men, women, and children of the town crossed the half-mile long bridge over the Dnieper to work in the eastern grain fields from sunrise to sunset, allowed adequate enough food to keep them strong and healthy for work. The water gates of the dam could be operated both electronically or manually, and Chenko had them raised at intervals for irrigation. But his control of the water gave him absolute control of the people.

“They should be grateful!” he proclaimed to his officers. “Millions are dead from starvation, thirst, and disease. The nations of the world have crumbled, their populations barely able to survive. But here in Samovar and Pavel, we live like kings in comparison, where I protect them from the wolves outside our gates!”

Although Pavel had no power at all, his acres of solar panels were still active eighteen years after the Flare, the thousands of batteries also kept charged by hydroelectric power created by waterflow from the dam. But even he had been unable to predict the ferocity of the colossal solar burst and the long-term devastation it would cause. By ordering careful conservation measures and rotating their use, each battery’s ability to accept a charge and store electricity had been stretched out for many years.

But Chenko knew they would not last forever.

For himself, he did not care... He was now seventy-three and in declining health. It was Sasha’s future he was most concerned about.

Elena had died years ago. Well, he couldn’t deny that he had killed her himself after discovering her riding his own aide, a panting Captain Sokolov, as she rolled her hips and moaned in pleasure, the one thing he hadn’t been able to provide for a very long time. A stoic Sokolov had taken his immediate execution like a man as Chenko watched him thrown off the top of the dam to the rocks hundreds of feet below, then walked inside to where a hysterical Elena was being held and strangled her with his bare hands, an act of personal vengeance that surprisingly revived his flagging libido.

For the first time, he took advantage of the Harem.

As Samovar Base was being built, he understood that his young, unmarried soldiers would need a way to find sexual release without molesting the working women of Pavel.

He ordered the construction of the Harem, a multi-level luxury compound that could house sixty women, with full-service spa facilities, a fitness center with pool and hot tub, a lounge and bar, cafeteria, library, and medical clinic.

Appointments would be held in the Pleasure Wing, where each suite was decorated in a unique sensual theme. Only an officer could schedule their appointment in an alternative location of their choice.

Before the solar disaster, the Harem had twenty well-paid women in residence, but afterwards, news of a way to survive the catastrophe traveled far and wide, and many wandering and starving young girls and women who had no other place to go made the difficult trek to the base.

After undergoing an interview by Dr. Orlov and his team to assess their beauty, personality, medical condition, and desirability, the woman or teenage girl was assigned to her own private bedroom and given immediate access to food, alcohol, and the Harem's luxurious facilities, including a new wardrobe and a professional makeover.

The central scheduler then distributed a photograph and short biography of the latest arrival to the officers and soldiers. Appointments were booked in one-to-two-hour time slots for a six-hour workday. It was sexual servitude and prostitution, but better than what awaited them out in the dangerous and chaotic post-Flare world.

Chenko had admired one of the newer women in passing and requested her name. The striking and sexy redhead was brought to his chambers an hour after Elena's murder, her amazing skills taking him almost to the brink of death. Anya was assigned to Elena's vacant quarters and reminded that unless she chose to meet the same fate as her predecessor, her lips and thighs were only for Chenko himself.

Yuri worked his section of the wheat field until dusk before hoisting his scythe over his shoulder and joining his fellow laborers, men and women, as they headed back across the bridge to town. They briefly glanced at each other now and then, their covert nods unnoticed by the guards.

It was on! The leaders of the resistance would announce their plan tonight! The meeting would begin at midnight at Stepan Petrov's barn, a short distance from town, when they could slip away while the night guards were in their towers and usually fast asleep. Could it be that his dream of a free Pavel and a safe and happy home with his beautiful, sweet, and loving Sasha could finally become a reality?

****

The three travelers stepped out of the mist into a rustling field of grain just as the sun was starting to drop below the horizon. Moses launched himself into the sky and headed in the direction of the setting sun.

"Where is he going?" Nylah asked curiously. "Shouldn't we all stay together?"

"Moses has a special mission of his own. He and I have been here before," Adam told her. "But there's someone I'm taking you to meet."

"I've never seen fields like this, Adam!" she exclaimed in wonder, entranced by the endless expanses of flat, open land alive with waving heads of grain. "So beautiful, and with so much plenty!"

"But at what cost? The Darkness has been hard at work in Pavel for many years, even before the Flare. What you see is only part of the picture, Nylah. Come on, there's a town not too far from here."

They crossed over the bridge and entered the outskirts of the village, hand in hand, the people they passed stopping in surprise. “Who are these two strangers?” they murmured to each other. “They are certainly not from Pavel. Who would travel through the dry and uninhabitable wasteland in the east to come here? And why?”

With a pleasant expression, Adam nodded at each of them politely, but kept walking until he came to a row of one-story bungalows. Without breaking his stride, he targeted the red brick house at the end, and he and Nylah stepped up to the porch. But before he could knock, the door flung open! An arm darted out, grabbed the front of his shirt, and hauled him inside, Nylah dragged in behind him.

“Do you want to get shot? They kill strangers here without even asking who they are!” A young man with dark blond hair and brown eyes ran to the window and carefully parted the curtains. Satisfied no one had followed, he sighed with relief as he turned to face them.

“Sorry to be so rough, but I’ve seen enough death to last a lifetime.” He held out his hand cordially. “My name is Yuri, Yuri Fedorov.”

Adam smiled and gripped the offered hand firmly. “I’m Adam Devereaux... and this is Nylah Kennedy. Thank you for taking us in.”

Yuri looked at Adam curiously. “You’re not Ukrainian or Russian... yet you speak perfect Ukrainian. Where are you from?”

“Have you ever heard of a place called the Bahamas? East of America in the Atlantic Ocean?”

“I’ve heard about America, but I can’t say I’ve ever heard of the Bahamas. Is it far from here?”

Nylah grinned. “Yes, it’s very far away.” Stepping towards him, he flinched uncertainly. “I would never harm you, Yuri,” she assured him softly, “but may I touch you?”

"Why?" he asked, puzzled by these two very odd people he had unaccountably tried to protect at his own risk.

She moved closer, her sparkling gray eyes mesmerizing.

"Will you trust me?"

Before he could even decide, his lips spoke. "Yes."

Her eyelids fluttered shut as she brushed his cheek with her fingertips, and when they reopened, her eyes glistened with mournful sadness.

But then, only a heartbeat later, she smiled at him in a way that almost made him forget his beloved Sasha.

She nodded approvingly at Adam.

"Yuri, can you take us with you to the meeting tonight?" he asked the startled young man.

"We need your help."

Chapter 24 A Forgiving Heart

Her luscious curves melted against his hard muscled body as Michael crushed her to him, her honey sweet lips parting beneath his urgent mouth with a moan of need, a sound that poured over his tortured soul like a healing balm. This was his Angel, offering him her precious love with a forgiving heart, a gift he would never again refuse!

He needed nothing more in this life than to keep kissing those soft lips forever, her taste, her warmth, her very breath resurrecting his lost dreams and fractured hopes. Time stood still, the very air poised and waiting as they clung to one another, at last drinking deep at the well so long denied.

Fused as one, they caressed each other, gently at first, then rougher, wilder... their desire, their passion, their need to merge, both body and soul, overwhelming! With a savage growl, he reluctantly tore himself away from her lips and swept her into his arms.

Carrying her to the bed, he laid her down, his eyes never leaving her as he ripped off his t-shirt and dropped his shorts. He stood before her, naked in the dim light, his manhood hard and alive.

"You're beautiful," she whispered, reaching out to touch the bronzed, rippled muscles of his belly, her expression one of both fear and desire.

"And you are a breathtaking vision." He knelt on the bed and slowly lowered himself on top of her, reveling in the feel of her long limbs and incomparable breasts against the length of his body.

Their eyes met... the reality of the moment they had both dreamt of for so long suddenly hitting home. A happy grin split her lovely lips and she began laughing with sheer joy, Michael's laughter joining hers as they rolled across the bed, tangled around one other!

Back and forth they rolled, like two young dolphins at play, their arms and legs intertwining. She maneuvered out of his grasp, then pounced on him like a frolicsome kitten until he tossed her on her stomach, clamping his teeth down on the back of her neck like a panther toying with his mate as she squealed with delight!

Still laughing, they collapsed on the bed, the light from the dying fire dancing on the ceiling above them.

"I can't believe you're really here!" she said in a voice full of wonder and laid her head on his shoulder.

His arm immediately wrapped around her and drew her closer. "I'm here, my love. And I'm here to stay." He kissed her shining hair and stroked it reassuringly. "You belong to me... only me."

Her happy smile faded. "Jordan..."

"Would you have married him, Angel, if I hadn't come back? I have to ask."

"Do you, Michael? I think you know the answer."

He pushed himself up on his elbow, his blue eyes intense. "I do now... but I would have moved heaven and earth to stop it." He swept a finger across her lips, then ran it down to her heart. "Because *this* is my home."

She quivered under his gentle touch, and he leaned down to kiss her as he cupped one of her breasts, caressing her nipple with his thumb. God, she was so responsive, the mere brush of his hand against her skin causing her to gasp.

Replacing his thumb with his mouth, his tongue swirled round and round before he began a warm, wet pull of suction that made her writhe, her sighs and whimpers causing him to grow even more excited than he already was. He was finding it difficult to concentrate as the enticing aroma from between her thighs filtered up to his nose.

"My beautiful iba, my beautiful ushu iba," he chanted softly in Mayoruna. "My beautiful moon, my beautiful white moon. Join with me, love, blessed and free, under the shade of the kapok tree."

He lowered himself again to her rosy nipple, enjoying the taste of the dainty appetizer. Oh, he had many more delights in mind for his beautiful Angel!

Rolling her on top of his broad chest, he stroked her smooth and silky skin, slowly, sensuously, as she found his lips with a cry. Gripping the firm globes of her rear, he pulled her against his hips so hard that her knees spread apart. The full length and girth of his engorged member lay pressed between them, throbbing with need.

"Oh, Michael!" was all she could manage to say.

Holding his breath, he prayed for control. "Hold still, my love. I want you so much and we haven't even started." It had been so long... and she was so delectable, but he didn't care about his own pleasure. Angel's happiness was his ultimate goal.

Flipping her onto her back, he began a leisurely crawl down her body until he reached her silken nest of blonde curls, already damp and fragrant. He slid her towards his hungry mouth as she stretched her arms overhead, the feel of his hot breath on her skin and the brush of his beard making her shiver with want.

Her delicate pink folds were spread before him like a feast for a starving man, and he groaned with desire as he dipped in for his first taste. The moment the tip of his hot, seeking tongue touched her, she screamed, bucking wildly, but he gripped her even tighter, worshipping his beloved with his eager mouth until she was clutching the sheets, her moans of passion exciting him beyond belief.

"Oh, oh, I don't know what's happening!"

He smiled at her uninhibited and innocent response as he flicked and teased her exquisitely sensitive pale pink pearl.

Then, as if he was indulging in a rich and creamy milkshake, he gently sucked the tender bud between his lips.

"Michael, oh my God!" she cried, her body trembling as she released a long, drawn-out sigh.

"Yes, baby, yes," he whispered before his lips and tongue continued on their loving mission, and she shattered again, her fingers running through his long, dark hair, unwilling to release him from between her quivering thighs.

As she relaxed, he began an easy stroking of her moist, velvety folds before inserting one finger inside her secret place and slowly drawing it out, making sure to brush her tiny bud of flesh before sliding it back home.

"Michael... what are you doing to me? It feels so good!"

"I'm preparing you, my darling." He added another finger, then another as he stroked her with a leisurely but steady rhythm. "You will be mine, my Angel," his deep, rumbling voice murmured, "and only mine."

"It's happening again! Oh God...." she breathed as wave after wave of exquisite fluttering pulsations rippled through her.

The picture of her spread before him in all her loveliness, her hair tangled and crying out in ecstasy, was just too much. With one last luscious lick as she melted into the sheets, he rose to his knees.

"Angel, I'm ready to take you now. But I'm going to have to hurt you, my love. I don't want to, but this will be your first time. If you tell me you don't want to do this, it's okay. I'd rather never have what I desire than to ever hurt you again."

She gazed up at him, unafraid. This was her Michael... her dark, passionate, complicated Michael... who she had loved all her life... who she'd love until she died.

"Please, Michael, I want you... no matter what."

She was startled when she first saw his manhood, honestly fearful at the thought of such an enormous thing invading an intimate part of her that no man had ever touched. But her love finally overcame her fears as she remembered the astounding pleasure he had just given her, drawing forth sensations from her inexperienced virgin body she never imagined in her wildest dreams were even possible! If she could give him the same joy, she would.

Unable to wait any longer, he leaned forward, positioning the head of his throbbing organ at her untried opening. She wrapped her arms around his neck and smiled bravely as he started to push, but as he expected, she began to struggle, her lashes wet with tears. He paused instantly.

"I can stop if this is too much for you, my love," he gasped.

"No!" She closed her eyes, panting, fighting the panic and the searing pain, but when she re-opened them, he saw the love and determination in their depths.

Clutching his buttocks with both hands, she drove him deep inside her to the hilt, her scream of agony breaking his heart as much as her tight, warm wetness electrified him!

"Oh, my darling, my baby, my Angel!" he cried out, the feel of her staggering his senses, but not daring to move, terrified of hurting her more than he had to.

So, she did it for him.

Every instinct, every nerve ending, every muscle, shouted to push him away, but instead, her hips began the rise and fall of the timeless rhythm of a man and a woman joining together in the most ancient and primordial of ways. With tears streaming, she pressed through the piercing pain, his impassioned groans satisfying her womanly soul.

Her virgin blood lubricated his path to bliss as he assumed command, each slow, deliberate stroke smearing them both with the evidence of her sacrifice as he finally claimed the woman of his heart.

He thrust again and again, feeling adoration, lust, remorse, and tenderness for her all at the same time, until at last, roaring like the mighty jaguar itself, he finally erupted, the volcanic flow of his male essence pulsing deep into her core in an unrestrained and powerful release.

She clung to him, licking the drops of salty sweat from his chin as their bodies relaxed into one another.

"Was it always like this for you, Michael?"

"It was *never* like this."

He enfolded her in his arms and rolled to his side. In only moments, they fell asleep, their lips touching in a soft caress.

The night was still with no wind, the gentle waves brushing the sandy shore and retreating with a soothing hiss. The stars were almost ready to relinquish to the dawn as they slept, an occasional ghost of a smile on the lips of one or the other the result of happy and contented dreams.

The door silently swung open, and for the second time that night, a shadowy form was silhouetted against the window, paralyzed in shock as it watched the naked lovers peacefully sleeping, wrapped in each other's arms.

An invisible tentacle suddenly shot down from the sky and viciously stabbed the still form in the back of the neck, its razor-sharp, needle-like tip injecting its vile contents deep into the oblivious host until the hovering Dark Master was satisfied.

The stunned expression on Jordan's face changed to one of bitter hatred. Defying her father's request, he'd snuck onto the property to comfort his fiancée, only to find her lying in bed with an unknown man on the very day he'd proposed to her in front of the entire town! And after all the effort he'd made to plan and orchestrate her 18th birthday party and his surprise proposal, even trading a new fourteen-foot skiff for her ring! Why, he'd be the laughingstock of Spanish Wells, mocked by every man, woman, and child who heard of his shame!

But not if he could help it...

Slipping carefully out the door and closing it quietly behind him, he vanished into the night, an ominous rumble echoing over the ocean.

"Yes," the Darkness thundered, "It was You, my Heavenly Enemy, who brought them back together, but it is I who will again tear them apart, and this time... it will be forever!"

Chapter 25 A Better Way

"Who are you?" Yuri shouted, backing away from the two strangers. "Are you spies, sent here by Chenko? Get out of my house!"

"We are not spies, Yuri," Nylah insisted. "Please, we can explain everything, if you'll give us a chance."

"I have nothing more to say to you." He strode to the door and flung it open. "Leave," he ordered harshly, staring at the floor as he waited.

"Wouldn't Sasha give someone a chance to explain? She gave you a chance on the day you met, when you bumped her elbow and spilled her tray as you passed her in the hallway."

His head snapped up. "Don't you dare even mention her name!" But he quickly shut the door.

"How do you know Sasha?"

"She's in love with you, Yuri. She stays late at the hospital every Wednesday, hoping you'll come. She has the only key to the storeroom for the medicines that her father provides to keep his workers healthy. That's where you meet to talk for an hour... and where you shared your first kiss. Her guards think she's safe, mixing powders and counting pills, so they go to Mrs. Balko's little cafe next door and drink tea."

He inched closer to Nylah. "There's no possible way you could have known that! We've never told anyone!"

She smiled at him, and the agitation and confusion in his mind somehow eased.

"You have a gift for her that belonged to your mother, Yurina, who was executed after the solar flare, when your people resisted Chenko's invasion of your town. Your father slipped her wedding ring from her finger before he buried her and gave it to you. It's a square-cut emerald in a silver band. You plan to give it to Sasha next week as a token of your love."

"Listen to Nylah, Yuri," Adam said reassuringly. "We're here to help your people, but we can't do it alone."

With an expression of astonishment, he studied them. The young man was handsome and sincere, with an aura of calm, controlled authority, the teenage girl breathtakingly lovely, with a definite air of mystery. How could they help Pavel? But after what she just told him, he somehow knew he had to take the chance.

"Tell me what you want me to do."

****

Yuri pulled his black knit cap over his blond hair as they slipped out of the house right before midnight. He had dug into his parent's closets and given each of them some black clothing to wear, any exposed white skin covered with soot from the fireplace.

Nylah looked incredibly sexy, he thought, in boots, a short leather jacket, and skintight pants, her long black hair in a ponytail that swung behind her back. Most of the women in Pavel were fair of skin and hair, and her unusual dark beauty was distracting.

"Follow close behind me and do not make a sound," he warned them. "The guards tend to get sloppy late at night and often fall asleep, but we don't want to risk waking them."

Adam nodded his agreement, and the trio silently worked their way through the streets and alleys of Pavel until they reached the outskirts of town. A lone guard tower stood at the entrance to the bridge, the lantern revealing only the toes of two crossed brown boots propped up on a tabletop, their owner obviously reclined and fast asleep.

Quietly slipping past the tower and crossing the bridge over the narrow stream of the Dnieper River, they pushed through a field of tall barley stalks until the silhouette of a farmhouse and its large, two-story barn appeared beneath the twinkling starlight ahead.

"We're late. Everyone else is already there." Yuri picked up his pace until they reached a side entry.

"I can't guarantee how you will be received, Adam, but I've done what you asked of me."

Adam clasped a hand to Yuri's shoulder. "You've done what you were meant to do, my friend, and your heart has been noted. Don't worry, I'll take it from here."

What he was meant to do? What did Adam mean by that? Did he not realize that he and Nylah could be killed by the very people they wanted to help… and that he himself might even be killed for bringing them here? The rebels would most likely see the strangers as spies sent by Chenko, just as he had, and as a dangerous threat to their secret plans. Their motivations were beyond his understanding. Why had he even agreed to do this?

Sasha's face suddenly appeared in his mind, and no other reminder was needed. If Adam and Nylah could really help end the tyranny they lived under year after year, he and Sasha could be together! And if not, what did it matter? He could never have her, and whether he died tonight at the hand of his own people or in five years from a bullet, it would make no difference. But it was the spark of hope that had made him agree.

Without another word, he pushed open the door.

The barn was filled with people, multiple lanterns casting low light on the bales of hay scattered around the floor where small groups were sitting, engaged in intense discussion. Even the second level haylofts were packed with onlookers, many of them the wives of the men below, with infants at their breast they were reluctant to leave at home, alone and unprotected. A few of the women were sitting at the unrailed edge with their legs dangling, their babies tight in their arms as they waited for the meeting to begin.

Yuri walked in first, followed by Adam, with Nylah closing the door behind them. All conversation stopped... the barn suddenly silent as a bearded, older man strutted towards them, bristling with anger.

"What have you done, Fedorov?! Who are these people? You may have sealed our doom!" He drew back his fist to strike the man he had once called his friend, but Adam grabbed his arm to stop the blow. Every rebel in the barn leaped to their feet, prepared to defend their leader.

"Yuri serves the will of God, who has come to save you, Alexei Andropov!" He released the man, who rubbed the spot where Adam had touched him, surprised by the jolt of power that had surged into his body.

"How do you know my name? Who are you?"

"I am Adam Devereaux, the Prophet of the Almighty God! He has sent me to free you from your fear and servitude to Boris Chenko and his troops at Samovar."

Andropov was silent as he stared at Adam and Nylah, then suddenly started to laugh.

"A madman! Yuri must have told you my name." He pointed at Yuri and frowned disapprovingly. "I'll deal with you later." Then, turning to the bewildered people with an amused smile, he held up his arms.

"We have nothing to fear, my friends! This poor soul has obviously wandered in from the wasteland, delusional from thirst and starvation." He waved to several of his men. "Seize them both. We'll take them to the guards tomorrow and say we found them in the fields."

Yuri stepped in front of him. "Please, Alexei, listen to him! He says he can help us defeat Chenko, and I think I believe him! Otherwise, I never would have brought them here to meet you."

The rebels started to murmur among themselves. Yuri had always been a strong backbone of the resistance. Why was he supporting two crazy teenagers who had appeared from out of the blue? Up in the hayloft, a frustrated man struggled to see better and maneuvered his way towards the front. But as he did, he tripped and fell against a woman sitting on the edge, gently rocking her baby boy.

The infant rolled out of her arms and began to fall to the floor below! But before she could even open her mouth to scream, every man and woman who saw the baby tumble off her lap gasped aloud in disbelief as the impossible... the unimaginable... unfolded right before them!

His eyes lit with molten fire, Adam's hands were stretched towards the child, suspended ten feet in the air, encased in a protective bubble of brilliant white light! As he lowered his arms, the child slowly drifted down until Nylah caught the crying baby and cradled him, the light gradually dissipating.

No one could move or make a sound as the mother shot down the rickety ladder and raced to where Nylah stood. With a sweet smile, she passed the boy to the woman, who clutched him to her chest.

Turning to Adam, she fell to her knees, tears streaming down her face as all around the barn, others did the same.

"You are truly His Prophet! We have been visited by God himself! Blessed be the name of the Lord!"

****

The awestruck rebels remained locked on the young man they now knew as the Prophet. He had given them a powerful infusion of renewed hope, and for some, an assurance of the existence of God, something that for so long many of them had good reason to doubt.

Alexei himself was not quite as eager to believe. He had seen some amazing and seemingly miraculous tricks on a trip to the capital city, Kyiv, before the solar flare, and had heard of the famous American magicians, Criss Angel and David Copperfield. He was impressed with whatever it was Adam did to protect the baby, but decided that for now, he would reserve his judgement.

Their faces wiped clean of soot, Adam, Nylah, and Yuri were seated on a bale of hay as Alexei revealed the plan that he hoped would disrupt Samovar Dam and bring the rule of its cruel dictator and his followers to an end.

"Our first move is to destroy their ability to recharge their batteries," Alexei explained. "Our technicians will sneak into the solar panel fields and sever the main connections from the panels to the wiring. The ends of the wires can then be shorted to ground, which will drain the batteries inside the dam in under thirty minutes. Chenko won't know what hit him when his entire security system shuts down! Then it will be up to our fighters to breach the outer doors.

"Yes, his troops have guns, and we have nothing but our farm tools, but we must try... for the sake of our children and our grandchildren. Every soldier we kill is another gun for our fighters... and it is rumored there is a significant cache of weaponry hidden deep within the dam itself. Once they are rendered powerless, we must find those weapons and quickly mount our own attack on the base. But until we can learn the configuration of the interior, we are hamstrung."

He drew a rough map in the dirt floor with a stick. "This is the exterior layout of the dam, but what's inside is anyone's guess. Chenko's quarters are maintained by workers from the base, and none of us have ever been permitted to enter. But the solar panel arrays are here, to the west of the dam. The military base is to the east, on the shore of Samovar Lake. They use the causeway on the dam to move back and forth to the solar fields, and to reach the west road leading down to Pavel.

"His two hundred soldiers have grown lax whenever they think Chenko and his Elite 20 won't notice. They enjoy the sensual pleasures of the Harem, as his officers and soldiers must remain unmarried, and of the bourbon, whiskey, and vodka they distill from the potatoes, wheat, barley, and rye we grow. I must say we make a decent vodka ourselves, on the sly," he said with a proud grin.

"So, you may be wondering, with the Ukraine and Russia both still trying to survive and rebuild from the grim and perilous world created by the solar flare, why would we want to upset the Chenko applecart that at least feeds and protects us from whoever else may want to invade us and take what we have? Let me tell you the truth of what occurs here.

"The guards conduct random beatings to keep us on edge, cowed and afraid. Their chosen victims are taken to the center square where the rest of us are made to watch as they are stripped, beaten, cut, and lashed, some permanently scarred or maimed. Other victims are not that fortunate... Yuri's father was beaten a month ago, but he died from his injuries."

Nylah slipped her arm around Yuri's shoulders, and he could have sworn he felt a healing strength flowing through her touch straight into his aching and angry heart.

Alexei took a long drink of water and wiped his mouth. "Last year, we refused to work for a day to protest the small amount of food we are allotted. In response, Chenko cut off all water from the dam into the Dnieper for three weeks. Have you ever known real thirst, Prophet? Your mouth and tongue swollen, your lips cracked and bleeding, your mind delirious, your children crying, too weak to move from their beds. And yet you must go to the fields as usual, under threat of being shot if you refuse. That is when the rebellion was born!

"We are watched to make sure we stay in line and provide them with their quota of vegetables, grains, poultry, pork, and beef, but we believe many of them are getting bored. A few of the more amenable guards have told us that they pass their off-duty hours gambling or betting on the winners of contests that challenge their fighting abilities. But I suppose it's a better life for them than struggling for survival in Moscow during a Russian winter.

"So, I have set a date before the end of summer to send our women and children into the wasteland late at night, with a small contingent of men to protect them, and enough food and water to survive until we send a courier to notify them it's safe to return home. You saw how lax the guards are in the wee hours... Their habit of inattention will provide the perfect opportunity for our families to slip away before we launch our offensive."

His expression grew solemn. "If we fail, our families must make a new life for themselves elsewhere without us. But their necks will never again be under the knee of Chenko."

"Can you tell me about the Harem?" Nylah asked.

He lowered his voice and patted her arm. "I don't think your young ears should hear such things, Miss Nylah."

She smiled at him, and his heart skipped a beat. "Alexei, there's nothing you could tell me that I can't discover on my own, but I want to hear your impressions of the Harem and of the women who live there. The feelings and attitudes of people towards others are important to God."

"I can tell you about the Harem," a voice called out from behind the closely packed circle of people surrounding them.

"Because I'm one of them."

****

The crowd parted as a woman came forward and planted her boots firmly in front of the newcomers. She was tall and lithe, her wheat-colored hair woven into a long braid, her intelligent violet eyes searching Nylah's face as if trying to read the secrets within. Alexei offered his seat to the woman, who nodded her thanks and sat down opposite Nylah.

"Why do you ask about us... you, who I can clearly see, is still innocent in the ways between a man and a woman?"

"I would ask about *you*, Sonya Smirnova, because your story will tell me all I need to know about your sisters in bondage at the Harem."

Sonya's lips twitched into a half-smile. "So, it is not only the Prophet who serves your God. I suspected as much. You are quiet, young one, but your own power shines from deep within your eyes." She surveyed the rapt circle of listeners seated around them and those up in the hayloft.

"Everyone here has already heard my story, but for you, Nylah, I will repeat it.

"Using the thickly forested, less traveled eastern side of the base, I left the Harem eight months ago, intending never to return. My life had become unbearable, my soul sickened by what I was doing and by what I saw happening to the other trapped and hopeless women like myself. Yes, we were kept in safe, comfortable accommodations, given food, alcohol, and good medical care, but we were nothing more to these men than erotic playthings, with no choice given as to who we served... or how many.

"Any romantic relationship that grew between a soldier and a woman was frowned upon, and if discovered, the couple was kept separated. Their cruel punishment was the soldier being forced to watch through a two-way mirror as his beloved was led into one of the pleasure suites, where three of his closest companions waited in anticipation, and was made to service them, none of them even aware of the woman's importance to their friend."

A shadow passed over her face and she grew silent. Nylah rose and went to sit beside her, taking her hand and lifting it to her own heart. Sonya did not resist her loving gesture, and the shadow gradually vanished. They sat hand in hand as she continued her story.

"Of course, many children were born of these unions over the years, although most of us became adept in clever ways of prevention. But once born, the infants were taken away, their mothers screaming in protest, never to be seen again.

"I'd had enough, but not knowing where else to go, I made my way down the hill to Pavel, uncertain as to how I would be received. I was a woman who had given herself freely to the soldiers of Samovar for food and shelter from the cold. Why would they choose to help me and put themselves at such risk... for a whore?"

"You did what you thought you had to do to survive, Sonya. The important thing is that your spirit moved you to search for something better."

Sonya looked at Nylah, any remaining barriers toppling like dominoes when she saw the non-judgmental love and acceptance in her eyes.

"I am still in love with Nikolai," she whispered. "He is a good man. We are forbidden to see each other, but I know he still loves me too. I have asked for his life to be spared..." She took a deep breath and nodded towards Alexei.

"Alexei and his wife graciously took me into their home, and after hearing my story, asked me to become part of the rebellion. But I could not stay in Pavel, where I would soon be found and executed. So I went back, telling them I had lost my way in the surrounding woods we were allowed to walk in. I am now the eyes and ears of the rebellion inside

Samovar Base, and my mission is to learn the layout of the interior of the dam.

"I have been requested by Lieutenant Baranov tomorrow, to meet him in his office before lunch... in the records room. I found a rare herb in the forest that has proven effective to put a man to sleep. That, combined with a glass of vodka, should do the trick. But what no one else but the rebels know is that I have a photographic memory. I should be able to locate and imprint all the blueprints for the dam before he wakes up. He'll believe we had a wonderful time as I take my leave."

Adam had remained silent, listening to Alexei and Sonya speak. The alluring, but inevitably false and deceptive path of the Darkness always led men to conflict, violence, war, oppression, and death. Would the rebels be willing to hear the alternative path that God preferred they choose, a path that would require faith and trust in the unseen... and not in themselves?

He stood, all eyes instantly turning to the Prophet.

"I have heard your plan, Alexei, but the Lord of Glory has sent me here to offer you a better way."

Chapter 26 The Die Is Cast

Michael stirred and groggily opened his eyes, the pale light of morning reflecting off the water. Had it just been another fantasy dream? Was he lying in his hammock on the deck of *Muchacho*, dreaming of his beautiful Angel turning to him, relaxed, satisfied, and happy, and pulling him towards her for a soft kiss that would light the fires of his passion one more time?

"Good morning," a voice mumbled sleepily, and he felt the warmth of her body cuddle closer, her leg sliding across his thighs as she nestled against him.

This was no dream! Angel was real... and in his arms!

She turned up her lips invitingly and he drank them in, savoring the lingering taste of their lovemaking, a taste he would require every day for as long as he lived.

"Oh, the way you kiss me, Michael... I can feel your love pouring into me, filling me, taking away my sadness. Kiss me again, my love, kiss me, kiss me..."

He captured her soft lips tenderly, his heart pounding with emotion. Angel was his woman now, and their new life together was about to begin! But there was something he had to do first.

"My baby, go back to sleep," he whispered gently. "I need to go up to the big house and talk to your parents. No one knows I'm here, and I want to be the one to tell them about us."

"Do you want me to come with you?"

"When a man asks a woman's parents for their blessing to marry her, he needs to do it alone."

She gave him a slight smirk. "Shouldn't you ask the woman if she even wants to marry you? This would make twice for me on that one."

"Not in this case. You're mine, and that's that."

She tugged the blanket higher and rolled to her side. "Well, tell Mom and Dad I said hi and set the date."

He leaned over and kissed her cheek. "Good girl! Hey, have I told you today that I love you?"

"I love you too, Michael..." and she drifted off to sleep.

As quietly as possible, he gathered his clothes and went out to shower. He decided to shave off his beard, using soap and a fillet knife left on a mirrored shelf in the shower stall for that purpose. Satisfied with the results, he soaped himself thoroughly, then pulled the cord and stood under the cool spray of water from the nozzle to rinse, watching the waves breaking onshore, the eternal cycle never-ending.

Bowing his head, he thanked God for reuniting him with Angel, and asked for His forgiveness for his many foolish sins in the past. He also sent up a prayer of grateful thanks for Moses, who had infused him with the courage to fight for his woman! Pulling his t-shirt back on, he marveled at the difference only one day had made in his life.

I need to talk to Adam, he thought. I'm overdue for a few of his words of wisdom that always helped me to see God more clearly, and to understand how to live in a way that pleases Him. Feeling hopeful and refreshed, he dressed and walked up the path to the big house. As usual, the door was unlocked, and he went inside.

The kitchen was packed with people from the Tribe, slicing bread, cutting fruit, and pouring glasses of milk. John was sitting at the end of the twenty-foot-long oak table nearest the screen door and heard a bang behind him. He turned around to see Michael standing there.

"Michael! Oh my God, everyone, Michael's come home!"

"My dear sweet boy!" Josey raced towards him, she and John wrapping him tight in their arms.

"Mom, Dad, I missed you both so much!" he cried, his tears mingling with theirs as they kissed each other over and over. Daniel and Alea were next, but Noah waited until everyone in the room had jubilantly welcomed him home.

Remembering their last conversation of a year and a half before, the two men smiled knowingly as they embraced, and Noah spoke directly into his ear in a low voice.

"I take it you've seen Angel?"

Michael leaned back and looked him straight in the eye. "She's mine now, Noah... since last night. As soon as my ship dropped anchor, I went to find her."

Noah nodded with a wide grin. "I would have picked you over Jordan any day! Welcome to the family, brother!"

"I figured I'd tell everyone at once. I want to marry her at home on Miracle Island, where we first met and grew up together." He smiled happily, looking like a teenager again. "I'm pretty sure we wiped out any problems we had between us. Our future is what I'm looking forward to now!"

"I wonder how Jordan's going to take this... He's really a nice guy, Michael, but he wasn't going to make Angel happy in the long run. She never showed the spark with him that she had with you. He was safe, and I think, a way to forget you."

"I'll ask Angel how she wants to tell him. But for today, I just want to enjoy being with her. We'll come up to the house when she's awake. I'll ask Mom to make her some of that potato soup she likes. I'm sure she'll be starving."

Noah met Gypsy's eyes across the room, and he smiled at his own wonderful memories of his wedding night.

"Don't be in too much of a hurry, Michael. A man only gets one first night with the girl of his dreams. All the wedding fluff can come later. A woman truly becomes your wife the second you freely give her your heart and soul, and she looks deep into your eyes... and believes."

****

Jordan scanned the shoreline across the bay and spotted the sixty-foot schooner still anchored near Gun Point. Pulling a ten-foot skiff out of the bushes and sliding it into the water, he began rowing towards it. It was almost dawn, and he didn't want to be seen.

The captain had been questioned the day before by the guards at the chained entry point, and ultimately by Mr. Curry himself, which led to uncertainty regarding the intentions of the unfamiliar boat. They hailed from Brazil and had sailed a very long way into Bahamian waters, but their reasons for wanting to dock in Spanish Wells were unclear. They carried no goods for trade, and except for the captain, the crew spoke no English.

"We have heard of your hospitable dock and its shops," the captain had said pleasantly, "and of your amenable people. We merely wish to rest for a time before beginning our journey back to Rio De Janeiro."

"You'll find safe anchorage and fresh water at Gun Point," Mr. Curry told him. "But with nothing to trade, I see no reason to permit your vessel into our harbor. Your skiffs are welcome to fish inshore or offshore as you please, but any reports of trouble will be quickly dealt with."

"So are my men and I to be denied the enjoyment of your restaurants and bars? We do carry a few items to barter for a hot meal and a shot of rum. It's been quite a while since my crew of twenty had anything to drink other than water."

Mr. Curry gave his request some thought. "No more than four of your men at a time can come ashore through the entry point, and only during daylight hours. No weapons are permitted, and you will be restricted to the public areas on the dock."

The captain's perfect pearly white teeth were displayed in a wide grin. "Bueno! My grateful thanks, Administrator. And I can assure you, there will be no trouble."

Jordan rowed until he reached the stern of the schooner. After tying up to the ladder, he climbed onboard, and was instantly surrounded by men holding machetes. He raised his hands to show that he carried no weapon.

"I bring a gift for your captain!" he announced.

"With your hands open and empty, what gift could you possibly bear?" The captain walked through the ring of his men, stopping right in front of Jordan. "And if you do have a gift, will it be of any value for the trade I deal in?"

"Would an eighteen-year-old virgin with blonde hair, blue eyes, and the full-breasted body of a goddess be enough to intrigue you?"

One black, bushy eyebrow lifted with interest. "I am Luis Escobar, Captain of *Diablo*. And you are?"

"My name is Jordan Russell. It didn't take me long to figure out why you're here in Spanish Wells."

"Oh? Please enlighten me, Mr. Russell."

Jordan held the man's cold stare unflinchingly.

"You're here for women... White. Blonde. Beautiful. My guess is that you procure them for someone very powerful in your hometown of Rio. You search for them, kidnap them, and take them back to your rich drug lord master to do as he pleases. Some vices from before the Flare will never change. And you are well rewarded. You heard about a Bahamian island where many women of that description live that would make such a lengthy voyage very valuable for you."

Escobar pondered him silently. How could this intense young man have discovered his real business? He was skilled at keeping his intentions a secret when he entered a port. It was only afterwards, when he'd finally sailed away and the girls were discovered to be missing, that his ship fell under suspicion.

But he never returned twice to the same location, and in the post-flare world, with all communication now only by word of mouth, his reputation had never preceded him.

"And what do you expect for this paragon of beauty? I find my own cargo."

"She's yours for free, Captain! I'll arrange for your men to have easy access for her abduction. My only request is that you keep me completely uninvolved."

"My, my, this unfortunate girl must have done something quite terrible to deserve her betrayal. I accept your offer, my friend, but you must tell me why you would choose to make such a deal with the devil."

Jordan's mouth twisted in anger, his eyes burning with hatred and humiliation as he remembered her ripe, naked body entwined with a stranger.

"She left me for another man!" he snarled. "And I want *him* to feel the same gut-wrenching pain of losing her that I do!"

****

Michael quietly closed the door of the cottage behind him, trying not to awaken Angel, who was still asleep and curled up in a ball.

Stripping off his clothes, he climbed into bed and pulled her back against his chest. She murmured softly and slowly eased herself around in his arms as she stretched out against him. Feeling his desire, her eyes opened, and he could see himself reflected in their azure depths.

Noah was right. This was their time. The world would just have to wait a little longer.

****

The Darkness gloated as Jordan climbed into his skiff and rowed back to Spanish Wells, pleased with the actions of his unwitting servant.

"So weak... so gullible... so easy to lead in the way I would have them go if they are not protected by the blood of the Son. A whisper here, a suggestion there, any idea I wish to inject that appeals to their human vanity and desires. This one will serve me well as a demonstration of my power to thwart His will!"

He drifted over the bay to the cottage where Michael and Angel were sleeping, their limbs tangled together.

"The die is cast, and very soon, the lovers will never see each other again for the rest of their lives!"

****

"I really should tell Bruno tomorrow that I'm going back to Miracle Island with all of you, Dad. He'll need a few days to find a replacement for me at the gift shop."

That evening, the Tribe gathered in the ocean view great room after the celebration dinner for Angel and Michael's engagement. They had finally come up to the big house at sunset, just as the barbequed chicken was being lifted out of the firepit. Angel snatched a few slices of fried plantain off a plate on the table unapologetically and wolfed them down, so hungry she didn't even care about her manners.

"Do you want him to come here, sweetheart, or do you want to go to the shop?"

"No, I'll walk over in the morning. It's only right that I give him my notice personally."

"What about Jordan?" Josey asked anxiously. "Have you decided when you're going to tell him, Angel? He wanted to see you last night, but your father told him he'd have to wait until you were better. The poor man was going out of his mind with worry."

Michael's arm tightened around her. "I never met him, but I know how I'd be feeling if I was in his shoes. Your father would've had to shoot me to keep me away from you."

She leaned her head against his shoulder and sighed. This was going to be the hardest thing she'd ever done, but she now realized she'd never been in love with Jordan. It had always been Michael... would always be Michael, and her strength and resolve came from that undeniable reality.

"I'll tell him after I meet with Bruno. And I need to do it alone. This is my mess to deal with, and it's going to hurt him badly. But the moment I saw Moses above me, I knew... God was sending me a message, and I received that message loud and clear.

"I'd allowed my life to take a turn that wasn't in His plan, and when, by some miracle, I saw Michael standing in the doorway of the auditorium, I knew He was answering the secret prayer of my heart and setting me back on course, back to where I was meant to be... with my dearest love and best friend. I'm so grateful, and I'll never stop thanking Him, even when I'm old and gray!" she uttered tearfully.

Morgan and Alea were unashamedly crying in the arms of an emotional Matt and Daniel, all four of them remembering their own story of the heartache and trials of their lives that had preceded the joy of ultimately finding the one they were destined to love.

Michael swept Angel against him as she wept, his spirit on fire. He understood exactly what she was trying to say... it had happened to him too. He had ignored his compass and strayed from his own course; into resentment at those who he blamed for his misery, into self-pity, and into anger at himself for the many thoughtless choices he'd made, using alcohol to dull the guilt and remorse of hurting Angel, and the constant fear of losing her forever.

But those days were gone for good! He'd passed through the fiery furnace and come out a wiser and better man, like gold re-liquified and refined a hundred times, now shining and pure. And Angel had been returned to him, their love, their life, resurrected by the grace of a forgiving God.

They were going home to Miracle Island, but he knew his real home, his forever home, was deep in Angel's heart.

****

As the sun rose the next morning, Angel walked down to the docks, her resignation speech rehearsed over and over in her mind, dreading Bruno's reaction to her news.

At such an early hour, the shops, stalls, restaurants, and bars along the boardwalk had not yet opened, and she was somewhat relieved when she saw the streetside door to his office closed. He was usually behind his desk before dawn, but perhaps he'd stepped away for a few minutes. The boat repair building on the opposite side of the main office was already echoing loudly with the sounds of clanging metal, hammering, sawing, and cheerful laughter. Grateful for a chance to unwind before she spoke to him, she decided to wait at the Red Starfish and unlocked the front door.

The smell of scented candles, paint, and mineral oil tickled her nose, and she felt a brief twinge of loss. She had enjoyed the time she'd spent here; the art she'd created, the friends she'd made, the classes she'd taught, her work giving her a sense of personal accomplishment and fulfillment. But this phase of her life was ending, with a new life to begin!

Stashing her backpack in the studio, she heard the entry bells chime. She came out to see four unfamiliar sailors enter the shop, one with an empty duffle slung over his shoulder.

Well, the least she could do was try to make a good deal for Bruno with these new customers.

"Good morning, gentlemen! Welcome to the Red Starfish! Please feel free to look around, and if you see something you like, I'd be happy to help you."

There was no sign of recognition on their faces. Darn it, she thought, they don't speak English. I'll try the little bit of Spanish that I've picked up.

"Buenos Dias, senors! Puedo ayudarte con algo?"

The sailor with the duffle grinned, his leering expression one of admiration and lust. "Si, senorita! Debes venir con nosotras."

Feeling somewhat uncomfortable, she shook her head with an apologetic smile. "I'm sorry, but I don't understand."

"But you will, my virgin flower." Captain Escobar stepped forward from behind his men. "Yes, you most certainly will."

****

When she hadn't returned by midmorning, Michael began to worry. Perhaps her talk wasn't going well with Bruno. But he wasn't waiting any longer.

Asking Noah to accompany him, they jogged down to the Red Starfish. The front door was locked, with no sign of Angel. Checking Bruno's office next, they found it open and went in. Bruno was sitting at his desk, going over his ledger.

"Ah, good morning, Noah! Nice to see you again. And is this Michael I see? Welcome back, my dear friend!"

"Have you seen Angel this morning, Bruno?" Michael asked, without beating around the bush.

"Why, no, I haven't seen her since her birthday party. That was quite a show, wasn't it, with that osprey flying in and disrupting Jordan's proposal! How did a wild bird like that even get inside the hall? I had planned on visiting her later today to see how she was feeling, and to find out if they've set a date for the wedding."

Noah and Michael looked at each other, now on high alert. "Would you mind letting us look around the shop?" Noah requested.

Bruno stood up. "Not at all, Noah. I just got back thirty minutes ago and haven't had a chance to open up. Jordan came racing in here first thing this morning and asked me to survey a thirty-foot sloop he's interested in buying as a gift for his bride." He unlocked the adjoining inner door, and they went into the display area of the shop.

Broken pieces of sculpture, glass, and shell were scattered everywhere! Racing into the studio, they saw the back door wide open, cans of paint, brushes, and rolls of canvas knocked off their shelves. But Michael's jaw dropped in horror at the sight of their next discovery.

On the floor was the streak of a bloody handprint.

Chapter 27 Nothing Is Impossible

Alexei's brow creased, the rebels whispering together in confusion. What other possible way could there be to take down Boris Chenko and his troops? The plan was good, and despite the risks and probable death of many of the fighters, might actually have a chance to succeed.

"I thank you for whatever you did that saved little Ivan," Alexei said. "But you are asking me to trust you with the lives of the over four hundred men, women, and children of Pavel, who Chenko will make suffer in unimaginable ways if you are wrong."

Adam's eyes began to flicker with golden light. "Alexei, do you believe in the Son of God?"

The leader was surprised at the question. "Why, of course I do. I attend the service every Sunday, and the priest prays to God for us."

Adam spoke again, his eyes locked on the man before him. "Alexei, do you trust in the Son of God, the Lord Jesus Christ, with all your heart, and with all your soul, and with all your might?"

"I try, Adam," he replied honestly. "But I am angry at Him too! Why has He put us in such danger, with no hope for the future? It is hard to trust in such a God."

"I agree!" someone shouted from the hayloft. "The priest tells us that He cares, but where was He when my daughter died of pneumonia?"

"My brother was tortured by the Elite because they were bored!" another cried out. "Where was He then?"

"Is Christ only a myth, a story meant to inspire... or is He real?" A middle-aged woman stepped forward and pointed at her empty right sleeve.

"The Bible teaches us that nothing is impossible if a person has faith. I pray and try to do as the church tells me, and yet I remain as I was born... with only one arm. Tell me, Prophet, if faith can supposedly move a mountain, was my faith too weak... or is God a liar?"

A gasp went up from some at her words, but others nodded in agreement.

Adam shook his head. "It's not that your faith was weak, Lina Pavlov. Your faith can be the size of a grain of wheat, but its power is in *whom* your faith is placed! God hears every prayer made by His people, but He answers them in His own time and in His own way. All we are asked to do is believe, trust, praise, obey... and then patiently wait."

He took her left hand, enveloping it in both of his own. "And this, I declare to you, is the day He chose for your prayer to be answered!"

Speechless, the woman could only stare. Still holding her hand, Adam addressed the crowd surrounding him.

"His Word proclaims... *I am The Way, The Truth, and The Life. No man comes to the Father but by Me.*"

His golden eyes delved into her soul. "Lina, the Lord Jesus loves you so much and has been calling to you! I know you have felt His presence before but were angry and fearful of being disappointed. If you choose to trust in Him now, with all your heart, and ask His forgiveness for your sins and mistakes of the past, you will be washed clean, and will live with Him for all eternity. How will you answer His call?"

"I do believe, Prophet!" she cried out. "I give my heart to Christ!"

Adam smiled, his eyes now a deep ocean blue, and released her. "Shall we shake on it?" and offered her his right hand.

She appeared confused before a look of staggered disbelief spread across her face. The empty sleeve on her right side was slowly expanding, fingers emerging from the cuff, and she uttered a sob as she lifted her newborn hand to shake his.

The barn exploded with exclamations of shock and praise, individuals who may have doubted before struggling to touch Adam and asking him to lead them to God!

In the midst of the mad house all around him, Alexei stood perfectly still, his mind reeling. This was no magician's trick, no sleight of hand or illusion! The Spirit of the Living God had come to Pavel, and at that very moment, he chose the better way.

****

Sitting in his comfortable swivel chair at his polished mahogany desk, Chenko raised his crystal shot glass in a toast to himself and tossed it back, the vodka warming his throat on its way down. He sighed in contentment, surveying the shelves upon shelves of books in his extensive library that contained the entire history of mankind up until the Flare.

Anya had been an exciting diversion after lunch, enticing him in a black lace bikini that displayed her large, shapely breasts, her long legs ending in four-inch black high heels. He shivered as he remembered how expertly she had manipulated the short leather whip that perfectly matched her waves of flame-red hair, cracking its tip with pinpoint precision on his body in creative ways that made him bellow like a mating bull as she rode him. The sensational and exotic Anya always made him feel twenty years younger!

He was about to pour himself a second shot when he was startled by the sound of a voice right behind him.

"Good afternoon, General Chenko."

As he spun around in his chair, he hit the silent alarm, but the gun in his hand was ready to fire.

A young man and woman stood together, hand in hand, against a solid wall of bookshelves.

Chenko took aim. "How did you get in here?!"

"*How* is of no importance, but *why* is the question you should be asking," Adam said pleasantly. "This is Nylah. May we sit down?"

Fists began pounding on the library door, muted voices shouting through the two-inch thick wood. Chenko could not understand why his armed Elite 20 had not prevented this incursion or already entered the room to protect him. Heads would roll after he disposed of these assassins himself!

He aimed at the girl and fired. She smiled at him sweetly and walked forward to sit in one of the guest chairs on the opposite side of his desk, not a single drop of blood to be seen anywhere! Was he losing his touch?

Adam lifted his hand and the gun glowed red hot, Chenko crying out as it fell to the floor, smoke rising from the metal. It was then that he felt fear for the first time in fifty years, his palm puckering with burning blisters. Adam lifted his hand again, and the blisters faded and disappeared.

"As I said before, may we sit down?"

"Who are you?" he asked, his face deathly white.

Adam seated himself next to Nylah.

"We are emissaries, sent to you by the Lord God of Heaven himself, on behalf of the people of Pavel."

Chenko sat straight up in his chair. After what he had just experienced, they had his attention. "And what exactly does Pavel... and God, want from me?" He was shaken by the sense of incredible power emanating from the young man as he began to speak.

"The solar flare was permitted to happen to mankind for their ongoing and terrible abuse of the earth that God gave them, and for choosing the Darkness over the Light. But a new world can now arise from the ashes of the old, a world that honors the Creator, and where all men can finally live without fear of one another!

"He asks you, the leader of Samovar, to find the love He knows is buried deep within your heart to stop the torture, killing, and repression of the people of Pavel. There can be plenty for all, without coercion. All of your soldiers and the women of the Harem would be more than welcome to join their community, sharing both the work and the harvest, and making families of their own.

"The Lord also asks that Samovar Dam be opened to fill the Dnieper River once more. Let its water at least flow freely enough to make the fields and gardens of Pavel, and of the many villages south of its borders, a Garden of Eden in a new world of cooperation and respect.

"God is greatly displeased with the depravity, selfishness, greed, and inhumanity He has seen here... that you have allowed to continue for so long. The Evil One, the Darkness, has taken you as his own. Your only hope is to renounce your sins and turn from the Darkness to the Savior of man, where forgiveness and eternal life is offered, if your heart is true."

Nylah rose and knelt at the side of Chenko's chair, his arm trembling under her gentle touch, her gray eyes sparkling with love. "Boris, He calls you... We have been sent to call you. He loves you, and He loves Sasha and Anya as much as He loves the people of Pavel. Won't you hear Him? Won't you help us build a life here for all, rewarding, safe, and happy?"

Chenko could feel her love vibrating in his heart. Sasha... he instantly thought, a new life for Sasha after he was gone.

"I'd like to think about this, if I may," he said uncertainly, and she nodded.

Why he was even considering this madness, he had no idea, but something strange and baffling was drawing him, and he felt a slight tremor in the solid wall of emotional ice he had slowly and carefully built since joining the Russian army at seventeen, where any weakness meant failure... or even death.

These two young emissaries from Pavel had inexplicably appeared in his library four floors down inside the dam. The Elite, with unlimited tools at their disposal, were unable to enter the room. He'd shot the girl, and she should be dead. His pistol had glowed red hot, blistering his hand, then the charred flesh had miraculously healed. And what they said about God had somehow, in some way, touched him.

"We will return for your answer tomorrow at this same hour, Boris. I bid you goodnight." Adam and Nylah both rose and walked to the bookshelf, their hands entwined.

"Wait!" Chenko called out to Adam. "You didn't tell me your name!"

They turned to face the general and Adam smiled, his eyes flickering gold.

"I am the Prophet." And they vanished.

****

"Are they insane, General?!" Colonel Caspar thundered. "Send the Elite to round them up! It's been a while since we executed anyone by firing squad. It might be exactly what the insolent peasants need to stay in line!"

Chenko had gathered his officers to tell them of the town's demands, leaving out any mention of the unexplainable events that occurred. The man he knew only as the Prophet, and the girl, Nylah, would be returning that afternoon, and he'd spent a sleepless night mulling their words.

"Would it really be so bad, Caspar?"

The entire table of men in the conference room stared at him in disbelief.

"Tell me, what are we holding on to here with clenched fists? It's been eighteen years since the flare... There is no

Russia anymore, only small communities of survivors who have learned how to feed themselves and live off the land without the advantage of electricity, as we will have to do when the batteries eventually die.

"Would it not be better to merge with Pavel now, as the Prophet suggested? There is food enough for everyone, and instead of using the heavy-handed tactics of the old regime to control the people by force, we can join with them, all of us together becoming productive workers. And you can marry and have children with a proper girl from town to carry on your names, instead of sleeping with whores."

One of the troop leaders pushed back his chair and stood. "After what we've done to them, they'd kill us in our sleep! And I am not a farmer or herdsman. I am a soldier, sir... a soldier of Russia!"

"Would they want access to the weapons as well?" another asked. "There are enough at the bottom level of the dam to conquer a nation. What if the tables were turned... and we became the slaves?"

A captain rose to speak next, with a half-apologetic smile. "General Chenko, I believe I can speak for all of my men when I say that we've grown accustomed to the way we have lived for the past eighteen years. Once we are off duty, we enjoy our vodka, our choice of beautiful women, a good meal, and some entertainment at the gaming tables. Why should I ask my men to exchange these pleasantries to labor in the hot sun?"

Chenko rubbed his gray beard thoughtfully, unaware of the tentacle of the Darkness re-injecting him with its poison.

"You all make excellent points. Perhaps I was simply in a magnanimous mood after a delicious lunch and one or two relaxing cocktails that I even entertained their preposterous demands without executing them on the spot. The girl was quite lovely, I must say, and a pretty face has brought kings to ruin. I am unhappy that they were even able to enter my quarters, but at least we are now aware that a rebellion is in the making. I appreciate your comments, but I have yet to hear your opinion, Major Nureyev."

Every head turned to the strikingly handsome man sitting quietly at the far end of the table. Major Nikolai Nureyev was built like a professional heavyweight boxer and fought like one too in the base competitions. With close-cropped blond hair, strong-boned, classic Russian features, and piercing green eyes, he was admired for his analytical thinking and excellent leadership skills and was one of the most respected officers at Samovar Base, his men loyal to the death.

"I have been thinking about the day when we lose the ability to recharge the batteries. With the exception of our weapons, we will then be on an equal footing with the people we depend upon for much of our food. When they are so inclined, our men hunt for deer and wild boar in the forest, and fish in the lake, but the cattle, pigs, goats, milk, cheese, butter, produce, and grains from Pavel keep us alive."

He realized his next words might not be well received. "It is inevitable that for Samovar to survive, we need at least a degree of détente with our Ukrainian brothers. Some minor concessions could be made without losing control, General Chenko. And you were correct when you said that the men could choose wives from the pool of available single women in Pavel, or even from the Harem. Many have expressed to me their desire to have a family."

"Bullshit, Nikolai!" a captain snorted mockingly. "It is well-known that you're in love with one of the sluts and have been ordered separated! Does your legendary dick now guide your decision-making?"

The room went silent.

The major merely smiled. “I am told that when you request a woman, Mikhail, the women draw lots, and the loser has to requisition a magnifying glass from the supply depot.”

“Enough!” Chenko chuckled as the officers exploded into laughter, knowing full well that what Major Nureyev had said was true... and he had his own secret video surveillance to prove it. Watching his officers and men engaging in sexual pleasures and perversions in the Harem was one of he and Anya’s favorite evening activities.

“We will take a vote. There is paper before you. Write either *No*, we continue our policies as they are, or *Yes*, we agree to make concessions to Pavel to prevent rebellion. You need not sign your name.”

As the vote was being taken, the Darkness whispered into the mind of each man, meeting a disturbing resistance from only one.

Chenko tallied the votes and stood, his officers rising with him. “It has been decided. The vote is 11 to 1 that we stand strong in our control of Pavel and its resources. And as a reminder of our power and authority, we shall be sending them a very special message. As soon as they arrive, I will inform their emissaries of our decision.”

****

Chenko waited in the library, puffing on a fine Cuban cigar, the entire unit of the Elite 20 standing guard, their pistols drawn and ready. This time, he would be able to see how the Prophet and Nylah had entered the room... but they’d never leave it alive. He’d display their bloody, bullet-ridden bodies in the center square of town and shatter any hope the rebels might have had for a peaceful agreement.

“Be alert, Caspar,” he said as he tapped the end of his cigar on the ashtray. “They should be here at any moment.”

But there was no response to his warning.

He glanced up to see Colonel Caspar and the Elite 20 frozen in place like stone statues. The cigar fell to the floor when he heard a familiar voice behind him.

"Good afternoon again, General Chenko."

He slowly swung his chair around, dreading what he knew he would see.

The Prophet stood exactly where he'd appeared before, Nylah at his side. "I see that you have chosen a different path than the one we offered. The Lord God, however, is gracious and merciful and extends His hand to you once again, hoping that you will now reject the evil ways of the Darkness and walk towards His forgiving Light."

Chenko smirked and relit his cigar. "Your circus tricks will not change my mind, Prophet, if that's really your name. You are speaking to General Boris Chenko, Minister of Defense, who ruled the military forces of Russia for over thirty years with an iron fist! Samovar would not even exist if it wasn't for me! We have the might and the power to conquer and control whomever we choose, and the peasants of Pavel are only kept alive to serve us. Tell your *God* that He is a fool and nothing more than a myth and children's tale to frighten them into obeying their parents!"

Adam could see the tentacle of the Darkness latched onto the ranting man before him, stimulating the most basic of weaknesses that had almost destroyed mankind... pride.

"He has already heard you, and has declared that by this hour tomorrow, as proof to you of His power, your mouth of scornful pride, as well as the mouths of your men, shall be sealed shut for an entire day. Not one word will come forth from your lips. Perhaps then, Boris Chenko, you will learn that He is the Lord of all the earth and will praise His Holy Name."

"Get out!" he screamed, "before I skin you alive!"

"As you wish, General. We will return in two days, to give you an opportunity to change your mind." Taking Nylah's hand, they disappeared.

One by one, the Elite unfroze and began searching the room for the two intruders who had appeared from out of nowhere, then impossibly vanished before their eyes while they were magically immobilized.

Caspar was in a state of shock. "Never have I seen such a thing! He had the look of a young Greek god! None of us could move at all... How can we fight against such power?"

"He's all bark and no bite, Colonel," Chenko smirked, "and is apparently a master of smoke, mirrors, and illusion. The mission is on for tonight as planned, Caspar. Let's hit them where it will hurt the most. And remind the men... only the married women."

****

Adam and Nylah sat on the bank of the Dnieper River, once a half-mile wide goliath of rushing water that was fed from the mountains to the north, now only a stream running along the western shoreline.

They had just left Alexei after telling him their offer had been refused. Alexei had been disappointed, questioning his decision to trust in the Prophet. But Adam had encouraged him to be patient and allow God to work it all out according to His will, and he had finally calmed down.

Leaning against his shoulder, Nylah quietly wept.

"Oh, Adam, does this have to happen? Is there nothing we can do to prevent it? The rebels have chosen to trust in God, but this may destroy everything."

He sighed and pulled her even closer. "God has given the Darkness permission to act as He did in the Book of Job, my love, but you can be assured, there is always a purpose for whatever He allows. And you are an important part of His plan, as well as part of the solution."

****

Disappointed after his meeting with the Prophet, Alexei walked home after work and hung his cap on the rack, the aroma of freshly baked bread and vegetable soup his wife, Elise, had made wafting through the house.

His two sons and daughter took their seats at the table, and they all joined hands as Alexei prayed, their usual ritual now rich with new meaning since each one had accepted the Lord into their hearts and were reborn as one of His own! But God's message of salvation still needed to be spread to those who had only heard about the Prophet.

Elise winked at him playfully, and Alexei knew what that private signal meant! After dinner, he tucked the children into bed with a goodnight kiss and shut their doors.

She tossed aside the blanket when he came in, her body still firm and shapely, even after bearing three children, and he knew she prayed for more. He stripped down and joined her, the candle burning with a soft and peaceful glow.

They were not alone. That night, God blessed every one of the married couples in Pavel with an uninhibited evening of passion and pleasure for a very special purpose, a purpose that the Darkness and his human servants, with their ugly and sordid intentions, could never have foreseen, a divine purpose that was soon to be revealed.

****

At midnight, the moon lit the streets of Pavel, outlining the dark shadows that crept along the buildings, disappearing into a home here or an apartment there.

Elise woke abruptly, uncertain if she had heard a noise in the hallway. Without disturbing Alexei, she got up to check on the children and closed the bedroom door behind her.

The two boys were fast asleep, little Alicia clutching her favorite tattered brown teddy bear close to her heart as she rolled over on her side. Carefully adjusting her daughter's blanket and relieved that nothing seemed amiss, she went downstairs to the kitchen for a glass of water.

As soon as she walked through the door, a gloved hand reached around and slapped a piece of duct tape across her mouth! A masked man dragged her down to the floor, zip-tied her wrists together, then lifted the heavy table leg and shoved her bound wrists beneath it before lowering it back into place and tearing off her nightgown.

The man callously laughed as she struggled helplessly to free herself. Slowly unbuckling his belt and unzipping his pants, he dropped to his knees, forcing her legs apart.

A lustful grin split his lips. "Now you will never know."

Chapter 28 Humbled

Angel turned to run, but one of the men grabbed her shirt to stop her. She crashed to the floor; display pieces knocked off their stands by her kicking legs. As she opened her mouth to scream, he gagged her with an oily rag.

She felt faint from terror but closed her eyes and made her body go completely limp. Thinking she had passed out, the kidnappers relaxed, removing lengths of rope from the duffle to tie her arms and legs, and congratulating themselves for bagging such an outstanding virgin beauty!

Suddenly, she bolted up and raced towards the studio, praying to reach the back door in time. Muttering curses in Spanish, three of the men chased her, one of them catching her by her hair and swinging her hard against a shelf, her head exploding with pain from the impact. She rolled onto her stomach, her vision blurring, and heard the sound of footsteps leisurely strolling up beside her.

"I do not tolerate disobedience, as you will soon discover," a deep, heavily accented voice told her. "Your beauty will not excuse you."

With difficulty, she raised her head to try to see who was speaking when the toe of a boot slammed into her cheek, and she saw stars. Her hand flew to her stinging face and came away covered with blood.

"Put her in the sack."

"No!" she screamed; her cry muffled by the gag. She tried to crawl away but was lifted off the floor and dropped into the duffle, unable to move at all in the bottom of the bag.

"Michael..." she mumbled, her body bouncing against the broad, granite-hard back of the man carrying her. The last sounds she heard before her world faded to black were the gentle lap of waves on a beach, and the piercing screech of seagulls greeting the day.

****

“Who was the last person to see her?” Mr. Curry asked. The Red Starfish was mobbed with horror-stricken people, the noise deafening. Angel Garner had been kidnapped, the news spreading like wildfire!

“I was,” Michael told him, his stomach churning in agony. “I was with her last night and this morning.” The men of the Tribe stood behind him as he was being questioned, sickened by the smear of blood on the floor, and what it might mean for Angel. Josey was sobbing uncontrollably in Alea’s arms, Morgan, Sarah, Pearl, Gypsy, and Essie doing their best to control themselves for her sake.

Mr. Curry looked at him curiously. “Isn’t Angel engaged to Jordan Russell?”

Daniel stepped in front of Michael. “Ed, she wanted to break it off with Jordan, but she hadn’t told him yet. She’s in love with Michael. They’ve been together at Bonefish Bay since her birthday party.”

“Ah, I see.” He thought about what he’d been told, then frowned. “Does Jordan know what’s happened?”

A shout sounded from outside, and the crowd parted as a disheveled Jordan rushed in. “Where’s Angel? Someone told me she’s missing!”

Taking his arm, Mr. Curry led him into the studio where it was quieter. “Jordan, I hate to be the one to tell you this, but it appears that Angel was kidnapped this morning.”

“How do you know she was kidnapped?”

Mr. Curry pointed to the bloody handprint, and Jordan’s eyes widened in shock. “Angel!” he shrieked. “We’ve got to find her! She’s my fiancée! I love her! Oh God, I swear I’ll kill whoever did this!” He spotted John watching him from the shop and pointed at him accusingly.

"You wouldn't even let me see her! And now she's gone!" he howled as he collapsed on the floor, weeping in despair. Rushing over to console him, Morgan and Pearl's eyes met across his bowed head. Someone was going to have to tell the poor man about Michael eventually...

"How could this have happened, Edward?" Bruno asked Mr. Curry, his eyes rimmed with red. "I was only gone for an hour while Jordan and I were looking over the sailboat he wanted to buy as a wedding gift for his bride-to-be. I didn't even know Angel was coming here to see me."

He laid a comforting hand on Jordan's shoulder. "I'm so sorry, my boy."

With his head still bowed and tears streaming, Jordan's shaking hand crept up and covered Bruno's.

"I've already ordered a search of all boats in the harbor, and my guards are searching house-to-house as we speak. Volunteers are flooding my office. If she's on Spanish Wells, we'll find her," Mr. Curry reassured him. "Why don't you get some rest, Jordan. I'll keep you informed."

Bruno helped him up to his feet. "Can I walk you home, Jordan? It's best not to be alone at a time like this."

"Thank you, Bruno, but I think I can make it. I do need to rest for a while. Then I'll join the search party."

Squaring his shoulders, he walked out to the shop, where concerned friends patted his back or stopped him for a hug. But before he reached the door, he saw the dark-haired man who had stolen Angel away from him sitting in a chair, his head gripped in his hands, crushed and broken, with the Miracle Island families trying desperately to comfort him.

Michael, they called him... Now he knew his name. He hadn't met everyone yet that lived on Miracle Island, but this man's features were vaguely familiar. Perhaps he had worked with one of the other Care Teams.

A group of four pirates had been instructed to come ashore every morning through the main entry, all legal and proper, and make a show of shopping along the boardwalk near the Red Starfish while they waited for Angel to return to work. But Jordan had stashed a skiff on the secluded northeast beach for them, where they could push off undetected with their unwilling cargo and return to their ship.

He'd been keeping a close watch on Bonefish Bay, and as soon as he saw her walking towards the dock alone, he set his plan in motion. Pedaling to Bruno's office ahead of her on his bicycle, he engaged the unsuspecting man for the boat survey six blocks further down the boardwalk. It was then up to the pirates to collect their prize after that.

Only the most observant person on earth could have spotted the flicker of contempt and glee in his eyes as he passed by Michael and pulled open the door. He'd gotten just what he wanted... and gotten away with it too.

****

Angel opened her eyes, a gentle rocking motion beneath her slowly bringing her back to consciousness. She stared at the roughly hewn beams of the unfamiliar ceiling, and they gradually came into focus, her skull pounding.

She was in the cabin of a boat! The mattress on the narrow berth she lay in was thin, and she pushed off the sheet that covered her. Relieved to see that she was still dressed, she sat up gingerly and touched the aching split on her cheek.

Why had those men taken her? And where were they going? Sniffing the air, she was reassured by the salty smell of the open ocean. If she could get up on deck, she could dive off and swim back to Spanish Wells! But how long had she been out, and how far had the ship sailed?

There was only one porthole for light and fresh air. She tried the latch, but it only opened a few inches. She rattled the doorknob. Nothing. She was trapped.

There was a small private head for the cabin. The tiny vanity had a plastic container of water, a sliver of soap, a comb, and a tattered towel. A cabinet on the wall held a container of salt, toothbrushes, and a packet of homemade feminine hygiene items. Apparently, other girls had stayed in this luxury suite before her.

She sat down on the bed, assessing her options. She didn't have the strength to overcome her captors, and what if they kept her in this cabin for the entire voyage? If that were to happen, she'd never get a chance to escape!

Oh God... Michael. They had just found each other again after so long. The thought of how devastated he would be when he discovered her missing made her bury her face in the sheet, muffling her sobs from the ears of her captors.

She heard a key turn in the lock and the door swung open. Prepared for the worst, she quickly dried her eyes with the sheet and stood, unwilling to let them see her cower.

"You're looking well, my dear. Was your nap refreshing?" Captain Escobar ambled in, his men standing guard in the gangway.

"I don't think dragging me here while I was unconscious qualifies as "*taking a nap*". My name is Angel Garner. You must have mistaken me for someone else, perhaps another girl with blonde hair you were looking for?"

Escobar removed his hat and sat next to her on the bed. She tried to get up, but he pressed her thigh down as he shook his head in displeasure.

"Do not make me remind you again, my delicate beauty, that obedience is a requirement on my ship. You will be well-treated, but any attempts at rudeness or disruption will be swiftly dealt with. Bruises and cuts will have ample time to heal before we reach our destination."

"Where are you taking me?"

He wagged his finger at her. "Where are you taking me, *please*, Captain Escobar? Isn't that what you meant to say?"

She stiffened with resentment, her first inclination to tell him what she really thought. But her anger would do her no good with dishonorable men like these... She now realized she'd been kidnapped by pirates!

"Yes, Captain Escobar, I'm so sorry. Could you please tell me where we are going?"

He smiled and patted her leg. "Now that we are at sea, it will do no harm to tell you whatever you wish to know." He moved to the chair opposite the bed, resting his elbow on the small table nailed to the floor.

"We are sailing to my home port of Rio de Janeiro, where I will deliver you to Don Carlos Ortega, the most powerful drug lord in southern Brazil. He will sleep with nothing but blonde virgins that he has deflowered himself, to be certain of their purity. He has grown somewhat tired of his current woman, the enchanting and ravishing Raquel, whom I am hoping he will pass along to me when I return, and offered me a king's ransom to find a masterpiece of femininity... a sparkling jewel... to stir his desires again!"

Angel stared at him in horror. "But I'm not a virgin!" she blurted out.

The captain's face grew solemn. "If this is true, I have been lied to, and the liar will most certainly be held to account if we ever meet again. I would be more than happy to discover the truth for myself, but unfortunately, were I to find that I had violated such a valuable vision of loveliness, I could not offer you to Don Ortega. I would then have no choice but to sell you to the highest bidder in Rio and continue my search for the woman of Don Ortega's dreams." He stood up and put his hat back on.

"I will have you examined by a trusted woman I know, who is skilled at ascertaining your present condition."

He turned to go, but risking his wrath, Angel jumped up and touched his arm. "Please, Captain, why did you choose me, and how did you know where to find me?"

He looked at her, a flash of pity in his world-weary eyes. "My dear sweet Angel, you were given to me as a gift... by your own fiancée, Jordan Russell."

****

"Every boat, home, and business has been searched, and their owners were very cooperative," Mr. Curry announced at the meeting that evening at the community center. The site of Angel's birthday party was again packed with people, but this occasion was no cause for celebration.

"However, there is an unclaimed tender tied up at the main dock. My guards said it came in early this morning with four sailors from the ship I refused to allow into the harbor, the Brazilian schooner that has been anchored at Gun Point for the last several days, and which departed at ten o'clock this morning."

Jordan leaped to his feet. "Why wasn't the damn schooner searched right away?"

Mr. Curry sighed under his breath but chose to remain calm. God knows, he'd be feeling the same as Jordan if it had been his wife or daughter that was missing.

"By the time our search was underway, they had left. And if a ship is anchored in public waters, they can refuse to be boarded, and there's nothing I can do about it."

The Tribe from Miracle Island was sitting in the front row, stoically listening to his report, but the men suspected what was coming next.

"I'm afraid to say, that in my opinion, Angel Garner has been abducted by men whom I believe are human trafficking pirates, and heading home to Rio de Janeiro, Brazil, which my atlas tells me is a distance of 4000 miles away. Even if we launched rescue boats tonight, we'd never catch them, and we have no way of knowing if they're planning to stop at other ports in the Caribbean before sailing south."

He made a point of speaking directly to the Tribe, and to Michael, causing Jordan to jump up again.

"Why are you talking to them, Curry? I'm her fiancée! She was mine! Mine!" he shouted and raced from the room.

Daniel stood up and faced the astonished crowd. "Okay, my friends, there's nothing more we can do tonight. Thank you for coming and supporting us in our loss." As the room cleared, the men of the Tribe gathered to confer.

"Something's not right," Michael said emphatically. "Of all the girls on Spanish Wells, why Angel? She left the cottage early, and Bruno said he was only gone for an hour. That's a very tight window to grab her. And how would the pirates even know where she'd be?"

"They could have been casing the shop for the few days she was with you, Michael," Matt suggested, "waiting for her to come back to work."

"This was a set-up!" Noah kept his voice low so their wives wouldn't hear. "And who do you think might have wanted revenge for Angel breaking up with him?"

"But he didn't know! She hadn't told him yet," Michael reminded them.

While they were talking, John had been rubbing his chin thoughtfully. "Well, Jordan did come over to see her the night you two first got together. I told him to go home until she was better, then I bid him goodnight and shut the door. But what if he didn't leave? What if he snuck down to the cottage and saw you with Angel? Would that have been enough to anger him?"

Michael gave him a sad half-smile.

"If he was there, he hates us both."

****

A tray of plain but decent food was handed to her by one of the guards, who grinned and locked the door as soon as she took it. She ignored the bowl of fish stew, but devoured the cassava root, vegetables, and bread.

The daily routine at sea had become monotonous as *Diablo* plowed through the waves, her bow rising and falling with the swell. Desperately missing the cleansing feel of the cool, salty ocean, Angel washed herself, brushed her teeth, and combed her hair in the tiny bathroom as best she could. She ate her two meals alone every day. She kept the cabin clean. She exercised, not only to distract herself during the long, empty hours, but to keep herself strong, limber, and fit in case the chance to escape ever presented itself.

The captain visited her occasionally, and she never failed to treat him with the respect he demanded, remembering that beneath his pleasant social veneer, he was a brute of a pirate who would not hesitate to slam her into the wall at the mere suggestion of impertinence. It had only happened once. He hauled her up by her hair, checked her over for damage, and stormed out of the room, ghosting her for days.

The worst times, however, were late at night, lying on the uncomfortable berth, thinking of Michael. He was never far from her thoughts, but in the dark, silent hours when the only sound was the creaking of the hull, Angel suffered the agony of his loss. The feel of his lips on hers, the taste of his skin, the warmth of his body as he held her, their joy as they drank fruit wine and watched the stars...

She cried out to God in her loneliness and pain, realizing for the first time that without the loving spiritual influence of Adam and Nylah, she had moved further and further away from hearing His Voice the way she used to. As a child, God had always been right by her side whenever she dove into the depths of the ocean, or when she sat in the sun on her special rock just outside of Hidden Cove. And He had given her the marvelous gifts of communicating with the creatures of the sea and swimming like a dolphin, gifts that she treasured and that made her who she was.

She saw now that her years of yearning for Michael had blocked Him from her sight, her desire taking precedence over worship of the One that would always love her in a way that no man ever could. Prostrating herself on the cabin floor, she prayed for forgiveness for her vanity, selfishness, and pride, and worshipped Him from a tearful, but humbled heart. When she finally stood up from the floor, her outer circumstances hadn't changed, but the inner woman had, feeling renewed, grateful, and full of hope!

No matter what, she reminded herself. *Trust Him, no matter what.*

Diablo's journey home was entering its fifth week after a stop in Havana, Cuba for cigars, rum, and women, and one in Caracas, Venezuela, where Captain Escobar brought aboard two more girls that fit his requirements. In his opinion, they were not nearly as beautiful as Angel, but were most definitely young virgins, and his insurance policy with Don Ortega, if Angel's examination by Felicia did not turn out as he hoped.

After the ship stopped the second time, Angel could hear girlish voices in the cabin next to hers, begging to go home, their fists pounding on the door. Then she heard Escobar's angry voice. The two hard thuds against the wall made her wince, and her eyes filled with sympathetic tears. If only she could have warned them first...

Her anger and sorrow made her stomach clench and she raced into the bathroom, vomiting her breakfast until there was nothing left to purge. Feeling dizzy and weak, she rinsed her mouth and laid on the bed.

The same thing happened the following morning. On the third morning, after flushing the regurgitated remains of her breakfast down the head, she opened the cabinet door to find her toothbrush and the salt. But as she reached inside, she suddenly froze.

The pile of homemade feminine hygiene items was still on the shelf, untouched. She had never used them since she was brought onboard over a month ago.

A joyful smile instantly lit her face!

She was pregnant!

Chapter 29 The Healer

"The mission was a complete success, General! Now the rebels will think twice before sending teenagers to defy you! Their wives will never know if the child they bear will be their husband's. What a clever way to assert your absolute authority and bring them to their knees!"

Colonel Caspar raised his glass of champagne to the crowd of men in dress uniform standing in the conference room, all holding their own glass of the cold bubbling liquid.

"To the power and glory of Mother Russia!"

With a shout, they all drained their glasses of champagne simultaneously. After pouring another round, Caspar nudged Chenko's arm.

"I know I had mine on her knees, Boris, before I flipped her over so she could see me finish! The woman was quite attractive, I must say. The most satisfying mission I've ever been on."

"You must strike at the heart, Caspar. Each one will be left with a lifetime reminder of our strength and dominance. And if the husbands choose to revolt, we will have an excuse to crush them without mercy until they learn to bow before us."

"Nureyev refused to join the mission, General. Shall I order him disciplined?"

"No, Colonel. You can't force a man to get it up if he doesn't want to. I asked for volunteers only to join the Elite."

He glanced around the room nervously. The Prophet and Nylah had told him they would return today. Would they dare to appear in a room with a hundred of his men, armed with semi-automatic pistols?

The usually reclusive Elite 20 were mingling with the men, all giving detailed descriptions of their conquests from the night before, with frequent outbursts of rowdy laughter and congratulatory backslapping's.

Long banquet tables were spread with favorite Russian foods that the men dug into eagerly. Platters and bowls of lake sturgeon caviar, venison stroganoff, borscht, slices of smoked pheasant and goose, dumplings, marinated rabbit shashlik, garlic roast potatoes, wheat rolls with fresh butter, vegetable salads, and bliny crepes were devoured hungrily, accompanied by Samovar's own premium vodka.

Chenko was starting to relax when a large white bird flew in through the open double doors and landed on the podium! The majestic creature folded its wings, the bird's unnerving black eyes staring straight at him, and he felt the hairs on the back of his neck begin to rise.

One of the men pulled his pistol. "How do you like your poultry, General? With stuffing or without?" and took aim as his companions roared with laughter.

But the gun never fired.

The men dropped their champagne glasses, the fine crystal shattering to pieces on the polished concrete floor, clutching their throats in agony, unable to speak, to shout, to scream, unable to make any noise at all!

His own throat burning with hot, choking pain, Chenko watched as a white mist arose from the floor in front of the podium. The Prophet and Nylah, their eyes glowing silver, walked out of the mist as the white bird flew to the Prophet's shoulder.

They strolled through the room of writhing men, studying each one as if memorizing their faces, then returned to the podium. Nylah took one final stony look before disappearing into the mist with the bird, but Adam remained.

"It has been decreed by the righteous and most holy God that for your refusal to honor Him, Boris Chenko, and for your proud and haughty words, you and your men will not be permitted to eat, drink, or speak for one day.

"But now, as the consequence for your deviant acts against the women of Pavel, you will also suffer terrible pain, pain that will remind you of theirs as you beat and violated them.

"I will return at this same hour tomorrow. I pray that by that time, you will have searched your hearts and sought the Lord God to ask His forgiveness for your grievous sins, and when your voice is given back to you, will use that voice to praise His Holy Name and do no further wrong.

"There can be peace between Samovar and Pavel, if you choose to relinquish the ways of the Darkness and pray to the One who is pure and good, the only One who can give you the joy of eternal life in heaven, if you seek Him with all your heart."

The white mist began to swirl at his feet, the eyes of the agonized men pleading for the same mercy they refused to give their weeping victims.

"If your leader failed to mention my name, let me make sure you hear it now," he said sternly.

"I am the Prophet, the Prophet of the Living God."

And he vanished.

****

Samovar Lake was so lovely, Sasha thought as she sipped her cup of tea on the wide balcony suspended off the inner side of the dam, the deepest waters of the lake right below her.

The multitude of raucous geese and ducks had been a source of entertainment for her over the years, the birds quickly learning that her appearance on the balcony meant tasty bits of bread were coming their way. She loved to hear them honking and quacking as their webbed feet skimmed across the placid surface, their wings flapping, in hot competition for their treat before it sank out of reach.

If only Yuri was sitting beside her and enjoying this lovely view... She couldn't wait to see him on Wednesday!

From the day of her arrival at Samovar, she never saw her gentle mother again, and her life became one of isolation and loneliness. There were no other children to play with, and the aides who maintained their quarters never spoke, although she had tried to engage them in conversation when she was a child.

It wasn't until she was ten years old that Chenko told her about the solar flare.

Elena had been impetuous, flighty, and vain, but kind to the little daughter of her lover. When her father left every morning for meetings across the causeway at the base, she and Elena would play card or board games, enjoying chess, Monopoly, Scrabble, or poker, or cook in the stainless steel and black granite gourmet kitchen with towering floor to ceiling windows that overlooked the lake, making a pan of honey cake or her father's favorite borscht until the chef and his staff arrived to make lunch and dinner.

Sasha was inconsolable for weeks when Chenko bruskly informed her that Elena had died of a sudden fever, her loss made even worse by the arrival of the arrogant Anya.

She had visited Pavel many times, riding in the backseat of a military Humvee whose engine and battery system had been modified prior to the Flare, its windows tinted black. Although never permitted to step out of the truck, she was thrilled by the sight of the vast fields of grain that stretched for miles, and the row after row of potatoes, cabbage, lettuce, tomatoes, celery, squash, pumpkins, onions, beets, and fresh herbs growing in the gardens.

But she longed to talk to the people she saw walking in the road, their hoes propped on their shoulders as they headed home from the fields. With her nose pressed against the glass as they drove through town, she watched the little children playing in the streets and listened to the women with baskets of laundry on their shoulders bantering back and forth.

What caught her attention as she grew older, however, were the bruises and gashes on both men and women, and how the people turned away when her truck passed them, many of them limping or with an arm secured against their chest, using an old shirt as a makeshift sling. The sound of harsh coughing rang in her ears during the cold of winter, and she was reminded of Elena's death from a fever.

Sasha decided that it was only right and humane to open a hospital in Pavel! She began campaigning her father to give her a large, unoccupied building and have it repaired, then set-up and stocked with equipment and medicine from the massive supply depot at the base.

She was seventeen now, she told him firmly, old enough to do something with her life other than bake cookies, study, and play Monopoly, or she'd go crazy.

Chenko could see the common sense of her request. The workers who kept Samovar Dam, Base, and the Harem fed needed to be healthy and fit to do their work, and many of them were getting older. So, with a tender smile and a hug, he gave in to her out of love, as he always did.

She pressed him to allow her to recruit any townsperson with medical experience to run it for a stipend of extra food, with the base physician, Dr. Orlov, to evaluate and treat the worst cases once a week. But it took a month to convince her father to let her train with him as his assistant.

He ordered a squad of ten armed men to accompany his daughter and the doctor to town every Wednesday. Under threat of dire consequences, the squad captain was told to prevent Sasha from witnessing any torture, and if a victim survived and was taken to the hospital for treatment, they were warned not to reveal the actual cause of their injuries to anyone, particularly Sasha, or their lives, and the lives of their family, would be at risk.

Every soldier at Samovar wore a rechargeable walkie-talkie for communication, and as long as Sasha continued to wear hers while in the field, with a special frequency he used only for her, Chenko was satisfied he could reach her at any time.

If only she could wear her blue dress for Yuri instead of her uniform, she thought as she took her last sip of tea. He loved the color blue.

She was twenty-two when they met and had been seeing each other secretly for the past year. When she asked him why he didn't want her to mention him to her father, that her papa would love him as much as she did, he was amazed at her innocence, realizing at that moment that Chenko had kept his daughter insulated from the cruelty he inflicted on Pavel.

So he kissed her, and told her that he hoped to meet her father very soon. He had never discussed the reality of what was happening in Pavel, and informed Alexei and the rebels that she was completely uninvolved with her father's brutal policies. There would be time enough to tell her the truth if the revolution succeeded.

A large white bird suddenly landed on the railing in front of her, his wings batting the air as he settled down, her cup of tea rocking precariously on its saucer.

"Well, hello there, my friend! Back again? This makes four days in a row. What kind of bird are you, I wonder? I've never seen such unusual, black-rimmed eyes before!"

Feeling no sense of danger, she offered him his favorite crust of oat bread.

The bird had first visited her a few days ago, appearing every afternoon right after lunch when she went out on the balcony overlooking the lake to sit with her cup of tea, her father disappearing into his library or visiting Anya's suite.

Today, he was hosting a luncheon in the conference room with dozens of officers and soldiers, events to which she was never invited. Too dull for you, my darling, he would tell her, and wave her away.

"I should give you a name if we're going to keep meeting like this," she told him with a playful grin.

She startled when he unexpectedly hopped over to her armrest. His beak was so close to her face she was afraid to move, but the bird only nestled down and gazed at her, as if inviting her to pet him.

"Okay..."

Her fingers lifted slowly and stroked the smooth, tight feathers on his head. He chirped softly, and Sasha could not help but feel an overwhelming sense of peace as she petted him.

"I have a book that will tell me what kind of bird you are, sweet one. I'm so glad we became friends."

He suddenly stood up, whistled twice, and flew into the living room behind her!

"No, no, you shouldn't be in there!"

She ran inside to shoo him out and saw him sweep through the maze of hallways and up a flight of stairs as she chased him, then dart straight into the crowded conference room. Sliding to a stop in the doorway, she clapped her hand over her mouth at the shocking sight before her!

Her father and every one of the hundred men in the room were clutching at their throats, many rolling on the floor in agony! But oddly, there was no sound at all coming from any of them.

The podium was shrouded in a strange white mist, with a young man and woman standing in the midst of it, her friendly bird perched on the woman's shoulder. The woman and bird turned and vanished into the mist, but the young man stayed behind, his voice ringing out with power and authority.

Hiding behind the door, Sasha listened in disbelief.

Terrible pain inflicted... grievous sins... women violated? Had her father and his soldiers done all those things to the people of Pavel? And who was this compelling young man, whose eyes glowed with silver light? Was he an angel?

Her mother had tried to teach her about God, much to her father's displeasure. She remembered very little of what she said, but the passionate words of this man seemed to ring true in her heart!

When he finally announced his name... the Prophet, and disappeared into thin air, the room faded from view as she wilted to the floor in a dead faint.

****

As if by some unspoken agreement, the married women of Pavel began to converge, one by one, at Yuri's house.

Why they were drawn there after the terror of the night before they did not know, but they continued to come despite their injuries, their black eyes covered with an old pair of sunglasses, or trying to mask their limp, or with an arm supporting a friend in too much pain to walk alone.

Yuri had already departed for work in the fields, as had their husbands, but everyone in Pavel knew where the Prophet and Nylah stayed, even if they hadn't met them yet.

They filled his house, sitting in silence, unable to meet the eyes of their neighbor across from them... but each one knowing why.

The door opened, and every woman looked up as the lovely young girl, Nylah, walked in. They were all here.

Her spirit message had been received.

Taking a seat in the congested living room, she lifted the hand of the woman sitting beside her... and waited.

"I could not tell him. I could not tell Anton of my shame." Yana began to cry, her chin dropping to her chest, pulling her collar even tighter around her neck.

Alexei's wife, Elise, took her other hand, her tears also flowing.

"Nor could I. And I have vowed that I will never tell my husband what was happening as he slept peacefully, unaware of what the brute was doing to me on my kitchen floor. I hid in the bathroom this morning until he left for the fields, so he would not see my broken teeth and split lips. I could easily explain away the blood between my legs as my usual cycle, but the ragged tearing of my intimate parts would be much more difficult to conceal."

Many nodded at her words. It was the same for them.

Her hand was quickly caught up by the woman beside her, then that woman took the hand of the next... and the next... and the next... until all the women were linked to one another in a chain, each one sharing their own terrible ordeal with their suffering sisters.

But now, they were no longer alone.

The echo of quiet sobs filled the room as the last woman finally finished her story, and Nylah rose. Their anguished faces turned to her, wondering what the companion of the Prophet would say.

"It is difficult to trust God when we do not understand why He permits tragedy to take place on earth... Why sickness ravages our bodies. Why death comes to a young child before the aged. Why one is born whole and another crippled."

Her eyes filled with sorrow and compassion.

"Why a man overpowers a woman and violates her."

Her body began to glow with an aura of shimmering white light, her eyes sparkling like silver stars, and the awestruck women gasped in amazement!

"The Lord God of Miracles offers three special gifts for you who have suffered so greatly at the hands of the Darkness."

She rose and began walking through the packed room, the tips of her fingers gently brushing each woman's cheek as she passed, a jolt of power from her touch surging deep into their core.

"The child you will bear is from the seed of your husband! You will know God's Word is true when you see the sign of the cross on the skin behind the child's right ear, and from the moment you see the mark, all memory of your abuse will be erased from your mind."

She continued her walk, the women locked on to every word.

"And to ease your spirits, if your abuser crosses your path again, he will not remember who you are, nor will his mouth ever be permitted to speak of his monstrous act."

"I believe you!" a young woman cried out as she touched the iridescent light.

"I had only heard of the Prophet's message of salvation and of his miracles, but seeing you and listening to you now, Nylah, I choose to follow the Lord!"

All those who had not been present at the barn joined the young woman in giving their hearts to God, and the sorrow on their faces evaporated as a feeling of joy and renewed hope replaced it!

Nylah returned to her chair, the shimmering aura slowly fading, and they gathered close about her.

"His final gift to you is very precious and of great power," she whispered. "A gift unlike any other given to mankind from the moment of his creation.

"He has decreed that from this day forth, no woman in Pavel will be able conceive a child unless she and the man she is with choose to do so. You must repeat the words I will tell you, but the words must be spoken by both the man and the woman before the gift of conception is given by God."

Her pronouncement was met with stunned silence.

To be able to enjoy their husbands without the worry of pregnancy was a privilege taken away by the solar flare when contraceptives were no longer available, and even then, not always reliable. And a woman would be certain that her mate truly wanted a child!

"Nothing is impossible with God," she told them. "But you must *believe... trust... praise... and obey*."

"All of us here, Nylah, have chosen to trust in the Lord," Yana said. "But we will not see the gifts you have offered for a very long time. Can you show us something now to help our newborn faith, to give us confidence in the words you have spoken?"

"You received wounds on your neck. Show them to me."

Surprised at her request, Yana unbuttoned the high collar of the blouse she had put on to hide the angry dark red bruises from Anton, bruises she'd received from the iron hands of the masked man who was strangling her and laughing as he raped her.

Staring straight ahead, she pulled the collar open and lifted her chin.

"This is how he held me down."

"I see no bruises," Nylah said softly.

"It's true, Yana!" her friend exclaimed. "They're gone!"

Cries of amazement rang out as the women uncovered their own bruises, black eyes, shattered noses, broken teeth, and bloody lacerations.

But their injuries were gone, their broken or missing teeth made whole, their humiliating wounds sealed closed, their skin unblemished and glowing with health!

As the celebration of blessing and glory to God began, Yana knelt at Nylah's feet, her face radiant despite her tears.

"Adam is known to us as the Prophet, but what are we to call you?"

Nylah smiled as the wave of joy in the room washed over her, silently praising the God of the impossible.

"I am called the Healer."

Chapter 30 Answered Prayer

Diablo sailed east from Venezuela, then curved southeast for the next three weeks, dodging a storm off French Guyana as they followed the coastline towards Brazil.

The two girls in the cabin adjacent to Angel could be heard moaning with seasickness, their captors indifferent to their misery. Angel had never been seasick, but she commiserated with the sound of their frequent vomiting.

Beyond her own bouts of morning sickness, that she made every effort to conceal from the smirking pirate that brought her breakfast and took away her plate, she was in good health. But that morning, before she had even eaten, she raced into the head and dry-heaved until she was dizzy, not knowing that her server had entered the room with her food.

A short time later, Captain Escobar burst through her door, the server right behind him. "Strip her, Umberto!"

The lecherous look on the man's face as he cornered her made her stomach convulse again, but threatened by the possibility of projectile vomit, he quickly backed away.

"Must I do everything myself?!" Escobar roared. Seizing her by the nape of her neck, he ripped off her clothes until they were nothing more than tattered shreds. She stood in the center of the cabin, naked and trembling with fear, her belly showing a slight, but definite roundness.

His eyes went cold. "So, it is just as you told me... you are not a virgin." He studied her extraordinary body carefully, then nodded as he came to a decision.

"You are much too valuable to sell to Madame Espinoza, although she is usually the highest bidder for my second-best wares, but only a few months of servicing rough, diseased degenerates in one of her waterfront brothels would most likely kill such a delicate flower as yourself, and certainly your unborn child. However, I believe this situation can be salvaged."

Releasing her neck, he handed her the sheet from the bed. "Cover yourself. We will talk." Angel wrapped herself in the sheet and sat on the bed as he ordered the server to wait in the hall, unwilling to risk his anger by speaking first.

He took the chair opposite her and crossed one leg over the other as he removed his hat, placing it carefully on the table. "I may still be able to offer you to Don Ortega, but my woman in Rio, Felicia, she must remove the child from your womb."

Angel leaped up, the sheet falling to the floor. "Never! This is Michael's baby! I'll never let you murder our child!"

Escobar didn't flinch. "You have no choice in the matter. Felicia will remove the fetus, implant you with a piece of tissue that will serve as evidence of your virginity, and Don Ortega will pay me much for such a prize. And if you value your life, you will speak not a word of what was done. He has eviscerated women while they are still alive for much less serious infractions to his ego, and needless to say, he would be quite angry with me, and that I cannot have."

Angel suddenly felt faint, and her knees buckled. Escobar caught her before she hit the floor, sat her down on the bed, and re-covered her as she slowly revived.

"I am tempted to partake of you myself, now that I know you have already been despoiled... Felicia will repair any damage before Don Ortega knocks on your sweet door. But I would prefer to seal the bargain between us without making you hate me, Angel. Rio de Janeiro is my home, and if Don Ortega becomes my enemy... well, I know you understand, my dear."

Angel lasered him with a scathing glare.

"No man who fears God would even suggest such horrible and despicable things, Captain Escobar. You will do with me as you will, this I know, but *you* must understand that the Lord has heard your words and has seen the intentions of your heart, and in Him will I trust for my deliverance!"

The captain blanched, her words sending a chilling spike of fear straight to his blackened heart. He didn't believe in God, a fictitious being meant to keep weak men under control, a myth that had certainly never earned him a dime in his entire life. No, it was power over people, and money... trade goods now, that he desired even more than the feel of a woman beneath him.

What had shocked him was the look on her face, a glowing look of confidence, strength, and power, after seeing nothing but submission since their first confrontation in her cabin. Was it simply the love of a mother for her child? Or did she truly believe that her God would save her?

"Accept your fate, my dear. Don Ortega will worship you, and as long as you fulfill his every desire, he will deny you nothing! You will have the finest of accommodations, your own servants, beautiful gowns, as well as food and wine fit for the gods! You and I will dance at his grand fiestas, and you will wear priceless sparkling jewels that once adorned the bosoms of Mayan queens.

"Or would you prefer the brothels of Rio, the remnants of your unborn child lying in a pile of trash in the street as you sweat for your supper under an unwashed, stinking body? I will allow you to choose the path you will take, Angel, but I will expect your answer before the sun goes down."

****

Angel stood at the porthole, gazing out at the deep blue Atlantic Ocean of the southern hemisphere. She had learned about the geography of the earth from the classes Josey taught the children until they were sixteen and knew the distance from Michael was growing farther every day.

She had overheard some of the men in the gangway as they passed her room saying that *Diablo* had already sailed halfway down the coast of Brazil and would arrive in Rio in several weeks, where Angel knew that her life would begin again in only one of two ways. Laying her hand gently on her belly, she closed her eyes to seek Him.

"My Lord, our baby has done nothing to deserve what is to come. I am so far away from home, and my beloved Michael will never know what happened to me, and that our love created this precious life inside me."

She fell to her knees, pouring out her heart, her soul, her very being into her next words.

"Please God, please save my baby! I can't even imagine how You would do it, but I have no doubt that You can! Whatever You ask of me, I will do, if it means that my child... Michael's child... will live! I have returned to You, my Lord, with all my heart, and I am calling out to You. Help me, in the name of Jesus, the only name that has the power to save!"

As she prayed, little did she know that chaos had broken out on deck! The lookouts had spotted a reef just beneath the surface, and the captain had ordered a rapid change of course to go around it. But as the helmsman frantically spun the wheel, a loud snap was heard. The line to the rudder had broken, and with no way to steer, the wind was pushing *Diablo* straight towards the reef!

She was jolted out of her prayer as the port side of the hull struck the reef and scraped along the jagged rocks, the wood screeching as it cracked and shattered. She jumped away from the outer wall of her cabin just in time as razor-sharp rock and coral tore through it, the forward motion of the boat creating a long gash in the hull. An outcropping of rock stopped *Diablo* cold, but the doomed boat began to slowly list toward the starboard side.

The gash ran along the portside wall, water pouring in fast from where the back edge of the reef met the open ocean. But her heart sank when she saw it would not offer her a way to escape, the opening only about ten inches high.

She scrambled to her cabin door, pounding as hard as she could. "Let me out!" she shouted, but there was no response. The girls in the forward cabin were screaming and crying, but there was nothing she could do to help them.

The water was rising rapidly, already waist deep, surging in hard with the ocean swell. Despite her gifted ability to hold her breath for long periods of time, once the water reached the ceiling, she knew that she, and her innocent unborn child, would drown.

She had been kidnapped, then trapped inside this tiny cabin for months, but still hanging on to hope. Now, with the end in sight, she placed herself completely in the hands of God. If this was His will, she would meet Him, having never lost faith and trust in His goodness and love, no matter what! And someday, she would see Michael again, and they would all be together as a family in heaven.

Angel stretched out, her nose brushing the ceiling, and as the water finally overcame her, she smiled.

She couldn't think of a better way to die.

****

Thump... Thump... Thump... Thump...

Angel could feel herself suspended in water, cool, wonderful water, caressing her skin. Was she in heaven?

Thump... Thump... Thump...

What was that noise? She took a deep breath. Oh, that was nice, she thought. It was as if she was breathing liquid life itself!

Thump... Thump... Thump... Thump... Crash!

She opened her eyes to find the source of the curious sound. The gash that had been too small for her to squeeze through was now at least three feet wide! Flipping over on her stomach, she realized she was still in her cabin, but it was entirely full of seawater!

How was she even alive?

She felt the water ripple beneath her and looked down. There was an azure blue and silver fish in the cabin with her! Wait a minute... Focusing on the large swishing tail more closely, her eyes grew wide in astonishment.

Her long, shapely legs had disappeared.

She *was* the fish!

She touched her neck with tentative fingers. Gills... she felt gills! She was breathing underwater with gills! Running her hands down her body, she felt delicate scales starting at her neck, running along both arms, and traveling all the way to her fins. It was as if she had slipped on the costume of a mythical mermaid... except she really *was* a mermaid!

Touching her belly, she was reassured by the presence of the soft, growing bump. Humbled beyond measure, she bowed her head, praising God for an astounding miracle she could never have predicted!

Are you coming out, Mermaid?

She turned to see a dolphin swimming through the gash.

We heard your call. We haven't seen one of your kind for many, many seasons. Come out of the mantrap and join us!

"You widened the hole! Thank you!" she said, speaking with her mind. "Can you help me save my friends? They're trapped behind this," and she tapped on the adjacent wall. Only moments later, frantic pounding from the other side answered, assuring her that they were still alive!

If you wish, Mermaid, yes.

The dolphin sharply swished about, its tail churning the water, and charged, ramming the wall hard with its bottle-shaped nose, and the thin wood cracked! A second dolphin swam in to take its place, and one after the other they came until the opening was large enough for Angel to enter.

She pulled herself through and lifted her head above the waterline. The two young girls were shivering and clinging to a post, the water at chest level. When they saw her, they both started to cry.

"Senorita, can you get us out of here?" the one with darker blonde hair whimpered.

The girl was speaking in Spanish, and Angel realized she could understand every word! Would she be able to speak in Spanish too?

"What are your names?" she asked in perfect Spanish. Yet another amazing gift from God, she thought gratefully.

"I am Sylvie. My sister is Solange. We are twins, kidnapped from our home in Caracas, Venezuela."

"My name is Angel, and I was kidnapped too. I've been living in the cabin next to yours, and I could hear you and your sister crying. The ship is sinking, but I know a way to get out. I need you to take a deep breath and hold it as long as you can, Sylvie. We'll have to dive underwater and swim to the exit."

"You will return for Solange?"

"Yes, of course." Angel smiled and touched her hand.

"Ready?"

With a nod, Sylvie inhaled and released the post. Angel guided her through the adjoining wall, her own cabin, then out into the ocean. The girl was hit in the face by a wave as soon as she popped up to the surface and started coughing and gasping for breath. The fin of a dolphin rose right next to her, and she shrieked in terror.

"It's alright, Sylvie, this is my friend. Hold on to her until I get back." She guided Sylvie's hand to the dolphin's fin, then lowered herself underwater. No sense frightening the girl any further by the sight of her new tail. She brought Solange up the same way as another dolphin swam in to support her.

Her tail swishing back and forth, she surveyed the wreck of *Diablo*. The hold of the vessel was still taking on water, and she watched as it gradually listed further and further over the edge of the reef, destined for a watery grave.

Captain Escobar was standing stoically on top of the hull, half the crew crossing themselves and calling out for God to save them, the other half desperately trying to salvage the partially submerged lifeboat before the ship tilted into the sea.

When he saw her in the water, his only reaction was to nod, as if he'd somehow expected to see her, but an eyebrow lifted when he caught sight of Sylvie and Solange clinging to the dolphins.

"Your God works quickly, dear Angel. You are free. But alas, you will meet the same fate as I, when the sea takes us both. We are still far from land."

A series of huge waves broke over the reef and the ship lurched and groaned, beginning a slow slide into the depths, the frantic men screaming. Angel looped the arms of both girls around her neck. "Don't let go," she told them, and looked up at Escobar.

"My God is the God of Miracles! You chose the Darkness, Captain, and there's always a price to pay."

She turned to face the open ocean, the girls turning with her, and as she began to swim away, she flipped her tail high into the air.

The last thing Luis Escobar ever saw before the Darkness finally claimed him was the miraculous sight of a beautiful mermaid, her white-blonde hair streaming behind her, her tail glittering with azure blue and silver scales, leaving the unrepentant and cold-hearted men of *Diablo* to their well-deserved fate.

****

With the pod of dolphins following her, Angel swam in the direction the Voice deep inside was telling her to go. With nothing but miles of open water before her, she was trusting in that Voice, not knowing what lay ahead, but in a way, not even caring. God had saved her... minutes after she prayed. If that wasn't enough to seal her trust in Him, nothing ever would!

The girls hadn't even questioned the speed at which she swam, nor the pod of faithful dolphins that guarded them. They simply clung to her tightly and said nothing. Angel knew they would soon need a dry place to sleep, food, and fresh water, items that were hard to find in the middle of the Atlantic Ocean. But she kept going... and trusted.

The sun was touching the horizon when she spotted a ship not too far in the distance. The Voice encouraged her to go to it, and she changed course.

The seas had grown calm, and it appeared that the ship was planning on anchoring for the night. Angel noticed that her vision had sharpened considerably, both above and below the water, and even from a distance could see sailors preparing the anchor line and lowering the sails. She had a good feeling about this ship, almost as if she knew them personally.

The lookout was scanning with his binoculars, stopped, lowered them in disbelief, then raised them back up. "Man overboard!" he shouted and pointed in Angel's direction.

The rails began to line with crewmen searching the water, and one of them saw her as she swam closer. "Yesu, it's a woman! No, I see three women! Call the captain!"

After being notified of the unusual situation, the captain climbed up from below deck and walked over to the rail.

"Well, what are you waiting for, Emilio? Lower the tender and go get them."

"Aye aye, Captain," and he began barking orders.

The captain watched as her crew rowed towards the three survivors. They hadn't seen another ship for days. Where had they come from? Suddenly, one of the women broke away, dropped underwater, and never resurfaced.

The rowboat reached the two survivors and hauled them over the gunnel, wrapping blankets around their shivering shoulders. Emilio questioned them about the third woman, but they only shook their heads. Once they were onboard, and after talking to the rescue crew, the captain went over to where they were sitting, drinking thirstily from the bottles of water Pepe had brought them.

"Welcome aboard *Muchacho*, my dears. I am Captain Rafia Gonzalez. You are safe now, and I will do all I can to get you home. Caracas, I am told? You were kidnapped?"

"Si, Captain. Thank you for your kindness! The pirates that kidnapped us sank on a reef, and another girl who had also been kidnapped pulled us out of our cabin before the ship went down. She brought us to you... carried us on her back through the water."

Now that was unexpected. "Where is she? We could see her with you, and then she vanished. Did she drown before we could reach you?"

"No, Captain. Just before she left us, she said she had to go home to Spanish Wells, an island in the Bahamas, where her lover waits for her, a man named Michael."

Rafia startled, her face growing pale. "How did she plan to get there? My ship would have taken her."

Sylvie and Solange glanced at each other. If they told this woman the truth, would she believe them?

"She was a mermaid, Captain, a real mermaid!" Solange whispered, her voice full of wonder. "She carried us for many miles without tiring, with a pod of dolphins following as our guard. She was so beautiful, with long blonde hair and eyes the color of a tropical sea, the scales of her body and tail matching her eyes... and her name was Angel!"

"Get these girls more water, Pepe! They're dehydrated and delirious. Then give them some hot food and bunk them in my cabin for tonight. I'll sleep in the lounge and speak to them tomorrow when their minds have cleared."

The deck emptied rapidly as the girls were carried below. When she was finally alone, Rafia strolled to the rail and gazed out over the water. Was it only her imagination... or did she just see a graceful blue and silver tail rise up out of the sea and slap the surface as if in farewell?

She couldn't help but smile.

"Ah, Miguel... so you did catch your mermaid after all."

Chapter 31 Tears Of Joy

The fog started to lift as someone gently patted Sasha's cheek. She quickly sat up, but weakly fell back again, her heart pounding wildly. Major Nureyev was hovering above her, a look of concern on his handsome face.

"Thank you, Major," she murmured. "I'll try to sit up now, but perhaps a bit more slowly." Sasha pushed herself off the floor, Nureyev's strong arm helping her.

"What happened here, Miss Chenko?" he asked. "I came in to find you lying unconscious on the floor, your father and the officers and men in the conference room writhing in pain and unable to speak. Except for myself, every soldier at the base is also mute, but not in pain, and for some reason, I was the only one able to walk past the gates."

She hadn't imagined it! What the Prophet had decreed had taken place! "If you could please take me to the kitchen in my quarters, Major, I'll tell you what I know."

The act of serving him a cup of tea calmed her down, and she told him every detail of what she heard and saw as they drank, even the story of her friendly bird, who had joined the Prophet and his companion as they vanished into the mist.

Nicholai listened without comment, her remarkable story difficult to deny after what he himself had just observed in the conference room. The powerful words of the Prophet impacted him greatly, especially since he was aware of what Chenko and Caspar had been planning, a night mission so shameful, so degrading, that he'd considered deserting his post and taking his chances in the wilderness.

But he'd have to find Sonya first... He could never leave her behind.

Sasha leveled him with an accusing glare. "Were you aware of what was being done to the people of Pavel all these years, Major?"

He refused to lie. "I was, Miss Chenko. How could I not be? My troop is in charge of monitoring the village at night, so we are less involved with the "disciplinary" measures that are doled out. But I make no excuses. It was not my choice to run Samovar in this manner, but I am a soldier of Russia, and I must obey my commander, even if I do not agree with him."

He then revealed to her the many orders that her father had given regarding Pavel over the years, orders that broke her heart, tears of distress and anger clouding her eyes.

Nureyev's position was completely understandable. He had tried to mitigate the effects on the people as much as possible, but how could she fault him for doing his duty, at the risk of court marshal and the firing squad? But there was someone else she found herself angry with, someone who should have been honest with her from the very beginning.

"May I call you Nikolai, Major? As it appears we alone are exempt from God's wrath, perhaps we should be friends."

He gave her a slight bow. "I would be honored... Sasha," he replied with a smile. "You have grown up to be a lovely and compassionate woman."

"Thank you, but I can assure you my compassion does not extend to murderers, torturers, and rapists." She rose, and he rose with her.

"Nikolai, could you please drive me to Pavel?"

****

Yuri swung his scythe, the wheat falling at his feet, the gatherers following behind him. He had stopped to wipe his brow when he heard the alert.

"Soldiers! A Humvee is approaching our field!"

Grateful for the warning, he resumed cutting. It was asking for the lash to be found loitering.

A rustling in the wheat ahead of him caught his attention, his surprise complete when Sasha burst through the stalks and marched right up to him, a tall, striking soldier following close behind. He had never seen her so angry!

"You never told me, Yuri! You never told me what my father was doing to Pavel... the beatings, the rationing, the horrible deaths!" She refrained from mentioning the mass rape until she'd had a chance to talk to him alone.

"Year after year, so much suffering and pain, and all the while, my father kept his despicable acts from me! I've been drinking tea and eating the finest of food that your people have been slaving for with their sweat and blood!" She burst into tears, and the major came forward to comfort her.

"Don't touch her!" Yuri shouted, not caring if he was shot dead on the spot, and pulled her into his arms as the major unexpectedly stepped back.

"Sasha, my darling, I wanted to tell you, but I couldn't! If I had made any slip of the tongue about our plans, we were worried that your father would somehow hear of it."

She pushed him away, now even more irritated. "Slip of the tongue about what plans, Yuri?"

He glanced at the major. "I can't tell you. Not with him here."

"I'm not what you believe, young man. My name is Nikolai Nureyev. Sasha will tell you what happened, and that you can trust me. Everything has changed. When you wish to talk to me, let Sasha know, and it can be arranged."

He bowed to Sasha. "I will wait for you at the car." Tipping his hat to Yuri and the other workers, he walked back into the wheat.

The workers were stunned. An officer of Samovar had left Yuri alive after touching General Chenko's daughter? And telling them he could be trusted? Ever since the arrival of the Prophet, their world had been turning upside down!

She took his arm, his lapses forgiven. "Yuri, my love, take me to your home, and tell all your friends to take the rest of the day off." Seeing their cautious expressions, she smiled reassuringly. "There is no reason to fear... Other than Major Nureyev, every soldier in Samovar has been incapacitated until two o'clock tomorrow afternoon."

She looked him straight in the eye. "By a man who calls himself the Prophet."

****

Yuri opened the front door of his house, letting Sasha and Major Nureyev walk in before him. As he led them into the kitchen, Sasha paused in the doorway.

"Why Yuri, what a nice, clean home you keep! And who made these lovely loaves of fresh bread on the counter?" She leaned over to sniff the delicious aromas of wheat, butter, and honey coming from the six crusty tops.

He didn't know what to say. It was as if a hundred fairies had entered his house, cleaned it from top to bottom, and left him a gift to boot! "Uh, my neighbors are good to me."

She grinned at him and winked. "You could use a wife."

Nikolai's mouth quirked into a half-smile. These two were perfect for each other!

Sasha cut off three thick slices of bread and spread the soft interiors with scoops of the butter she found sitting in a bowl of cool water. Making a plate for each of them, they sat at the kitchen table and ate as she relayed the events of that afternoon to Yuri. But she was taken aback to discover that her astonishing story came as no surprise.

"Yes, we have all met the Prophet. He came to us several days ago and set us on a new course of change, one that does not involve our original plan of insurrection and violence. He has already met with your father twice, to encourage him to join forces with us and create a better life here for everyone, villagers and soldiers alike. Each time, General Chenko has either delayed his answer or outright refused his request for equity and peace."

He lifted her hand to his lips and kissed it. "If you truly trust Major Nureyev, I will share with you both anything I know."

Sasha looked at Nikolai, his face unreadable. "I do trust him, Yuri. He's a good man."

"The Prophet makes one feel like that too, both he and his companion, Nylah. But there was no bird with them that I saw."

"Nylah?" she asked. "Is she the dark-haired woman who travels with the Prophet?"

"Did someone mention my name?"

They all turned to see Nylah and Adam in the doorway, the bird on Adam's shoulder. Moses suddenly lifted off and flew to Nikolai's arm.

"Moses appears to approve of you, Major Nureyev," Adam said. "He's a very special osprey."

"How do you know my name, sir?"

Yuri took a bite of his bread and waved his hand. "People need to stop asking him that." He swallowed the delicious morsel. "He's the Prophet, for heaven's sake!"

Nikolai immediately stood, and Moses flew to Nylah. "You are the one who cast the spell on the soldiers of Samovar?"

"It was no spell, Nikolai. They were judged by the God of righteousness and found wanting. But they will all have a final opportunity to receive the gift He offers freely, if they choose to believe in the name of His Son."

"Why was I not affected?"

Adam approached him until they were face to face. "I think you already know," and gripped his hands.

Nikolai paled and began to tremble. Adam's eyes flared with golden light and slowly, slowly, Nikolai dropped to his knees, a distant look in his eyes.

"I see Him, Prophet!" he whispered. "He tells me I am one of His own beloved people, chosen by Him from before the dawn of time! I hear and I believe the Word of Truth from the lips of the Master Himself!"

Bowing his head as the Spirit of God entered his willing and repentant heart, Major Nikolai Nureyev, a decorated officer of the Russian Army, received the gift of eternal life from His Lord and Savior.

****

When Nikolai began to weep in Adam's arms, Sasha wept with him, but their tears were tears of joy! As the Prophet led Nikolai to faith in the Lord, Sasha remembered his powerful words to the men in the conference room. Nylah took her hand, and Sasha felt a love pour into her that she hadn't felt for many years. For the first time, she silently prayed to the God she remembered from her sweet and gentle mother.

Her own faults and sins, as small or inconsequential as they may have appeared to others, were still sins in the eyes of a perfect, righteous, and holy God, and as she tallied them, they felt like lead weights crushing her very soul. Even her many good deeds could not satisfy God's most important requirement, belief in His Son, Jesus. But the moment she confessed, a sense of God's forgiving love filled her, and she felt joyously reborn, the weights gone forever!

The Prophet encouraged them both to read the Bible, God's own Word and instructions to His people, and spoke to them about how to walk in the ways that pleased Him. He and Nylah then departed, taking the osprey, Moses, with them, and Sasha, Yuri, and Nikolai sat down together once more in the kitchen.

"Yuri, I'm leaving Samovar. May I stay here with you?"

He was surprised by her request, but he couldn't deny it was his dream come true! "Of course, my darling. But won't your father send troops to take you back?"

Nicholai nodded his agreement emphatically. "He'll have Yuri taken into custody, Sasha. You'll never see him again."

But she was unrelenting. "I plan to live in Pavel from now on, but I must return to the dam at least for tonight. I have to be there tomorrow when the Prophet arrives to hear my father's decision, and then I need to speak to him myself," she said, the firm, resolute look on her face reminiscent of the general.

"I'm going to make sure that my father sees the light, if it's the last thing I do."

Chapter 32 The Pod

With her charges safe on *Muchacho*, Angel dove to join the pod of dolphins waiting for her below. The rush of saltwater across her newly created gills was exhilarating, life-giving oxygen pouring into her lungs! She felt so free!

Twisting and turning joyfully, her arms stretched out like wings, her long hair streaming behind her, she experimented with her amazing new appendage, discovering she was able to swim at uncanny speeds and change direction in fractions of a second. Her hearing was so acute she could hear the swish of the dolphins' tails and the scraping sound of small bottom rocks shifting in the push of the current. The ocean had become her highway to distant lands anywhere on the globe!

But right now, there was only one place on earth she was determined to go. Back to Michael... because wherever he was, was her home.

Mermaid, where is your destination? The female dolphin she had spoken to before swam up alongside her.

"What is your name, my friend?" Angel asked.

I am Sola. Do you have a name, Mermaid?

"My name is Angel. I'm trying to find my way home, Sola, er... to my birthing grounds, and that place is very far from here. Is there any way you can help me?"

We follow along the unswimmable hardness to find our food. Sometimes we swim to the cold, sometimes to the warm. Which way do you want to go?

Angel considered what the dolphin said. In the southern hemisphere, *to the cold* must mean swimming towards the South Pole, and *to the warm* towards the Equator and the Caribbean. The unswimmable hardness? Ah, that had to be the coastline!

"I need to swim to the warm, Sola. Can you guide me?"

Our food now moves to the warm, where we go to birth our calves. You may join us if you'd like, Angel!

The rest of the dolphins surrounded them, gently rubbing up against Angel as they ingrained her scent, her shape, and her sounds. Once they finished their perusal, she was an accepted member of the pod.

Let's go! Sola clicked and the pod fell in behind her. Angel took her position at the rear, not wanting to offend anyone with higher status. She found it easy to maintain their pace, resting when they rested, and engaging in conversations with other members of the pod. But when they located the school of mahi-mahi and began tearing into it, Angel held back.

Angel, you must eat! Sola swam up with a mahi between her teeth and offered it to her.

"I... I don't eat creatures of the sea, Sola. I just can't. I love them."

The dolphin gazed at her with kind eyes. *It is the way of the sea, Angel. We speak to them too, but we all understand that to live, we must eat one another. We have done so from the beginning, and it is not forbidden. It is the only way you will reach your birthing grounds.*

Her face paled at Sola's last comment. She raced into the frantic school and snatched a mahi. Without any hesitation at all, her jaws opened to bite, and as she did, rows of sharp, pointed teeth emerged from her gums! She tore off a piece of its flesh and began to chew, the delicious fresh flavor of raw mahi melting in her mouth! She took bite after bite until even the bones were gone, and when she was finished eating, the sharp teeth retracted into her gums.

They loved eating lobster and fish on Miracle Island, and so had she, before she gave it up as a young child for her conscience's sake. But there was nothing more important than keeping her baby alive and healthy, and if it took eating the creatures of the sea to do it, then sushi it would be! With a grateful smile at Sola, she darted back into the school.

****

The pod kept moving north, veering in and out from the coastline as they followed the teeming schools, and when the pod came up for air, Angel did too. She didn't need the air like they did... she was quite fine living underwater. But whenever she rose above the surface, her human lungs allowed her to breathe the air, and she was able to enjoy the sight of sky, clouds, sun, stars, and moon once again.

The first time she saw a shark, she ducked behind a reef, not sure of a mermaid's place in the food chain. She'd been friends with Charlie and his family a long time ago, but for the baby's sake, she decided to be cautious. Sola eased her mind when she told her that mermaids need not fear any predator but could not explain why this was so.

They occasionally saw a ship, the curious pod swimming over to investigate, where they would entertain the thrilled passengers and crew by leaping high out of the water and spinning like tops, or dancing backwards on their tail above the water, flaunting their amazing abilities in front of their less aquatically inclined viewers.

During these playful performances, Angel stayed out of sight, watching from underwater until Sola finally decided she'd had enough fun and they continued on their journey. But one time, as they were passing the delta of the Amazon River, discovery had been unavoidable.

Angel had briefly veered away from the pod to collect a large lobster from a hole at the base of a deep coral reef. On her way back to the pod, she was surprised to find herself caught in a net that was being hauled in by a lone fisherman in a skiff, the man ecstatic over the heavy weight of his catch.

As he pulled with all his might, he was impatient to see what kind of monster he had captured, anticipating the meal his wife would cook for him and his children.

He was appalled to see a head of blonde hair coming out of the water! Worried that a woman had drowned in his net, he was relieved to see an indescribably beautiful girl smile up at him. “Senorita, I am so sorry! Please, let me help you into the boat!” he cried out.

But the vision only shook her head as she worked herself free. Then, to his utter amazement, she flipped out of the tangled mess, a tail where her legs should have been! As he sat in stunned silence, a giant lobster flew out of the water and landed in his boat! When he told the incredible story to his wife, she accused him of trading his entire catch of fish for a bottle of rum.

The pod had been moving steadily for two weeks, and as they curved west towards Venezuela, Angel knew she’d need guidance from Sola, the time of parting coming up fast.

“I must leave you soon, my friend,” Angel told the sad-eyed dolphin, “but I’m not sure how to find my way.”

Don’t go, Angel. Stay with us. My own calf is ready to be born. There is a safe place for us both I can show you.

Angel had to smile. “I wish I could, Sola! But my birthing grounds and my mate are past the warm and towards the other cold, a direction I call north.”

The dolphin swam around her in a slow circle as Angel gently stroked her smooth skin.

As you wish, Angel. The push of the water will want to take you where I am going. But you must resist it. Feel the push here, and she nosed Angel’s right hand, *and swim in the direction of here,* and she nosed Angel’s head. *When you first see unswimmable hardness, or land, as you call it, find the path of water in between. Then the push will take you wherever you want to go.*

Angel tried to visualize what Sola had told her. Once they reached Venezuela, she would have to swim as hard as she could through the west-flowing current and find the strait between Cuba and Haiti. As soon as she entered Bahamian waters, she would only be days away from Michael's arms!

But where was he? Had he remained on Spanish Wells to continue the search? Or had he finally given up hope and returned to Miracle Island? She'd never know until she got to Spanish Wells, because that's exactly where she was going... to confront the man who had tried to ruin her life, her old fiancée, Jordan Russell.

Chapter 33 Freedom

Anya stood under the nozzle of the shower, the steaming hot water washing away every trace of Boris Chenko from her body. If only it could wash him away from her mind and her memories too, places the water couldn't reach...

She stepped out of the marble shower and wrapped herself in a thick white towel. The shower alone was bigger than the wooden hovel she had lived in with her parents at the edge of the lifeless wilderness, where they had survived by begging, stealing, and scrounging for food after the solar flare turned their hometown of Kursk into a graveyard.

Her mother was the first to perish, the bitter cold of winter more than her thin, weak body could endure, having secretly shared half of her rations with her eleven-year-old daughter. When Anya turned sixteen, her father sold her to a band of traders out of desperation. The five men traveled along the border of the wilderness in a horse-drawn trailer, negotiating trades for food and necessities with the small communities of survivors they encountered.

They paid whatever he asked for the beautiful young girl, and took her straight to their trailer, kicking and screaming, where the inexperienced and innocent Anya learned what it meant to be a woman in the worst possible way. After an agonizing miscarriage four months later, lying on the floor of the filthy trailer as her abusers laughed and drank at the fire outside, her damaged womb never conceived again, and she began waiting and watching for a chance to escape.

By chance, the traders came across a military base near the Ukrainian border called Samovar. They were stopped at the entrance by soldiers with high-powered weapons, but as the trailer struggled to turn around, Anya flung open the door and raced towards the soldiers, her round bosom displayed in a low-cut blouse, her long legs revealed by a mini-skirt, her flame-red hair falling in waves down her back.

Colonel Caspar was entranced by her beauty and ordered the gates opened. She immediately ran to him, threw her arms around his neck, and kissed him. Despite the traders shouting curses and demanding the return of their property, Caspar ordered them driven off. She became a woman of the Harem, but Caspar managed to keep her to himself for a month until Boris Chenko caught sight of her.

The day the general unexpectedly called for her, she knew it was a golden opportunity! She'd heard that he respected strength, cleverness, and daring, and that his relationship with Elena had cooled, so she planned accordingly.

When she entered his chambers, he was pacing back and forth, his eyes wild, his forehead beaded with sweat, having just strangled Elena to death. Dressed only in a short black trench coat and spike heels, her flaming red hair untamed, her eyes exotically lined in black, and her lush lips painted blood red, she strutted right up to him and slapped him as hard as she could!

Roaring with lust, he ripped her trench coat apart, his once dormant member straining towards her. She then proceeded to do everything she had learned... and so much more. When he finally left, Anya Kournikova was escorted to Elena's luxurious quarters, and had been living there ever since as the Queen of Samovar Dam.

She finished drying herself off and went into her wardrobe to select her ensemble for the afternoon. Boris was hosting a luncheon with a hundred of his men in the conference room, and although he kept her from socializing with the officers and soldiers, he liked to see her dressed like the wife of a rich Russian oligarch. She was, however, permitted to watch the proceedings from the sixty-inch-wide screen in her bedroom, fed by the cameras positioned in every room at both the dam and the base, which served as a source of information and entertainment while she waited for Chenko's summons.

Tossing her clothes over a chair, she flipped on the screen and adjusted the input to the camera in the conference room. What she saw made her drop to the bed, her ruby lips parted in shock!

Boris, Caspar, and every soldier in the room were rolling on the floor, clutching their throats in pain! An incredibly handsome young man and a beautiful girl watched them, a white bird sitting on the girl's shoulder. But her mind reeled in confusion when the girl and bird vanished into a white mist!

She fumbled about for the remote and quickly turned up the volume as the young man began to speak. She listened intently as he admonished them for harming the women of Pavel, and that they would be incapacitated for twenty-four hours with intense pain and the inability to speak. He also spoke about a righteous God, who had judged them for their crimes. After he told them his name, the Prophet, he walked into the mist, and when it finally cleared, he was gone! The room suddenly began to spin, and she fell back on the bed.

When she awoke, the men were still flailing on the floor, the bedside clock telling her she had been unconscious for thirty minutes. She switched cameras to scan the room for the Prophet but stopped at the view facing the doorway.

Boris' daughter, Sasha, was lying on the floor in a faint and was being revived by Major Nureyev. As he helped her to her feet, he told her that all the soldiers at the base, except for himself, were unable to speak or pass through the gates. When they left the area, she found them again in the kitchen, where Sasha was making him a cup of tea. Were they having an affair? That bit of information could be useful...

She watched and listened as they spoke. No, it wasn't that, but Nureyev was telling Sasha the unvarnished truth about

Pavel, and she asked him to drive her there! Was something happening that could possibly jeopardize her comfortable life here? Despite having to deal with Chenko's perversions, it was better than the horrible existence she'd come from.

Were the women of the Harem affected the same as the soldiers? She checked the cameras in their central lounge, cafeteria, and in each of their rooms. Nothing seemed out of the ordinary. But since all the soldiers were incapacitated, and with no keys to a Humvee, she decided to take the rare opportunity to walk over by herself.

She was occasionally escorted to their compound to visit with the two good friends she had made since she arrived, Sonya and Kira, the only women that Anya felt were worthy of her time and attention. Sonya had suffered terribly after being separated from Major Nureyev. Anya had envied their love, bound to Chenko as she was, and under threat of a merciless death if she strayed. But he was old, and she was still young! After he died, and another high-ranking officer took control of Samovar, she would charm him as well, without the constant fear of execution hanging over her head if she was even seen talking to one of the officers.

Casually dressed in stretch leggings, a comfortable top, and her gym shoes, she peeked into the conference room, unnoticed by Chenko, who was lying under a banquet table, curled into a ball. After a quick stop in the video control room, she rode the elevator to the main level, hit the button that automatically opened the heavy steel entry doors, and started a slow jog across the paved causeway of the dam towards Samovar Base. She always enjoyed the breathtaking vistas that extended for miles beyond the town of Pavel to the south and Samovar Lake to the north.

Without Chenko or an escort by her side for the first time in years, she finally felt free!

****

"You've refused every appointment request for two days, Sonya, claiming you're still sick." Kira handed her a glass of lemonade, giving her a disapproving look. "After cancelling twice with Lieutenant Baranov, he demanded that Dr. Orlov examine you. If he says you're not really ill, they'll send you into the wilderness. What's going on with you?"

Sonya sighed and stretched out on the bed. After accepting the Prophet's call to salvation on the night of his miracles, she shuddered at the thought of returning to the Harem, with its sordid expectations. But trusting in the Prophet's promise to lead Pavel to freedom, she went back, feigning illness as her excuse to cancel her appointments.

A loud knock startled them both.

"Still faking it, Sonya?" Anya pushed open the door and strutted in, claiming the chair next to the bed and propping both feet up and across Sonya's legs.

"Oh, I could tell, but I certainly can't blame you. If I had an appointment with Baranov, I'd publicly announce that I had a contagious and incurable disease!" Seeing their nervous glances at each other, she grinned.

"Don't worry... I disconnected the camera and audio to your room. Are you her servant now, Kira? Well then, bring me a drink too, but make it something a little stronger!"

Kira snorted. "Fetch it yourself!" and plopped down at the foot of the bed as they all laughed.

"What are you doing here, Anya?" Sonya asked. "Isn't this about the time that his majesty needs tending?"

"Yes, but not very observant, are you? Anyone notice yet that none of the soldiers can speak a word since about, oh, an hour ago? Or that none of them can physically leave the base, or eat and drink?" She couldn't help but laugh at the confused expression on their faces.

"At two o'clock this afternoon in Boris' conference room, a man who calls himself the Prophet, a woman, and a white bird appeared out of nowhere as he was entertaining a hundred soldiers. The woman and bird disappeared, but the Prophet proclaimed that for twenty-four hours, every single one of the cocky bastards will be in horrible pain as God's punishment for something they did to the women in Pavel! Then, the droolingly gorgeous Prophet walked into a white mist and vanished! I saw it all on camera, and I brought the disk to show you!"

Sonya leaped out of bed to grab her remote as Anya loaded the disk, and they watched the incredible footage from start to finish. She froze when Nicholai came into view, breathless as he and Sasha Chenko drank tea and talked for a while before leaving for Pavel together.

Kira looked fearful when the screen went blank. "Should we of the Harem be worried? Would this Prophet punish us for our sins? If many of us hadn't agreed to join the Harem, we'd be dead. What else could we have done?"

"If he can control dozens of highly trained Russian soldiers with weapons, what else is he capable of?" Anya asked with a frown. "And what does all of this mean for me?"

Sonya stood up, re-energized and on fire, her jacket already swinging around her shoulders. "I'll tell you what it means, Anya, what it means for all of us!

"It means freedom!"

****

Sonya left the Harem compound, immediately noting the absence of any guards as she headed towards the gates. They were probably in a panic over their sudden inability to speak, eat, or drink, she chuckled, and standing in a long line at Dr. Orlov's clinic, discipline and rules forgotten because of the bizarre disorder that had struck them all. For the first time ever, the entry gate into Samovar Base was left unguarded. She broke into a run across the half-mile long causeway, then headed down the road to Pavel.

She was recognized by many of the rebels, surprised to see her in daylight and dashing through their streets. But she continued her search for the Humvee that Nikolai would have driven to bring Sasha Chenko into town, finally locating it at the end of a row of homes not too far from the bridge.

Leaning on the picket fence to catch her breath, she was about to climb the stairs to knock on the door when she saw it open. Sasha, Nikolai, and Yuri Fedorov came out, but as soon as Nikolai saw her, he stopped in his tracks.

"Sonya!"

He turned to Sasha and Yuri and spoke quickly. They went back into the house and closed the door as he came rushing down the steps. But before she could speak, he pulled her hard against him, murmuring her name before covering her lips with his own. She cried out under his mouth, and they melted into one another, their tears mingling as they kissed.

"I can't believe you're here, my darling! But how did you find me? Come... come inside. There are people I want you to meet."

"Oh, Nikolai, so much has happened!" She clung to him, searching his face. "But I must ask... do you still love me?"

He stroked her hair tenderly as his other arm held her like iron. "I never stopped loving you, Sonya."

Nothing more needed to be said, their passion burning in their eyes. It had been so long...

"Nikolai, bring her in. Sasha is asking to meet her," Yuri called out from the doorway.

Their eyes still locked, Nikolai smiled. "Our world changed forever today, my love, and more is yet to come! I can only hope you'll believe my story."

"I have already met Yuri. We have a few stories too, but at this point, I'd believe anything you told me!"

****

Sasha led Yuri, Nikolai, and Sonya into Samovar Dam, where Sasha invited them all to spend the night before the Prophet, Nylah, and Moses returned the next afternoon. But before showing them to their suites, she led them to the two-way mirror viewing room attached to the conference room, where she and Anya would occasionally be invited to sit and observe important events.

Seeing it with their own eyes was even more horrendous than on the disk! Unable to function from the constant and excruciating pain, not one man had been able to leave the room, hard-boiled career officers so completely exhausted that their waste-smeared bodies quivered like jello.

Sasha finally said what they were all thinking.

"According to the Prophet, this was the judgement of God for their terrible crimes against the women of Pavel, and for the sin of pride, especially for my father. Although we don't know who the affected women are, we must never speak of what we have seen and heard, for their sake."

"I agree," Yuri said as he watched the suffering soldiers through the glass. "If this judgement was just for twenty-four hours, can you imagine what it would be like to endure this kind of torment for all eternity as a victim of the Darkness? The Prophet told us of the ancient enemy of the Father, the one our Pavel priest calls Satan, and even his crusty heart has been reborn and softened by the Prophet's message of faith and love! I am so grateful that Adam and Nylah chose my home the day they came here!"

"There is much I do not yet know about God and His Son," Nikolai confessed, "but Sonya and I will learn these things together." It had been a happy revelation to discover that his beloved had also become a believer, and her incredible story of the miracles the Prophet had done on his very first night in Pavel had astonished him. The vision of a new Eden was closer to becoming a reality than ever before!

Anya had already retired for the evening in her suite, and after the four enjoyed a dinner of delicious extra leftovers in the refrigerator from the banquet, Sasha and Yuri went out to her balcony with cups of tea to talk and watch the geese. She had shyly asked him to spend the night with her, but he gently declined. When he made love to his Sasha, it would be on the day she became his wife.

Sasha had offered Sonya and Nikolai a single suite, but Nikolai made the decision for them both. Standing in the doorway to Sonya's room, they clung to one another, neither wanting to let go.

"Goodnight, my heart," he whispered softly, leaning down to capture her sensational lips one more time before they parted. "I'll see you in the morning, but you'll be lying next to me in my dreams all through the night."

"My lion... Your valor and courage keep me strong. How will I sleep when I know you are near?"

"We must try to be patient, my love." He guided her inside and reluctantly closed the door, his gut clenching at the sight of her disappointed expression. As much as he longed to stay, he wanted her to rest. Tomorrow would determine the course of the rest of their lives.

Sonya glanced around the beautifully appointed room, but there was only one place that drew her. Filling the large tub with hot water and scented soap, she turned on the powerful jets for a full-body massage. Uncoiling her braid of wheat-colored hair, she shook it out, undressed, and stepped into the tub.

She allowed the jets to pommel her skin until every last particle of grime and sweat had been vanquished. Turning them off, she submerged herself in the lavender-scented, steaming water with a sigh of pleasure, and when she finally rose to the surface, she felt baptized with a sense of peace and serenity.

Sensing him before she saw him, she slowly opened her eyes. He was standing in the doorway watching her, his hard, muscular, naked body causing her to draw her breath, a rush of desire coursing through her veins.

"I don't know what tomorrow will bring, my Sonya. All I know is that we have tonight, and if it's to be our last night on this earth, I want it to be with you."

She held out her arms as he stepped into the tub.

Chapter 34 Why?

It was lonely without Sola and her pod, but Angel kept heading steadily north. The west-flowing current was strong as it moved through what seemed like bottomless waters between South America and Cuba, requiring all the strength of her powerful tail and the vision of Michael's loving face motivating her forward. With no shallow reef structure to draw upon for food, she hunted as the opportunity presented itself, a fish or two from a passing school more than enough to satisfy her hunger.

She saw other pods of dolphins as she swam, and they passed each other with a friendly greeting, the surprised mammals chattering amongst themselves at the sight of her, but also in a hurry to reach their birthing grounds.

Finally crossing the 25,000-foot-deep abyss of the Cayman Trench, she reached the strait between Cuba and Haiti. She could see fishing boats above her and dove as deep as possible to avoid their hooks or nets, but once through the strait, the water began to change its hue from dark blue to turquoise, and she knew the Bahamas lay straight ahead!

Picturing the old maps she had studied of the islands, she calculated the route to Spanish Wells, but it was the urging of the Voice that drew her in the direction she should take.

She decided to trust in nothing but the Voice, stimulating in her the same silent message that told birds when it was time to fly south, that drew the male to the female in the spring, that the homing pigeon used to navigate the skies... *Instinct*... the mystical sixth sense instilled in all of God's creatures, and in man, if he chose to heed it.

She rose to the choppy surface and rotated in a circle. The Voice whispered a direction in her ear, and she came to a halt facing the northwest. Her tail flipping into the air, she began sprinting towards Spanish Wells. She'd be there in two days, and as she swam, one word kept repeating over and over in her mind.

Why, Jordan? Why?

****

Her eyes slowly rose above the water, the cove at Bonefish Bay five hundred feet before her. James' sailboat, *Sapphire Blue*, was bobbing in the low rolling swell, but she saw no one outside on the backyard deck.

Was Michael still here? And how could she get up to the house with a fishtail instead of legs? As she pondered that question, she felt a nudge from the Voice.

Swim towards the beach.

Without any hesitation, she obeyed. As she grew closer to shore, her sparkling scales began to fall away until she was left in nothing but a flesh-colored material that resembled a thin dive suit. A few more strokes and her tail split in two, and as she entered waist-deep water, her legs re-formed! Praising God for yet another amazing miracle, she walked out of the water, her first steps on dry land in three months.

Judging from the position of the sun, it was almost noon, and she knew the family would be gathering in the kitchen to make lunch. She skirted off to the left, her heart leaping when she saw the cozy cottage where she and Michael had made such passionate love, their baby alive inside her, by the grace of God!

She ducked under the kitchen windows until she reached the rear screen door. She could hear people talking, but none of them sounded like Michael. Quietly opening the door, she went in. Armand and Nadia were standing at the sink with their backs to her, and she was about to announce herself when James appeared, a basket of sapodillas in hand, with his wife, Elizabeth, right behind him.

The sapodillas fell to the floor.

"Angel!" He clutched his heart with both hands. "Angel, you're alive!" he cried and ran towards her, enveloping her in his arms. "It's a miracle!"

Elizabeth threw her arms around them both, Armand and Nadia doing the same, everyone sobbing at once.

"Where have you been all this time?" James asked, his voice cracking with emotion. "We searched everywhere! But you're alive, child, and that's the most important thing!"

"I was kidnapped by pirates at the Red Starfish. I'll tell you the whole story later, but please, Grandpa, I must know, is Michael here?"

Still in complete shock, he drew her to a kitchen chair as they gathered around her. "The Tribe left two weeks ago, but Michael left last week with Gypsy and Noah for Adam and Nylah's wedding! Armand and I just got back from Grand Bahama, so we're going to host a wedding party for them the next time they come to Spanish Wells.

"Michael searched for you, Angel. Not a day went by that he wasn't going house to house, talking to every captain and sailor at the dock, even combing the bush and caves for your body. He never gave up, not even for a second!"

"Wow, Adam and Nylah are getting married! Then Gypsy and Noah probably won't be back for three or four weeks?"

"Yes, my girl," he told her. "But we'll take good care of you until they return! Perhaps you could wait to tell us your story until I let Mr. Curry know you're here. He'll want to hear it too. Let's get you some food, then I'll send for him."

She smiled at the wonderful man who wasn't really her grandfather but felt that way to all the children on Miracle Island. "That would be fine, Grandpa James. What are you having for lunch?"

"Oh, I'm sorry, Angel, it's grilled lobster. But Elizabeth and Nadia can make you something else."

Angel grinned. "No need... lobster sounds great!"

****

"What an interesting dive suit you were wearing, Angel," Elizabeth remarked, curiously fingering the fine, ultra-soft material. "So unusual... and it has no zipper. Where did it come from?"

Angel slid back the curtain of the outdoor shower; a towel wrapped around her. Nadia and Elizabeth had refused to leave her alone, fearful she would disappear again. They sat within a few feet of the shower stall as she bathed, holding an armful of clean clothes in her approximate size.

"Something the pirates made me wear. It's very stretchy." She dried off and selected a sleeveless top and shorts from their offerings.

"When will Mr. Curry arrive?"

"He'll be here shortly," Nadia said as she folded the rest of the clothes. "You can't imagine his excitement when Armand told him the good news! I'm sure he'll want to ask you a million questions. I know I do!"

Angel had already perfected the story she would be telling the island administrator, a true story except for three very important omissions... Jordan's role in her abduction, her miraculous transformation into a mermaid, and maybe a bit of the stretch of the truth on how she actually reached Spanish Wells.

As for Jordan Russell, she had no plans for revenge. She had tried to make herself love him until Michael's sudden return exposed her true feelings, feelings she had suppressed out of anger and the pain of rejection. Her real concern was *for* him, the close friendship they had once shared making his uncharacteristic act even more upsetting.

Although she needed to hear an explanation, he had most likely been influenced by the evil of the Darkness, and she felt the Voice urging her to fight it, to try to save him from an eternal fate she wouldn't wish on anyone, no matter how vile their crime.

The meeting with Mr. Curry and the family went on for hours, the room dead silent as she told the story of her kidnapping, the long voyage towards Rio, and the ultimate demise of her captors. Everyone was relieved to hear that the pirates had not seriously harmed her, and that she and the other two captives had been rescued by a passing ship that took the girls home to Venezuela first, then dropped her, at her request, just offshore of Spanish Wells, where she swam the rest of the way to Bonefish Bay. Only the families knew about the God-given aquatic gifts she'd had all her life, but no one was yet aware of her amazing new gift of being able to move between land and sea as a mythical being.

Already analyzing her incredible story, Mr. Curry barely heard her final sentence, dismayed by the blatant chink in security that her startling abduction had revealed. "Well, you've certainly given me a lot to think about, Angel.

"My initial suspicions about Captain Escobar's ship were correct. I should never have allowed them any access to our shores, and we need to brainstorm how to prevent such a thing from ever happening again. They obviously planted a boat in a secluded location so they could remove you without going through the formal entry point."

"Edward, don't be so hard on yourself. No one could have foreseen something like this. You've done your best for many years," Armand reminded him, "and our island has always been safe and secure. After talking about it, we believe that Angel was deliberately targeted by someone with a grudge against either her or Jordan, and we have to accept the fact that we may never know why. But merciful God brought her back home to us, and whoever did this will someday have to face His judgement for their actions."

Angel was only half-listening to their intense discussion, because as soon as Mr. Curry left and everyone went to bed, she knew the person who did this would most definitely be facing some well-deserved judgement.

****

Parting the bushes at the edge of his property, she saw a lantern flickering inside Jordan's bedroom. Staying low, she crept along the rear of the building until she reached his window and carefully peeked in. He was in bed, his naked buttocks thrusting rhythmically, the attractive blonde-haired woman beneath him moaning with pleasure, her legs tight around his waist. Backing away, she tip-toed in through the kitchen door.

"I imagine the last person you'd want to see right now is your fiancée. Oops, sorry... your *ex*-fiancée."

He rolled off the woman, who yanked a sheet over herself.

"Holy shit.... Angel?"

She was leaning against the bedroom doorframe, casually examining her fingernails. "Bet you never thought you'd see me again, did you, Jordan?"

He frantically struggled to pull on his shorts. "Oh, thank God, sweetheart, you're alive!"

"Jordan, who the hell is this bitch?" I thought I was your fiancée! the girl shouted indignantly.

"Shut up, Donna! This is Angel, my old girlfriend who went missing before I met you." Now dressed, he stood, holding out his arms, and walked towards her.

Her interest suddenly piqued, the girl swung her legs over the edge of the bed. "You're the one they tore the island apart looking for? Wow, where've you been for so long?"

Angel dodged his embrace and sat on the bed next to Donna. "That's a fascinating story that would take quite a while to tell, but would you mind giving Jordan and I a few minutes alone to talk? You know, catch up on old times before I go?"

The girl fidgeted uneasily. "So, you're not angry that I'm engaged to Jordan?"

Angel had to chuckle. "No, definitely not. He's all yours."

Donna breathed a soft sigh of relief as she stood up and knotted the sheet. "I'll wait for you in the kitchen, Jordan. Let me know when we can... finish up," she whispered as she brushed past him, closing the door behind her.

He didn't answer, standing like a stone and staring daggers at Angel, who was staring right back.

"Why?"

"Why what?"

"Why did you do it?"

"I don't know what you're talking about, Angel. I was a mess after you disappeared. And now, you waltz in here and accuse me of... what?"

"Does the name Captain Escobar mean anything to you?"

He remained silent, but she caught the gleam in his eyes.

"Yes, Captain Escobar, the pirate you offered me to... for free. The pirate you hoped would take me as far away as you could get me, a blonde virgin sacrifice, to be sold to a rich degenerate as his plaything. Oh, but if they discovered I wasn't a virgin, to be sold into a brothel and used until I was dead... or killed myself out of hopelessness."

He said nothing, his face cold.

"He told me everything, Jordan, before his ship hit a reef and went down! But thanks to God I got out in time, along with two other kidnapped girls. A passing ship rescued us and brought us all home."

"You were never supposed to come back!" he hissed. "After how you betrayed me, I wanted you dead! But it could have been pinned on me, so I arranged for the pirates to take you. Now, I'm the object of everyone's love and sympathy instead of the town laughingstock!" He spit on the floor in front of her in disdain.

"I saw you, naked, your legs wrapped around him in your own bed, your lips touching as you slept! I should have been the one to have you first! And you gave yourself to him like a common whore on the very night of our engagement!"

She leaped off the bed. "You never even let me answer you! It was my birthday party, and you arranged for your surprise proposal in front of everyone. I was going to have to break your heart with the whole town watching, Jordan! At least Moses spared you from that."

"I've seen your lover, running all over the island for weeks, desperate to find you. I busted a gut laughing, knowing he never would! Who was he to you anyway?"

"I've been in love with Michael since I was a little girl. And I carry his child."

Oh God, what had he done? If Curry found out he had instigated her kidnapping, he'd be run out of town for good.

She felt a gentle prodding from the Voice. "I've already spoken with my family, and with Mr. Curry. Don't worry, I never mentioned your name."

He looked at her in shock. "You... you didn't tell them?"

"I didn't come here to hurt you, Jordan, but I needed to hear why you did it from your own lips."

She moved closer and took his hand. "I was going to tell you about Michael, but I deliberately delayed because I was afraid of hurting you. Michael is the only man I've ever loved. I'm so sorry you had to see us together that night, but it was still going to hurt, no matter when I did it."

She pressed his palm against her heart. "Please forgive me, Jordan."

He snatched his hand away, his guilt overwhelming. "You want *me* to forgive *you*, Angel? After what I did?"

"You always were a good and decent person, Jordan, and I care about you very much. What you did to me is not the Jordan I remember, nor the Jordan I choose to remember. I want you to be happy."

At that, he fell into a chair and burst into remorseful tears, and with those tears, the tentacle pouring its manipulating poison into his mind dug in even deeper.

"Help me, Angel!" he cried. "I feel like something is trying to drag me down to the bottom of the sea, choking me with rage and hate... making me do and say things that chill my soul!"

She immediately gripped his hands and knelt at his feet.

"Pray with me, Jordan! There's only one way to defeat the power of the merciless Darkness... Open your heart and let me introduce you to the Lord of everlasting love, forgiveness, and peace."

****

Nadia never woke up until she smelled the coffee brewing, leaving that task to Armand, the early riser of Bonefish Bay. At the first aromatic whiff, however, her robe went on and she joined James and Elizabeth at the kitchen table, where they all enjoyed a fresh hot cup before starting their day.

But on this morning, she walked in to find Armand holding a piece of paper, the coffee forgotten.

"She's gone... Angel is gone."

"What do you mean, Armand?" James asked as he and Elizabeth came in. "Isn't she in her room?"

"Read for yourself." He passed James the note.

My dearest family, as you read this letter, I will be on my way to Miracle Island. I'm catching a ride this morning with some very special friends that will drop me at San Salvador. Then I'll find my way home from there. I'm so very sorry, but I just couldn't wait for the Gypsy Queen to show up. Michael doesn't even know I'm alive, and I can't stand the thought of him suffering any longer. I love him, I love him, I love him! All my heart, Angel

"Oh dear." Nadia glanced at the pile of clean laundry. "She didn't take any clothes with her at all."

Elizabeth riffled through the pile. "She did take one item, Nadia.... She took her flesh-colored dive suit."

Chapter 35 The Face Of Fear

"The Prophet will return today to release my father and his soldiers from God's judgement. Oh, Yuri, I pray it will all go well!"

Sasha and Yuri were sitting at the breakfast bar, waiting for Sonya and Nikolai to join them. Sleep had been sketchy at best... The future of Pavel depended on whether or not the Prophet's message from God to these men had been heard and accepted in their hearts.

Would General Chenko finally yield to the request of the Prophet for peace, or would his pride and lust for power lead him to seek revenge against the people?

"Well, this is cozy." Anya sauntered into the kitchen and poured herself a cup of coffee. "Who is this, Sasha? No longer Daddy's sweet little girl?"

Yuri enfolded Sasha's hand protectively in his own. So, this was the mistress of Boris Chenko everyone whispered about! She was indeed stunningly beautiful, but he could sense the vulnerability lying beneath her sarcastic exterior.

"Good morning, Miss Kournikova," he said politely. He stood and offered her a bow. "I am Yuri Fedorov. A pleasure to meet you."

Well, at least he wasn't a rough and tumble peasant... and quite good-looking too. She nodded once and took a sip of her coffee. "Likewise." She waved a finger between them with a knowing smirk. "Are you two sleeping together?"

Sasha jumped off her stool. "Please, Anya, don't start! Yuri and I plan to marry. Then we can start our family."

"For heaven's sake, Anya, can't you leave the poor child alone for five minutes?" Sonya and Nikolai walked into the kitchen, arm in arm.

Anya's eyebrows lifted. "A day of surprises! You never told me that you and Nureyev were seeing each other again on the sly. I'm all in favor of true love, but aren't you in danger of a serious reprimand, Major?"

Nikolai poured Sonya a cup of coffee and pulled up a stool. "It may be a moot point very soon, Miss Kournikova. As you are aware, the Prophet will be arriving in the conference room at two o'clock, and all our lives will be changing in one way or another."

Anya frowned. This was exactly what she was afraid of. If Chenko gave in to the Prophet, her easy and comfortable life at Samovar could end. She refused to work in the fields or with the animals, but her stomach churned at the thought of what awaited in the wilderness if she was forced to leave.

"I must return to the Harem before he arrives!" Sonya told her new friends. "They need to hear the truth of God's Word and have a chance to choose for themselves."

"Shall I go with you, my darling?" Nikolai was loathe to let her leave his sight.

She kissed him, feeling his love and desire to protect her. "No, Nikolai." But her eyes met Anya's. "Anya will come with me. But if we're delayed, the three of you must be there to hear the general's final decision. Rest assured; we'll rejoin you later."

****

Sonya and Anya walked back across the causeway, but this time the base guards were on duty, despite their inability to speak. Appearing embarrassed, they waved them through.

Once inside the Harem compound, Sonya went into the scheduling office. Finding it unmanned, she picked up the handset for the intercom system.

"Good morning to you all, my dear sisters of the Harem. This is Sonya Smirnova. Please, stop whatever you may be doing and meet me in the cafeteria, where I will explain to you why the soldiers have been unable to speak."

Replacing the handset, she took Anya's hand. "Come on, Anya. You need to hear this too."

They headed further into the compound, passing the party lounge and the double doors that led to the Pleasure wing until they reached the cafeteria. The chairs and tables were already filling with the beautiful women of the Harem who had hurried downstairs, some still in their bathrobes, their skin damp from their shower, a few with their makeup and hair only partially complete, others hurrying over from the fitness center in their swimsuits or workout clothes, but all asking the same question.

What was so important that one of their own had been given permission to use the intercom to call for a meeting?

Anya received a few spiteful looks and catty comments as they entered, but Sonya kept her hand tightly clasped in her own until she climbed up on a table, and Anya took a seat nearby.

"Sisters, I have come to make you aware of the events that have taken place in the last five days here at Samovar and in Pavel. The villagers were planning a revolt against General Chenko, a risky rebellion that would have cost the lives of hundreds, both villagers and soldiers alike! The solar fields were to be destroyed, all power lost to the dam, the base, and this compound."

The women looked at each other. A rebellion? Were they to be slaughtered along with the soldiers?

"But a miracle happened! Instead of war and bloodshed, a man and a woman appeared from out of nowhere to offer a better way! The man is called the Prophet... and he has been given incredible powers by God! He saved a falling baby from certain death! A woman born with only one arm now has the use of two! And he used his power to bind General Chenko and one hundred of his men at the dam for the last twenty-four hours, unable to make a sound and in terrible pain as punishment for crimes against Pavel!

"You have seen how the soldiers here at the base have been mute since yesterday? He performed that miracle too! And he is returning today, to release the general and his men from their torment and to ask for a decision. Will General Chenko join with Pavel to create a new life... a new Eden, as the Prophet describes it, with peace and plenty for us all? Or will he refuse the call for unity and wreak even more grief and heartache on an already suffering people? We will soon know his answer, but the Prophet assures us that no matter what, God is for us!"

There was a ray of hope on the faces of some, confusion or disdain on others.

"You're asking us to believe in impossible miracles, Sonya, and in a fantasy superhero who supposedly has powers we only saw at the movie theater!" one woman declared, with many nods of agreement. "There is no such thing!"

"And *God* supposedly gave him these powers?" a younger woman said bitterly. "I lost my faith in a merciful God when a band of raiders held my husband's head underwater in the Dnieper and laughed until he drowned... before turning to me. A Samovar soldier found me, almost dead, and brought me here, where I was nursed back to health. I joined the Harem of my own free will after that. There is no God, and if there was, He certainly wouldn't want me after the things I've done."

Sonya answered her, her face alight with joy. "But He does! I asked Him for forgiveness, sisters, and He cleansed me from all my sins! The gift of freedom and eternal life can be yours as well, if you believe in Him with all your heart! I saw the miracles of the Prophet with my own eyes. The new Eden will be a safe and wonderful home for each of us, free from sexual servitude, free to find love, bear children, and have families of our own!"

"How do you find Him, Sonya, to ask for His forgiveness?" a girl of sixteen asked uncertainly.

The women suddenly gasped as a white mist began to arise from the top of the table! Sonya fell to her knees, unafraid, but an ashen-faced Anya jumped up and backed away. A mysterious, rose-scented breeze brushed their cheeks as it slowly parted the cloud of mist, and cries of astonishment echoed throughout the room at what was revealed!

A young and beautiful woman stood in its place, her body shimmering with radiant light, her long midnight hair lifting behind her, a gentle smile on her ruby lips as she surveyed the thunderstruck women before her.

"Look!" one of them whispered. "Her eyes... her eyes are like sparkling diamonds!"

"My sisters, my daughters, my mothers, my friends," Nylah said, her soft and loving voice like the ripple of cool rushing water over pebbles in a stream. "You ask how you may find Him?"

She held out her arms. "Let me show you the Way."

****

Chenko lay on the cold hard concrete floor, barely able to wipe the drool from his mouth with the back of his hand. If the excruciating pain didn't stop soon, he swore he'd find a carving knife and plunge it into his own heart!

Caspar lay next to him, crying like a baby, his uniform smeared with feces and drenched in urine just like all the others, one hundred officers and soldiers of Russia, as weak and helpless as infants. And how was this done, he thought angrily? By a teenage boy who claimed that God had given him the power and authority to render punishment for his order to dispatch a hundred of his enthusiastic soldiers to beat, rape, and impregnate the married women of Pavel in retaliation for their men's plan for rebellion?

The parts of his brain that were not desperately trying to cope with his pain refused to accept that absurdity. A more likely explanation was that the champagne had been poisoned in some manner... yes, that was it! The coming and going in an artificial white fog... Las Vegas showmanship! And the girl must have been wearing a Kevlar vest for his deadly shot not to have killed her! There was a reasonable explanation for all of this, and when the poison finally ran its course, he would issue orders that the people of Pavel would never forget.

Sasha, Yuri, and Nikolai took their seats in the observation room. Nikolai was worried about Sonya, but it was almost the appointed hour, and she had told him to go on without her.

Sasha was also worried. She had to convince her father, who she knew would be livid with fury, not to seek vengeance on the people of Pavel for his righteous punishment from the messenger of God. She prayed he would have the humility to accept the consequences of his grievous actions, and to change course and join with the leaders of Pavel to steer towards a better future for them all.

The current regime was destined to fail with her father's death, and with the death of each soldier as they aged, alone and childless. But how many innocent lives would be lost in the meantime?

"Look!" Yuri exclaimed, pointing to an area in front of the podium where Adam and Nylah began to materialize, with Moses riding on Adam's shoulder.

The suffering eyes of the men turned to them, pleading for release, Chenko and Caspar's burning with hate.

Adam raised his hand... and their pain was instantly gone! As each man struggled to his feet, the sounds of coughing, sobbing, and groans of relief filled the room.

"The merciful Lord has called an end to your punishment for your transgressions. But now, He wants to hear the intent of your heart towards Him, He who is ever ready to forgive and bless those who fear Him."

He placed a gentle hand on the arm of the man standing closest to him and smiled.

"If you're ready to tell Him, He is ready to listen."

The bedraggled captain met Adam's searching eyes.

"Prophet, I am a man who has never believed in a higher power. How could I, with the evil I saw in the world around me? And I justified my own actions by telling myself that my superiors would not require such inhuman things of me if they were not necessary for the good of my country, or now, for Samovar. But as I lay on the floor drowning in pain, I remembered your words, and something in me called out to your God. I suddenly saw myself reflected in His eyes, and I hated what I saw."

He slowly knelt before Adam. "I would tell Him that I'm sorry... that a God who has the power to do what He did to me is to be feared and respected... and that I don't deserve His mercy or His help... but I'm asking for it anyway. That's what I would tell Him, Prophet."

"Traitor!" Caspar shrieked wildly; his pistol aimed at the captain's head, those in the line of fire jumping back as the celebrated marksman pulled the trigger.

But the bullet hit nothing but a golden bubble of light that instantaneously surrounded the humbly kneeling captain, ricocheting off with a metallic clang, a chandelier high on the ceiling shattering into splinters of glass!

Caspar stared at his gun in disbelief and again took aim, but Adam covered the muzzle with his palm.

"Enough, servant of the Darkness." But the colonel only laughed, the earsplitting shot echoing off the walls.

The soldiers were stunned to see Adam pull his uninjured hand away and brush tiny bits of metal off his shirt, the semi-automatic lying in pieces, the bullets rolling away! A moment later, they felt movement at their waists, and saw their own holstered guns disintegrating into dust!

Screaming obscenities, Chenko and Caspar backed out of the room, warning them of the dire consequences of siding with the Prophet. Traitors, they shouted indignantly, all to meet the firing squad the very next day!

Once they were gone, an Elite walked over and shut the doors. Then, returning to where Adam stood, he fell to his knees next to the repentant officer, the other ninety-seven men behind them doing the same.

"Prophet, I believe every man here is now ready to talk to your God."

****

In the observation room, Yuri held a trembling Sasha as Chenko and Caspar disappeared. But one of the monitors above the two-way mirror showed them entering Chenko's office, the live video captured by a hallway camera.

"I must speak with him! I've never seen him like this! Now that I know how he has governed Pavel in the past, I can only imagine what he might do."

Nikolai spoke softly but firmly, anxious to keep her from speaking with her father until they knew his state of mind. "Sasha, there must be a camera in his office. We should try to learn what he and Caspar plan to do. With that information, your talk with him may have a better chance of success."

"Yes, yes, that's a good idea, Major! Here, let me see, on this console... Okay, watch monitor six!"

Chenko was sitting at his desk, wiping his face with a towel. Caspar had poured them each a stiff drink and handed one to the general before taking a seat across from him.

"This ends today, Caspar! I can see now that I've been much too lenient with the peasants, and I'm through playing games with this fucking Prophet! You have your orders, Colonel... Use your walkie-talkie to direct the men at the base on what to do. I want them all in Pavel in thirty minutes! Then take your post on the causeway watchtower and await further orders."

"Yes, General Chenko! I am yours to command. You can count on me, sir."

Chenko leaned back in his chair. "I know, Caspar... and you will be rewarded for your loyalty. Now, go up to the main level and carry out my orders. I'll see you on the causeway shortly."

Colonel Caspar shot to his feet and saluted, downed the rest of his drink, then swiveled on his heel and left the room.

Nikolai was worried. They'd been too late to overhear the orders Chenko issued to Caspar, but whatever they were, it was time for Sasha to try to change his mind.

"Sasha, your father won't remain in his office much longer, so if you think you can sway him, now's your chance."

Without a word, she gave Yuri one last kiss and left the room. Nikolai immediately turned to Yuri.

"Yuri, you must run to Pavel and warn them! The troops from the base will be on their way there in minutes, and we don't know what Caspar has ordered them to do! Tell them they must leave at once and cross the bridge into the fields, then keep going until they reach the wilderness!"

With a firm nod, Yuri darted out the door, and Nikolai refocused on the conference room. The Prophet was sitting in a chair with Nylah and Moses standing behind him, the men listening intently as he spoke. Nikolai could see their faces, lit with a fire from within, their souls now awakened, some weeping with joy, just as he had done when the Spirit first filled him.

But he also realized the grave danger these men were in. Chenko had threatened to execute them for the treasonous act of giving their hearts and loyalty to God. To the power-mad general, this meant an unacceptable loss of control, something that his egotistical and dictatorial nature could never permit. He didn't really care about these men, denying them families and children merely to serve as his puppets, and to enforce his will on innocents who had no means to protect themselves.

If the remaining one hundred troops at the base were following orders, as he knew they would, they should already be heading across the causeway. The safest place for these newborn Christian men was somewhere that no one would ever suspect them to go, and if they had to fight their own comrades for their lives, could re-arm themselves.

Right back at the base... and when the Prophet was done speaking, that's exactly where Nikolai Nureyev was going to lead them.

****

Sasha pushed open the door and stepped inside, the first time in her entire life she had crossed the threshold of her father's office without his express permission. He was still sitting in his chair, speaking harshly into his walkie-talkie, but when he saw her, he quickly signed off.

"What is it, Sasha? I'm very busy, my dear."

Squaring her shoulders, she marched over and sat down in the same chair Caspar had recently vacated.

"Papa, I know everything... about what you've been doing in Pavel all these years, about the rape you ordered of their women, about where you've been since yesterday... and that you plan to do something terrible to people who have done nothing to deserve such a fate."

She paused and swallowed hard. "And I also know about the Prophet."

As she spoke, his expression never changed, but she caught a steely glint deep in his eyes that made her tremble with fear. The father she loved had disappeared. She didn't even know this stranger.

He lit the tip of a Cuban cigar and slowly leaned back in his chair, his black, soulless eyes never leaving her.

"Did I ever tell you, Sasha, how Elena really died? I found her with another man, betraying me, betraying everything I'd ever done for her, all I'd ever given her. After I ordered her lover thrown off the top of the dam, I strangled her to death on the beige leather couch you love to read on... with my bare hands."

The stranger smiled, reminding her of a cobra about to strike. "And regarding your mother, your beautiful, Bible-reading mother, who I came to despise for her weakness and planned to divorce until the solar flare made it unnecessary. I took you away from her and brought you here to Samovar, leaving her to starve in Moscow, for all I cared."

He suddenly jumped up and slammed his fist on the desk. "I built Samovar for *you*, Sasha! A place where you would be safe, secure, and happy, protected from the monsters that surrounded me in the Kremlin, and from the demons who emerged from the ashes when the world as we knew it finally fell. Everything I've done here, whether you agree with my decisions or not, was done for you! And this is how you repay me? With judgement and recriminations?"

"Father, you know I love you, no matter what you've done! You don't have to say painful things to hurt me. But I don't want any of this, bought with slavery and blood and tears! Please, if you love me, call back your troops! There is a better way, the Prophet tells us, where all men can be free to build happy lives and honor the God of heaven who loves us! He calls it the new Eden, Father, the world intended for us from the beginning. And I heard his invitation to become one of God's family and have accepted the Lord Jesus Christ as my Savior!"

He shook his head, his hatred of the Prophet multiplied a hundred-fold. "You always were a dreamer, child, so in need of a strong hand to guide and protect you. But now, I see you are nothing but a fool."

"And I'm in love, Papa! His name is Yuri Fedorov, and we are going to be married. I want to live with him in Pavel and give you grandchildren someday! But you'll destroy our lives and our happiness if you punish the town for wanting justice, for wanting freedom, for wanting food, and not to be beaten or tortured! I beg you... if you built all of this for me, then give me a future here, give us all a future here!"

Chenko felt himself start to waver, his love for her almost tipping the scales. But the tentacle of poison twitched in his brain, fearing the influence of the Light, and the Darkness renewed its efforts to keep him firmly under control. Every word of the Prophet, every imagined slight, every challenge to his ego, every flaunting of his authority, hammered his mind. Rage, anger, pride, and bitterness surged through him afresh, and his heart hardened against her.

"You are forbidden to see this peasant ever again! Colonel Caspar will assume control of Samovar after I'm gone, and you will marry him! If he has to lock you in your quarters until the wedding, then so be it," he barked. "And as for the Prophet, his crude attempts at sorcery will never prevent the lesson I have ordered, a lesson that, as we speak, my troops are heading to Pavel to teach them, a lesson the rebels will never forget!"

Sasha slowly rose. She had tried to make him see the truth, and her failure to do so was tearing her heart in two. She so desperately wanted to remember the father who had always treated her with love and kindness.

But she could now see the ruse... *This* was the face that Pavel had feared, a cruel despot and murderer who had no remorse whatsoever about what he did to others.

Tears of sorrow spilled down her cheeks. "I will love you forever, Father, but I'm going to Pavel, home to my Yuri. I will pray for you, that you will finally listen to the Prophet and see the truth of God's Word. On that day, you would become a welcome part of our lives, and of the lives of your grandchildren. But until then... this is goodbye, Papa," and she ran out the door.

He leaped up. "No, Sasha, no!" Falling back into his chair, his lined face was now that of an old and tired man.

"I don't want you to see the nightmare that I really am."

Chapter 36 God Of Miracles

Yuri rushed to the elevator and pushed the button for the main level, still amazed by the unlimited power available at Samovar, power he hadn't seen for eighteen years.

Reaching the causeway level, he felt a rumble beneath his feet. From where he stood at the west end of the dam, he could see a convoy of Humvee's and trucks rolling towards him from the base. If he was to cover the half-mile to town before they got there, he'd have to fly like the wind!

Breaking out into a full run, he raced down the road to Pavel, a hail of bullets hitting the trunk of a tree just as he passed it. They'd seen him! Breathing a fervent prayer and drawing on every last ounce of strength he had, he pushed himself even harder.

"Run!" he shouted as he entered the village. "Run to the wilderness! Soldiers are coming to kill!"

Straining to get to Alexei's house, he pounded through the streets, calling out the warning to everyone he saw. But the people seemed confused, and instead of heeding his cry, began to gather in groups to talk.

"No, no! Don't delay! Run... run for your lives!"

But he was too late. The Humvee's were already moving into town and fanning out. Heavily armed soldiers in full military gear jumped out of one and stormed into a home, forcing the terrified occupants to first line up in the street, then shoved into the back of an empty truck.

He ducked into an open door, panting for breath. Alexei, Elise, and their neighbors were being herded into a truck, but he froze when he saw their three young children being led away and marched by armed guards towards the bank of the Dnieper. What was going on?!

A scan of the block revealed the same thing happening at every home! Crying infants and toddlers were being carried in a soldier's one arm, their rifle in the other, dozens of children bound together with rope and being led towards the river!

Oh God, the butchers were going to murder the children of Pavel!

Yuri collapsed in the doorway. There was no way to stop this! Where was the Prophet, his power... his miracles, when they needed him the most? They had relinquished their plan for revolution because of what they'd all seen him do in the barn, two undeniable miracles that caused them to believe his promise that God would help them!

Well, they needed help now! So where was God?

A line of trucks, packed with older teenagers and adults, started up and began rolling towards the bridge. Elise was screaming wildly and struggling to climb out to follow her children until one of the soldiers butted her in the head with his rifle. Alexei pulled his bleeding and unconscious wife onto his lap, his expression one that Yuri never wanted to see again.

"You there!" The cold barrel of a rifle pushed into his ear. "Follow me!"

****

"What the hell, Captain! You're ordering my squad to round up all the children and stake them down in the middle of the Dnieper River? Except for the stream on the west bank, it's dry as a bone! Are we supposed to shoot them out there, so their blood won't get your socks wet?"

The squad leader was not happy. It was one thing to keep the town under strict control for General Chenko, but this was the outright murder of innocent children!

"Are you telling me you're going to disobey a direct order, Corporal?" The captain pulled out his pistol and waited for a response.

The corporal's men shifted uncomfortably. They knew the captain wouldn't hesitate to shoot any soldier who refused a command from the general.

Sheepishly kicking a loose rock with the toe of his boot, the corporal backed down. "No, sir... I, well, I just never expected to be told to kill a child."

"You won't be killing anyone, soldier." The captain grinned as he reholstered his gun.

"We'll be letting the river do it for us."

****

The truck containing Yuri and two dozen of his neighbors stopped at the bridge.

"Get out, peasants! This is the end of the line."

They climbed down and were immediately steered towards the walkway that was already filled with people. Yuri could see soldiers on the opposite end that led to the fields, any hope for escape now cut off.

As they stepped onto the bridge, a soldier called out, "Last bunch, Captain!" A twelve-foot-tall roll of chain link fence was then spread across and secured on either end, leaving the entire adult population of Pavel trapped like rats.

The flow of the once mighty Dnieper had been reduced to a stream by the controlling gates of the dam. Since the Flare, its only purpose for the town was to provide potable water and irrigate the crops. The stream ran closest to Pavel, the rest of the half-mile wide riverbed dry, except when it rained. The disabled drawbridge was eighty feet high, and before the dam was built, the Dnieper ran thirty feet deep, which had allowed most size boats to easily pass underneath.

A woman in the center of the bridge suddenly screamed. “The children! They’re staking the children in the middle of the river!”

All eyes locked onto the horrifying scene of the bound and weeping children, the soldiers securing their ropes to the ground with rebar stakes hammered deep into the earth. The untied babies were spread out and lying directly on the dusty ground, their tiny arms and legs squirming as they cried.

All at once, a voice was heard coming from the top of the dam, the voice of General Chenko himself on a loudspeaker at full volume, clear as a bell, even from half a mile away.

“Subjects of Samovar! For your crime of planning a violent insurrection against me, and for sending your representative, the man you call the Prophet, to incite my troops to revolt against my authority, I now sentence you all to death!”

Alexei clutched Elise, a loud gasp and cries of fear arising from the prisoners!

“But I will extend my benevolence to every adult on the bridge. Your lives will be graciously spared, but in your place, the children of Pavel must pay the price for your crimes!

“The sentence is to be carried out immediately! I will now open the gates of Samovar Dam, which will slowly begin to fill the Dnieper River with water. As you watch your precious infants drown, as your young ones draw their last breath when the water finally covers them, remember your crimes, and never forget that I... I alone... have the power over you of life and death!”

****

Nikolai entered the conference room, but the Prophet and Nylah had already vanished, the men sitting quietly, deep in prayer.

The question of where their loyalties might now lie hadn't even occurred to them, the glow of their rebirth still strong and vibrating in their souls. But they accepted the respected Major Nureyev's reasoning, and after the convoy of trucks rumbled by, followed him to the base, where they found the entry gates open and unguarded.

Sonya and Anya were leaving the Harem compound and saw them coming, with Nikolai leading the way. Sonya raced down the main access road and threw herself into his arms.

"Oh Nikolai, something I never believed was possible has happened!" she exclaimed. "Nylah appeared in the Harem and led every woman to faith in God! She spoke to each one as if she already knew the innermost secrets of their hearts and the wounds that no one else could see. And before she disappeared in a cloud of white mist, she revealed her true name... the Healer!"

He smiled at her excitement, the soldiers directly behind him also chuckling. "Well, as you can see, my love, the same miracle took place in the conference room." He waved the men on before tugging her over to the side of the road.

"God is at work, Sonya! It is indeed wonderful how the Prophet and the Healer have encouraged many to seek the Lord, by their words, by their miracles, and by their obvious love for God and for people.

"But I have much more disturbing news to report... After the Prophet released the soldiers from their bonds of pain, we overheard General Chenko ordering Caspar to send all the troops at the base to Pavel for a mission that I fear will lead to the deaths of many."

Sonya nodded. "Yes, when we heard the call to muster, I told the other women to remain in the compound, but Anya and I watched as they prepared. Full battle gear, Nikolai, and every man on base left in the Humvees and trucks."

He frowned as he pondered what their next move should be, but no solution was coming to mind.

"They were armed to the teeth, Major. When Boris wants someone dead, it's done quickly. If the troops are already in Pavel, there's little we can do to stop them," Anya said as she joined them. She was the only one of the women who was still uncertain whether she was ready to accept the call of God and had remained silent as the others rejoiced.

The watchtower loudspeaker crackled on and the voice of Chenko began to speak. When he was finished, every woman in the Harem and every soldier ran to where Nikolai, Sonya, and Anya were standing, their faces white with shock.

"He's going to murder the children!" Nikolai exclaimed. "And their parents will be forced to watch as they drown! I've seen the remote that operates the gates of the dam. With the press of a button from any location, the gates will open!"

Anya seized the hands of Nikolai and Sonya and started pulling them towards the viewing area on the southeast side of the dam. "Come on, everyone! If your God is real, this is the time for you to pray!" and all the others followed.

From the expansive overlook, one thousand feet above the Dnieper River, they could see the bridge packed with people and guarded on both ends. Three hundred feet away from the bridge was a mass of at least ninety children and crying babies lying in the dirt, only fifty yards from the stream.

Suddenly, they heard the grinding of engines deep inside the dam, and the four flood gates started to rise, lake water cascading into the river!

"No!" Sonya clutched the rail and burst into uncontrollable sobs at the appalling scene below, the others surrounding her also wailing as the stream began to flow faster and faster!

Nikolai squinted as a lone figure emerged from a grove of trees and raced to the riverbank. Climbing down into the stream, the figure waded through the chest-high water and headed straight for the children. He knew that person...

"I need a pair of binoculars!" he shouted.

One of the men raced to a nearby vehicle, located a pair, and rushed them back to the major, who slammed them up to his eyes.

"My God, it's Sasha! She'll be killed by the rushing waters of the river, along with the children. What is she doing?"

He clasped Sonya to his side and turned to the born-again believers who stood with them at the overlook. If there was ever a test of their faith in the God of Miracles they had all just come to know in the last few hours, this was it!

"My friends and fellow Christians, the Prophet told me only yesterday to never fear, that the Lord will always go before us, to fight for us! Our job is to *believe... trust... praise... and obey*. Shall we pray to Him now, placing our faith completely in the One to whom nothing is impossible? He has forgiven our terrible sins and healed us. Let us honor Him by trusting that He will save the children of Pavel, in whatever manner He chooses."

Joining hands in one unbroken chain, the entire motley assortment of prostitutes, rapists, torturers, and killers bowed their heads before the Lord of Heaven and Earth, confident in His love for them as one of His own, and that whatever they asked of Him, in the name of Jesus, would be granted.

****

By the time Sasha got to Pavel, the homes and streets were empty. The troops had gotten there before her, but where had they taken all the people? As she walked further in, she could hear voices, and followed the sound.

Hiding in a small grove of trees, she watched in horror as soldiers forced groups of crying children down the muddy riverbank, and dragged them by their ropes, coughing and choking, through the stream and up onto the dry riverbed. They were roughly corralled into a tight cluster as the men who carried babies in their arms laid them in the dirt in a circle around the perimeter.

Once the ropes had been staked deep into the earth, the soldiers returned to shore and headed towards the bridge to join their comrades guarding the adults of Pavel.

Sasha was aghast as she listened to her father's revolting announcement, his ruthless voice as cold as ice. No one in their right mind would even dream of doing such a terrible thing, and she was convinced he'd gone mad! But perhaps, just perhaps, there was a way...

Darting out from behind the trees, she ran down to the riverbank. Holding her walkie-talkie high above her head, she waded the rising stream and sloshed up to dry ground, and as she approached the children, they begged her to let them go.

There was only one possible way to help them! She turned to face the dam, raised the walkie-talkie to her lips, and switched it on. The single frequency programmed into it was used to communicate privately with her father. She was not permitted to hear his discussions on the other frequencies.

"Father, this is Sasha. Do you read me?"

His response was immediate. "Sasha, where are you?"

"Look down at the children you are about to murder."

There was a few seconds delay. "Get out of there right now or I'll send soldiers to haul you out, do you hear me?!"

"No, Papa. If you murder these innocent children, I choose to die with them." The stream was rushing faster and faster, the water beginning to overflow onto the dry riverbed.

His tone changed. "Please, my daughter, you know I must maintain control if Samovar and Pavel are to survive. These children are unimportant. The peasants will breed again, but I cannot condone rebellion! An example must be made!"

"This is immoral and wrong, Father, and I no longer want to live in a place where such evil deeds are considered merely *an example*... We must say goodbye forever if you do not reverse this insane decision."

She felt a sudden gust of cool wind blow across the river, and the Prophet and Nylah appeared on either side of her, the bird, Moses, hovering in the sky above them.

"God is love, Sasha," Adam told her gently, "and He has seen the love in your heart for Him, and for others. It is what He searches for most of all... the spirit of sacrifice. You are to be greatly blessed." Nylah's smile was radiant with joy for her friend as Moses whistled softly, the Angel already well aware of Sasha's unique and special spirit.

From his position in the center of the causeway, Chenko saw the two anarchists materialize out of thin air next to his daughter! His logic fought for a rational explanation of the unexplainable, but the Darkness overcame him again, the foul concoction of evil pumping into him from the tip of the tentacle.

He switched channels on his walkie-talkie. "Caspar, are you in position?"

From thirty feet above on the watchtower catwalk, Caspar responded. "Yes, General, I'm ready."

Chenko smirked at the Prophet. "Take him out!"

With his sniper rifle stabilized on a bipod, Caspar scanned with the scope until the Prophet was dead in his sites. He decided to go for the chest... one shot straight to the heart!

The Darkness watched as his human puppets prepared to shoot his nemesis. Such fools, he sneered. The powers of Heaven would never permit the messenger to be killed! But a better idea occurred to him, one that would bring even more death and destruction than he had originally planned.

The most decorated sharpshooter in all of Russia, Caspar began the slow depression of the trigger, but at the very last millisecond, he was buffeted by a strong gust of wind just as he squeezed off the shot. A body fell to the ground! He was about to celebrate when he saw who it was...

Sasha Chenko lay dead in the river, blood pouring from a bullet hole in her heart.

****

Yuri had watched as Sasha crossed the stream and ran to join the children. If there was any hope to stop this madness, he knew Sasha would find a way! If her life was in any danger, her father might finally come to his senses.

When the Prophet and the Healer suddenly appeared beside her, his hopes soared! But when he saw her drop to the earth, limp and bloody, his soul shattered into pieces!

"Sasha!" he screamed, his sobs echoing across the river. He threw his leg over the railing, trying to jump off the bridge to go to her! Alexei grabbed his other foot just in time, but it took six men to prevent him from plunging to his death a hundred and ten feet below.

He sank to the walkway, unable to breathe. There would be no Garden of Eden for him.

Boris Chenko had won.

****

"What have you done?!" Chenko roared.

Pulling out his pistol, he took aim, pumping round after round through the steel-grated catwalk. The bullet-ridden body of Caspar fell from the watchtower, blood and brains splattering the causeway.

"Sasha, my darling!"

All desire for power, for control, for victory, drained away. There was nothing left... it had all been for her, his beloved Sasha!

He looked at the remote-control in his hand. The device was not simply for the opening and closing of the flood gates. Unbeknownst to anyone currently living at Samovar, when the dam was first built, he'd had explosive charges installed at intervals from top to bottom in the center. Always a proactive thinker, he'd planned for any and every possible scenario, but never believed until this day that he would actually consider destroying the pride of his life's work with a push of the red button on the right side of the remote.

Pride of his life's work? The dam? Samovar Base? *Sasha* had been the pride of his life!

He looked down at the Prophet and Nylah, who were both looking up at him, their faces expressionless, as if waiting for something. Sasha lay still, their white bird now standing in the dirt of the riverbed at her feet. The children and babies were crying, their parents pleading with him for mercy, his own troops shaken by her murder and wondering what his next move would be.

What did any of them matter? It was over... Life had no meaning without Sasha.

He flipped open the cover over the red button.

****

Nikolai and Sonya clung to each other in disbelief as they watched Sasha fall to the earth. Had Boris Chenko killed his own daughter? What kind of demon had Nureyev loyally followed as his leader for twenty years?

He focused the binoculars on Chenko, who was standing like a statue on the causeway directly above the Red Star of Russia, with the remote-control in his trembling hands. He was obviously upset and seemed to be pondering something before he flipped open the protective cover on the remote... and pressed a button.

The force of the explosion knocked them all backwards, toppling like a row of dominoes! Nikolai leaped to his feet, but the Red Star... and Boris Chenko, were gone!

The second explosion was even stronger, earthquake-like tremors shaking the overlook violently and again knocking them down. But by some miracle, it remained intact.

Water began pouring out of the missing section of the dam wall, the Dnieper River rapidly spreading in the direction of the bound children and where the Prophet and Moses stood with the body of Sasha, Nylah kneeling by her side.

The third explosion finished the job. Samovar Dam split open, the lake now a thousand-foot-high mountain of water that would sweep away everything in its path in barely a minute, including the entire town of Pavel and every soul on the bridge!

The soldiers deserted their posts and ran towards higher ground, leaving the villagers trapped. Alexei wrapped Elise in one arm and Yuri in the other.

"I will see you and our children again in heaven, my wife, and Sasha will be there, Yuri, waiting for you to join her. I choose to believe that our death must be God's will, or it would not be so. Blessed be His Holy Name!" Together, they fell to their knees and began to pray, everyone on the bridge doing the same.

The Prophet quickly turned to the people preparing to die, and the power of the Lord God Almighty suddenly ignited in his heart, surrounding him with a brilliant aura of dazzling multicolored light, his dark hair blowing wildly in a ghostly wind, his eyes fierce golden orbs of blazing fire!

"Do not be afraid!" his commanding voice rang out. *"For the Lord your God is One, and of great and awesome power! The outcome of every battle, whether in war or in the lives of His people, belongs to Him!"*

Adam spun around to face the monstrous deluge of death rapidly approaching.

"Stand still and see the salvation of the Lord!"

With a final shout of praise, he swung his arms up towards the giant wave, his hands spread wide, sending lasers of light brighter than the sun itself hurtling towards the racing wall of water, the twin rays striking the wave with an explosive and fiery hiss! The towering tsunami instantly slowed its forward momentum, then suddenly came to a stop... only fifty feet away from Sasha's body, a living mountain of shimmering blue!

No one moved, no one spoke, the sweet song of a bird in the forest reverberating over the river like the beat of a drum.

Adam smiled as the Darkness roared in defeat, enraged by the celestial intervention ordered by Heaven, the staggering power given to the Prophet holding back the torrential wave of destruction!

"He who believes in the resurrected Son of the Living God will never see death!" he cried out.

With a wave of his arms, the colossal wall of water began to retreat! Like a motion picture played in reverse, the water rolled backwards towards the dam, an unseen force pushing it up into the lake, the concrete wall repairing itself foot by foot until the dam was whole and strong once more!

A thunderous shout of joy burst from the bridge and the overlook! God had shown them a miracle, an astounding, awe-inspiring miracle not seen since the days of the Bible!

As those on the bridge praised God, the chain link fences at either end disintegrated into dust! The soldiers who had fled up the hill began to re-emerge, dumbfounded by what they had seen, their guns also turning to dust and blowing away in the breeze.

Nikolai held Sonya as Samovar Dam sealed itself shut, not a crack or flaw to be seen.

"It's a miracle, Sonya! The Prophet has saved us all! The new Eden is here, just as he promised!" They looked down at Adam and Nylah standing hand in hand as Yuri waded the narrow river and raced towards Sasha's body.

"Yuri... We must go to him, Nikolai," Sonya said sadly.

Adam glanced up at the overlook, and Nikolai paused.

"We've been asked to wait, Sonya, just a little bit longer."

****

"Sasha, my darling!" Yuri tenderly kissed her cheek, his tear drops falling on her cold white face. "How can I live without you, my love?"

Her blouse was saturated with blood, her body limp and lifeless, the tiny bullet hole in her chest no longer oozing.

He looked up at the Prophet, his vision hazy with tears. "She was using herself as a human shield! Her life was the only thing her father would have stopped the extermination of the children to protect."

He dropped his forehead to hers, his heart breaking. "Why did he shoot her, Prophet? His own daughter?"

Adam laid a gentle hand on Yuri's shoulder.

"He didn't do it, Yuri. He ordered a sniper to kill me, but the Darkness made certain that the shooter's aim was deflected away, knowing that God would protect me from any harm. The Evil One must have determined that arranging for Sasha's death would incite her father to an extreme reaction, which would then result in the drowning of the entire town and of all the soldiers guarding them."

As they spoke, the parents of the children had rushed into the riverbed to cut the ropes and remove their loved ones from harm's way. Infants were being nursed by relieved mothers, young children tightly clutched in their parent's arms, their joyous reunions taking place only yards away from where Yuri mourned Sasha's loss.

He lifted her hand and kissed it. "I loved her so much, Adam, but I believe I will see her again in heaven."

"Yes, you will, Yuri, but not just yet!" Nylah knelt down next to him, holding a perfect red rose.

"Where God sees the sacrifice of unselfish love, there can be no death." She kissed the delicate, moist petals, and laid the beautiful flower over Sasha's heart.

A glow of soft, luminescent light began to flicker around Sasha's body, her white skin flushing with a touch of pink. Yuri watched in wonder as her lips curved into a hint of a smile, her chest rising and falling with the breath of life!

"Sasha," he whispered incredulously, and her eyes slowly opened, their hazel depths full of love.

"I'm home, Yuri. He sent me home... home to you."

****

Anya sat on the stone border of the overlook, well apart from the others, who were celebrating the miracle that had finally freed Pavel from the ruthless and brutal tyranny of General Chenko, her mind and heart in turmoil.

She had feared the changes that the rebels had been willing to die for, but after what she saw today, the Healer appearing to the women of the Harem like an angel from heaven, and the Prophet's mind-boggling miracle of the dam, the hardened fortress encasing her heart was shaking and threatening to crack.

She struggled to control her quivering lip. Sasha lay dead in the dirt below, innocent, gullible, sweet little Sasha, who she had enjoyed teasing unmercifully in her own sarcastic way. Now she was gone... murdered... her dream of a home and children with her Yuri lost forever.

But wait... Snatching up the binoculars, she focused the lens, straining to see what was happening in the riverbed below where Sasha lay.

The Healer was leaning over Sasha's bloody body, holding a dew-kissed red rose, and laid the flower on her heart.

Anya leaped to her feet, thunderstruck, when Sasha sat up and threw her arms around a sobbing Yuri!

The Healer and her God had brought Sasha back to life!

From that moment on, there was nothing left to doubt... nothing more to question. Anya Kournikova, the beautiful, arrogant, and decadent mistress of Boris Chenko, fell to her face on the dusty ground of the overlook and gave her heart completely to the Living God.

Chapter 37 To Have And To Hold

"Do you, Yuri Fedorov, take this woman, Sasha Chenko, as your lawfully wedded wife? To have and to hold from this day forward, for as long as you both shall live?"

The hastily built pavilion on the bank of the Dnieper River overflowed with the jubilant crowd encircling the couple, with the surplus of the exuberant guests spilling over onto the surrounding grassy area.

Yuri gazed at his lovely bride, unable to contain his pride and happiness, their hands intertwined.

"I do!" he said firmly and slid his mother's emerald ring on her finger.

Alexei turned to the bride, dressed in a simple white dress with a crown of sunflowers on her hair, her expression of joy bringing tears to every man and woman watching.

"And do you, Sasha Chenko, take this man, Yuri Fedorov, as your wedded husband? To love and to cherish, until death do you part?"

Yuri would never forget the look she gave him, even when he grew old and gray, as the simple silver band was slipped onto his own finger.

"I do!"

"I now pronounce you man and wife! You may now kiss the bride!"

The crowd burst into cheers and applause as Yuri pulled his wife into his arms! A hero and son of Pavel had married the woman of his dreams! But they had all been living in a dream, ever since the miracle one month before.

The soldiers who had staked their children in the river to drown and kept their parents imprisoned on the bridge also saw the Prophet restrain the wave of impending destruction and resurrect the dam! When they came down from the hills, they fell to the earth before Adam and Nylah, pleading for mercy and forgiveness. Yuri carried Sasha to his house to rest while the Prophet and the Healer led the remaining soldiers of Samovar to faith in God!

The townspeople approached the repentant and kneeling men, who looked up at them, fearing vengeance. Holding her youngest child, Elise walked up to the soldier closest to her and lowered her daughter into his arms.

"I forgive you," she whispered. The soldier burst into tears and clung to Alicia as he wept in shame, his comrades also greeted with love and invited into the fold as brothers.

Now, with Samovar and Pavel as one, the new Eden began to take shape. When the doors to the secret cache of weapons were finally opened, it was found empty except for piles of dust, not a grenade, land mine, rocket, cannon, mortar, or nuclear device remaining! The only ammunition and guns found intact were at Samovar Base in an arms locker, to be issued strictly for hunting purposes by Major Nureyev, the new leader.

But the Prophet gifted Pavel with another miracle as well! He blessed the thousands of batteries that powered Samovar and gave them infinite life, never to lose their ability to hold a charge from the solar fields! He requested that the power lines be extended to Pavel, where for the first time since the solar flare, each home would again have lights and the use of electrical devices to make their lives easier.

Given their choice of where to live, many of the soldiers remained on base, but traveled down to Pavel every day to commune with their now welcoming Ukrainian neighbors, and to learn about farming and animal husbandry.

Some chose to become game hunters, others to fish in the lake and now almost fully flowing river, while the rest of the men renewed their pre-military interests and training in construction, carpentry, welding, plumbing, electrical and automotive repair, and solar technology.

Dr. Orlov and his staff alternated between the base clinic and the old Pavel hospital, a new hospital currently under construction to replace it. With an eye to the future, Alexei asked if he would also become the instructor for physician and nurse trainees, to which he readily agreed.

The women of the Harem were provided with apartments and homes in town, choosing their own special interests to pursue, and no longer obliged to serve as any man's sexual companion. The hospital and clinic now had a ready supply of medical personnel in training, while others chose to help by sewing, baking, cooking, tending the gardens, teaching, or running the daycare. And with the influx of single men and women from the base, the newly instituted Saturday Night Social had become a popular event.

The pews of the Pavel church overflowed every Sunday morning, with the priest, now a born-again pastor, delivering inspiring and heartfelt messages that kept the fire for God alive in every heart! But it was merely icing on the cake... the Savior was very real to them all, each one communing with their Lord personally and intimately, words of praise often falling from their lips as they worked and played. But today, Alexei had been asked to preside at the wedding ceremonies.

He turned to his left and smiled at the next couple waiting their turn.

"And do you, Nikolai Nureyev, take this woman, Sonya Smirnova, as your wedded wife? To have and to hold from this day forward, for as long as you both shall live?"

Nikolai gripped Sonya's hands, all his love in his eyes.

"I do."

"Do you, Sonya Smirnova, take this man, Nikolai Nureyev, as your wedded husband, to love and to cherish, until death do you part?"

Her lashes brimming with tears, Sonya raised her chin and gazed at the man she had loved for so long, the man she had fallen in love with the first time she was sent to him. By the end of that night, they were entranced with one another, but ordered separated two months later when Nikolai foolishly confided in a man he thought was a friend, Colonel Caspar, of his love for a woman of the Harem.

Sasha had given her a flowing, floor-length yellow gown, and she wore a tiara of chamomile flowers, the daisy-like petals symbolizing rebirth and renewal, her long waves of wheat-colored hair tumbling over her shoulders.

"I do!"

A round of enthusiastic cheers erupted for the couple as their lips crashed together, the exchange of wedding rings forgotten.

"I now pronounce you... oh, go ahead!" Alexei grinned and waved them on. "Please, don't wait for me!"

When the laughter finally died down, Alexei smiled and turned to his right.

"Do you, Adam Devereaux......"

Adam gazed into Nylah's sparkling gray eyes as Alexei spoke the vows that would seal her as his wife forever before God, one hand resting in his own, her red rose in the other, her dress a soft pale blue, her midnight hair cascading to her thighs like a veil.

She had been given to him by the Almighty, destined to serve God with him as One, as Skylark had prophesied before her death. But he had been in love with her from childhood, her sweet spirit, her love for God, her luminous dark beauty drawing him like a magnet. And today, she would become his wife!

"I do," he said proudly, his heart surging with love.

"Do you, Nylah Kennedy, take this man, Adam Devereaux, as your wedded husband, to love and to cherish, until death do you part?"

Before she could answer, a whistle sounded from above. Moses sailed down from the sky, landing on the floor of the pavilion in front of them, his wings glowing so brightly that the people were forced to cover their eyes. But when they could see again, the osprey had vanished!

An Angel now stood before them... beautiful, terrifying, colossal, emanating an unearthly power, his wings spread wide, his eyes multifaceted crystal prisms of ever-changing color and light!

Adam and Nylah fell to their knees and bowed their heads before the Angel, as did all the people.

"Thus saith the Lord," the Angel spoke, *"I am the Lord Thy God, that divided the sea, whose waves roared; The Lord of Hosts is His name. I have put My words in thy mouth, and I have covered thee with the shadow of My hand. The Lord will bless you and keep you as you go forth to bring His Light and Hope to the new Eden of earth."*

Placing his hands on their heads, Adam, Nylah, and her red rose also began to glow with angelic light. "I do take thee, Adam, as my beloved husband," Nylah murmured softly.

The Angel smiled, his crystal eyes flashing with power.

"The Almighty now pronounces you man and wife!"

Raising Nylah to her feet, Adam enfolded her in his arms as their lips met in a tender kiss.

His benediction complete, the Angel lifted into the sky, his majestic wings beating the air. As Sasha watched him in wonder, he suddenly caught her eye, and to her complete surprise, the Angel of God, who had once visited her at teatime in the form of an osprey, and to whom she had fed crusts of bread... gave her a friendly wink.

****

Nylah leaned over the railing of the causeway facing Pavel, holding a glass of dandelion wine. The lights below twinkled in the dark, the happy wedding celebrations continuing far into the night. Adam quietly came up behind her and kissed the alluring curve at the nape of her neck.

"My beautiful bride," he whispered softly in her ear, and wrapped his arms around her slender waist.

"Nikolai and Sonya decided to take Chenko's old suite. We'll be staying in Sasha's quarters one level down, as she and Yuri are spending their honeymoon at his house. We'll be all alone, my Nylah, just you and me... for as long as we choose. Then we go home to Miracle Island."

Setting her glass down on the rail, she slowly turned in his arms and drew him close, her full red lips moist and inviting.

"I can't think about the island right now, Adam. Tonight, this is our home... and all I want is you."

Chapter 38 Gifts From The Bride

Matt tossed his backpack on the bed as Morgan followed him in and stashed her bag in the closet, making a mental note to thank Nylah for how neat and clean the house looked.

"Nylah must be out somewhere with Adam. Alea said he wasn't home either," Morgan commented.

The Tribe had just returned from a distressing month in Spanish Wells. Michael had stayed behind to continue the search for Angel, refusing to give up. Despairing as they all were over her puzzling disappearance, their relief at being home again was short-lived when everywhere they looked held precious memories of their own little mermaid.

Matt went into the living room while Morgan changed her clothes, but when she came out to join him, he was standing at his desk, shuffling through several pieces of paper.

"What's that, sweetheart?"

He looked up at her, his expression causing her concern.

"We need to talk to Daniel and Alea... now."

****

"I can't believe Adam never told us!" Alea finished reading Nylah's letter and handed it back to Daniel.

"All these years... I mean, we knew Skylark had prophesied they were both destined to be used by God in a wonderful way, but this is unbelievable! Instantaneous travel anywhere they choose to go on the planet... Moses accompanying them and revealing himself in his true angelic form... both Adam and Nylah able to perform astonishing miracles... If we were to tell anyone other than the Tribe about this, they'd think we were crazy!"

Matt was still in awe of what he'd read. "They traveled to the Mi'kmaq tribe, where she met her grandfather and her mother's people... My friends from *Four Winds*, Bjorn and Marcel, and the rest of the crew are still alive and well and have families of their own! What an amazing experience for my girl! And she wrote, how did she put it, that she, Adam, and Moses were *stepping out* for their very first mission for God? I wonder where they went and how long they've been gone? She said time had no meaning to God."

An amused smile curved Morgan's lips. "And to think... I once almost shot Moses with my bow and arrow!"

Daniel listened quietly as Alea, Matt, and Morgan spoke. He had always believed this day would come for Adam, the Prophet now his new name. He was excited for his son, as any father would be when his child found their destined path in life. And what a path! To bring the knowledge of the reality, might, and power of God to the survivors of the Flare, and to encourage mankind to bring the earth back to its original intended form as a Garden of Eden, clean, pure, and full of life, with men worshipping their Creator and living peacefully as brothers!

They had tried to do the same for the last eighteen years, he and Alea's journey on *Into The Mystic* leading them to their own Garden of Eden on Miracle Island, an incredible journey guided by Moses, an angel of God disguised in the form of a white osprey, a journey that brought the message of peace and unity to Spanish Wells, Eleuthera, and all the other islands of the Bahamas, and even beyond their quiet, isolated shores, a journey that gave them Adam!

He reached out and they all joined hands.

"We are the blessed families of the Prophet of God and of the Healer. But before we share this with the rest of the Tribe, let's give special thanks for Skylark's sacrifice, and pray for our two children, Adam and Nylah, as they venture out into the unknown, challenging the evil of the Darkness with the Light of God's perfect love!"

****

The coals in the firepit were burning low as Daniel laid the lobsters on the sizzling grate. The first day home after an extended trip was always busy and tiring, and dinner would be running late. The emotional meeting with the Tribe about Nylah's letter had eaten up a good portion of the afternoon, and the dive had been targeted and quick. They were waiting for Matt and Morgan to join them when they suddenly heard a familiar voice.

"Did you guys miss us?" Adam and Nylah emerged from the dark, hand in hand, as Moses flew to his regular perch on the back of Adam's chair.

"Adam! You're home!" Alea cried out. Racing to her son, she captured him in her arms, but then stopped herself and drew away in awe. "You never told us, Adam... I don't quite know what to say, but I'm so glad to see you!"

He grinned and pulled her back in. "Good, you found our letter! I missed you, Mom, but I wasn't allowed to tell you until the time was right."

Daniel moved in to hug his son. "You're safe, and that's all I care about, my boy," his voice cracking with emotion.

"Dad!" They clung to one another, no words needed, the bond of love they had always shared unbreakable.

When they finally parted, Adam slipped his arm around Nylah's waist. "I'd like you all to know that Nylah is now my wife. We were married a week ago."

"What's this I hear?!" Matt exclaimed as he and Morgan walked into the firelight.

"Papa!" Adam released her and Nylah ran to her father, flinging herself into his open arms as they both burst into tears, neither one able to let go.

"My sweet little girl," he wept. "You're all grown up and a married woman! And I couldn't be happier for your choice of husband!"

"Can I hug you too?" Morgan asked shyly, and both Matt and Nylah grabbed an arm to pull her in. Adam caught her eye as the three clung to one another, giving her a grateful smile for keeping his secret for so many years.

The rest of the Tribe crowded around them to offer their congratulations with a flurry of warm hugs and kisses, the realization of who they really were starting to sink in.

"You need a second wedding on Miracle Island! None of us even got the chance to see you get married!" Sarah said, all the women nodding in full agreement.

Adam and Nylah looked at each other, knowing they were already outnumbered by their loving island family.

"Well, as long as we get a second wedding night too," he replied with a twinkle in his eye, "I'm all for it!"

****

Michael said goodbye to the family on Russell Island he had interviewed about Angel's possible whereabouts. They were sympathetic when they heard he was her fiancée, and even let him search their boat and grounds.

It was the last house on his list...

He walked back to Bonefish Bay, completely disheartened. Armand and James were in Grand Bahama, but Nadia met him at the door, always hopeful. He shook his head. She'd made him a plate of food, but he couldn't eat, offering his apologies for her kind effort.

He trudged up the stairs to his bedroom on the second floor. It was too painful to sleep in the beachfront cottage where he and Angel had found such happiness. He threw himself on the bed, the spectacular ocean view unnoticed.

It was over. Never to hear her joyous laugh... never to gaze into her intoxicating blue eyes... never to feel her warm body beneath him. The realization that she was gone forever shot through him, and he groaned in despair.

Should he go back to sea the next time *Muchacho* docked? But it might be months before they came this way again to trade... Perhaps another vessel would take him on. He felt lost and adrift but couldn't stomach the thought of staying on Spanish Wells any longer.

He suddenly heard loud voices and excited exclamations downstairs, then nothing but silence. Worried about Nadia and Elizabeth, he was just starting to get up to check when Noah and Gypsy barged into his room.

"We came back to get you!" Noah told him as his smiling wife flung herself on the bed next to him.

"We'll give you all the details later when we're underway," Gypsy declared, "but the big news on Miracle Island is that Adam and Nylah are getting married... again!"

****

Adam and Nylah's wedding had been a jubilant event! The simple but touching ceremony was held at the top of the cliff where the weatherworn cross overlooked the Atlantic. The Tribe stood in a semi-circle as John officiated, the bride and groom silhouetted against a sapphire sea and powder blue sky, with Moses perched on top of the cross.

Daniel and Alea's wedding gift to their daughter-in-law was Alea's own three-carat diamond engagement ring, but what caught everyone's wide-eyed attention was that Nylah was holding a flower that appeared to be fresh cut, a flower that only the oldest of the Tribe had ever seen before. Alea, Morgan, Josey, Sarah, and Pearl marveled when they first saw it in her hand! It had been eighteen years since any of them had seen a rose, and yet it was perfect, the petals still moist with the dew of dawn.

After the young lovers shared a tender wedding kiss, the party moved to the beach to enjoy a buffet of conch salad, lobster, fruit, and cake. They gathered around the fire after dinner, where the bride and groom shared stories about Thunder Hills, New Hope, Pavel, and Samovar that elicited gasps, tears, and cries of awe and amazement.

Michael sat somewhat apart from the festivities, his mango wine untouched. He was delighted for Adam and Nylah, but their stories of miracles and happy endings only made his own hopeless situation feel worse.

When they first came home and were told about Angel's disappearance, their reaction was curious. "She is safe in the hands of God," Nylah proclaimed, with Adam nodding his agreement, leaving everyone with the belief that the Prophet and the clairvoyant Healer had confirmed her death.

When Michael arrived, Adam took him aside. "Your great love and devotion for Angel has not gone unnoticed." He wasn't quite sure why Adam's cryptic words should comfort him, but somehow, they did.

But the evening's surprises were not yet over. Nylah stood up, so lovely in the firelight in her wedding dress of a fringed and beaded buckskin tunic and eagle-feathered headband, her waves of soft, midnight hair flowing free, her ruby lips smiling.

Matt's heart quivered with emotion when he saw her. She was Skylark reborn! Morgan felt him trembling, and gently took his hand. When she had once traveled the spirit world during her many Mayoruna Festivals of the Moon, she had seen Skylark too, and felt no envy, jealousy, or resentment, having loved Skylark herself.

"I know it's supposed to be our wedding, but Adam and I have gifts for all of you," she announced. "And for you, Papa, I brought something very special."

She opened her palms to the sky, and an object suddenly materialized in her hands! Matt's eyes filled with tears, and he slowly rose from his chair.

"*Starfire*!"

His treasured Mi'kmaq bow gleamed in the firelight; its black oak limbs carved in a flowing replica of his beautiful Skylark!

"Where did you find this, Nylah? It was stolen by Karen and her gang in Boston while you were still in your mother's womb! I never thought I'd see it again." His voice shook, his arms reaching out for it as he spoke.

She passed it into his hands, and he held it against his heart reverently. *Starfire* was the only image he had of Skylark, except for the memories in his mind.

"I went to get it for you, Papa. It was tucked away in the closet of a deserted penthouse. I wanted you to have a little bit of Momma back in some way."

He passed the bow to Morgan and enfolded his daughter in his arms. "But I have you, my Nylah! Morgan and I wish you and Adam every joy, every happiness."

She turned to Alea. "You are now my mother too, Alea, and the gift I bring you is something you have wanted for many years. The Lord has heard your prayers, Mother! Your womb has been opened, and the child you both have long desired grows inside you!"

Alea clutched her heart as Daniel's arm encircled her. "I believe you, Nylah," he said, "but we're in our mid-forties. Wouldn't it be dangerous for Alea, and for the baby, at our age?"

"No, my father! God has assured me that the child will be healthy, and the birth will go well. May you bear as many as you choose to bring you joy!"

Completely overcome, Alea wept on Daniel's shoulder. Her deepest wish was finally to be fulfilled by the child she had nursed after Skylark's death, the girl she had always thought of as her own. "I don't know how to thank you, Nylah," she sobbed. "You have healed a great sorrow in my heart."

"Thank *Him*, Mother! It is His love and power through me that demonstrates His will."

She turned to the other women, her eyes sparkling. "As Adam and I continue to travel the earth, God has shown me an important part of my mission... To bring a special gift to all the women of the new Eden and their mates, and today, to you of the Tribe.

"The choice will now be yours whether to conceive a child or not! Unless you and the man you are with both repeat the poem I will give you at the same time, no seed will take root within you. This gift will ensure that every child born to man will be treasured by their mother and father as thc blessing they are from a loving God."

They could enjoy intimacy with their husbands without concern? And if they chose to have a baby, all they had to do was recite a poem together? This was a woman's dream come true!

"What is the poem, Nylah," Sarah asked, "and should we write it down?"

"If you wish, but I will engrain it in your hearts." Everyone took a seat, waiting to hear her next words.

"God's great love waters the root,
And when the fig tree blossoms,
It is the sign of its fruit."

"All Ryan and I have to do is recite that poem at the same time when we both decide we want another baby and I'll get pregnant? Otherwise, we can, uh, honeymoon whenever we want to?"

"Yes."

"Already got it memorized!" Ryan exclaimed triumphantly, the men moving off into their own circle as they high-fived one another and started talking rapidly.

"Women have dreamt of this for millennia, Nylah!" Pearl declared. "The ability to choose to bear life will completely change everything between men and women! Everywhere you and Adam go will truly become a Garden of Eden!"

"Yes, Pearl, it is a wonderful gift. But the Darkness is still out there, and those not sealed by the blood of the Son will be doomed for all eternity. God has prepared us for many years for a mission that will take all our heart, all our soul, all our strength, and all our love, for the rest of our lives, or until He returns."

Her eyes began to shimmer with flashes of gold.

"The Prophet, the Healer, and the Angel are being sent out to change the world!"

Chapter 39 The Vision

Michael left the group of excited men and wandered up the beach to Alea's Secret Spot. Adam and Nylah's gifts were a shock to everyone, a true demonstration of God's power! But he was the only one alone and miserable tonight, and there had been no gift to make *his* dreams come true.

The two worn chairs were still in the same place they always were, set under a grove of waving palm trees and lit by the light of a full moon. The last time he was here he had broken sixteen-year-old Angel's heart by rejecting her at the very same moment he was confessing that he loved her.

No, instead of acting on the truth in his heart, he'd gotten lost in social appearances, unable to see her as the woman she'd become... and he had suffered for it. He dropped into a chair and stared out morosely at Osprey Bay, glittering like diamonds in the moonlight. He barely noticed.

"Mind if I join you?"

He saw Matt walking towards him from camp. "Sorry to interrupt, but I decided to follow you. I've been watching you tonight, Michael. You're still in pain, and I think you could use a friend. Mind if I sit down?"

Michael nodded, and Matt took the seat next to him. They sat quietly for a while, listening to the whisper of the gentle waves of the bay brushing up on the beach, the roar of the Atlantic pounding in the background.

"I once sat in that same chair, right where you are, many years ago, Michael, mourning Skylark, unable to let her go. I chose to hold on to my grief for years until Morgan was sent by God to free me, years that I made everyone in the Tribe worry... because I couldn't trust in His plan."

Michael kicked the sand angrily. "And just what is God's plan, Matt?" he shouted. "I left because Noah told me it might be a good idea to separate myself from Angel for a year or so, to allow her to get some perspective and let her find herself. So I did, and it almost killed me! And when we were finally reunited again, it was perfect! I loved her so much, Matt! Then God took her away from me... We were only at the beach house for two days when she disappeared."

He started sobbing, his head clenched in his hands. "I don't know what to believe anymore. I thought God had brought us back together... I rejoiced! I praised Him! What am I supposed to believe now?"

"You never give up!" Matt sprang to his feet and grabbed Michael by the shoulders, lifting him out of his chair.

"And you never give up on God! You offer Him all your trust and fall to the earth, thanking Him for every second you had together... for every kiss, every touch, every smile you shared with the woman of your heart! Then you pick yourself up, brush yourself off, and move forward, trusting that His plan for your life is proceeding exactly as He wanted... and that maybe He has someone else out there, waiting for you to find her, and made especially for you!"

He caught himself and released Michael from his grip. "Sorry. It's just that I care about you, and don't want to see you go through what I did."

"It's okay, man. I needed to hear that." He leaned against a palm tree, staring out over the bay.

"What do you think I should do now, Matt? She's gone... There's nothing left for me here on Miracle Island... it's not my miracle anymore, not without Angel."

"Michael, do you believe in God?"

"Yes, I believe in God, and in His Son, Jesus Christ."

"And if you believe in a Supreme Being, do you trust Him? I know you feel lost and alone, but He's calling for you to come back to Him, Michael, calling for you to come home, calling for you to make Him your first priority and trust in Him with all your heart, no matter what."

"I like to think that I trust Him."

"Then why are you suffering at all? If the God of the whole universe, who made the heavens, who formed the earth and everything on it, who created man, is alive and real, why are you worrying about anything?"

Was it that simple? Was it really that simple? Deep inside, he knew that it was. But it took Angel's devastating loss and Matt's caring words for his heart to truly open wide.

"Will you help me, Matt?" he implored, reaching out his hand. "Will you help me find my way back home?"

Matt took the offered hand and squeezed it tight. "If you asked me that question, you're not far, my friend." And they bowed their heads to pray.

****

After Matt left him to return to the wedding celebration, Michael leaned back in his chair and blew out a long, deep breath. The tranquil waters of Osprey Bay reflected the full moon like a mirror, and now, with his soul finally at peace, he could appreciate its beauty.

The dark blue water spread before him like a soft aquatic carpet, curving to his left along the sandy shoreline past the camp and out to the cliffs that bordered the Atlantic, and to his right, to the entrance of Hidden Pass.

The protected bay had saved Daniel and Alea's lives after the Flare, when they had drifted in the Atlantic, powerless and alone on *Into The Mystic*, until a white-winged osprey guardian angel guided them to the haven they eventually named Miracle Island. And for very good reason.

They found an abundance of food. They were safe from hurricanes. Alea's frightening fall when the rock collapsed beneath her revealed a limitless supply of fresh water from the Black Hole. Dr. John Garner and his family were led to them, sailing in on their catamaran, *Barefootin'*, bringing them friendships and a wind-powered boat.

On their first Christmas, they found the key to a built-in locker on *Mystic*, filled with tools and medicine, a surprise wedding gift from Daniel's old friend, Ben Knowles. Adam was born here, and most importantly for Michael, so was Angel, she and her mother miraculously resurrected from death on the day of her birth.

The island had also been a miracle for many others over the years, and turned out to be his own miracle too, when *Piranha's* long journey from the depths of the Amazon River of Brazil finally ended there, driven up onto the rocks by a raging storm that came out of nowhere, the surviving crew rescued by Daniel and Matt.

He was thirteen when he arrived on Miracle Island... the same day he first met the adorable five-year-old girl who would eventually become the love of his life... Angel.

Overcome by emotion, he humbly bowed his head.

Father, I thank You once again for Your perfect guidance and care, not only of myself, but of all the souls here on this beautiful island of miracles, a gift that You gave us from Your loving heart. Your perfect plan brought us all together, to find comfort, support, and love, not only in each other, but in You, at a time when our world was brought to its knees by a catastrophic disaster. We heard Your message, Lord, a message that brought us all back home... to You, our true Garden of Eden.

If my Angel is out there somewhere, or if she's standing by Your side, holding Your hand, tell her I love her. And for the rest of my life on earth, I will always be watching for her in the ocean she loved, to come swimming towards me, joyful and free, until she rises up and walks out of the water and into my arms once more. In the precious name of Jesus I pray, Amen.

He wiped his eyes and lifted his chin with determination. It was time to move forward... Standing up to stretch, his mouth curved into a smile when he heard off-key singing and raucous laughter coming from the camp. He knew he was missing the party of the year, but it felt so good to be free from the burdens of his heart!

A loud splash near Hidden Pass drew his attention. A pod of dolphins perhaps? Whales had come into the bay before too. He decided to watch a little longer before rejoining the wedding party.

Whatever it was, it was heading straight towards shore... and straight towards him! The form breached and dove again and again, and he thought he saw an unusually large, finned tail. He walked down to the water's edge, hoping to catch a better glimpse in the moonlight.

But much to his dismay, an ominous-looking dark cloud slowly passed in front of the moon, and although he could still hear the repetitive splashes coming his way, it was too dark to see the creature at all.

A rumble of thunder rolled in the distance, and the dark cloud drifted away. But as the moon's light illuminated the bay once again, Michael froze.

The finned tail of the creature was clear, but he now also saw long locks of silken white-blonde hair streaming in its wake. As it grew closer to shore, the tail dipped below the water, and to his utter amazement, a woman rose up from beneath the surface!

He rubbed his eyes in disbelief, but when he looked again, the woman was still there! She dove back in and started swimming to where he stood, her shapely body covered in shimmering azure blue and silver scales and glowing with a soft, blue bioluminescence, her face in shadow.

The sight of her instantly transported him back in time... back to his youth with the Mayoruna, to the Festival of the Moon celebration, to his vision of the magnificent crystal woman in the moonlight as she rose from the depths of the sea, her face veiled and indistinguishable.

Chief Bedi suddenly appeared in his mind, nodding at him with a wise, kind, and knowing smile, and all at once, he understood!

His powerful youthful vision had been a prophecy of his future! The mysterious woman, no, *mermaid,* was Angel! She had always been his... the crystal woman of his heart, right before his eyes all along!

As she reached the shallows, the tail divided into two long slender legs, and she waded towards him, blue and silver scales falling away like sparkling confetti in the moonlight, her naked body wet and gleaming. Her joyful smile stopped his heart, the love shining in her eyes searing straight into his soul like lasers of brilliant white light!

She reached out her arms... and Michael knew he was finally home.

Epilogue Standing As One

The old wooden cross at the top of the cliff was silhouetted against the sky above the Atlantic, the strong winds blustery but warm as Adam and Nylah came up over the rise and sat down on their log. Moses landed on his usual perch on the beam of the cross and began preening his feathers.

Nylah lifted her red rose to inhale its delicate fragrance. "I love my flower, my husband! It brings me such joy." She held it out for him, and Adam closed his eyes, breathing in the glorious scent.

"I love *you*, my wife... you are my beautiful flower," and he kissed her tenderly.

Moses whistled, and they drew apart.

"I think he's jealous," Adam chuckled, and the bird stared at him disdainfully.

Nylah slipped the rose into her pocket and sighed. "So much happiness! Michael and Angel's wedding was lovely, don't you think? We kept her return a surprise, but it gave him time to find his way, to find his real strength in God alone. And he accepted her gift to transition into a mermaid whenever she chooses quite well. Our Lord is so creative!"

"My mother is also happy, and soon I'll have a brother!"

"Yes, that's what Moses told me. I think he's really looking forward to having both Angel and Alea's babies to play with."

They gazed out over the ocean, their hearts awash with love and joy for their island family. But Adam's expression slowly changed, becoming serious and thoughtful.

"The Darkness is angry, Nylah. His attempt to tear apart Angel and Michael failed, nor could he at last carry out his destructive plans for Thunder Hills, New Hope, Pavel, and Samovar. They are sealed forever by the precious blood of the Son, as is everyone on Miracle Island. No doubt he will try to influence them, but they now have the weapons they need to defeat him... the helmet of salvation, the shield of faith, and the sword of the Spirit. But in his bitterness and hatred of God and the Savior, the Darkness will never stop trying to manipulate and ultimately destroy mankind, who hold a very special place in the Lord's heart. Our work has only begun."

"It's time, isn't it?"

"Yes, my love," and they both stood.

The Prophet turned to Moses. "And you, Angel? Are you ready?"

Moses whistled and flew to his shoulder, his black-rimmed eyes intense, his wings glowing with radiant light.

"Where are we going, Adam?" Nylah asked softly.

His eyes ignited with golden fire as he took her hand.

"Have you ever heard of a faraway land called Iran?"

Standing together as One, they stepped out over the edge of the cliff... and were gone.

Thus saith the Lord, which maketh a way in the sea, and a path in the mighty waters. Remember ye not the former things, neither consider the things of old. Behold, I do a new thing, now shall it spring forth; shall ye not know it? I will even make a way in the wilderness, and rivers in the desert.

Isaiah 43: 16, 18-19

Acknowledgements

Amal & Dennis Playlist Mood Song
**When You Say Nothing At All – Ronan Keating*

I just wrote the final words of this book... and I'm crying. I will miss my characters so much now that the Trilogy is complete. But as Matt, Nylah, Angel, and Michael finally learned, you have to release... but that's when Miracles can happen!

Thank you, my wonderful beta husband, Dennis, for your wisdom, patience, and contributions to this incredible story.

And to the Lord of Life, thank you for giving me the chance to show your greatness to the world of men, in my own little way.

To my dear Readers, your opinion matters to me, so if you enjoyed Prophet Of Eden, please consider writing your review at Amazon.com, Kindle, or Goodreads.

The Power of Love can change the world, one heart at a time!

About The Author

Chicago born poet, dancer, and artist Amal Guevin enjoyed her career as a physiotherapist, but always dreamed of writing a book. She and her husband Dennis have traveled the Bahamas and the Caribbean for over 25 years, diving, surfing, fishing, and boating. Now retired and a full-time author, Prophet Of Eden is the final novel in the Into The Mystic Trilogy.

Facebook.com/Amal Guevin

Made in the USA
Columbia, SC
06 May 2025